The Alan Burns

Omnibus: Volume One

Alan Burns

The Alan Burns

Omnibus: Volume One

Alan Burns

Verbivoracious Press

Glentrees, 13 Mt Sinai Lane, Singapore

This edition published in Great Britain & Singapore

by Verbivoracious Press

www.verbivoraciouspress.org

ISBN: 978-981-11-0971-3

Printed and bound in Great Britain & Singapore

First published in Great Britain.
Buster in *New Writing 1*, John Calder, 1961.
Europe After the Rain, John Calder, 1965.
Celebrations, Calder & Boyars 1967.
Babel, Calder & Boyars, 1969.
'Essay' & 'Wonderland' published in *Beyond the Words*, Hutchinson, 1975.

CONTENTS

The Shadow Behind Each Word:
An Introduction

DAVID W. MADDEN

Alan Burns (29/12/1929—23/12/2013) was an important voice in a group of experimental writers who came to the fore in Great Britain in the post-World War II era. While not necessarily prolific, Burns worked in multiple genres—essays, interviews, drama, non-fiction, and short fiction—however, his reputation is based primarily on his eight novels, the first four of which are collected in this volume.

Burns was born in London into a comfortable, middle-class family, the second of three boys. At thirteen, however, his mother died suddenly, and two years later, his older brother, whom Burns adored, also died. These losses left an indelible imprint and shaped the writer's impression of life as tenuous and unpredictable. Thus was established what Burns has described as his family pattern in his fiction, "With no preconception or conscious decision I repeated my family pattern. Powerful father, absent mother, slaughtered son, surviving son, one woman: 'the woman about the house' as my mother was in our family of five. Whatever random techniques I used this pattern remained inescapable" (*Beyond the Words* 66).

Burns graduated from school, entered military service, and became a barrister and vetted copy at Beaverbrook Newspapers for libel and copyright issues. From the time he was a boy, he was a voracious reader and someone who had an enduring fascination with language, often coining his own words and in so doing running out of favor with his teachers. A second life-altering experience occurred one day while walking down a street and glimpsing a photo of a couple kissing in the window of jewelry store.

> It recalled the relationship between my mother and father and between them and me, which I had tried to define but had been defeated by its complexity. I solved the problem simply, by describing the photograph, the image. This was the key to my being able to write my first book, *Buster.* Using my memory intensely, I found I could review my life in pictures and describe them in sequence. At the same time I discovered I could lie. I had been held up by the need to tell the whole truth. Now I described the couple in the photo as if they were my parents although they weren't really. I could invent fiction" (*Beyond the Words* 63-64).

Buster (1961) is easily Burns's most accessible novel, and a work that superficially resembles other kitchen sink dramas of the era. The story recounts the childhood and maturation of Dan Graveson, a middle class boy who experiences the death of his mother and older brother at a young age and who wanders from one undertaking and profession to another. Graveson is deluded into thinking that he is unique and a genius, though he cannot point to any overt accomplishments or indications of that extraordinariness.

After flunking out of school, he joins the military, in partial emulation of his older brother, and moves through the ranks until he is cashiered for presumed Communist sympathies. In civilian life he turns to social protest and starts a peace committee, with which he quickly loses interest. His next endeavor involves studying for the bar, studies he executes with his now characteristic diffidence, and fails twice. Penniless and depressed, he is evicted from his apartment and wanders home, where he devours the family dinner and culminates his adventures by sponging off his ever-generous father.

Although the narrative unfolds in a chronological fashion, it is characterized by abrupt shifts in time and location and transitions are often non-existent. Burns has labelled this his "snapshot method" because of the inspiration of the photo in the shop window, and for the reader the impression is one of thumbing through a family album or baby book, catching glimpses of key moments in Graveson's life. Burns will develop this method of presenting photo stills or disparate images and events in increasingly startling fashion in later novels. In a few instances, the narrative simply lists disparate actions or perceptions, as for instance during the funeral of his brother:

> Doors of expensive cars slammed heavy. Husbands waited while wives titivated. Thicker greyer overcoats from Leeds greeted slick tight London ones. Stretched-and-skinny car reflections had squeezed waists, bodies split into two shrinking pears, or tears. Ladies' sharp high heels spiked between the new grey gravel stone; men trod the gravel down. Stone cemetery arch, square cemetery building of stone. Foreign, clean, preserved from contact with the countryside. . . . They filed in, past a pile of broken prayerbooks heaped on a backless chair. They edged round the walls, chatted hushedly, continually. No coffin, only an oblong space of floor. Outside, somewhere, the body lay in its warm brown varnished box.

In this instance the technique mirrors the emotions and psychology of the protagonist; however, in later works the technique of presenting snippets or fragments has less to do with evincing character than destabilizing the perceptions and expectations of the reader.

The family theme is clearly overt in *Buster*, and the pattern replicates the outlines of Burns's family history. He uses the family structure as a skeleton upon which he can experiment with his play of images rather than as a controlling device. As he explained in one interview, "I don't think of the structure as a rigid thing, but as a flexible thing, an organic, a growing thing, with a capacity to grow and change. As soon as the structure gets fixed, the book is ended, in a way" ("The Value of the Image" 21-22). As he moves into later novels, the domestic situation morphs from a literal to an increasingly figurative arrangement.

In one scene where Graveson is wooing a young woman, he plays a verbal game that is a harbinger of Burns's aesthetic predispositions. After yoking disparate, often absurd images together, he explains, "Words don't describe, they point, and poets hit the source in history, the shadow behind each word. Don't slip so quick from step to step. Rest. Words are abstract isolate ancient huge, flipping and floating in coloured balloons in fanlight air." In later novels, Burns often arranges unlikely words in combinations that confuse and startle but often illuminate. As he commented in interview, "As well as the attempt to convey experience, it occurs to me now that there's also aesthetic qualities of words themselves—their sound, the way they look on the page, and in relation to each other—I am particularly interested in that" ("A Conversation With Alan Burns" 136).

With his second novel, *Europe After the Rain* (1965), Burns takes a leap away from coherent, linear plotting to create an atmosphere that evokes powerful emotional reactions. As he remarked in interview, "The lunacy of war is certainly at the heart of my politics and my writing" ("A Conversation With Alan Burns" 123). Burns has said that the inspirations for the novel emerged from three sources: Max Ernst's painting, *Europe After the Rain*, a record of the Nuremberg trials, and a journalist's report of life in Poland after the war. The novel is set is in a temporal limbo, some indeterminate time in the future and can remind the reader of nearly any conflict in recent or current memory. The physical landscape is some ravaged place, where life has been reduced to its most brutal and inhuman aspects, and overwhelming narrative is the emphasis on atmospherics. Early editions of the novel often included a print of Ernst's painting, which depicts destroyed buildings and decomposing tendrils surrounding a threatening birdlike man and woman in the center.

The atmosphere is haunting and the sense of imminent violence is palpable. Such is the same atmosphere that Burns creates in the narrative, which centers on a lone man searching through the ruined landscape for a young woman with whom he may have had some relationship. Bandits and para-military figures wander about the countryside, and the reader is never certain with whom the unnamed protagonist has allegiances. At one moment he is described as a figure sent to study documents, at others he appears to be an assassin sent to kill either the girl's father (a commander of one faction) or his chief adversary. The air of ambiguity and uncertainty never lifts and leaves the reader in a condition of logical suspension.

The abrupt transitions of *Buster* are more dramatically pronounced in *Europe After the Rain*. With this novel, Burns moves clearly into a surrealist aesthetic, one in which non sequiturs, the absence of rational motivation, and surprising juxtapositions predominate. As he explains in his revealing essay, "Writing By Chance," the point of such art is "to create an environment, a relationship between the artist and material in which the material 'speaks', non-rational perceptions prosper, unpredictable connections arise" ("Writing by Chance" 11). The novel assaults the reader with the overwhelming chaos of armed conflict, the horrors that ensue, and the sheer brutality that is engendered by dehumanized activities. Thus one finds scenes of animal slaughter, people fighting over the gold teeth in corpses, and acts of cannibalism by starving villagers. Indeed, in Burns's world, people are less human and more like Ernst's bizarre, unrecognizable bird-man.

What further adds to the horrors in the novel is the narrator's sense of emotional detachment. He dedicates himself to the search for the girl, but never seems particularly engaged, emotionally or psychologically. Burns has said that the quality of detachment matched this own reaction to the deaths in his family, but his method of composition also explains the odd sense of dislocation.

> I bought a journalist's report on life in Poland after the war. This last provided most of my background material. I had this badly written guide-book on my desk and I typed from it in a semi-trance. My eyes glazed and in the blur, only the sharpest and strongest words, mainly nouns, emerged. I picked them out and wrote them down and made my own sense of them later. I dug up characters' from that book though as a mere travelogue it hardly contained any. Perhaps some of *Europe After the Rain's* 'numbness' derives from this distanced technique of writing from the unconscious. Painters often screw up their eyes when looking at a landscape so that in the blur they catch the essence" (*Beyond the Words* 65).

The notion of writing from the unconscious and creating new methods of composition Burns further explores in his third novel, *Celebrations* (1967). Although like any artist, Burns was reluctant to evaluate his works, he did admit that *Celebrations* was his favorite, and that appreciation was not only for the narrative but for his emerging aesthetic. "Thus *Celebrations* might loosely be called 'more extreme' than *Europe*, getting further away from the traditional novel. Thus the leaps between the images are greater, the juxtapositions bolder, the risks crazier, and so on" ("A Conversation With Alan Burns 127). The novel presents another obvious domestic investigation in which an aging paterfamilias and his two sons work at the family business. The younger son dies on the factory floor as a result of dubious circumstances, and the older brother soon marries the younger's wife, who carries on an affair with the father until he eventually dies.

The title is actually ironic for the "celebrations" involve an inquest into the son's death, the remarriage of his wife to his brother, the funeral of the father, and in short all the rituals that surround this rapacious, unscrupulous family. These rituals often highlight the abrupt transitions, turns, and reversals in the narrative, and these reversals are the conscious products of Burns's narrative choices, "As soon as I become aware of a certain characteristic, I instinctively look for an opportunity to show its opposite. For the brave to show fear, the innocent guile, the timorous courage, and so on. An example of this is early in *Celebrations* where Williams [the father] is given one blue eye and one brown' ("A Conversation With Alan Burns" 123).

The reversals also reveal Burns's increasing interest in surreal juxtapositions that take the reader more deeply into a unique sense of awareness. Burns deconstructs popular clichés, such as the virtues of family life and the productiveness of unfettered industrialism. Thus Williams refers to his sons as his "pets, he called them his animals"; as the son lies mortally injured the father unhurriedly glances at his notebook and asks "if he would like a game of golf"; and Jacqueline (the wife) transitions from dutiful, grieving widow to sexual opportunist. Nothing in this world is ultimately what it appears to be, and at the heart of these displacements is a growing reliance on surreal images.

Many of these surreal effects are the result of what Burns called his "cut-up" method, a term taken from William S. Burroughs but executed in his own unique fashion. At the outset of writing a new novel, Burns often visited used bookstores, purchased "good junk fiction," searched for clichés and then folded the pages or cut trenchant phrases and sentences out and reassembled them on drafting table. The result, he commented, "was a wonderful fragmentation, a chaos of language in which I can find new connections and images of language" ("Slash and Burns" 12). Another inspiration was talk radio, which he would transcribe on his typewriter; at other times he sat atop a staircase with his typewriter and recorded stray bits of conversation he overheard.

The results are evident throughout the novel with nearly each page offering a startling perception. As his son lies dying, Williams feels "the end of life was the sound of yellow, rattling across the floor." The surviving son, at his brother's funeral, has a "beard that battled and leapt to be seen before he fell back, wedged against Jacqueline, she slipped away, a flare of white thigh, a glacier surrounded by feathers, her skirt soiled and black . . . ." The judges at the inquest "retired to consider their verdict. The two drank the think white wine, the green and tasty stomachs stood on the polished table, their wigs and hats on the convenient shelf, each day a brandy in a balloon." Such passages reveal Burns's insistence on creating powerful images on every page, images that startle and disorient but which "create an environment, a relationship between artist and material in which the material 'speaks', non-rational perceptions prosper, unpredictable connections arise" ("Writing By Chance" 11).

Burns extends this technique even further in *Babel* (1969), certainly his most challenging, but also most forbidding, novel. Burns, in fact, did not want to label the book a novel but was encouraged by his publisher to do so for commercial and possible libel issues. The book has no continuous narrative thread and no chapters; pages are arranged in blocks of text separated by white space, and in some cases the text appears to be arranged in newspaper columns or like a concrete poem, with lines that can be read horizontally or vertically. There is also an appendix which lists the personages who appear in the text, in a seeming parody of nineteenth century Russian novel.

The text offers a panoply of voices, each competing for the reader's attention as they present aphorisms, newspaper headlines, social observations, anecdotes, and fragments of conversation. Like its mythical namesake, the text offers one snippet after another without clear continuity or coherence. This book represents Burns's most extreme experiments with the cut-up method, very much like a Godard film, "I work, as he does, without any preconceived idea. I create a great mass of fragments, and then I search in and live with those fragments. As Picasso says, I do not seek, I find. I find in those fragments a pattern and build up from there" (The Writer's Place 60).

In spite of its seeming chaos, the text does present some unifying characteristics, the first of which is an anonymous narrator/protagonist, who periodically intrudes on the observations to comment or evaluate. This "I" persona is male in some passages and female in others, and in these inconsistencies Burns undermines traditional storytelling and an audience's expectations. Still another unifying feature is the domestic theme found in his other novels, here presented metaphorically. The patriarch of early works is positively autocratic, "In *Babel* the despots of the earlier books, camp commander, factory manager, death, are re-constituted in the subtle dominance of the amorphous State" (*Beyond the Words* 67). Obvious examples are the Queen and members of the royal family, but the coercive powers of the state can be found in religion, Jesus, Billy Graham, news commentators, celebrities, police, ministry officials, etc. As Burns says elsewhere, "The prevailing culture of any society is the culture of the ruling class. Capitalist culture rewards those concerned to perpetuate the myth of stability" ("The Disintegrating Novel (1)" 7).

Surreal passages abound and push the audience to extremes of perception, "The quick horn handle at the side, the Mercedes was pregnant, the pedals covered with flesh, the bucket seat looked chic, the coloured beautiful automobile drove narrow like a dirty knife." "Playing the adult beautiful, she behaved like a pound of bacon." The point, as in surrealist paintings is to challenge and subvert in order to free the mind to explore the unconscious, dreamlike possibilities.

In the midst of such mordant seriousness, Burns often embeds ironic or downright amusing passages such as, "He was allowed a reduction in the old age pension on condition he died"; "The famous court and prison afford lovely views over the airfield, intercourse is not allowed, though permits are issued for limited periods"; or one of Burns's favorites, "Most people will claim to be people, usually."

I had the pleasure of interviewing and corresponding with Burns and know what a generous, caring person he was. In one interview, he remarked, "It sounds pathetic—this avant-garde novelist wanting to change the world—but I do, I simply want to leave it a little bit better" ("Alan Burns" 22); in all my dealings with him this concern about others was evident. Since we had never met outside of letters, I sent him a picture of my family on vacation, and he in turn sent me one of his younger brother, a couple of his children, and himself, and he commented about how convivial it was to share something other than literary ideas. In all his works I find a deep vein of humanism and a strong desire for intellectual and physical freedom. "The bold use of chance is a liberating experience; it is also fundamentally democratic and anti-elitist. The belief that art can happen by accident means that it is all around, not confined to the painter's studio or the writer's study" ("Writing By Chance" 12).

WORKS CITED

"Alan Burns." *Minnesota Alumni Association*. July-August 1989: 22-24.

"The Value of the Image." *FallOut* Spring/Summer 1980: 20-22.

Burns, Alan. "The Disintegrating Novel (1)." *Books and Bookmen* September 1970: 6-8.

---. "Essay." *Beyond the Words*. Ed. Giles Gordon. London: Hutchinson, 1975. 63-68.

---. "Writing By Chance." *The Times Higher Education Supplement* 29 January 1982: 11-12.

Gillen, Shawn. "Slash and Burns." *The Minnesota Daily*

Hall, John. "Novels from the Unconscious," *Guardian* 30 April 1970: 10.

Kitchen, Paddy. "Surrealism and Sculpture in Words." *The Times Educational Supplement* 18 September 1970: 21.

Firchow, Peter. "Alan Burns." *The Writer's Place: Interviews on the Literary Situation in Contemporary Britain*. Ed Peter Firchow. Minneapolis: U of Minnesota P, 1974. 50-62.

Madden, David. W. "A Conversation with Alan Burns." *The Review of Contemporary Fiction* 17.2 (1997): 122-45.

BUSTER

BUSTER

BUSTER:

A small new loaf or large bun
A thing of superior size or astounding nature
A burglar
A spree
A dashing fellow
A Southerly gale with sand or dust
A piece of bread and butter
A very successful day
Hollow, utterly, low
To fall or be thrown
                         (Dictionaries).

1

THEY stood over him.

Grandma shrieked:

'Let me look at you! What a big boy you've grown! Have a chocolate! Have a pear! Have some more seedcake darling! You're not eating anything! How can you be a big man without eating anything? What is he going to be when he grows up?'

'Lord Chief Justice,' said his father.

'Prime Minister,' said Grandma. 'Danny, who do you like better, your mother or your father?'

'Both the same,' he said.

That night he wrapped the sheets round it, then a mountain of blankets, then the eiderdown tucked in. Small pig hot inside. Then wet.

In the bath his mother had told him never play with that. Never. It's dirty. It will make you go mad, like being bitten by a frothy dog. Told him again and again how his cousin had stood up to make himself soapy, but his heel felt the curve of the bath and his spine cracked the edge of the bath and the nerve was crushed and the bone splintered and the track for the nerve from the brain to the legs was ruined and he sits in a chair all day now. Dan had seen those legs in their grey flannel trousers, skinny knees poking through like pins.

But this was so easy and lovely. He watched moonlit clouds slide evenly between him and the moon.

His mother's hand held his hand, pointed at the sheets. His face pushed into the smelly sheets.

'You wait till your father comes home. You just wait.'

She had locked the dining room door. He walked slowly round the table squeaking his fingers on the polished wood; he slid his penknife along the grooves, collected threads of dirt. He stood on the windowsill, looked out over the hedge into the road. A soldier posted a letter. He jumped on to the couch, his feet sank in as he pranced about on it. He waited. He reached up for the sweet dish; it fell on the carpet. Liquorice allsorts. He crawled round picking them up: one for the dish, one for his mouth. He poked under the tails of the green monkeys climbing the vase; when they reached the top he'd get a Rolls Royce. He sat on the couch and waited.

He saw the car through the window. Quickly he put his father's slippers in front of the big chair. It was his job. He banged on the door.

'Let me out!'

He wanted to be first, to run down the path, be swung up on to the garden wall, given a piggyback. The door stayed shut. He heard them talking. He kicked the slippers across the room. They lay in the empty fireplace. They were black and red tartan wool.

Upstairs to the spare room, his father treading behind. He pulled his trousers down, they wouldn't come over his shoes. 'That's enough!'

He hobbled to the bed, lay across it. The prickles of the hairbrush touched his bottom.

'Get up and get dressed. You'll go straight to bed without supper.'

He heard them arguing. His mother brought him snap crackle pop with milk.

He heard his brother coming up the stairs. He bounced up and down making the bedsprings prink. Bryan came in, sat on the bed, smiled, waited.

'I hate her,' Dan said.

'You shouldn't. She's your mother.'

'She's got sticking-out eyes and frizzy hair.'

'That's only because she's not got enough iodine.'

There was an old brown photo of her kissing under an orange tree.

'I'm a cruiser with six-inch guns,' Bryan said, 'and father's a battleship and mother's the Ark Royal stuffed with tuck instead of planes.'

'What about me?'

'Oh you're nothing. You don't want to be in this fleet.'

'I do.'

'Well you're a brilliant destroyer, the fastest ship in the Navy. And you've got torpedoes which can sink anything.'

'Where are we going?'

'We're steaming across the Bay of Biscay to fight for Spain.'

'Then what happens?'

'Tell you tomorrow. Go to sleep.'

'Now.'

'Tomorrow. Good night, sleep well.'

'Goodnight. I don't want to be Lord Chief Justice.'

'You haven't got to be.'

'They all say I will.'

'Never mind them. Good night whippersnapper.'

'Night.'

2

Bryan was home all day because he had finished school and not found a job yet. They played french cricket in the garden and read a story in *The Wizard* about U-boats and Dan made a speech in Parliament:

'Why should the rich have pears and cake and the poor can't even have bread?'

Bryan said: 'Hooray!'

Boys came round and they held Dan between them and raced him along the street, flying him into the air.

'Let me down! Let me down!'

But when they stopped, he cried: 'Do it again!'

'Come in and listen to the wireless. Sh! It's important.'

Mr Chamberlain. The war had started. The air-raid siren went. Dan got under the dining room table. His mother was making tea; she bent down and looked in:

'You all right down there?'

He hugged the cross-piece between his legs. He was nine.

They were talking about boarding school.

His father said: 'It's too much for you dear. Bryan can look after himself. But the other one.'

His father stood at the foot of the bed:

'I'm sorry Dan. It's the war. We didn't know there was going to be a war did we?'

'Here's a pound for spends,' his father was shouting as the train moved off.

'What?'

'Not what, pardon. Look after your mother and write every week.'

Staring out of the train windows. Boring. Just fields. Reading *Woman* and *Melody Maker* with mother.

Strange roads. Greygravel path. Grey walls. Eyesocket staring windows. Standing while mother mumbled with Headmaster. Unbroken tradition. Evacuated. Discipline. Horse-riding and Music extra. Tall boy walked slowly past the open door, twisting his head to stare. Matron. Cash's name tapes. Down a corridor, clicking a radiator. Mother grabbed his arm. Corridors leading off. Hundreds of doors. He would never find his way around.

'He will have to be inspected.'

Trousers down round his ankles, getting creased. Hobbling, taking the fawn rug with him over the slidy floor. Mother getting up to help.

Doctor roaring: 'He'd better get used to undressing himself!'

The carefully balanced timetable cut up the days. Mr Hoffman took Geography. Two sweets after lunch followed by compulsory rest period. Miss Lazarus took French. Desks in rows. Mr Hoffman walked up and down, sometimes he was in front, sometimes behind your back. Miss Lazarus had a special high desk she had bought herself, in France. Diagrams on the walls. A woman cut through the middle, green kidneys, orange heart. A fat minim, black crotchets, quavers, semiquavers, demisemiquavers. The British Empire rolled down red, and on a dusty table in the corner a relief map of the neighbourhood with cardboard roads and bits of green sponge trees.

He stood on the cold bumpy football field, by the white goalposts. The others charged around. If only he could dribble right through them and smash the ball into the net. But he was glad he wasn't one of those who just ran near the ball, shouting, pretending.

Mr Beezley made Dan sweeping prefect, and in front of everybody showed him how to hold the broom so as not to sweep the dust on to his own shoes. Mr Beezley took Latin. O table. Smack smack smack smack Dan's eyes went flat on four walls.

Anything could happen on Sunday. He walked through the garden at the back, looked into the greenhouse at the black grapes dangling in bubbled bunches from the green vine spreading out. Over the fence, scratched by rusty wire, down the middle of the road past the chestnut tree with the cobbled wall round it, into a wood he'd never been in before. He sensed the deep heat of autumn, saw it gobbling up the green, scraped thick moss on to his hand. Out into a new wide field, hunting for mushrooms. Hand down in wetness, fingers at the base of the stalk, gentle snap, then peel back a strip of skin to make sure it wasn't a toadstool, nibble a bit. Puffball, puff, brown smoke. He pocketed hazelnuts. He wrenched a stick from the hedge and swiped the hedge with it. He struck the neck of a drooping flower, the dark head slipped off and down into damp dark grass. The split stalk shivered, showed sticky white blood. A tremble fixed his hand, held his stomach, legs, head. Stockstill unbelief. A hawk hovered. He pointed his stick straight at the one pin dangerous eye. At school he was bumped awake. He told them about the fox he had seen close up.

Harry Finegold made him go horseriding. Such tough necks. Dan was too skinny. When the horse chewed grass, shoving his neck down, he couldn't pull him up. Harry Finegold gripped with his knees, got the horse between his legs. Dan sat on top. He trotted, bumping. The horse saw home a half mile down the road, his back hooves slipped as he jerked forward in a sudden gallop. Dan sat straight as a Bengal Lancer. He could not believe he was galloping. Then slowly he slipped sideways.

'Up you get!'

Harry's voice. No.

'You're going to be Prime Minister and you can't even ride a pony!'

He dreamt he was searching for someone among shopping crowds. He caught up with her, she changed, he saw her further on. He held her sleeve, it came away, it was a German, blackclad Germans swung from parachutes, columns of Germans with rifles marched over him. He clung to a bomber's wings, diving into trees, rocketing up, looping through the clouds. And at night he found easier suppler ways, unobtrusive sexy ways.

That lovely feel of between, squeezed between his slippery thighs, or under him. And in the garden lavatory, wooden bucket seat, stinking pail, he found old soft sweets, covered himself with them.

He worked at the piano. He held his hands and wrists correctly, tapped each note separate and clear. All Sunday he practised the first page of his piece.

'Quite good. A little wooden. Go on.'

'That's all I've done.'

'Better play it right through, even badly.'

'What's the use of playing badly? I want to play it brilliantly, perfectly, better than anyone else has ever played it.'

At half-term he gave up the piano.

The Headmaster took General Knowledge. He explained about docks, Parliament, motor cars, the Armed Forces, icebergs, telephones, pollination, traffic lights, Mount Everest expeditions, orchestras, railway engines. It was Dan's best subject. For his Task he gave a talk on the Russian Revolution, and made a coloured map to show the dispositions of the Interventionist armies. At home, when his Report came, his father was proud of the second in General Knowledge and told Grandma and Uncle George. That his position in form was twelfth out of fifteen was only because he hadn't settled down yet.

At home Dan missed the countryside, and he walked often in the park. He would whistle *The Trumpet Voluntary* or *The Blue Danube* as loudly and perfectly as he could. Perhaps a composer or a violinist would come up and say: 'You whistle very beautifully young man. You have an exceptionally sensitive ear. You must take up music — one day you will be great.' Or he sang *The Marseillaise* hoping that a Frenchman would recognise it and reward him for Loyalty to the Republic.

Bryan one morning marched off to the park to help dig trenches and fill sandbags. He held a garden spade riflewise and did a 'P-r-e-s-e-n-t Arms!'. Dan went to watch. At lunchtime they sat together on a park seat. Bryan tried to rub the clay off his flannels.

'You're the first to know, Dan. I'm joining the Army.'

'God! Dad won't let you.'

'I must —'

'But Dad says you're doing war-work.'

'As his Secretary! Any woman could do the job. I'm nothing. I didn't even go to Spain.'

'You weren't old enough.'

'It's the same war and I'm old enough now.'

'I'm going too.'

'You stay at school and work like mad. You're the clever one. You've got a big chance.'

Dan wandered round the park, and arrived back at the trenches to go home with his brother. They walked along without speaking. Dan was annoyed: 'Why don't you say anything?'

'I'm thinking. And I'm tired.'

'But I love having proper conversations with you.'

'You can't order "one conversation" like a pound of apples.'

'You talk with Philip all the time.'

'We exchange ideas.'

Dan was silent. Then, near home, he said:

'Plato did all the talking and the others just said "Oh yes" or "I don't agree" to set him off again. I could do that with you.'

Bryan said: 'Okay. You win. But it's a bit late now.'

'Yes. But after the war.'

'Of course.'

Bryan spoke quietly, coolly, explaining. His mother sobbed: 'You mustn't go, you'll get killed, don't go, please, for my sake.' His father said: 'Why didn't you discuss it with me first? But we understand how you feel. You must do what you think is right.' Dan listened.

Bryan's Training Camp was 'Somewhere in Scotland'. Dan watched him go on the nameless Express. The thread linking their eyes pulled and pulled and snapped. Dan sat with his arms folded. An iron shovel shovelled bricks behind a planked wall of advertisements. Above, dirty panes of tough glass backed by steel netting shut off the sky. On the wide platform people walked in various directions, away from each other, unconnected, yet together making a pattern. Clip clink tread pad in time with tinned music from loudspeakers. Fat pigeons walked among them, heads bobbing out of time with their feet. An unprepared roar and shriek of steam frightened the young ones, made them jump and fly a few yards. The people took no notice. A little boy was dragged along by his mother as she hurried off somewhere; his spare hand wiped his runny nose. Three young soldiers, sweating in thick uniform, drifted by, grinning. Whippersnappers raced in and out of telephone boxes, pressing button B. Nuns looked funny and young in light blue, their big white hats turned up like paper gliders. They chatted and nodded. An Irish voice: 'It was a wedding present. He picked it out with a pin.' Two girls in skyblue shorts were glared at. *I Speak Your Weight* spoke a lady's *Fourteen Stone Four Pounds* to everyone as she giggled. Sticks dropped and bounced on the platform. Porters shoved trolleys loaded with cartons of kippers Deposit Four Shillings. A girl from India stood blinding in orange. The fruit stall was a box on the platform, a spare bit in the train set. A pound of apples, paid for, was left on the counter. A face looked out, then a hand took the bag inside. Men wandered into the Gents' Hairdressing & Brush Up, emerged unchanged. A tramp searched for fag ends; his head was twisted so that his cheek was forced permanently against his shoulder. Ticket collector touched the hands of girls and watched them on to the train. Yorkshireman talked extra loud in London. A kid swung on his father's hand: father smiled wide and lovely. People walked in various directions, away from each other, unconnected, yet together making a pattern.

He took the War Map from Bryan's room to his own. He replaced the little flags on pins which marked the positions of the armies: union jacks, tricolours, swastikas. He stretched coloured cotton across the pins to mark the Maginot and Siegfried lines. He cut out a big flag, marked it with a red 'B' and stuck it in Scotland.

Bryan sent letters to his brother at school, and in the holidays enclosed a separate note for him in the family letter. Once he mentioned that on his first leave he would 'sell a lot of old junk including my bicycle.'

Dan hauled the bicycle out of the garage, mended the punctures, cleaned the chromium. He looked through the 'Wanted' columns of the local newspapers, cycled miles around reading cards in newsagents' windows, and in the end sold it for six pounds which he kept in his brother's room. Another letter advised Dan to: 'do some proper reading. Less newspapers and politics. You're old enough to read the classics. Only real learning counts.'

Dan took *War and Peace* from his father's bookcase and read it in five weeks. He talked about Pierre who proved his philosophy by algebra. In each letter Bryan told him to work hard and look after his mother.

Bryan came home on leave and told them he had been posted to India. He tied a knot in the corner of his handkerchief and danced it round the table, like a Rajah with a turban. 'It takes more than a World War to get you down,' his father said.

'When I die put three hundredweight of marble on my grave, and inscribe it: "Laugh This One Off",' Bryan replied.

At school Dan tried to study, had few friends, rarely wrote home. Each term he won the form prize for Poetry Speaking. He enjoyed standing alone on the broadstage, pronouncing the words of poems perfectly, making his voice break with emotion. He received his prize to a patter of clapping.

In the holidays there were air raids. An oil bomb dropped on the park. It seemed more real than other bombs: a tank of oil falling from up there onto the ground. Oil seemed heavier than steel. A morning bomb shattered the bathroom windows, covering the floor with powdery glass. His mother screamed and weeped:

'Your father always shaves at eight o'clock and today he didn't. Thank God. Thank God. There is a God after all!'

Dan helped her sweep up the glass; she held the newspaper while he swept the glass onto it. The monkey vase had got broken, so he went out for some Seccotine.

Where the corner newsagent had been still smelt of charred wood and dusty rubble. He wondered about the paper bill.

At home his mother called from the kitchen: 'Mend it in here, Danny, and keep me company. And put some newspaper on the table so the glue won't make so much mess.'

'It will make the same mess but it won't matter so much,' he said.

He popped the monkeys into the vase and said he'd like his Rolls Royce with grey Hooper coachwork. The cat got a piece of paper glued to his fur, and raced round the kitchen chased by the paper. They laughed and she hugged him till he had to push away to breathe, still laughing.

One morning very early he started off to cycle into the country. He heard his mother running after him.

'Wait Danny. I'll walk with you a little way. I'm taking some cheesecake over to Dolly's. Jack's not well.'

He called back:

'I must get to Hertford by lunchtime.'

But he waited for her, and they went along together, she holding the handlebar while he rocked his feet against the pedals. He wobbled over the road.

'I must get on,' he said, impatient.

He heard the hum of a plane.

'Please leave go.'

Heavy sound of the plane, throbbing. Gurrumgurrumgurrumgurrum loudsoft loudsoft loudsoft a heart. He was fifty yards down the street when the noise stopped and the thought flashed 'Buzzbomb'. Roar and boom into his eyes. The front wheel yanked sideways. He felt his elbow slithering against asphalt. His sleeve filled with blood. He ran to his mother. She lay on her back, stretched out as he had seen her sunbathing in the garden. Only her foot seemed twisted. The weight of that foot on the ground. The brown leather shoe, lace pulled tight and neat, double bow tied precisely. The leather had the glow that comes from unthinking morning polishing over years, brown turning to black with work. The force of the blow against the asphalt road had torn open the outer leather in one place exposing its yellow inside like the slit belly of a pussfilled pig.

A policeman wrote in his notebook: *Scratch on left shoe approx one inch.*

The foot had a slight unnatural twist at the ankle. She could not have bent her foot like that if she had been alive. The difference was small, an angle of ten degrees. But alive she could not have done it without breaking the bone, gouging one bone into the other, wrenching the muscle enough to make her scream with pain or come as near to screaming as an ill middle-aged woman can, not a young clean scream, but a choke, a sob, a cough, a constriction in the throat caused by too much trying to escape at one time. Weight is being drawn into the earth, pulled to the middle of it. Her foot weighed.

'She's bought it,' the policeman said.

He dragged the body into a doorway beside a butcher's shop. He bawled up a steep flight of stairs:

'Someone give us a 'and?'

A man came downstairs. He unlocked a door into the shop and helped carry the body inside. Dan could see them standing up in the shop, the body between them on the sawdust floor. They took no notice of him. He ran up the stairs and stood on the unfamiliar landing. A door was partly open, and through the E-shaped gap he saw a woman in a yellow electric lit room. She wore a yellow flowered dressing gown. She was kneeling in front of a fireplace, trying to pull the string from a bundle of firewood. It caught on splinters. She poked one stick through, then another, then two or three at a time until the whole bundle collapsed. She threw the sticks on crumpled newspaper. She added small coal to the pile, then put a match to it. She dropped the string on the flames.

He was freewheeling downhill homewards. He had ridden into the country, as far as Hertford. Smoke rose straight from the chimney. Through the windows he saw his father playing chess.

He stood in the dining room, waiting for the solemn talk. He looked at her empty chair, remembered seeing her white bottom once when he'd gone into their bedroom without knocking.

He was taken upstairs to the spare room. He had stationed hundreds of lead soldiers over the floor, flicked marbles at them. An unused bookcase held Bryan's old books, Left Book Club, Thinker's Library. He tried to cry.

'You'd better go back to school. It would be best.'

'But it's holidays. There'll be no one there.'

'Never mind. We'll ring them up.'

From the country railway station he cycled to school: through the village, along a muddy lane, bumping down into puddled hollows, watching the marks of tyres in thin mud. The camouflaged waterworks crawled with yellow monsters. His head felt queer, like blotting paper. He stopped. He looked up at the flat sky. It was empty except for those specks floating past his eyes which he knew were caused by minute particles slipping between the retina and the iris, and slowly easing down.

That term he missed the big food parcels from home. So he stole from the Food Cupboard: he slid back the brown door just a few inches, pushed his hand inside and picked up whatever was nearest, a bar of chocolate, a tin of sardines.

He was senior enough to have a study. He shared with Michael, a smoothfaced neat boy whose father was a Member of Parliament. Michael was to enter politics.

'I think my first step will be to obtain a position in local government,' he told Dan.

'A job with the Council? I wouldn't do that.'

'Why?'

'Haven't you seen that notice on their carts? It reads: 'Gratuities Forbidden'. I'd like a job where you can make something on the side.'

Michael talked about his family, proudly of his father, glowingly of his sister. Dan was invited to Sunday lunch. The father gave him orangeade and remarked that the weather was pretty frightful for cricket. Dan said that today was not good but it was better than yesterday. The day before had been perhaps a little better than yesterday but not quite so good as today. Tomorrow the position would be complicated still further, and the day after that the complexity would become unbearable. Suicide, and an eternity of good (or bad) days, seemed the only solution. Michael got the biggest helpings of roast beef; his sister was tall and wore thick stockings. Over lunch Dan talked about incest and the Oedipus complex.

Michael used the study less often. Dan enjoyed being alone. He ate fingersful of Radio Malt. He looked up words in the dictionary. Rape is an administrative division of Surrey. He began to write an Epic Poem. He borrowed his brother's typewriter. His father sent him a ream of foolscap typing paper. Dan typed on the first sheet, a word: *Onion*. And then, brilliantly: *Man. Onion Man.* What a picture! Was there another mind in the school that could have conceived it? In the whole county of Gloucestershire, in England, Europe, the Universe? Time was grander. Multiply together all the billions of minds and moments there had ever been: had one once deliberately and self-consciously thought: Onion Man? Pause. Knowledge. How many men there were whose life was onions, whose sons had onion seller owner eater dealer digger Dads. Uniqueness demanded disjointedness. Irrelevance was the key. To Onion add the word least like onion. . . .

He was picked for the House chess team and decided to become a professional. His father sent him untidy parcels of books by Lasker and Capablanca and he swotted the first chapters. He played chess with Montague who had been brought up in Chicago and Paris, had a motor bike, girl friends, cigars, coloured waistcoats and a thousand gramophone records which he and Dan listened to on sports afternoons. They conversed about composers.

'Of course the move from Beethoven to Brahms reflected the growing complexity of the contradictions inherent in capitalist society,' said Dan.

'Say bud, you don't say so!' Montague replied.

'Yearh, Clodface, I do say so.'

The music formed a background to Dan's thoughts about himself.

They played word games.

'Describe midsummer in terms of sound,' Montague said.

'Beethoven's Ninth performed by an orchestra with ten million first violins and the Massed Choirs of the Universe. And midwinter?'

'The sound made when T. S. Eliot taps his teeth with his spectacles.'

They discussed genius. Was Dan a genius?

'You're obsessed with the word,' Montague said.

'But what does it mean?'

'Genius is another name for pride,' said his friend, 'and pride is the cardinal virtue.'

'Genius is the ability to achieve extraordinary things,' said Dan.

'No, it is the achievement, by work, of extraordinary things. For example, could you spend the entire week at school, saying only "fish paste"?'

'I am unique and I will amaze people,' said Dan.

'Unique? That's very ordinary. And who fails to amaze their mo— father?' his friend asked.

'Aren't you a genius?'

'You mean will I exchange recognition? I'm afraid not. You remain the supplicant.'

Soon after he was made a Prefect, Dan walked into Montague's formroom:

'You're making a shocking noise. This is a sixth form and should be an example to the others.'

They looked at him, silent. Montague was smiling.

'And don't smile when you are being admonished.'

As he left he heard his friend's French-American drawl: '*Quel sang froid! Queue savoir faire!*'

The boy bent over correctly and touched his toes. The skin on his bare legs and buttocks stretched tight. He was trembling.

'The other way,' Dan said.

The boy straightened a little, touched the edge of the washstand with his hands. He was thirteen. At the daily 'hands inspection' he had been caught three times with dirty fingernails. The traditional punishment was a caning by the Duty Prefect. Dan wanted to thrash him. He was beautiful and Dan wanted to hurt and bruise him. He let the cane touch the boy's skin.

'Get to bed. You're lucky this time.'

Dan was reprimanded. He said he could not support capital punishment, no he meant corporal punishment. The dignity of man, Tom

Paine, scientific humanism, principles. His Prefect's tie, red with a gold stripe, was formally taken away from him at a special ceremony in the Prefects' Common Room.

'You have precisely one hour left, gentlemen.'

The invigilator's plummy voice, artificial as a Bishop's, sounded through the examination hall. Dan's school-leaving certificate, English Literature. The main question read:

'Dr. Johnson was the Hero of his Age. Discuss.'

Dan wrote:

Johnson in the Modern Eye

Johnson was god. And typical of his age. Era of Goodsense worship, sameness the ultimate ideal, piggery and prudery rife, nonsense wisdom, pomposity prestige.

So the Nightmareman Must — mountain of conventional revulsion, foul-mannered filth loving big boar beast — of course he Must be part of every mantelpiece. A great lumping tasteless victorian grandfather clock, stumpgomping on top of and right through the pretty coffee cups and sniki simplicities. How he bounds! And Boswell is his weak-tea shadow And the drawingroom clusters and the Dryden Chandelier and the Johnson and the titters are blushed and the boom begins. . . he would not like little cracker nuts but with big lumping joll stump off with blugging beaf hunks. And guzzle. And cover his ear with gravy. And guffaw. And stuck his feet and glush his mouth

the modern dainty mind reflects recedes back back

But now when the cooling stonily creeps me and I can see him just plain big, not glumping, clumsy yes but his thud was live and he jollily glowed in thrilling proudness of Town and culture and coffee house fine conversation and rightness (who will read it?) of the good occasion and the truth

And he warms his behind by the redfire large and lust and he glows. His great brown pipe I can see in his great brown fist and his boots. Gleaming black and sturdy. The socks must be wool (hand woven quite good) and the lack of a bath quite foul. Thank God I'm here and I'm now away from the stench feast and the big fug   for I'm modern and fine young man.

'Idiot!' Montague said, 'they'll fail you.'

Dan knew it. He felt sick.

'I won't fail. I don't care if I fail. I'll show them. I won't join the Army. I won't get a job. I won't queue. I'd rather walk. I'll go to London. I'll get a girl and go up West. She'll curve and have a curvy dress. I'll jive with her. I'll sling her round the room. I'll pull her between my legs. She'll be jumping mad. I'll kiss her cheeks. I'll slap her bum till it stings. I'll burn her name on my arm. I'll sleep with her. I'll sleep in the park. I'll get soaked. I'll march. Hope it pours. Hope we get soaked and drenched and drowned. I'll have a long wet crazy beard. I'll slosh through the gutters. I'll smash their windows. I'll yell. I'll knife you. I'm going up West. Coming? We're dead tomorrow.'

'I'm not coming,' Montague said.

3

Plank from collar to bum. Head back, eyes set, chin in, shoulders back, tummy in, bottom in, legs straight, heels together, feet at an angle of forty-five degrees, thumbs stretched down the seams of the trousers. Cap band polished, best serge pressed and creased to cut, webbing belt and straps tight clean and tough, pack emptied cut square and plywood-stiffened, slices of brass set slick as a flicknife, polished to whiteness. Cap, collar, pack, each precisely parallel to concrete slabs beneath the boots. Boots. Eyeblinding scintillating brilliant boots.

The cartoon Brigadier treads slowly by, unbelievably moustachioed, inspecting.

'Completed basic training?'

'Sir!'

'Category?'

'Clerk. General Duties. Sir!'

'Enjoying the Army?'

'Sir!'

Behind, walls of dirt. Deadgrey walls, dirt colour. Narrow jail windows. The plaster, hard and flaky with age, crumbles: at a touch powdered wall snows on the scrubbed wood floor. Rifles will not be leaned against walls.

Condemned as uninhabitable each year since 1905, Talavera Barracks were most suitable for the accommodation of National Servicemen during basic training.

'Carry on Sergeant-Major.'

'D-i-i-i-i-isMiss!'

A thousand men swivel right on the right heel, bring left leg up till thigh is parallel to the ground: crunching crash as a thousand boots slam down.

The men grumbled across the parade ground. They went to the Naafi, queued for tea, strained forward to see the cakes and bacon sandwiches and Irish girls and sausage and mash. The food was served on bakelite plates by girls in sexless overalls.

The Church of England Hall had dusty lampshades and cobwebs on the walls and you were served by old ladies in floral dresses and hairnets and spectacles. On Tuesdays the Naafi had cod and chips and the C of E was empty. As usual the ladies apologised for not having 'frying facilities'.

'We've applied so often, but there isn't the money today.'

Though tonight was cod night Dan preferred to sit alone in the C of E with *Titbits* and a cup of tea. He had just heard that the Naafi put something in the tea 'to make you sleep well'.

'I don't like being done good to on the sly,' he said.

He worried about his rifle. The bolt was missing. How could it have happened? Bayonet practice tomorrow. Bound to be rifle inspection. And some idiot had kicked his toe-cap on parade. Need a good two hours work to get it right again. They said burning the leather with a hot iron gave a smooth surface that polished up beautifully. It was a gamble. Perhaps it would ruin them. That bolt. 'Pull bolt back for inspection of magazine.' Had he failed to 'ram bolt securely home' so that it had slipped back onto the ground? He left the canteen quickly and ran to the parade ground. He tried to find the spot where his Section had been having rifle instruction. It was dark. He got down on his knees to look. The smooth-looking concrete was rough and jagged to touch. Like a razor blade under a microscope.

'See a pin, pick it up, and all that day you'll be in the bleedin' shit. What the hell are you doing?'

It was Bert.

'Riding a bloody bicycle. I'm looking for my rifle bolt,' said Dan.

'Blimey! It shouldn't happen to me ma-in-law. You'll get ten years jankers!'

'That's why I'm looking for it.'

'Bet someone nicked it. Well, be 'ung for a bleedin' sheep. Come on to Parsons Field.'

'What for?'

'Apples. Lovely red ruddy apples.'

Dan didn't want apples.

'Okay, I'll come.'

In the dark they climbed among fruit trees, pushing apples into all their pockets. Bert had brought his kitbag and they saw him heaving it on his shoulders, heard a loud whisper: 'I'm off.'

Ginger, Dan's partner in latrine fatigues, was mooning about in the shadows. Dan was giving him a leg up a tree when a huge hand thudded on his shoulder. He fell back, Ginger on top of him. Sprawling on the ground they saw standing over them a giant with a shotgun.

'Look at that shotgun,' whispered Dan, 'he can keep his ruddy daughter.'

'None o' your lip.'

He was enormous. Dan kept quiet. They were taken into a brightly lit kitchen and stood against the wall 'to wait for the military'. Sergeant Lewis came:

'You'll be up before the C.O. for this.'

'Ya yah yah yah yah yah YAAAAAAAAA!' screamed Sergeant Bussel. 'That's the way. Yell as you charge. Scare him to death. Hands grip the butt, and up into his guts. No slashing about the face. UP into his guts. There's no second chances with bayonets. It's him or you. And those Ruskies know a thing or two I can tell you. Right now. First man.'

A man ran at the dummy and prodded it with his bayonet. 'Yell!' yelled the Sergeant, 'and HATE him! There's no hate in you lads. You don't last long with a bayonet without hating. Next man!'

The dummy on the rope was still moving, and Dan went to steady it before the next man charged. He saw that someone had painted a moustache and spectacles on the face.

Sergeant Bussel shouted like a madman: 'What do you think you're doing? Come back here! Now! At the double! Who's in command of this exercise? Who's been running this lot for twenty years? You or me? Who told you to touch the target before the charge? Want to get sliced up? And who'd carry the can back?'

'I thought it should be straight, Sergeant.'

'Who told you to think? Would Ivan sit "straight" while you went up nice and polite and stuck a bayonet in his guts?'

'No, Sergeant.'

'Right then. Next man. And YELL.'

No rifle inspection. There was a God after all.

The bolt wrapped in paper, lay on Dan's bed. On the paper a word: 'Thanks'. Dan checked the number, rammed it home, sat on the bed, thinking about apples.

'We're on the Board,' said Ginger, 'C.O.'s Office, 1400 hours.'

'Christ,' Dan said.

Roaring at them, the Regimental Sergeant Major drove them into the Office, marching them in treblequick time. Bareheaded, they stood stiff at attention, rigid. Across the wide desk the Commanding Officer looked up from a file of papers.

'Sergeant Lewis?'

'Sir. At 1700 hours I relieved Sgt. Watkins as Orderly Sergeant—.'

The C.O. snapped: 'Where did you find the accused?'

'Sir. I proceeded to the premises where I found the accused with apples in their possession which they admitted were not their property. Sir.'

'Thank you Sergeant. You men, have you anything to say?'

Ginger said: 'I didn't know they were private apples sir. I just saw them and nipped over and nicked them. I thought it was all right sir. Everybody —.'

'Yes yes. Graveson?'

'I only want to say I am very sorry indeed sir for all the trouble I have caused and—.'

'Very well. I have carefully considered the facts of this case. . . . Far too much disregard for the property rights of neighbouring landowners. . . . Fine of ten pounds.'

'No C.B. and no fatigues!' Dan was laughing. 'He couldn't wait to get back to his brandy!'

'I'd rather fatigues. It's a ruddy fortune,' said Ginger.

'It'll be stopped out of your pay. You'll hardly notice it.'

'I already send my mum a pound a week and she keeps saying that's not enough. She thinks I'm made of money.'

'A pound a week!'

'I gave her four in civvy street. Now what can I tell her?'

'Write and explain what's happened.'

'Tell her there's a thief in the family? She'd never laugh that one off.'

'Thief? Still, you can't send her anything for the next ten weeks. Haven't you an uncle who could help?'

Ginger shrugged his shoulders.

'Perhaps I could—?' Dan said.

'Nah.'

He walked off, hands in pockets.

Dan wondered how he could pay his own fine. His father's five pounds a month had all gone. He would ask Bryan. He composed a letter. It was difficult. He remembered Bryan's return 'after the war'. The special troop train. The first glimpse in the crowd of the white shirt, red tie, blue jacket worn by troops in hospital. Bryan had just been re-classified 'walking sick'. 'My biggest thrill in years.' The absolute change. Thinning hair, nervous glancing eyes, no concentration. 'No wounds, no gallantry in action,' he said, 'just dreary killing malaria.' Bryan sent the ten pounds in a registered envelope, without a message. But the fine was paid, that was the main thing.

Queen's Regulations, War Office Orders, Army Orders, Standing Orders for Division, Regiment, Battalion. These were all transmitted down to Battalion level. Battalion headquarters was neck-deep in Orders. More important, all Orders were continually revised and amended. Important for Dan because he was Orders Clerk. He had scissors and paste. He cut out the new revised version, and pasted it over the old. The amendments were specially printed to cover entirely on the page, the paragraph they were intended to replace. Dan was instructed to paste the slivers of paper by their edges, so that they could be lifted up and the old Order consulted, because certain matters remained governed by the old Orders. For example, stores purchased in 1946 would stay governed by the Orders of that year; amendments to the Stores Purchasing Orders therefore must not be allowed completely to obscure the 1946 Orders. Dan became skilled at amending amendments to previously amended Orders. And, like all H.Q. personnel, he was allowed to wear shoes instead of boots and gaiters. He did not have to clean his boots or blanco his gaiters.

He was waving Queen's Regulations over his desk, the latest amendments, flowing paper tails, looped the loop, flapped backwards and forwards. Captain Ames came in, with a young Gunner. The Captain wanted all Forms and Regulations relating to signing on in the Regular Army. 'They will be sent to your office, Sir.'

'No, better do it now.'

The Captain pulled two chairs up to Dan's desk, motioning the Gunner forwards. They sat down, and the boy, hunched over his pen, filled in the forms slowly and carefully. His nails were bitten and dirty. Dan could read the black capitals. *Donald MacAndrew. 18 years.* He looked nearer fifteen, had spots on his chin. *Crane Driver's Assistant. Expresses a desire to join Her Majesty's . . . Twelve years engagement.* Typewriters clicked. The boy peered about the office, as if trying to find his way about. The Sergeant nodded and smiled. Captain Ames said:

'Jolly good show.'

The boy seemed pleased to have pleased everyone. Dan tried to catch his eye but did not manage to do so.

*   *   *   *

'Get up, you lazy bastard!' Bert hurled a pillow against the wall above Dan's head, bringing a shower of plaster down on him.

'You're on the Board.'

'Not again!'

'It's all right mate, you're going to be a ruddy Officer.'

Twelve foot drop. Impossible. Better stay in the ranks for ever. Why did they need an Assault Course with a twelve foot jump to distinguish between Officer Material and the Other Stuff? The Colonel had talked of 'modern methods of Officer selection,' but this was feudal.

'Hurry along Gentlemen, only thirty-seven seconds to go.'

'Gentlemen'! Dan strained for the New World. With a look straight down, he jumped.

The Selection Board psychiatrist dropped his handkerchief on the floor, looked up at Dan, and said:

'Well?'

'Well what?'

'Talk about what I have just done.'

Dan talked, very rapidly: 'You have just dropped your handkerchief on the floor. It's a queer thing to do, just like that. It's a dirtyish floor, but your handkerchief is fairly clean, so apparently you don't drop it often. It was queer because it was disjointed, it bore or seemed to bear no relation to what had gone before. That is unusual in a human action. The causal relationship between successive actions is usually apparent. Which sounds clever but is in fact a platitude. No, it is profound and also untrue. My confusion results from my avoiding complex subjects like free will and determinism which are the roots of the question. Things drop with varying velocities, depending on their weight. No, the velocity is constant. I think it called G2 but I don't know what G2 is—.'

'That will do. You may go now. Thank you.'

As Dan went to the door, the psychiatrist called after him: 'What is that propelling pencil doing in your pocket?'

'It is being a propelling pencil.'

'Do those white bits, then, mean that you are a proper Officer Cadet?' his father asked for the third time.

'Fully-fledged. And I carry an Officer's stick. If I get through the course

I'll be Second Lieutenant Graveson in three months' time.'

'Well Dan, I'm proud of you. You've done something at last. That uniform. Doesn't he look smart Bryan?'

Bryan, from his armchair, said: 'Thank God someone in this house looks smart. He looks healthy too. Vitamin packed.

'Killing must be good for you.'

'I haven't slaughtered any Japs, like you did.'

'I'm sorry. I got it all wrong. It is training to be a killer that is so good for you. Instruction in annihilation stimulates the hormones. Do you suffer from spots or backache? Have you got a bad leg? Have three months' fun with a bayonet and feel young again!'

'Just because you took five years to reach a Corporal—.'

'That's enough!' their father said. 'We're going out to dinner. To celebrate. I've booked a table. So stop quarrelling you two while I go up and shave.'

'Doesn't he shave in the morning any more?' asked Dan, when he had gone.

'It's Saturday,' said Bryan.

But he would not let go.

'Yes, we're proud of you Dan. We'll sit at home in the next war, being blown to atomic smithereens happy in the knowledge that you're at the Front winning glory!'

'You were mighty glad of the Atom Bomb when it stopped the war and brought you home.'

Bryan stood up.

'Glad? You bloody fool! You sodding bloody little baby!'

'I'm sorry.'

'Perhaps I was just nearer to it than you were. But since that Bomb I've felt like I had leprosy, like bits of me were dropping off.'

'It brought you home,' Dan insisted.

'Half-dead.'

Dan said: 'You used to be a scientific humanist.'

'Labels going cheap! Scientific what? Tell it to the Japs. They're still dying from an overdose of science. Have you heard the latest from the States? They say a cure for radiation sickness is theoretically possible. Spread the glad news in Hiroshima and Nagasaki. Scientists may even now be tackling the theoretical problem of raising the one hundred and twenty-eight thousand Japanese dead.'

'It's not the scientists, it's war, and the causes of war—.

'General Graveson begins to think! Who ordered you to think?'

Their father came in, in his dressing gown, soap frothing his face. A white blob fell on the carpet.

'You'll wear your uniform Dan?'

'Of course. I'll have to press it though. Have you got an iron?'

Bryan said: 'In the kitchen, by the bread bin. Sorry Dad, I can't come tonight, I don't feel so good. Got the shivers. Perhaps I'll join you later for a drink.'

'Please come,' Dan said, 'I want you to.'

'Some other time. Sorry.'

Dan went to press his uniform, his father to finish shaving. Bryan watched the soap bubbles sink into the carpet.

Gilt and green nudes danced among flowers round the walls. Tablecloths and waiters' shirtfronts glistened in the artificial gloom.

'It's very smart. Costs a fortune. But you don't get made an Officer every day,' his father said.

'I've told you so many times. I've got a three months' course to get through yet.'

'You'll do it. You can get anything you really try for. I've always said you were the clever one.'

'No. Bryan is.'

'Why don't you two get on these days? You used to.'

'He's so ratty. He blows up over nothing.'

'You must give him time to settle down,' his father said. 'I'm worried about him. He never sees anybody or wants to do anything. He doesn't sleep, just walks about all night — we meet in the kitchen at two in the morning and eat cornflakes! If only he had some friends, especially a girlfriend. He needs one. Any man does.'

'I suppose so.'

Waiters handed them each a huge Menu.

'Have anything you like, Dan. Have the best. Do you like smoked salmon? And there's a whole capon cooked in wine, with asparagus or mushrooms.'

'I want something extraordinary and rare that I've never had before.'

His father ordered oysters, Lobster Newbourg, Boeuf Stroganoff. He studied the Wine List.

'We'll have a good claret, Léoville Lascases '28. You'll have to learn about these things now, Dan.'

There was a Cabaret. A fat little man played a grand piano. He composed medleys from popular songs shouted at him by the diners. '*Smoke Gets In Your Eyes*,' shouted his father. 'That's a grand old one. Your mother's favourite.'

A girl sang. The lights went low and she danced, chased by a white spotlight. Her shiny dress fell in a heap on the floor. Two chorus girls joined her, hiding her with long fluffy fans. She held a fan herself and moved around followed by the two girls. For seconds at a time Dan could see the girl's white-lit nude body as the fans hesitated. It was intentional. He glanced at his father.

'Have a liqueur, Dan. For Officers only. Green Chartreuse.'

'I'm sozzled.'

'There's someone I would like you to meet, Dan.'

'As long as it's not Auntie Lulu. I can't stand Auntie Lulu.'

'I haven't seen Lulu for a long time. We've been very alone, your brother and I.'

'I know.'

'It's been too much. But you could help, Dan, if you wanted to'.

'Me help you? That's a new one!'

'We'll see. Let's go now.'

They drove through the West End. Dan sat in front next to his father. He felt warm and sleepy. The car pulled up outside a block of flats.

'Let's have a goodnight drink, Dan. And you can meet Helen.'

In the self-operated lift there were six black studs with clear silver numbers. His father pressed '3'.

'Darling! What a lovely surprise!' she said.

She was thin. Red hair. Young.

'And I know who this is. Come in Daniel. Let me take your coat. What will you have?'

'Nothing thanks, had too much already.'

'Don't be silly, have a small gin.'

'I'm not silly. No thanks.'

His father said: 'Helen's only trying to —.'

'I know that. It's very nice of you. But I just couldn't take a drop more. Specially as I think I'll have to drive Dad home!'

'We'll have coffee,' she said, 'I'll put the kettle on.'

Dan sat in one deep armchair, and his father sat in another.

'It's a lovely room,' Dan said.

'Yes. Dan, I've known Helen for some time. She's been wonderful to me. I know you'll get on well with her.'

'Of course I will.'

She poured the coffee:

'It's a wonderful machine, darling, it doesn't clog up like the French one.'

'I thought the chromium sieve-plate would be an improvement.'

'It makes very good coffee,' said Dan.

She uncrossed her legs and got up to pour Dan a second cup. She leaned over him.

'My, you look swell in that uniform.'

'Thank you. And that's a very nice dress.'

His father smiled.

'I'll take them in,' Dan said.

He collected the coffee cups, put them on the tray, carried them into the kitchen. He washed them under the tap and placed them on the stainless steel draining board. He looked for a drying-up cloth. He went back to the room to ask Helen. They were standing up and kissing hard in the well-lit centre of the room.

'I'm sorry.'

'Come and kiss Helen goodnight, Dan,' his father said quite loudly.

'No.'

Dan could see he was holding her hand very tightly.

His father said: 'Well we've had our goodnight kiss. So it's time to go.'

Dan picked up his Army greatcoat from the back of a chair.

'You stay. I can easily get home by tube. It's a direct line, no changes.'

He had one arm through his coat-sleeve.

'Don't be silly,' his father said.

'Seems to be my silly night.'

He was feeling vaguely for the other arm-hole.

They drove home together, with the car radio playing dance music.

He blabbed out the first big triangle. Two triangles left, eight oblongs, fifty-six circles. An infantry officer must excel the best of his men in anything he may order them to do. Assault course, route march, musketry, manoeuvres, rope-climbing, weapon-training, swimming, fencing, rugger, drill. Drill. No time to think? It is intentional, you are going to be an officer not a philosopher. Lectures on tactics, man-management, venereal diseases, regimental history, Russia, Korea, Malaya, mess-etiquette, signals, strategy, leadership. Cadets when dressed in civilian clothes will wear trilby hats. Cadets will not engage in conversation with Other Ranks. Dan stumbled from day to day, counting the days. On Sundays after Church Parade, when he walked in the town he wore his officer-type raincoat, carried his officer's cane and once or twice was saluted by young national servicemen.

He didn't care that he was an officer.

'Congratulations! Of course you'll be coming home for your leave,' his father wrote. It seemed Bryan was shamming ill again, sitting in a deckchair in the garden, staring, or lying in bed all day. The idea clearly was for Dan to sit with him, spend his leave playing chess, reading Proust aloud, making coffee, being polite to Helen, chatting, visiting relations in his new uniform. No. He was going to have a good time.

He drew his first month's officer's pay, wrote home to say that he had already arranged a holiday 'with some newly-commissioned Officer friends'. And by the way he would not need the five pounds a month any more, thanks for sending it so regularly.

He packed a bag and alone in a taxi went to the railway station.

'Single to Llangollen, please.'

He loved the sound of the name, that was why he had chosen it.

He booked a room at a hotel. A steamy hot day. He walked in the park, searching. He knew he didn't care what she was like as long as he could have her without you or anyone or her knowing.

A girl lay on the grass in front of him. Her hair spread a pool of blond on the green. Her body spreadeagled, arms and legs wide, cheek against the warm lawn. The earth curved against her tummy and thighs and breasts. He felt the weight of heat in the leaves. Minute eyes of birds winked. A slow plane murmured by. She raised herself so he could see into her blouse. Her breasts moved with her breathing: lowering to brush the ground then rising barely to touch it. A grasshopper, conspicuous on the smooth lawn, was jumping away to shelter. He caught it gently: pale green, dark green, streaks of hazel brown. He took it to her.

'Look at this.'

'He's lovely,' soft Welsh voice, let him go now.'

She pulled his fingers apart and the insect hopped out and away.

'Did you hear about the pea-catcher? he asked.

'Tell me.'

'A man stood on a high flat roof, threw a pea up, took a step back and caught it in his mouth, threw a pea up, took a step back and caught it in his mouth, threw a pea up, took a step back, fell a thousand feet, feet first. It's an old Welsh folk-tale taught me by my Granny.'

'No.'

'No. I made it up.'

'I can see you talk a lot.'

'Too much.'

His hand played with her heavy fair hair, slid inside her blouse, held her breast, squeezed till his nails bit deep, felt the nipple rise hard in his palm. He strayed, searching and feeling, beneath her wide skirt.

'Let's go over there, to the trees,' she said.

They walked easy together, arms round waists, to the shadow of the trees. He stretched beside her, moved closer, lay over her, in.

'I love you,' he said.

'You say that easily.'

'Can you make love without loving?'

'Don't be silly, of course I love you. I saw you come into the park, wandering round, and I thought you were lovely.'

'What's your name?'

'Deirdre Watkins. I work in a shop. But I'm studying fashions, to be a designer.'

'I'm Lieutenant Daniel Graveson — just call me Dan.'

'My brother's in the army,' she said, 'I thought you were something like that.'

They lay close, without talking.

She said: 'Have you seen our swans?'

She took him to see the lake, over the other side of the park. They watched the swans floating slowly, careful, deceiving. He was dizzy with them, felt their softwhiteness. Two swans together suddenly whizzed off the water skinning the surface with their feet, like waterskiers. They fluttered heavily around, realised the air was not for them, came skidding down, bottoms first. Ducks bounced on the small waves.

An alien starched Scottish Nanny sat on the bench beside them, lecturing her neat child:

'It's fesh not wishes, fesh not wishes. It's time you were learning to say the few words you do say, properly. Do you want a sweet?'

'No.'

'Thank you.'

'Fank you.'

A moment later: 'Nanny, can I have a sweet?'

'Please.'

'Pease.'

Across the lake a herd of mauve and white schoolgirls giggled and yelped, like flamingos drinking the Amazon. An intermittent 'peep' came from an angry schoolteacher blowing her whistle, the toneless cry of an unimaginative bird.

A brilliant scarlet speed boat went mad in the middle of the lake, whining round in small circles. A big boy in a striped blazer told them:

'It's got enough petrol to keep that up for three days.'

'Hurrah!' Dan said.

'We'd better be going, Dan, there's a storm coming.'

They hurried back the way they had come. They reached the trees just in time. Came a maniac intensity of the sun; the shadowed side of sunlit leaves showed black, veinless. Pearly pregnant evening light invaded the afternoon. Rain fell grey against blueblack trees. They moved to where the trees were so thick that the sunlight was always shut out: no grass, only bare earth under layers of dead leaves. They were safe and dry. They looked out. A huge weight of rain drove like iron across the park, soaking drenching flooding, making the lawns wallow in water, forcing water into the flowerbeds, compelling the flowers to gulp and swallow hundredweights of water.

It drizzled. Raindrops filed along twigs. Budge up. Budge up. Drops dropped from leaf to leaf to ground. 'While it's pouring it's driest under the trees, but afterwards it's wettest,' she said.

It stopped. The last waters sluiced away. The air was clear.

A Police car zizzed past them, microphone bellowing. Among the incomprehensible syllables Dan heard 'Graveson'. Impossible. The car was away and turned a corner. A grave young policeman walked on the other side of the rainshining street, impregnable in helmet, cape, waterproof boots. Dan told her about his brother's mock-German:

'LuftwaffenBomben, Watford-By-Pass gebomben, Auntie-Dolly gebomben, Ark Royal ein zwei drie gebomben, Corporal Graveson gebomben, Schikelgrüber über alles gebomben . . . .'

They held hands past the hotel receptionist. In the corridor he joked:

'Do you come here often?'

'Of course not. Do you think I'm that kind of girl?'

'At least you've heard about "that kind of girl". I didn't know they had them in Llangollen.'

'If you don't stop I'm going straight home.'

'Only kidding.'

Arm round her waist, hand on the door-knob, he kissed her.

On the carpet, just by the door (it had been pushed under the door) lay a telegram.

NO.

'Your brother.'

His fist was through the wardrobe; the mirror inside was shattered. He waved his fist about so that it bled all over the fawn carpet spattering it with purplish stains.

The girl stood still, one hand white on the mock-walnut dressing table, looking at the stains. She packed his things into his bag, went downstairs to explain to the manager.

'He was very understanding,' she said.

She handed him his bag.

'I'll never see you again.'

He didn't say anything.

He could not decide whether to walk to the station or get a taxi. It was not far, yet the bag was heavy. Platform one. Which platform? Platform one.

Early morning. He fumbled at the burglarproof double-lock. Helen opened the door.

'Hello Dan. Glad you could come so quickly. Your father is upstairs.'

The house was ordinary. The dead body had been taken to hospital to make sure it was dead. He opened the door of their room. His father was sitting up in bed, backed by pillows, reading the *Daily Mail*. Dan said nothing because he could not think of anything to say.

Doors of expensive cars slammed heavy. Husbands waited while wives titivated. Thicker greyer overcoats from Leeds greeted slick tight London ones. Stretched-and-skinny car reflections had squeezed waists, bodies split into two shrinking pears, or tears. Ladies' sharp high heels spiked between the new grey gravel stones, men trod the gravel down. Stone cemetery arch, square cemetery building of stone. Foreign, clean, preserved from contact with the countryside. Chemical sprays and regular scrubbing with disinfectant killed small creepers and scraps of moss. Not a fleck of grass, not a living insect survived to spoil the stone. They filed in, past a pile of broken prayerbooks heaped on a backless chair. They edged round the walls, chatted hushedly, continually. No coffin, only an oblong space of floor. Outside, somewhere, the body lay in its warm brown varnished box.

'Move in a little closer if you please thank you,' the priest said. Like a market salesman to his customers. Were they the customers, or was the thing in the box? It depended whether the funeral expenses were charged to the deceased's estate, or were paid by the surviving relatives. Dearly beloved. The priest was enjoying his rich voice. Cut off in his prime. Splendid young man. Loyal son and brother. Credit to his church. Brilliant mind and wonderful promise. Mourned by all who remember his loving nature. Dust unto dust. Recitative without end. He towed them down the long path to the yellow trench to watch the coffin dumped in. The body in the sheet in the coffin in the earth was in the universe.

> 'Unassuming, Unpretending,
> Straight the Path of Life he trod,
> May his Bliss be never ending
> Thro' the Mercies of his God.'

Oh God.

4

Brother officers gathered round him.

'Fighting for freedom and democracy with the Yanks in Korea? You can't believe that rubbish!' Dan was saying.

'Another whisky?' Lieutenant Crabbe stooped over the siphon; hard head, thick ginger stubble. He had a parachute badge, and medals.

'Here's a stiff one. Or would you prefer vodka?'

'Thanks. Remember Hiroshima. A hundred and twenty-eight thousand bodies. What colossal contempt they must feel for us with our measly machine guns.'

'You mentioned that before.'

'Then tell me, who profits from the war? Korea? China? The answer may show who started it.'

Someone said: 'Those yankee millionaires you were talking about, with their arms factories—.'

'Yes,' said Dan, 'and there were five million American unemployed before the arms drive solved that problem overnight. There's no unemployment or arms manufacturers in the New China.'

'They produce a deal of arms.'

'But not privately,' Dan said.

'Does that make any difference?'

'It's a long story. And I must get to bed. I'm drunk.'

'Wait a bit,' Crabbe said, 'so the North Koreans are fighting for peace and independence? Is that right? Let's get the whole thing perfectly clear.'

'That's an over-simplification . . . but I can't think straight. I must owe you all buckets of whisky.'

'Think nothing of it. It's been a pleasure.'

Lieutenant Gerson, an attached Officer from the Education Corps, spoke for the first time:

'Let's talk about something else for heaven's sake.'

'Hey, don't spoil the fun,' Crabbe said.

Dan blinked.

'Fun?'

He walked over to the mantelpiece, stood with his back to them. Eleven sharp tings sang from the glasscased clock. He knew they had followed him across the room. He watched the moving parts inside the clock swinging and linking, teeth biting precisely into delicate revolving cylinders. He heard the scrape of windows being fastened. He looked down at his reflection in the polished silver tray on which letters addressed to officers were laid. He turned round. They had formed a halfcircle close to him.

'I must get back,' he said quietly, 'I've some reading to do.'

(Lenin on Imperialist War; not one of them had read a book like that.)

'Don't go yet, it's been so interesting listening to you. Quite an education.'

He wondered where his hat was, he couldn't leave without it, had to have it for parade in the morning. He moved towards the door. A Major stood in front, his tummy stuck out. Dan half saw a brown boot flick out, felt his ankle crack. He put his hands out as he fell, felt the carpet slide against his palms. A hand of iron grabbed his wrist, another twisted back his arm. Crabbe knelt down and spoke to him:

'Now look here, we don't want to break up the Mess. Will you come out like a man?'

'What's happening? . . . Yes.'

He was bundled outside in the middle of eight or nine of them. The cold foggy air hit him. They marched him along a gravel path, then onto grass.

'What good will this do? There's problems to solve, but this is not the way.'

'Christ, he never stops.'

He thought God what are they going to do to me. I can't speak to them. No way of getting at them. He slithered his heels against the ground. They pushed and punched him along.

They were behind the cookhouse among smelly piles of rubbish and open dustbins. They stopped and held him. Two of them levered up the cast iron cover to the grease pit. Stink came up. They shoved him in. He managed to hold his body above the slime, there was only the smell. Then a hand at the back of his neck pushed his face into the grease, held it there.

He was out, spluttering, yelling after them: 'Fascists! Fascists!'

They'd gone. He sicked up onto the grass.

He arrived at breakfast very late next morning, after all the junior officers had gone. A Major and a Colonel sat at one end of the long oak dining table. He sat on his own. On his way out he picked up an envelope from the silver tray, and read, on a piece of cheap lined paper:

'Meet me for coffee at Lyons, 7.30 p.m. this evening. Gerson.'

Lyons was crowded. Everyone seemed old or middle-aged. He could not see Gerson. He queued up, bought two cups of tea, sat next to an old grey man who was excitedly reckoning figures down the side of a newspaper. Dan poured sugar into his tea aiming the stream to burst the bubbles round the side of his cup.

Gerson came in, sat opposite, saying:

'Glad you could make it.'

Dan looked straight at the eyes pale behind steelrimmed spectacles, pale lips, thin fair hair. Gerson asked the waitress, an old African woman, to bring him a packet of cigarettes.

Dan said: 'What do you want to see me about?'

'I want to have a talk with you.'

'Hullo.'

'Seriously. I want to know what you are trying to do.'

'What do you mean?'

Dan was annoyed to see Gerson continually glancing round the room. A nervous habit.

'All this revolutionary talk,' Gerson said. 'Red Flag wagging like a ten year old.'

'I have certain principles—.'

'Why not keep them to yourself?'

'It's those Captains and Majors. I want to kick their teeth in.'

'You are in a bad way. Don't you know they're laughing at you?'

'I don't care.'

'Yes you do, you're not so stupid. I don't know what your job is or what you're trying to do. Frankly I don't trust you enough to tell you anything M.I.5. don't already know. I've been fifteen years in the Party, too long to take chances. But if you care about Peace, and want to do something effective—.'

'What could we do?' Dan asked.

'Make a demonstration, a gesture. Have you ever gone chalking?'

'Slogans on walls? No. But that's brilliant. Let's cover the camp with hammers and sickles.'

The old man on Dan's left looked up, interested.

Gerson smiled: 'Lucky we live in England. Tell me, what is the main political task here today?'

'Peace—.'

'Right. The reaction to hammers and sickles would be "Help! Russian spies!" Would that tend towards peace or war?'

'The symbol of workers and peasants—.'

Gerson interrupted: 'Have you seen many peasants lately?'

'Thousands.'

'Being peasantless,' said Gerson, 'is a British peculiarity of great political significance. But that's another matter.'

'Then what shall we do? Let's decide now.'

'No, I must go. Think about it. But for Christ's sake keep your mouth shut. If you must talk, talk to the men, that way you may learn something.

Go down to their lines, or to the Public bars, even the Education Centre. Get to know them. You'll find one or two good ones.'

Dan sat looking at Gerson's tea cup. A pale brown skin had formed on the untouched tea. The waitress asked:

'You want this sir?'

'No, thank you very much indeed.'

He put the cup with the cups, and the saucer on the pile of saucers on her tray. He looked at her tea-stained overall, the blue cotton skirt with yellow flowers peeping beneath it, thin liquorice legs. How could those skinny ankles bear her weight, hold up that huge bottom? How steeply under her skirt those legs must swell out into giant thighs. She should be sitting in a rocking chair surrounded by grandchildren. Gerson had not said thank you for the cigarettes.

Standing in the Officers' Latrine, a week later, they decided to paint on the Ammunition Store: *Join the Movement For Peace*. It was, in Gerson's phrase, 'the correct slogan'. Dan thought it was too long.

Gerson said: 'It can't be helped. Those words are essential. There may be another comrade along to help us.'

'Another comrade'! Dan felt he had been knighted.

Hidden by a rolling heavy midnight fog, Dan waited just outside the camp. He felt safe in the fog and darkness. Gerson loomed up, nosing around, looking for him. Dan skipped round behind him, pushed a stick in his back and roared:

'Welcome Comrade!'

'For Christ's sake have some sense,' Gerson snapped.

'Can't you take a joke?'

'Yes. Where's the brush?'

'You were bringing it.'

'Hell. Now what can we do? We can't paint with our bare hands.'

'I'll find something,' Dan said.

He ran off and returned twenty minutes later, bearing like an Olympic flame, his shaving brush.

'The best I could find. All the paint brush shops are shut. It's a capitalist conspiracy.'

'Watch out for sentries,' Gerson said, 'you know what happens if we're caught.'

They crept across the battalion football field, then through lines of elephantoid field guns.

'Down!'

Dan flopped on the squelchy earth. Ten yards ahead a sentry stood, heavy like a lead soldier, staring. His slung rifle poked awkwardly out of his khaki cape. Gerson, crawling correctly as he had been taught in basic training, moved away, quick and quiet. Dan crawled after, feeling ridiculous.

They reached the ammunition store. Gerson unwrapped a paint tin.

'Take it,' he said, 'you paint first and I'll keep watch. A short whistle means danger.'

He folded and pocketed the brown paper.

'It's oil paint I'm afraid, which is tricky because it stains your clothes. Be careful.'

The hut was built of corrugated iron sheets. It had once been painted light green. In places the paint had come away showing rusty orange beneath, elsewhere it bubbled up in wide blisters or formed a separate corrugated skin of thin green. Dan scrubbed the paint on. Green specks and slivers mixed with dollops of white showered over him. The letters began huge and got smaller and smaller as he tired. He did the final 'E' and went back to Gerson. But Gerson had gone. He returned to the wall and with the last of the paint added an exclamation mark. The hairs of the brush were rubbed away, only the small bone handle remained.

Huts and guns and piles of junk, grey animals, jumped from the fog, lurched at him. He found he was swinging the paint tin; Gerson had not said how to get rid of it. He passed an empty oil drum which had been stood straight and painted shiny black for a General's inspection. He lifted the edge and pushed the tin inside.

In his room Dan tried to get the oil paint off his hands and uniform. He used paraffin from a lamp kept 'For Emergencies'.

As soon as he woke he longed to go and see the slogan, but Gerson had forbidden it. He waited by the Naafi, hoping to overhear excited conversation; he was disappointed. However, on the Regimental Notice Board a paper had been pasted over the 'afternoon programme'. It read:

Important. All ranks will attend parade, Regimental Parade Ground. 1430 hours. A. Digby-Smith. Adjutant.

Dan thought of going sick, or deserting. He could not find Gerson.

He marched at the head of his Platoon, hearing the crunch of their boots on the concrete. His Battalion formed up. The high bawl of the Sergeant-Major:

'Talyar-r-r-n, Talyarr-r-r-n, Shun!'

The Adjutant walked slowly up and down the ranks. Dan held his breath, stared straight ahead. The Adjutant came right up to him, stood glaring, inches away.

'Stand easy, Graveson. Now, let's have a look at your chaps.'

Dan relaxed.

'Just a security check,' the Adjutant murmured.

'Now men,' he turned to them, 'each Section in turn will come smartly to attention and all ranks will hold their hands smartly in front of them.'

As each man begged for alms, the Adjutant walked gravely by, accompanied by Lt. Graveson. With the tips of his fingers he turned over each pair of hands, and looked at them keenly.

A man with big grimy hands and dirty bitten nails, said:

'I work down the boilers, sir.'

'Hold your tongue man! Don't you know you're on parade? Speak when you're spoken to!'

The Adjutant looked up at the man, who was a foot taller, and snapped:

'A disgraceful turnout. No excuse. Take that man's name Mr Graveson.'

He smiled at the Sergeant and glanced at his hands too.

'Carry on Mr Graveson!'

'Yessir! Platoo-oo-oon, by the right, qu-i-i-i-i-ck March!'

Since 1747 Friday had been Regimental Mess Night. From seven o'clock until nine all Junior Officers stood about the Mess Lounge in dress uniform, drinking, chatting, waiting for the C.O. to Lead the Regiment into Dinner. Dan stood fingering the stem on his glass. He heard Gerson's clear clipped voice:

'. . . Hunt Ball on Tuesday.'

'Where the devil is one to procure scarlet tails these days?' Crabbe asked.

Dan stood near them.

'That's a problem for you regulars,' said Gerson, 'I think I'll trot along in my D.J.'

A pause. They sipped whisky.

'So you're a National Serviceman,' Crabbe said. 'What were you in before?'

'I'm a lawyer,' Gerson replied.

'Defending swindlers and murderers eh?'

'Not exactly. I dealt mainly with land law and property.'

'Oh yes.'

Crabbe finished his drink.

'What'll you have?' Crabbe asked Gerson.

Dan stood quiet.

'And you old chap?' Crabbe turned to him.

'No thanks,' Dan said.

Crabbe brought back two whiskies. On the way he had been thinking.

'What is land law exactly? Sounds a bore.'

'Strangely enough land law is ninety per cent of the law, although less than a tenth of the people own land.'

'Why is that?' Dan asked innocently.

'Because most of our laws were made by nineteenth-century landed gentry whose first concern was with their own property.'

Crabbe left them. Dan said to Gerson:

'Next week he'll be telling the Mess that land law is ninety per cent of the law and what are they going to do about it.'

'Really?' Gerson said, 'Please excuse me a moment.'

Dan rolled the stem of his glass between his fingers. The chat rose and fell around him. He lit a cigarette.

At a quarter to nine something unusual happened. The Adjutant stood at one end of the lounge banging the table with his glass, calling:

'Quiet Gentlemen. One moment please Gentlemen. Quiet.'

There was some whispering. The Adj had drunk only two gins the whole evening, a sign something was brewing.

'I do apologise gentlemen. But the Security chaps have a thing on their mind. And you know what that means. We'll just have to play along with them. This afternoon we had a special parade and inspection for all non-commissioned ranks. Now Intelligence is so damned thorough, suppose we should thank heavens for it, it seems it will be necessary for us in the Mess to undergo a similar check. A mere formality for completeness, you understand gentlemen. All junior officers then, if you please gentlemen, form along that wall, and we can finish in five minutes.'

A roar of voices all talking at once, some protesting, some making jokes, all asking what it was all about. Rapidly the Adjutant walked past glancing at their hands held out. He made it clear that it was not his idea, but that he was formally carrying out superior orders. Dan remembered the early morning spent scrubbing his hands almost raw with pumice stone and scalding water. By electric light the streaks of white across his hands barely showed. The Adjutant checked and passed him without a sign. Perhaps he lingered a moment. Dan could not be sure.

A week had passed. The slogan had been blacked over by Military Police before more than a dozen men had seen it. No one had quite understood it; there had been some puzzled talk, a paragraph in the *Movement for Peace Newsletter* under 'News from the Branches'.

'How's it going old boy?'

The Adjutant's hand rested on Dan's shoulder. This treatment was reserved for Field Officers and RSM's.

'Quite well thank you sir.'

'Could you take ten minutes off this afternoon? The C.O. would like a word with you.'

'Yes sir. What time would be convenient sir?'

'What about 1430 hours?'

'Well I'm down for firing practice then sir.'

The Adjutant frowned.

'Never mind about that Graveson.'

'Very well sir.'

Rarely did the Commanding Officer talk officially with a person of inferior rank, without being supported by his menials: Second in Command, Adjutant, Regimental Sergeant Major, Aide de Camp. Dan was relieved therefore to find Colonel York quite alone.

'Glad to see you Graveson.'

The Colonel did not get up from his heavy leather chair. He sat like an old lion, with whiskery brows, paws for hands, and a way of turning his head round slowly.

'Do sit down. Smoke?'

'No thank you sir.'

'Wise man.'

Dan sat straight on his wooden chair, his hands on his lap. The Colonel glanced down at a file of papers and a copy of Queens Regulations. He pulled at the lobe of his ear, flicked the bristles of his moustache. Dan had seen him behave like this when talking with very senior officers.

'It's about this security report, Graveson. It seems that on the afternoon 3rd July, that is Monday last, during the delivery of a lecture to 'P' Company, you were guilty of conduct which amounted to incitement to mutiny. What have you so say?'

'I have absolutely no idea what it is all about sir. There must be some mistake.'

'I don't think so,' the Colonel murmured. 'You were giving instruction on the twenty-five pounders?'

'That is possible.'

'You initiated a discussion on the value of the weapon?'

'I prefaced my lecture with a general description of the gun, including its cash cost. I had obtained the information from Regimental Office.'

'Indeed. What followed?'

'I'm not sure sir.'

'Come come Graveson. I have the details here. But I prefer to know your side of the picture. "*Audi alteram partem*" you know.'

'Well sir, the figures in thousands of pounds meant nothing to the men. So I may have translated them into terms they could understand. One gun equals twenty motor cars, for example.'

'Or so many council houses or hospital beds? Did you even find it necessary to discuss the position of old age pensioners?'

'No sir, that was one of the men.'

'Did you not ask the men to "vote" on which they would "prefer to have their money spent on"?'

'It was not quite like that sir.'

'You understand, Graveson, that I cannot have one of my officers carrying on like this.'

'Sir.'

'No one sympathises with the pensioners more than I do, but this kind of talk, in the Regiment's time, it's sheer pacifism. Or worse. You join the Army to do a job. A job for your country. If you would prefer to be on the other side, very well then. But you cannot have it both ways.'

'It seems to me—.'

'Don't argue with me. And don't interrupt. The fact is Graveson, I am instructed to request you to resign your commission with effect from the 1st of next month. You will have twelve days leave until that date.'

'It's a terrible shock sir.'

'I'm sorry Graveson. I've never had a thing like this in my Regiment. I cannot concern myself with personal feelings. It's more than a question of regimental discipline, the matter is out of my hands.'

'I must have time to think about it.'

'That is impossible. I formally request you to resign.'

Dan stood up.

'I cannot do that, sir. I consider I have the right of any citizen to hold political views and express them, so long as I do not break army or civil law. If I am charged with an offence, then I wish to be tried by Court

Martial. The publicity will no doubt create—.'

'You may take whatever action you think fit,' the Colonel said decisively. 'But I must warn you that a number of other matters, including a recent occurrence you no doubt have in mind, would certainly be raised against you in the event of your acting foolishly. A court martial needless to say has the power to award the heaviest penalties. I still hope we may settle this matter man to man without unpleasantness.'

'I am only asking for my democratic—.'

'Yes yes yes. Very well, that will be all Graveson. I advise you to consider your position carefully.'

'I will sir. Thank you sir.'

In the outer office, the Adjutant handed him a typed document:

'. . . commanded by Her Majesty to inform you that, following certain admissions, the Army Council have decided that Lieutenant Daniel Graveson should be called upon to . . . resign his Commission. . . . Should he neglect or refuse to submit his application to resign within fourteen days . . . steps will be taken with a view to terminating the said Commission with effect from. . . .'

'Will you sign for it, sir?' the clerk said.

'What?'

'To show you received it, sir.'

'No.'

The clerk looked towards the Adjutant, who said:

'Never mind about that now.'

He marched smartly across the parade ground among the drilling squads and companies. Orders of command whined and roared over his head. He tried to appear as if he had important business to attend to. But he did not know where to go. A Sergeant glanced at him sideways: did he know? How long would the news take to travel round the camp?

He found himself at the Education Centre. Forlorn and empty. Dusty posters told stories in pictures about first aid, fire drill, artificial respiration. Men with moustaches demonstrated life-saving. Old coloured maps showed the distribution of barley, wheat and sugar beet in the neighbouring fields. Who cared? A film of dust covered the globe's northern hemisphere. The Centre was mainly used as a source of drawing pins. The bottom pins from all the posters had been borrowed, leaving pinholes and blobs of rust in the flapping corners. Old Major Caulfield came in:

'What can I do for you, Graveson?'

'I'm waiting for Mr Gerson, if that's all right sir.'

'By all means.'

Dan watched the sagging face, the huge dark veins in the hands.

'Did I ever show you these, Graveson?'

Glossy photographs of a chubby bouncing man.

'I was Army breast-stroke champion in those days, nineteen-thirty-two.'

He still wore his Army Swimming Club blazer and tie. Gerson came in. A spot in the palm of the Major's hand was then travelling towards his heart, a thickening, a slight thickening of the blood, easing towards the muscular heart to cover over and close two hefty pounding vital bloodfilled arteries and stop the flow of blood. He'd be gone, and turned to slime.

'The granting of a commission,' said Gerson, 'is part of the Queen's prerogative. There need be no court martial, no appeal. That which Her Majesty giveth, she may also take away. But you can make a political fight. Do you want to?'

'I'll do anything.'

'Don't underrate the strength of the forces against you. Don't start a battle you can't win. Will your own platoon speak up for you? Can you depend on any of the NCO's, or your brother officers? What about your family?'

'I don't expect much help from anyone else.'

'I see. Well how do you propose to start the campaign?'

'I am prepared to follow out any plan the Communist Party proposes.'

Gerson said nothing for a minute, then:

'In my opinion you should resign with as little fuss as possible.'

*   *   *   *

'Dan! We're going to Helen's. Put your uniform on,' his father called up the stairs.

'I'm sick to death of the bloody uniform.'

'Do as you please.'

Then, on the last day of his leave, a letter arrived, addressed to '265546221 Pte. Graveson, D'. His father held it out to him:

'What's all that about?'

Dan read the short printed letter.

'Good news. I've been posted to another unit. It's quite close by, Epping Forest. On the Central Line. I'll be able to get home for the weekends.'

'Aren't you an Officer any more?'

'The envelope? That's just a typist's error.'

In the car, outside the tube station, his father said:

'You're in some trouble.'

'It's nothing.'

'Then why the long face? I'm a bit older than you—.'

'Old enough to be my father.'

'And I still know a thing or two. If only you'll tell me what kind of a jam you're in—.'

'Raspberry. I've been demoted, temporarily.'

'I knew it. What happened?'

'Well the C.O. is an absolute tyrant. Real Guards disciplinarian. Punishment parades for the slightest mistake. He's completely inhuman. I lead a deputation of the men to complain, I threatened we'd see our M.P.s and get publicity in the papers. . . . It was nearly a mutiny.'

'What about your Communist friend, whatsisname, Gherkin?'

'He thinks I did a good job.'

'But he's leading the troops from behind?'

'No. In the developing political situation—.'

'I don't give two pins for the blasted situation. He got you into this mess, can he get you out?'

'The Government is tottering—.'

'And a puff of your adolescent emotion is going to bring the Government down! You've been cashiered and ruined your career and you still shout *Daily Worker* slogans at me.'

'You're doing the shouting, Dad.'

'You'll miss your train. Better go now. I was going to tell you: I've been trying to get you into the Inns of Court, to read for the Bar. I only hope they don't ask me for your Army record.'

They went into the station. His father bought the ticket, handed it to him, with a five pound note.

'You'll be needing this now, Dan.'

'Thanks.'

'Don't thank me, keep out of trouble. And you'll find a law book in your bag. No harm in a bit of swotting if you get the chance.'

'I will. Thanks for everything. Give my love to Helen. Cheerio Dad.'

'Goodbye.'

Alone in the carriage he dumped his bag beside him. He put his feet up and glared horribly out of the window. A bald old man, unperturbed, got in and went to sit where the bag was. Dan swung the bag up to put it on the rack. Plunk! He hit and smashed a light bulb and bits of glass pattered over the miserable blue suit.

The girl opposite crossed her long legs, lifted one leg to fiddle with the heel of her high-heeled shoe. Past the band at the top of her stocking (reinforced to give the suspender something to hook into) that inner surface of her thigh was her softest and sweetest part. In a tunnel the train stopped dead. The one bulb gave a bead of light.

'Aren't you frightened?'

She didn't answer. He stretched to get something from his bag. As he did so his army boot struck her leg hard. When the train brought them out of the tunnel he saw the heavy dark mark on her leg caused either by a bruise on the skin showing through the stocking, or by the black polish from his boot. As she got out at the next station, she said to him, in a strong cockney voice: 'If you're the kind of miserable little sod who takes it out on young girls, the sooner you're locked up the better.'

The train swung out towards the strange fresh air, rising from a concrete ditch topped by level railings, passing another train sliding in the opposite direction into the long hole: first the head then the long body last the tail light spinning away and down. He looked into the back windows of grey slum houses, grey lace curtains, bits of kitchen, geysers and cupboards. Further from London life got easier. Hundreds of oblong back gardens, trees, television aerials, multicoloured clothes on clotheslines, shirts, upsidedown trousers held by pegs one to each ankle. Outside stations in desirable residential areas massed cars waited: some for wives with spare keys, to do the shopping; others till evening to save their masters ten minute healthy walks. Came odd hopeless triangles of desert: long grass, planks, patches of stinging nettles, pram bits, small hills of gravel; nobody owned them.

A monster black and yellow Army sign shattered the countryside. He obeyed the arrow, walked across open heath, among 'beach trees and blackberry bushes. The berries were hard and green or having-been-picked with a morose scrap of hay left behind. The kids must be on to them as soon as the green gets tinged with pink. They are forced to eat them hard and sour because if one leaves them as uneatable, others will risk the tummy ache. He dreaded arriving at the camp, pictured it again and again. He remembered the radio blare and the cursing, the purposeless parades, being ordered about by unintelligent Sergeants.

His job was to push trolleys or carry shelves of supplies from the Food Store to the Kitchens. He put both hands under the heavy wood shelves which were piled with loaves, slabs of lard, bacon, bowls of potatoes. His neck muscles and the backs of his knees ached. The trolleys, mysteriously, were always empty, so they were light and easy to push. He liked pushing trolleys best. It was the most useful work he had done since joining the Army.

5

He was downstairs early, before them. The maid on her knees in the lounge was laying the fire, her bare legs stuck out from under her skirt. Among the plates on the breakfast table there were as usual two butter dishes. One, between his father's place and Helen's, held yellow heavy butter. In the other, convenient to his own place, he recognised the white flakiness of margarine. He changed the dishes over. At breakfast he spread the butter thickly, asked for more toast, kept the dish close to him. He smiled at Helen.

His father was calling for him to come out to the car immediately, he couldn't wait all morning, he at least had some work to do. Dan went quickly to the maid's room, stood holding the door open. She sat on the cheap bed, darning her skirt.

'Could you spare just ten bob, Joan?'

'You know I'm not paid till Friday.'

'Sorry.'

'Wait, I think I have two shillings.'

She opened the wardrobe with a little key that had survived three owners and two second-hand shops. While she searched in her handbag, he looked, ashamed, at the bits of worn carpet which didn't match. A porcelain Christ hung from a nail on the wall. Catholic pamphlets and women's magazines were piled up, tattered from being read religiously. She gave him half-a-crown.

'I'll pay you back. It's damn nice of you.'

'It's nothing of the kind.'

He walked from his father's office to the public library. Intently, he indexed things: a charwoman washing the tiles in the doorway of a chemist's shop, her broken shoe; a cubic yard of white hot coke in a machine thugathugathugathuga making asphalt; a chap looking up at a lorryful of fruit.

At a table in the Reference Library and Reading Room he struggled to study, learned rare words, wrote sexy stories. A tired woman dragged a child to the *Nursing World* in a rack on the wall, hisswhispering:

'Michael I'm not hurting you. Now stop it. I've got you so your hand can't slip.'

Situation vacant. *The Law of Master and Servant.* Preface. The author could not forbear to mention the generous assistance afforded him by. A ragged tanned man asked at the counter for the *Bankers' Almanac* please. The librarian, a thin girl with tight curls permanently waved, consulted reference books about reference books.

He said: 'It's all right, I'll find it.'

She hurried, touched his elbow.

'It's BA 332.8.'

She pointed to the shelves.

'I can get it,' he said.

He hovered in the middle of the room. Reaching up on tiptoe, she put her hand on a large blue book, tips of her fingers at the top of it, her palm resting along the spine. He looked down at her shoes.

'Thanks, I'll get it,' he said.

She eased the book out so that a triangle of it was away from the shelf. She walked back to the counter, past him. He stood before the books, reading their heavy-lettered titles. Hummed a bit. His long brown forefinger touched *Bankers*, did not move the book. He took his hand away. He scratched his neck inside his collar. Chapter One: Nineteenth Century. Conditions of employment. The early Workmen's Compensation Acts. Whereas. A girl shook the table as she scribbled hard, notes from the *Encyclopedia Brittanica*. Rubber products. She leaned across the book, resting her bosom on it. As she wrote, the end of her pen, which was soured and scratched where she had nervously sucked and bitten it, jabbed into her rhythmically. He bent down to tie his laces, looked up at her beneath the table. Shadows. KOJE yelled from a newspaper headline. And the prisoners at the gateway sang their international song. 'One miner's worth ten lawyers,' he had said to Gerson. 'Yes,' Gerson had replied, 'down a mine.' He moved to another table, and worked. As he left, at twelve, for lunch, an old lady was explaining to the Chief Librarian: 'It was an anthology by Herrington, I have it so firmly in my mind. And so have you, haven't you?'

'I wouldn't say that madam.'

'You'd remembered you'd seen it.'

'Well I might have seen it on a list.'

'Yes, that's right, on a list.'

*   *   *   *

'Helen tells me you've been borrowing money from the maid again.'

His father was tired.

'I'll pay her back.'

'That's not the point. It's not nice. And I've given you twenty-five pounds this month. That means you're spending over six pounds a week. Families live on less, and you've got to.'

'I don't know where it all goes. If you exploited the workers less intensively I might qualify for a government grant, and then I'd be on my own.'

'Is that what you want?'

'Maybe it's what many people want.'

'You're quite wrong Dan, only the other day Helen was saying—.'

'I know: "how much she liked me".'

Dan heard the kitchen door slam. He said quickly:

'Saw a loony boy this afternoon.'

'Mmm.'

'He was making a pig in the sky with string.'

Helen jerked the door open. 'Perfect timing' he thought. She saw him smile.

'What was that?' she asked.

His father said quickly: 'Only a boy Dan met.'

'Didn't he say "pig" or something?'

'Yes? There's a marvellous programme on tonight. Danny Kaye.'

'He's brilliant,' Dan said.

'I wonder if he passed his law exams first time,' Helen said.

'Well I'm certainly going to, if that's on your mind.'

'Of course you are,' said his father. 'There's time for a cocktail before dinner. Dan, get the ice. Have we a fresh lemon and a little grated nutmeg, Helen?'

* * * *

He sat for his exam. It would be a month until the results were published in *The Times*. He had to do something. Anything. He walked into the Town Hall. 'I'm forming a branch of the Peace With China Committee,' he announced.

'Oh, well—' said the young clerk.

'I'm told you could give me a list of local organisations.'

'I'll see.'

He called through a door: 'Young gent here from the China people wants the Orgs file.'

Mumbles. Squeaks. A card board folder.

' 'Fraid you can't take it away. but you can copy the addresses.'

For ten days he knocked on doors, asked Beekeepers, Octogenarians, Pacifists, Conservatives, Folkdancers, Scouts, Labour and Communist Party members, Rose-growers, train-spotters, curates, trade unionists, stamp-collectors, youth leaders, to Stop MacArthur, Prevent International Conflagration and keep their hands off China.

Sixty enthusiasts were invited to the Inaugural Meeting at Dan's home, Thursday evening, 7 p.m. sharp. Helen and his father went early to the cinema. Joan was told she could go after she had prepared the egg sandwiches. Bottles of light ale which his father had ordered from the Off-licence stood in rows on the floor, and on trays tall glasses waited in twelve columns of five. Dan brought down the old Left Book Club books and strewed them around.

At seven, Rickie came, from the big house next door. He was middle-aged, a vegetarian, ran a cycling club for boys; he wore shorts. By seven thirty, two nice old ladies from the Peace Pledge Union were sitting in armchairs talking with Bert a cross-eyed chap in a blue suit with a rucksack. At eight o'clock Bert said they needed a Chairman and would Dan open the meeting. Dan stood by the fireplace, said yes, well they all knew why they had been asked, and if they agreed with the Aims of the Committee they could form a Branch and try to do something about it because it was a mistake to think that the People were powerless. That was playing into the hands of the Reactionaries. The People flew the bombers and fired the guns and the People could make war impossible. They ate sandwiches and Bert drank a quart of beer. They agreed to hold a public meeting in the Church Hall. Bert had some pamphlets about Peoples' China, and they all bought one. They decided to meet monthly at Bert's home. Dan was elected Secretary by four votes to none.

Helen complained about the mess. His father said cigarette ash was good for the carpet, it made it grow, and he told everyone that Dan was Secretary of the Peace Movement.

Dan was still in bed on Saturday morning when Helen brought up the papers.

'I can't find your name in *The Times*,' she said.

'Then I've failed.'

'You're very calm about it.'

'There's no point in getting hysterical,' Dan said.

'What will your father say? You might show some feeling for him, after all he's done for you.'

'He's a very generous man. Don't you find that?'

'You're his biggest disappointment—'

'Mind your own business.'

'Your father's happiness is my business.'

'Quite a profitable one.'

'Take that back! Take that back!'

She was crying. He heard her sobbing and shouting in his father's room. He thought, good he's got something else to think about apart from my bloody exams.

His father came in, sat on the bed.

'Do you want to give up law?' he asked.

'Of course not.'

'There's no "of course" about it. You could have passed that exam. You're not a fool. You just didn't work.'

'Other chaps fail.'

'You're not like them. You can do it, Dan. I only wish I had your chances, I'd be working day and night. I'll help you all I can, but you've got to do the work.'

'I could study better in a place of my own. Nearer the College to save travelling.'

'All right. I'll find you a room not too far away, so you can come home for the weekends.'

The three of them had become expert at mealtime chat, but lunch was like an escalator suddenly stopped, everyone having to climb the unaccustomed stairs. Dan sat quiet, looked at his face upsidedown in a spoon. Helen chatted in little swoops. Up she went, then, hearing the brittle brightness, stopped awkwardly. His father knew the weight was on him, and cautiously avoided forbidden places. He pointed with his knife at the electric clock:

'That was a bad buy, Helen, it's never been right since we bought it.'

Helen said: 'And the trouble is you never know whether it's going to gain or lose, but our bedroom one is—'

Dan interrupted her: 'It's caused by minute variations in the electric current, you know. But that steady sweep of the big hand. It's so impressive. Gets people every time.'

He wondered whether they would leave his chair by the table, or put it against the wall. The table was going to be very big for the two of them. Joan brought in three cups of coffee on a green plastic tray. His father glanced from her breasts to the coffee cups and back again.

Dan went to Bert's house, to see about the Committee. 'I'm sorry dear, Bert's not back from work yet,' his wife said, 'I know he'd like to see you, he's told me about you, come in and wait, I'll make a cup of tea.'

She was pregnant, about seven months gone. She shut the front door behind him. 'Clack' of a Council house, not 'Clonk' like the door of his home. The house seemed as full of kids as she was: four of them, 'the eldest is nine', ran around the kitchen, into the garden and back again, up and down the stairs, got legs caught in the bannisters, swiped each other with sticks, knocked over milk bottles, pushed a rusty old pram round and round the garden, climbed into the dustbin, got bits of grit in their eyes, used the dustbin lid as a shield while the others threw stones, pulled each others hair, burst into tears, yelled, laughed, wiped dripping noses with greasy hands, sat in a puddle eating dirt, asked questions, painted on the wall *it's our wall*, stood staring at flies, poked a tortoise with a stick, held it up by its shell, screaming:

'Don't drop Mr Wooby! Don't drop Mr Wooby!'

'They dropped him once and cracked him,' she said.

She walked round all the time, following them, telling them off, listening to Dan, talking to him. The kettle went on whistling. Her belly pushed at him. She had a wheelbarrowful of childbelly, she wheeled it in front of her. He sat harmless on a kitchen chair waiting for her navel to shove into his face. Her belly was covered by a skirt wrapped round it, huge pink and white blobs and big white buttons. The last three buttons hung down by their cotton threads pulled by the kids scrambling beneath her. Like a huge mother sow she didn't crush one of them. She bent down, showing her pink under-slip, and wiped or swiped bits of fluff and hair from the kids' sticky mouths, and yellowish snot from their noses.

Bert came in.

'Glad to see you here, Dan.'

Hefty handclench. He poured himself a cup of tea. Through the cabbagey smell of the kitchen his sweaty smell came over. His wife lifted a baby from a pram in the corner:

'It's time for his bath.'

And she pushed herself upstairs.

'Been digging trenches in the park,' Bert said. 'Foundations for a new school. They must have heard about my lot.'

'I'm terribly sorry Bert, I've got to give up the Peace Committee.' Dan knew he was talking in a special way, slurring words and dropping aitches.

'That's all right mate. Didn't your mum approve?'

'It's not that. I'm getting a flat in town, on my own.'

'Well well,' Bert said.

6

Unshaved and unwashed because a spider stayed circling shrivelling still crawling round the washbasin, he lay on the hard bed, looking at the nude on the wall, the blackblistered cold fireplace, the gas ring squatting on the lino. He sat up. Some bright bits on the carpet were spots of daylight from the other side of the earth. Tunnels made by needles. He remembered when Grandma swallowed a needle and a year later it came out of her heel. Faces, camels, goblins, birds lived in the patterned curtains; behind the window but almost flush with it, a darkbrick neighbour wall shut out the night.

He trod down the quiet creaking stairs, got outside. Street lights shone yellow madly at nobody. Sky men in purple overcoats and floppy pink hats played moon-football. His nose was cold. Fresh on his face light rain fell. He pounded over the ringing pavement. 'Be twenty. Poise dizzy at an angle on a waterfall edge. Look down, see the white gas there. Plunge, splutter, shoot away and race away downriver.' Rain fell, bounced, danced, on his pavement which he'd put there on purpose.

He looked in at a workmen's café. He wasn't a workman. Water trickled down the misted window, it was warm inside and cold out.

Home, he flopped on the bed. Spider's a long time dying. Up once more, he put the bacon he'd bought into the saucepan he'd bought, watched the warmed fat become lucent, ooze, begin to crackle. He sniffed.

Downstairs again, to the lavatory, taking things with him. The slightly slimy stone rim refused his body warmth. He stretched his leg forward, pressed his foot against the door to keep it shut. He read the brownpapercovered book he had taken from his father's wardrobe. First acne, underwear, the Orient, spiritual awareness, conducive foods: cloves and saffron, black molasses. Then at last, Love-play, Coital Positions, Perfect Courtship, Ideal Marriage, Advanced Coital Positions, Notes for the Obese. The other book, twisting nudes, lay on the floor. He tried to read the two together. O manufacturers of frosted glass for the windows of suburban lavatories.

The gas ring still flared in the dark room. The bacon was charred dust on the ceiling and out the window, the floor wet with liquid saucepan. He offered himself a saucepan sandwich.

*　*　*　*

Helen's precise hand: two neat strokes sliced through the old address and small clear letters announced the new. The envelope contained an Invitation to a party, from Montague.

Frantic in the frantic centre of the frantically crammed room Montague stood with his hairy hands in his hairy jacket pockets. Dan walked right up to and on top of him talking immediately loudly continuously. *Quelle savoir faire.* He wore his pipe and Montague told him how well it suited him, made him look much older. Dan joined the homosexual cowboys chatting cleverly at bubbly girls. What do you do? Me Yugoslav partisan – part-time. What's your favourite colour eyes? The great eyes of camels and the eyes of men in Sainsburys. He stopped. He'd climbed over himself. Embarrassed girls looked at each other's feet, drifted away. But she circled, dancing, a glance for him each time round. Her northern hemispheres bounced, wobbled, jumped. She looked, double-chinned, down at them, a basketful of puppies. He took her drunk damp hand, led her into the room reserved for sexual intercourse. It was going to be lovely.

He said: 'Bell fling float kite cap kiss shell hill plough panther antler elegant bending rainbow rain garden grave—'

'What are you talking about?'

'Just a game.'

'Kid's game,' she said, 'one word leads to another. One two three. We all know that.'

His head lay on her lap, he spoke to her tummy.

'Words don't describe, they point, and poets hit the source in history, the shadow behind each word. Don't slip so quick from step to step. Rest. Words are abstract isolate ancient huge, flipping and floating in coloured balloons in fanlight air. Yelp. Out it flasht. Flashtitout. Timmy begoodboynow. Guttergone. Autumn eats trees with amazing flames, leaving the indigestible bones for deadwinter.'

She stared across at the bodies fiddling and squeezing and heaving.

'Why go on?' she said.

'For the prize, to dirtily prise your knees and thighs, to deliberately split your delicious infinitive.'

'Oh. Well you can get off me.'

In the main room people sank by stages to the floor, spilling drinks over each other.

'Somebody stole yo' gal?' Montague asked.

'Seizing abandoned property is no larceny,' Dan said.

'So you're going to be Lord Chief Justice after all?'

'Never. My heart's not in it. I don't care who owns things.'

'Your father—'

'Forget him. One death was tragic, but two made him ridiculous. Now the weight's on me, and brother he's in for a disappointment.'

'Does he ever talk about Bryan?' Montague asked.

'The dirty words in our home are dead wife and dead son. Never mentioned. Not a picture, not a word.'

'Because the alternative to silence is a scream?'

'Because Helen's a doll, a real doll, and she mustn't be made miserable.'

'If it weren't for her,' Montague said, 'if you were left alone with him, you'd soon find him hanging by his braces. Your father is living with Helen, and he's alive with her. But you want to camp in galleries of tinted photographs. Why dwell on death?'

'Why not wallow in it? Hell how grandma would have wallowed and wailed and bellowed and punched herself blue! With us each emotion is clipped like a privet hedge or a slick moustache. Throw away your lines, be polite, and after two gins be charming. That's all. But I want to learn Latin, be in the desert, kill with an axe, cover my ear in gravy, piss on their carpet, fill that bloody television set with old cod. Ours is not an ikon, it's got doors, it's a triptych. Them, their actual heads and legs I love all right. But they've been suffocated by junk. They can't even cry for the dead.'

He belched.

His friend stood up: 'You'd better go home.'

'It's too early,' Dan pleaded, 'let's go to the pictures, or —'

'I'm taking you to the nearest Underground.'

Alone and singing in a huge lift going down. No, there was a man with him, working the lift, listening, chewing. Two big eye teeth and a thin loose lip, which he chewed. He prodded a bellysoft thumbshape into shadow. A strong spring flung the steel gate across and slammed Dan's ear out.

'Eye teeth!' Dan bawled, 'You've knocked my bloody ear out! You and the Senior Lift Operator and the Assistant Station Master and the Station Master and the Designer of Lifts and the Constructor of Lifts and The Minister and Her Majesty and Hieronymus Bosch and the Bishop of Bath and Wells. And I'm gonna boot the lot.'

Carefully he balanced on one foot, gave a quick swing and kicked himself out onto the non-slip floor. Eyeteeth picked him up, leaned him against the tiled wall and told him he'd had a drop too much. Scraps of rag and paper lay in the lift hole, cables and weights and wheels moved steadily. Miles above, a metal voice cried:

'Stand Clear of the Gates'.

Two hundred times a day he used to yell that, yelled himself hoarse. Now he does a new recording once a year and switches on whenever he wants. Dan saw three sharp little black studs with clear silver letters: nonsec; bel; bug. He tried to hang on to the smoothtiled wettish wall.

Suddenly he was deep in people rushing on and off and anyhow. Crowds of girls, a porter with a watering can, soldiers, boys in striped scarves, actresses, dreary gentlemen. He swam along. He was going home.

*   *   *   *

They dined in the Temple, formally, on benches, enclosed by ancient coats of arms, by King Charles tiny and pointed on his thirty foot cart horse, a gorgeous woodcarved ceiling, stained glass windows scarlet and ultramarine, pockmarked servants, a macebearer with a mace, glossy collars and cuffs and teeth pinpointed against dark suits and the solid brown of panelled oak. Montague, Dan's guest, was impressed.

'When I went into my Dad's dress business,' he said, 'I never knew what I was missing. Twelve hundred a year and the night plane to Rome when the peaches are ripe is all very well, but this, this is Big, Dan. It's grand, it's historical, it's feudal. The yanks should make a colour film of it.'

'You ain't seen nothin' yet,' said Dan. 'Here comes the Procession of Judges. Something to tell the grandkids.'

The line of old men doddered along between the tables, near close enough to touch. The Senior Judge thanked the Lord beautifully for His bounteous liberality and everyone sat down.

'Man, they're the ancientest,' said Montague.

'They are indeed incredibly old, and diseased,' said Dan. 'And remember that I, if I sweat and strain, I may become one of those.'

'It's a great incentive,' said Montague. 'Look at that little one, he's fantastic. Those facial muscles, that premature bulldog look. How does he do it?'

'Each morning,' Dan replied, 'after gargling, he informs the bathroom: "I, Mr. Justice Presley, Enshrine the Constitution. I have never heard of rock and roll". He repeats this to his wife who says: "Yes dear". He pulls on his long pants, eats a very big breakfast, is conveyed to the Courts, where, robed and throned, ten miles above the multitude, he tells working-class witnesses to "Speak up man!" because he can't hear a word.'

'Seriously,' said Montague, 'what makes you so bitter?'

'Tell me why in all history a Judge has never once said: "Put a sock in it", "Fuck you Jack", "My leg itches", "I feel awful", "You look a lovely bit of stuff"?'

'I'll answer your question if you answer mine.'

'I failed my exam.'

'Again?'

*   *   *   *

'You have proved that Property Law is a swindle and therefore not worth studying,' his father said, 'but you failed Divorce too?'

'Divorce is as big a fraud as marriage. Let people do as they please. They're grown ups. Live-together or not-live-together. Who cares?'

'The children?'

'Farm them out to mass-crèches supervised by trained male nurses.'

His father was counting pound notes from his wallet.

'Here's ten pounds,' he said. 'Make it last two years.'

'Did you discuss this with anyone we know?'

'Don't be stupid, Dan. Why didn't you work? If you were a bloody fool I could excuse it, but you're just drifting. Life's been too easy for you. You need a shock. If only I had my time over again. . . . I got to London with a five pound note in my pocket and a wife and child in the back of the car.'

'You had a car then?'

'You know what I mean, Dan.'

'Yes I do.'

'You think you do. You heard about the young man of nineteen who thought his father an idiot, and at twenty-one he couldn't understand how —'

Dan chimed in the last words: '— the old man had learnt so much in the last two years.'

They smiled.

'I mean it Dan. When I was your age I worked from six in the morning till twelve at night. Sometimes drove up to Lincoln to fetch a big load, then a quick turn round and down to the Garden by early morning. The other firms had drivers, but I was on my own. We lived on sandwiches, that's what ruined my digestion.'

'I thought it was booze.'

'I did things then I'd never do now. I'm old.'

'You're a success. You're well off. You've built up a business. You smoke cigars and drink whisky. You've a beautiful redhead and a 21 inch T.V. What more do you want — ulcers?'

'I was born at the wrong time. Ten years earlier and I'd have made a million. But those days will never come back. There isn't the money to be made any more, not that kind of money. I remember them coming to me with the first idea for football pools, but I'd been caught too often.'

'So you're rich and successful and full of regrets. Why can't you understand when I say my heart's not in it?'

'Who gives a damn if you heart's not in it! My heart's not in it! Go to your beloved workers on their way to work in the morning, if you can get up that early, and ask them if their hearts are in it. You'll get some funny answers.'

'Then what's the point of it all?'

'The posing of that question is a luxury you can no longer afford. You can start worrying about philosophy when you are in a steady job.'

7

He found Montague seated in his maroon upholstered swivel chair, using his two white daily-sterilised telephones, consulting his stainless steel filing cabinet, blinking at graphs, confiding in his suedette secretary, fiddling with the thermostatically-controlled central heating system. Fitness for function. Montague's function was to meet foreign buyers, note carefully that they were all unable to state precisely the quantity and quality of the goods they wished to import, and to have lunch every day with Dad and the other Directors. He was able to spare Dan a few minutes, lend him four pounds, and give him a note of introduction to Max Spencer, an appeals organiser for charities, who required an assistant secretary with a public school background.

Spencer carried a yellow glove in his yellow-gloved hand. Dan had worked for him for a fortnight, and was learning to keep a special boyish grin for the Chairmen of the various Committees, to create an attitude rarely cringing, yet always sufficiently deferential.

'I wonder, Graveson, whether you could take the Minutes for the A.O.'s tonight,' Spencer asked.

His tone of voice implied: although I speak jauntily, this, young man, is your chance to prove yourself.

Dan's navy suit and blue and gold old school tie contrasted with the virgin whiteness and special glossiness of a brand new Van Heusen collar style eleven. He travelled by taxi to the Mayfair address. A pretty starched white and bright blue maid opened the fine front door:

'May I take your coat sir? The A.O. meeting is in the front lounge sir. Thank you sir. This way sir.'

Three chaps in middle-aged sports jackets sipped sherry together. Dan stood close to the wall holding the cardboard file Spencer had given him. He walked over to the table, took a glass of sherry from the silver tray, felt himself in the middle of the room.

More people came: ladies with expensive legs, company directors who looked like company directors, talking together of maids and motorcars.

'Mr. Graveson?'

The hostess beckoned to him.

'Have you everything you need? A pen? Do use this card table for your papers.'

Like a Jane Austen curate he sat straightening his papers while the guests finished their sherry and slowly settled elegant bottoms in elegant chairs.

In a cultured voice Dan read the Minutes of the last meeting at which it had been decided that the Ninth Annual A.O. Ball should be held at the Saveloy Hotel. The meeting then proceeded to the discussion of the main item on the agenda: the question of prizes for the Tombola. The chairman of a whisky firm offered a case of whisky as first prize. He was congratulated, thanked, held up as an example. 'Simply splendid,' said the treasurer, 'if we had a few more Gerald Felthams all our problems would be solved.'

The price of Tombola tickets was debated passionately. Finally a compromise motion referring the matter back for decision by the Annual Ball Tombola Sub-committee, was carried by eighteen votes to nine with eleven abstentions. The treasurer estimated that the Tombola should make approximately two hundred pounds profit.

'What's that in terms of A.O.'s?' he asked Dan.

Dan read from the illustrated leaflet:

'Two and sixpence will buy enough dried milk to maintain an Asian Orphan in good health for approximately five days.'

'Simply splendid,' the treasurer said.

Dan didn't go to Spencer's office the next morning, or ever again. Spencer wrote, at first politely then rudely, asking for the return of his A.O. File.

8

Multilith operator, Adrema embosser, accounts clerk, upholsterer, Burroughs P 600 operator, invoice checker, delivery man, marine engineer, Capstan lathe operator, warehouseman, stove enameller, reinforced concrete engineer, window dresser, pig man. He was none of these. He wasn't even a Hairdresser's Assistant. Two columns of vacancies for shorthand typists. He bought a Teach Yourself Shorthand book, explained to the landlady that as soon as he got through it, say twenty-four hours solid work, he would be earning at least ten pounds a week. He reached Chapter Three.

He was thrown out of his room. Bodily. There's the rent and the state you leave your room in it's not nice the smell and tins everywhere the bed unmade dust all over sink blocked up it's not nice for the other tenants not that they've complained but it's not nice. Be out by morning. He wasn't. Her brother came. Headbutting bastard. Armwrenched body-buffeted buttockbumped bullied and socked downstairs and out.

Bums in lines queued for jobs and thirty bob odd doled out by clerks from behind heavy wire.

'Report three times a week to get your card stamped.'

To make sure you've not got a job same time as you're collecting. Dan waited all morning between tough blokes, Irish and Jamaican. Didn't talk to them. Shuffled up as queue moved forward. One bloke bounced on his toes, swinging a violin case so that everyone knew he was not an ordinary bum but a musical bum.

By hungry lunchtime Dan found out he was in the Manual Labour queue. Bricklayer's assistants only.

'All right, I'll take that.'

'No son, you've got school certificate. Come next Thursday, ask for the clerical department.'

He walked down streets, strange ones. Camden Town. He sat on a seat placed on a triangle of grass between busy roads. Good to sit down, lots to look at. Bless the Victorian philanthropist. Then women carrying shopping gooped at him.

Parkwandering, somewhere, he set a deckchair on its feet, wiped the birdshit off, sat. Got up, altered the back strut, sat again, more stretched out, nearer the ground. An attendant tinged close by. He leapt up, sat on a wooden seat, a free one. Nowhere to sleep. Lucky it was warm.

He went to the free lavatory. The door was lower than the penny lays. He moved with bent knees so that his head should not be seen. A spade and two brooms were kept there. One broom soft for dust, the other, thick copper red spines wet with disinfectant. No pick-up seat; only a rim of stained wood. Advertisements for venereal diseases. A metal notice above an empty box: *Toilet paper must be obtained from the Attendant*. A tramp with dirty bum must hobble out and ask for paper, please.

He found a sheltered place to sleep, protected from the slight evening wind. He took off his jacket, bunched it into a pillow, lay his cheek on it. Shivered. Picked up a fallen log for a pillow. Beetles. Flung it away. Stood still. Bells rang ArangArangArang.

'A-a-a-a-l Out! A-a-a-a-a-a-l Out!'

Hide. Down quick on his knees in the leaves, heart bumping. No. He got up, brushed the earth off his clothes, ambled out of the main gate. It was damp and cold now.

Raw noise. Tens of thousands of wheels on roads. Heaps of persons, hives of them, pouring from and into buildings, crowding up steps from underground, crouching in cars, stopping up the street gaping at gadgets in windows, getting pinched elbowed killed drunk dazed, reading evening papers, obeying policemen, selling (and buying) fruit. He bored through them, out to Holborn and the dead City where the daytime moneymagnet was switched off and it was empty. Greenish light lay on the windows of banks, insurance houses, tobacconists. Policemen shone square lights at doors, and tested locks.

Blitz sites. He was walking with conscious leverage from leg to leg. His legs weighed impossibly heavy. He came to a thudding hellplace, gleams of fires, men swung shovels, the ground shook, it was between mountains.

'What's happening?'

'Government contract. Double shifts.'

The steepening road grew bendier, slummier. Tramlines whipped away, shining. He looked at the headlamps of cars spinning round roadbends, coming and going, like spies signalling, but not to him. Asphalt now, to fall and cut your knee on. Everyone's got a scar on his knee from falling off a bicycle or something, onto a gritty road; an inch of blue grey dead. The regular street lights passed him one to the other. He was lit by two lights making two faint shadows; the third substantial shadow where the two overlapped, had an unhuman shape. Tremendous lorries bound for Glasgow Strasbourg Benghazi thundered past him onwards paralysing as panzer divisions. A dog barked. Bing beng, quarter past something. He found a nameless place with smashed windows and swinging door and a man on a backless chair. He crept in, lay on the floor, felt his head and spine against stone. His feet swing high and round and round in gorges, canyons.

Slammed in the ribs by boulders:

'Out you get, out of it. Railways property. Out with you. Come on out of it.'

Very slowly the morning sun warmed him. It was going to be another fine day. He stood with his back to a lamppost, turned his face into the sun for a moment. He'd ended up at Billingsgate of all places. The insane fish smell drove him up the hill, spitting. He passed a dead bus stuck in a hole, and early workers whistling.

'Ullo Ken, 'ow yer goin'?'

'Can't complain.'

He had been here before, ages ago, with his father. He found a halfpenny on the pavement. A kid pointed at his shoe: 'Look mum, it's got it's mouth open.'

Policemen glanced at him.

He finished the tea and the ham roll and walked slowly to the door.

'Not so fast. That's tenpence.'

'So sorry. I clean forgot.'

He felt in his trouser pockets. Halfpenny. He looked intently into his wallet. An old woman pushed in, past him. A wrinkled stick from an Irish hedge, crimson hair tangling from under her hat which had berries on it. She hooked her man's umbrella on to the counter, and in a sharp Belfast voice asked for a cup of tea. But the man looked past her:

'Well?'

'I haven't a penny on me,' Dan called from the door, keeping his grip on the handle. 'Now what do we do? I'm really most dreadfully sorry. A cheque for tenpence, of course, would be ridiculous.'

'Buzz off. Go on, get moving. And don't come this way again in a hurry. I'll know your mug for next time.'

He had to get decent. He got back to his father's home, knowing his father would be at work in the afternoon. Helen came to the door, wiping her hands on her apron.

'Dan! What a state you're in! So that's how you've been carrying on. I thought you were meant to be studying.'

'I'd like some lunch please.'

'It's half past three. Nearly tea-time.'

He shoved past her into the kitchen. She followed, stood holding the door. He opened the fridge, took out a bottle of milk, a cold roast chicken, a carton of potato salad.

'That's your father's supper.'

'He'll understand.'

'But there's nothing else in the house. What am I going to tell him? What will he say?'

They stood over him.

EUROPE AFTER THE RAIN

1

WE WERE APPROACHING THE RIVER. The modern bridge had been demolished, a wooden one constructed. Passengers were ordered to get out and walk across. The way led from the metalled surface of the road over deeply-frayed planks. Seventy yards away the permanent bridge, massive steel and concrete, was still half completed. Danger threatened the wooden bridge, ice pressed against the log piles supporting it. Explosions broke the silence as a soldier with a pole placed packages on the ice. 'It's moving', she said. Slowly the ice-pack oscillated and a large piece broke away to be carried by the current fast beneath the bridge.

In the bus, all the seats were occupied. 'Don't worry', she said, 'when the control comes the people will have to get out.' Two passengers could not find their tickets. They were taken off to some sort of centre, or so I was told. Genuine passengers were driven to the outskirts of the frontier town. The driver was pleasant enough: 'Of course it is bad here, but not so bad as you might think.'

At the first building, I asked her: 'Won't it be closed? It's already well after seven.' Someone is bound to be on duty.' A light shone. 'You were right, someone is here.' In a room lit by a bulb, a middle-aged woman sat knitting. She did not glance at us. I was left alone with her, a man came in, the three sat in silence, I wrapped in my coat.

The girl returned. 'Drink?' 'I don't drink,' she replied. 'Never?' 'I don't like alcohol.' The man asked her to dance, she glanced down at his boots, and danced with him. 'You'll have to dance with all of them. Let's leave, it's no use waiting. I'll pay the bill.' The man made a movement with his hand. 'We must pay the bill.' He did not reply.

We were separated. I objected: 'She is in my care, until she has contacted her family.' We had to stand in front of a desk. She understood that the words used were a message of welcome. They appeared to have a most enjoyable conversation. He walked backwards and forwards, I waited, I knew I would have to wait.

The rooms were littered with paper and rubbish. Room after room showed the same sight. A photograph lay in the dust on the floor of one room, she picked it up, glanced at it, then flicked it back to its former place. 'Upstairs it's a bit risky,' she warned, 'have you got a torch?' Everything had gone, even the floorboards. The staircase to the top floor was planks battened together. 'That's the door,' she said, 'I shall wait for you here.' The door opened slightly, the eye of a girl. 'Do you mind waiting a little? Someone isn't really dressed yet.' She showed no marked sign of being other than healthy. 'We were two patients to a bed. My fellow patient was a man who died. They left him with me for two days before taking him away.' There was no trace of hysteria. 'It was nice of you to come.'

We walked fast in a strong cold wind, among loose stuff lying about. A viaduct led to the destroyed bridge, we ran down stone steps to reach the street, whole steps were missing, the gaps protected by wire. Single walls crashed. Music sounded from a church, people with dogs waited at the entrance, the stairway was packed with a stationary crowd of listeners. Two new trolley buses were being tested. I counted thirty wooden huts. Girls stood in a circle singing a patriotic song. She would not join them.

We knocked. We said we could not stay.

We went to two cinemas.

Someone called for her. She discussed her plans. 'As a matter of fact I have not got any plan.' You have names and addresses.' I am probably standing on a dead body.' She bought two and a half pounds of sweets. Anyone could buy sweets. Everyone did a little buying and selling. Loot. Though there was little left. There were other ways. Casual labour received high wages. She did private work in the evenings. Quality work. One house was famous. The owner sang those songs. She sang the one we had heard in the street.

At the orphanage we were told that orphans arrived in a number of ways. 'The police find them. Or neighbours bring them. Some arrive on their own.' A boy of twelve had just arrived. He presented himself. A woman came with two children, she was their neighbour, their father had had an accident. They were disinfected and medically examined. They went through the hands of an examiner, a heavy woman with a strong face, cold, distrustful, a woman on the other side of the writing desk. She tested the children. She showed us her equipment. 'I have to carry out my tests. Most of the children are of normal intelligence. The history of each is written down. When it is a case of a brother and sister, this is marked on both cards. The building has three floors. Each floor is isolated to prevent the spread of infection. Children from three to eight are encouraged to play with toys.' 'Who sends them toys?' 'And there are kitchens, and there are laundries.' The interview, though it produced no useful information, was most pleasant. There were no armed guards or admittance permits. She was a member of the aristocracy. We could speak direct. 'What do you want? Where would you like to go? No, it is too dangerous.' Someone must make a start.' 'I shall see what I can do.' We saw the kitchens. We tasted the food. It was the same. The food was available. They achieved the maximum flavour, by careful cooking. 'A soup well made is the best means of deriving the most benefit.' The shops were filled with food. The children got milk for breakfast twice a week. A fine piece of work.

A boy. The sun. The windows. The rays of the sun streamed direct from the heavens. The boy talked to her: 'We got on a boat, a train, they caught us, back you go, they bought us tickets, we hid till the train went, we came out, why are you not on that train? It's gone, it's your fault, you told us the wrong time. Wait here for the next train. Before we started out we collected anything we could find, and our friends gave us things. When we got hungry, we sold everything.' They asked his name. No one knew his parents, they had disappeared, absolutely, he wasn't sure of his name, it had been signed away to someone else. They took his clothes, bathed him, turned him over, gave him other clothes. He asked for his own. She said: 'With very little you do a great deal, and do it well.' On our way to the dining room the boy stopped us: 'I'm glad you've come. I thought I had been forgotten.'

Up two flights of steps, a room, forty feet by forty feet, thirteen feet high. The walls and ceiling were painted white. On each wall, a fresco: undamaged cities, a dancer, an eagle five feet square, done in black on scarlet, no intention of flight, massive legs, it was not an eagle. A continuous table, along three sides of the room, had been laid for supper, plates of excellent ham, thin slices of sausage made from meat, fish in oil, boiled eggs salted and spiced, various salads, and cheese. But eating would not take place for some time. Sweet biscuits of several kinds were placed on the table. Conversation started. They recalled the tortures in the building. An undercurrent of recklessness. 'We can stand anything, if you know what that means.' We had to ask questions. It had been agreed that I was to remain. I asked about the boy. 'I don't know whether I should tell you. It was done without my knowledge. These young people. If I had known I should not have allowed it.' I noticed her eating the biscuits. 'Look at the roof, just above the room with the high windows. You see? The yellow tiles are new. Crawling and working on a steep roof. A drop of forty feet from the gutter.' A hasty whispering took place. It was time for us to go. 'Do you mind waiting? We shall have to give you an escort, that is, if you wish to return.'

We drove back across the bridge. The river ran past the town from south-east to north-west. We went round two sides of an open square. The doors of the car would not close properly. The driver demanded to be paid. I refused.

I bought her a belt for her birthday, a broad band of lemon yellow. She said: 'Today is a day. I don't notice any difference from other days. We visited the blind. Nurses gave their lives. I have no time. I have work to do. But now I must go to sleep.'

We had identical conversations with high-placed officials. I asked if we had a chance of finding the right direction. They laughed. She said afterwards: 'If you overwork them, they collapse. Something happens. They break down.'

They worked by candlelight. The electric cable had not been relaid. Hesitation was not tolerated. Each was required to correct mistakes. The standard of attention demanded was high. Questions were snapped at them, incorrect attitudes eliminated.

Police headquarters had been repaired. Electric lights functioned. I was standing at the back of the office when she entered. She explained the reason for her visit. It was not always easy to understand what she was trying to say. She would have to have lessons. She had no map. She tried to draw a map.

For years she had lived an abnormal life. She had been intensively trained. This had lowered her capacity to concentrate. She had formed habits of thought. Here was a powerful and unknown force. Her structure had been completely destroyed, in blood and burning. The structure of this girl was a new and unknown factor in history. It would be known only in the future. It would be something quite different from what her teachers had intended.

I had a haircut, a shave, my suit pressed, I collected clean clothes from the laundry. At my door a shoe cleaner waited, he cleaned my shoes, and with his assistance I bought some books, locks and bolts, a basket of bread, a pail of eggs, cakes, and flowers. I put the cakes and flowers in her room. The flower shops were filled with flowers. No one was allowed to have more than one room, few had more than the corner of a room. They needed a few flowers, and rich cakes with layers of thick cream, twenty shops sold such cakes, cakes had never been so rich or so plentiful, every woman who could made them at home and sold them to the shops.

Carrying my case, I walked back to the hotel. I had a pleasant surprise. I had not expected to be allowed into my room, but the hall porter handed me the key. On entering, I found her things lying about. There was no handle to the door of the room, so that should I have closed it, I could not have opened it again. Someone knocked on the door and pushed it open: 'Remember me?' I saw a young girl, I knew that I knew her well, and that she was someone I really liked, but I could not place her. Asking her to be seated, I went to my suitcase to fiddle about with its contents while I was trying to remember who she was. 'How did you know I was here?' I asked. I remembered buying her flowers a few days before. 'There are lots of things I should like you to explain, for example, the flower shops.' She replied: 'Flowers are good. Every office has a canteen. The hundredth trolley bus has been repaired. Thank you for the flowers. They are a great help.' 'And the man who cleans my shoes?' 'Offices have canteens.' She showed me hundreds of duplicated typewritten sheets. She handed me one. Her views were sane, but they were not her own.

I asked her questions. We had continually to change the place to avoid attracting attention. Carts hauled away rubble, these vehicles were long and narrow, wedge-shaped troughs, the sides were loose planks, the wheels had been taken from army lorries, as had the tyres, balloon tyres, and the ball-bearing axles. The standing figures, in groups of twos and threes, watched. She made some futile remarks about them. She was reading as she walked along, licking a finger tip, turning over a clinging page. It was late. The building was being cleaned and repainted, they were cleaning the high crystal windows. We discussed *Gone with the Wind*. I tried to attend. The crowd was too dense. I studied the outside of the buildings, house joined to house in a continuous row. The height of the rooms was eleven feet and the floors were one foot thick, the houses were dead and derelict fortresses, vitality in one or two rooms, warm and lighted. This was the heat of the life of the town.

We sat on benches along the walls, the centre of the room had been cleared for dancing. We played draughts with the board between us on the bench. The dancing was due to start. I mentioned the songs. She said something to one of the others who immediately, but without interrupting his game, started a song. The girls sang as a choir, the boys played instruments. They broke off to gaze at me. A hurried talk, then three of them formed themselves into a row, and three stood behind them. By keeping close they made a compact group, their bodies rigid, they kept time with sharp marionette movements of hand and head. It was effective, even menacing, but I could not interpret it. I knew it portrayed something powerful and perhaps reckless. She said that the choir prepared concerts for its own pleasure, it had never performed outside the building. While they were singing, she cut strips of coloured paper and stuck them on to a piece of white card. She made an intricate paper box, a square building freshly painted white. She talked to me. She had found some books belonging to her father, her trouble was where to hide them. It was not easily done. They had strict control over the bridge. She had taken the youngest and prettiest girl, and they had pretended. The books were stored and completely lost, she could not find where she had hidden them. She became hysterical. We moved to another room. The windows were holes in the walls, the plaster had fallen away, there were gaps in the floors. Her two brothers had been killed, her father had disappeared, she wanted to get back to a normal life. 'I was mad with joy. I could not understand it. I thought they wanted to kill just as I wanted to kill. After this I do not believe anything. My brothers were sent to work in the forests. I don't know where. I have not heard of them since.' Forty people were jammed in the room, everyone was compelled to stand upright. They formed against the walls, leaving a small square free. Her group was to sing as a choir. There were nine of them. I had a special interest in them. There was some bustling in the next room and from time to time the connecting door opened. Then it was flung open and she ran in, dressed in odd bits of coloured material and a few ribbons, in an effort to resemble a gay costume. She sang the same song and finished with an attempt to dance. She had shown great ingenuity in using coloured paper for her costume. She wore a coloured paper cap, and concealed her hands from everyone.

In the morning I found her with the children carrying steaming pails of soup across the courtyard. I watched her cross the cobbled stone yard. The steam was dense. She was in charge of ladling out the soup and could not be disturbed. The old woman told me that she could not be interrupted. Through a glass door on one side, the old woman in a black jacket, in the dim light of a boxlike room, on and on, motionless body. She got up from her chair, opened the glass door and invited me to enter: 'It is warmer here.' I said I wished to speak to the girl. She needed help. 'We give help,' the woman replied. 'We have a list. We make inquiries. We have had contests in swimming with eight hundred spectators.' I said I had to see the girl on official business. I was informed that she was engaged, I would have to wait. There were several men there, they seemed worried, and whispered together. A man walked from the room. The woman spoke to me: 'What shall I tell her?' 'Tell her I want to see her.' I heard a voice behind a closed door: 'Who is there?' I went in. 'This is no place.' The room was half a room, screened, two beds, a small table, a coke stove with a pan on top. 'It's too dark to read here. We have a window but it is boarded up, the boards are warmer in winter.' I replied: 'So far the winter has been mild.' Twice I have lost everything. This time I hope I shall be able to keep what I have got. Nothing is going to be stolen from here.' She showed me the bread she had made. The walls were decorated with paper figures from fairy tales, the home seemed so rich, with things of wood made by hand. 'I am sorry I came so late,' I said, 'and now I have come at an awkward time.' 'I'm afraid I must break off this conversation.' 'I hope I am not making things difficult for you. I know where you intend to go. It is a prohibited area. No foreigners allowed.' 'I don't need you. I can travel alone.' 'They are at war. You have heard of their attempts to pacify.' 'There are all sorts of rumours.' 'How do you manage alone?' 'It is difficult. I have to fight. I have to say to myself loudly and continuously that I can fight and win, I can save myself. When you failed to come I sent a message that you were not to come back.' 'What happened then?' 'You came.' There was a bed, with one thin blanket. We lay on the bed. 'Show me your hands.' She held out her hands. I wore my coat. We discussed my proposal to visit the town where her father had last been seen. It was a question of transport, the state of the road, the actual condition of the surface of the road, the presence of bandits. Buses had been stopped and the passengers robbed.

2

THE TRANSPORT ARRIVED. The driver was ready to take the risk. The car had a hood, and planks on each side, we were wrapped in blankets. The hooded interior was a small room. We faced each other and carried on a conversation. We were going to the town where her father, so she had been told, had been recently buried.

All bridges were broken. The front wheels were over a trench in the road. We got help, with concrete blocks we built a way across the trench. It was dark. We clambered out of the hooded wagon. We quarrelled. It was not clear what it was all about. We fought. She did not want to be forced. There was silence. I needed help. 'We are lucky to be in a town. I shall get help from somewhere.' A clock struck nine, the street was empty, no light shone from the houses. 'I shall find a place.' She remained in the wagon. She called out: 'I want some hot tea. Can I have some tea?' 'No.' 'Please speak. I like to hear it.' 'Tea?' 'Do you understand?' 'I'll get you some tea.' 'Don't leave me.' I must look for a place, we must get somewhere to sleep, otherwise we will have to answer more questions.'

The streets were quiet. I found a man, I argued with him, he directed me. The place was closed. I smashed down a door. A man with a gun waited. I told him what we wanted. He did nothing. The wind was blowing sleet. I passed a church tower. Cavalry clattered by, followed by men on foot carrying long, straight scythes, the wind bent the peacock feathers in their caps and the sleet beat on our faces as we tramped through the slush.

We stayed in her father's house. In the living room were two beds, a round table with a lace centre piece, a carpet on a polished floor. We were welcomed as guests. The caretaker heated the stove, his wife prepared some tea, eggs, and bread and butter. The room was not warm enough. The old man took the best bed out of the living room and carried it into the next room. It was two o'clock in the morning. On the wall was a large oil painting. Whether it was an original or a copy was open to doubt. The point interested me. I had noticed two indifferent paintings hung in the living room, old portraits of generals, or priests, leaders of some kind.

She asked about the doctor who had attended her father. 'That fellow is not—the doctor is no good. He ought to be kept in prison, but like the last time, he will be let out after a few months.'

The doctor was dead. She called on his deputy. It was a huge organisation. The deputy's assistant saw her, she learnt that her father had suffered from tuberculosis in an acute form and from a condition of the heart. There had been one curious feature, deep-rooted, fascinating.

We had coffee. A baker's assistant carried on his head two large wooden trays loaded with cakes, pastries, loaves. Hot milk poured steaming into glasses. She ate four excellent cakes, reaching for another cake she almost upset her coffee over me. She was under twenty, illiterate, completely untrained. She had been taught a certain occupation. 'When did you learn,' I asked her, 'that you were going to be sent here?' 'Last November. I was told that it had been agreed that you were to take me.' 'How long will you stay?' 'I am supposed to stay for ten days and in that time find the grave. But I'm ill, not fit for work, so I must look after myself. I know there is no grave. I should like to see him back, but it is not safe for him. People disappear, no one knows where they go. Probably it will change, I don't know what to do. I should like to stay here, but I don't know how long they will allow me to. Certain people are not seen in the streets any more and so it is forgotten that they are in control.' 'If it is a question of your father—' 'I am not interested. I must get a good job. I have found jobs in flower shops, many times it has happened, but the work, I cannot get used to it. The reason is clear, poverty is a sin, the good man is rewarded, he is successful. I shall found a new kind of institution for orphans. It will be a garden. Any country would be proud to possess such an orphanage. The building will be designed to give the children the maximum sunlight when indoors. The children will be poorly clad and ill-shod, they will be kept in a massive building with automatically regulated furnaces, the ovens will be on the same high level of modern design.' I preferred not to ask where she had learnt all this.

I took her back to her wooden room. She lifted her coat, she had no clothing underneath. 'I have access to stocks of clothing. Would you like me to treat you differently?' She said she had no need of money. I asked her if the others had money. She said yes. 'If you worked hard would you get the chance to earn more?' She was not sure about this, first she said yes, then no. I asked her how many there were in her family. 'One.' I did not ask you how many now, I know that, I wish to know how many you were.' 'Five.' 'And how many are left?' Silence. 'How many?' 'One.' 'And the others?' 'Gone.' 'Children?' 'Yes.' 'Did the others die?' This produced some confusion. Experience had taught me to be cautious about accepting statements at their face value. Information had to be extracted. She sat there thinking, preoccupied with survival. She divided her attention between watching me and having some game with crumbs of cake. She was indifferent, no emotion, yet I was asking questions often of the most intimate nature. It had a sinister meaning. 'I gave you a fresh set of clothing, but you will not help me, you sit and do nothing.' 'Give me better clothes and I will help, don't give me these rags, don't lock the door.' I made sure the door was locked behind me. Everything had turned to iron, six million pieces of iron, with appendages.

I woke her up, I stood by the door. 'My friend,' I spoke quietly. 'Who are you?' she got out of bed, 'why are you here?' 'You said you were too ill to work, you must be looked after, you are going on a holiday, now behave yourself.' 'What can I take with me?' 'Personal belongings, no furniture.' 'I have no furniture.' 'It is not important.' Her fingers were clumsy, she fumbled with the buttons. I noticed her long and curved lashes. I kicked her clothes into the corner of the room. A steel comb dragged through her hair. 'My eyes hurt.' 'You are ill,' I said, 'you need hospital treatment.' 'I must get a new coat, I'll sell my coat and buy a new one, there are new long coats on the market.' I was wearing my overcoat as the place was unheated. 'Get in.' She climbed into the bath, the level of the water was below the knee, she splashed the water over herself, trying to cover her body. 'Could I have some more water?' 'Not allowed, scrub yourself clean.' She stepped out of the bath, she looked cold. I gave her back her clothes and she put them on. I felt the twitch of my lips as I turned away and started to lock the shutters. 'Why do you block out the air?' The windows were barred, a metal shade protected the light. I handed her a slice of buttered bread. She put the bread on the floor. I stood over her, my face irritable with impatience. 'Take it. Quick.' She couldn't hold it properly, she was cold. I watched in silence. 'Get back to bed.' The room contained nothing but a bed, a chair, a tin bath. No pictures, no book, no jug of water, no calendar, no mirror. Her lips were counting numbers. I heard someone pass in the corridor outside. I asked her how old she was and whether she liked the food. She picked up the chair and came towards me, I twisted it out of her hands, it was too heavy for her.

She lay back, face upwards, looking at the ceiling, her face a piece of paper. She could not make the effort to stand up. She tried to avoid contact with me by turning towards the wall. 'Do what you're told, go and get ready.' 'No.' 'It's for your own good.' I don't want to, you can't make me.' But she began to pick up her few clothes from the floor. 'I can't go, I have a horror of hospitals, I once went to the doctor, he wouldn't examine me, I had no friends, no one, I had had my teeth out, all my teeth drawn, my father paid the bill, it had to be paid, the doctor came to see me, he asked how I was, I said I was well and he went away.' She was waiting to see what I would do, for something to happen which would prevent her having to go. 'I worked in the kitchens, I had swollen legs, you can see they are still bad. My father said I grew too quickly, I should not have done so. While I was working, I drank a lot of water, and I ate boiled fish, but the kitchens, all the steam and heat, it put you off your food, and my nerves were bad, I tried ointments, I put black paste on the painful parts, I had advice from everyone, I was told to eat stews, and soup, to avoid the terrible heat and the dampness. I still use drops twice a day.' She stooped close to the floor, unable to go on, waiting for me to move. When I left her she lay on the low table, her head pointing towards the door.

Hurrying downstairs, I was delayed by men carrying out bodies, they forced past me, one shoved a fist into my face. They grinned as the bodies came out. I looked straight ahead. They did not appear to know that I had been living in the house. Crowds on the stairs filled every foot of room, trunks had been left in the hall half-packed. Fugitives who faced exposure filled the hall with shouting to be allowed out, but the uniformed traitors dragged them from the door. At the door stood the caretaker of the building, the man who had welcomed us and made us tea. 'Without exception all are to be turned back.' I tried to touch his hand, to get closer to him and explain. 'All persons are to remain here. No exceptions whatsoever.' No one could deprive them of their sport, the scenes of fear. They forced the girl down on her hands and knees and made her scrub the stairs with acid preparations which bit into the skin, she was surrounded by jostling men, they put a scrubbing brush into her hand, splashed it well with acid. 'Now you need more water.' They slung a bucket of filthy water over her, then jerked her up by the wrists and made her show her hands.

They were intent on their enjoyment. The stairs were black with happy onlookers. I did not know one of them. She stared up at them, her mouth could not keep still. I got to the door and spoke to the man guarding it. 'I must speak to you at once.' 'Who are you? I don't know you.' I told him what I knew about the girl, and her father. 'If they discover who she is, it means her life. Certain information may help, so may money. I told her to ask me for money. I don't know her real name, I have no idea what will happen to her.' She is one of many. Things will get worse. She won't be heard of again.' He gave me a paper with instructions. 'Someone will come within a week. If no one comes, destroy it, it is all over.'

The doors were kept locked, we were shut in for twelve hours, we were examined, those who were ill were dragged into one room. They had lists. She was one of those taken away by lorry. I should have stayed and searched for her, but I was not sure how long they would allow me to remain. The main thing was that I should not lose contact with her. Everything was stolen, mirrors shot to pieces, the paintings ripped with knives, plates and glasses smashed, all with the utmost indifference. They telephoned for more lorries.

Food. The movements of waiters. I learned. Those mysterious persons. While at lunch one came to see me. 'Is there anything I can do for you?' Certainly, though his face . . . He conferred. It was a question of transport. 'Is there a lorry?' 'Yes. One of my men will go with you.'

An empty lorry. My luggage was placed on the seat beside the driver, I chose the most comfortable place in the back. Soon the back of the lorry was crammed, every space was filled with bodies and cases. The luggage remained on the seat. It was an order.

Later, when I had made it clear that I was going to co-operate, they placed a car at my disposal. It was built for military purposes, but I was not going to miss the opportunity of having a car. The seats were cut and torn. A person lay across the seats, and had to be thrown out.

The armoured cars I was compelled to follow were scarred by war, each carried a pennant, three different pennants, three divisions. Their commander greeted me in the friendliest way, so that I felt I need not worry too much over whether or not I was travelling in the right direction.

The road was a straight strip between high hedges, the rays of the winter sun were unexpectedly warm. When we stopped at an empty house, people came to look at us, old people arrived in procession, women whose houses had been burned down, who had gone for months without food, saving so that they could rebuild, faces dull purple, women blood-red tipped, men faded. They brought us tea which was excellent. They talked about their houses, but these people could not be reached, until they had their own homes they could not hope. The range of food carried by the convoy, and which they allowed me to share, was limited, though it included some remarkable delicacies.

The missing persons office had a new wooden roof, light yellow, the only roof that had been repaired. The office was closed. I was not concerned. I had a good road, a fast car, a reckless driver. The troops carried in the armoured cars went round systematically burning and blowing up buildings. They had sixty-four houses, then they had three. The troops repaired two. They helped them get going again. I asked the commander: 'What about the people who used to live in these houses, are they still here?' 'No. Deported to work in factories. Others drift back, others have been murdered, burnt.' 'I don't understand why.' 'You don't know them.' His face showed signs of strain. 'We brought them thirty tons of D.D.T. We organised squads. We broke the back of epidemics. Without D.D.T. typhus would spread without any hope of stopping it. That powder is one of the best things we have done. The girl? It is one case only. With migrations, changing populations, and fresh troops in the district, new batches of cases are continually being notified, and we have no idea of the number of unreported cases. We need help badly. We are cut off here. Can't you do something? Are you content to sit and take notes?' 'Today I am going to visit a person who, I believe, is living in the district and who may be able to help in tracing her.' 'Perhaps you can get us some medicine.' I heard him say that, and I decided to do what I could to help him.

The troops had gone. The house was in darkness. A woman with brown hair welcomed me, she couldn't sit still, leaning her face against mine she continued to tremble. She started to tell about the hanging, she tried to explain why she got the words twisted, but she could not. She held the light, the words got lost. I waited. Her thin face, she lived in the dark. She sat beside the light and started to talk. Soldiers had been in her home. She had tried to take care. There had been men outside the house, she had seen them in the street. A knock on the door, we have four prisoners, could you go to another house, of course not. The prisoners came, the most terrible people, it was painful to hear their treatment, when she complained she was told that soon they would be going home, with a rope. Through the window she saw them, their hands tied, four men, they were led aside. It was not that I was indifferent, I was not, but I was calm, I had no part of her trembling, there seemed no place for me. I felt that I did not care for the means by which this woman's mind had been broken, but I was relieved when I was no longer with her. This was deplorable, but the fact remained. There had been a number of factors and their effect had been cumulative. At first the troops had welcomed me, the sincerity of their welcome had been difficult to assess, it had been largely artificial, but they had had to be certain of my loyalty. I had proved that I could be trusted, but they had kept me outside and so I had become isolated. This had made for a double action. The mutual dislike had increased. Then there had been a horrible incident. They had held up a car and robbed the passengers, the driver had been taken out and shot. And I had discovered the fun in such business.

3

I KNEW where to find the person I was looking for. After scrambling up the path I arrived at the building and was asked to wait by a young girl in grey uniform. She explained that she would leave me with him. As she left he gazed after her. I found at first that I could not talk to him in any language that he knew. 'So, you live here,' I said. He was not at ease. I smiled at him, said his daughter had told me about him. He led me into a small room. I was seated on a red plush couch and he sat on my right in a red plush armchair. Before us was a round table. Two small windows facing me lit the room. Outside I could hear animals bumping and rubbing themselves against the walls of the house. 'Am I to be allowed to visit her?' I asked. 'No.' 'Does she live openly? Does she still use the same name?' 'Yes.' 'Tell me, what is her position?' 'She is safe. While she continues to work for us she will be protected no matter where she may be taken, don't worry, we will not lose sight of her.' He got up: 'I must offer you hospitality.' He left the room to return carrying a bottle of wine. 'It is home-made wine.' Chains hung round his thick neck, rested on his heavy body. We sipped the wine. We conversed. The sun cut sharply into the room. He smiled. He tried to entice me. I refused. I was aware of the animals moving around. He told me he was head of the family. In a burst of energy he shouted that she was his child, his family must not die out. Out of his wallet came photographs of the girl. My interest was qualified by hesitation and reserve. I noted the great variety, her talent for adaptation, her wide range of mood which was not at first apparent. He showed me another and another, without being aware of the differences, the backward slope, the white skin, the canopied eye, the arm, slender and colourless. They could have been different people. She expressed a jumbling of use and fancy. In one she came running through a doorway, the stones of her necklace swinging above her upper lip, in another, younger, she covered her fingers in long grass. There were none above a certain age. I asked him, in a calm uninterested tone, when she had left home. 'She said she would leave. She came towards me, to kiss me. I seized a chair. I had a bad temper. I meant no harm. I had always admired her.' He held a photo of his wife, but he did not show it to me. He said it was a poor likeness, the others had been taken from him, he had stolen this one. 'I'm sorry,' he apologised, he had knocked the table and spilt the wine. 'I don't seem to be able to manage this.' With his handkerchief he mopped up the wine from the table and from the floor at my feet, wiping off a few drops that had fallen on my shoes. 'I am getting old, though my nerves are still good, I sleep soundly. As long as I can keep going and complete the work.' 'You still work?' 'I am a worker.' 'But what exactly does that mean?' He looked slightly embarrassed. 'I obtain meat, and the town buys it. More or less.' 'I see. Is that all?' 'More or less.' He had tried, clumsily, to avoid my question. It was too hot. I was getting drunk. I opened the window. I could see the outside of the wooden building, a large hall was set behind the main part of the house and screened from the road by trees. The commander's armoured car drove slowly past. 'I had to buy meat. Everything was wrecked.' 'Where did you get the meat from?' 'The countryside. It came by lorry.' I smiled at him, and got up from my chair. He said quickly: 'I shall tell you everything, the bad as well as the good. What do you want to know?' I knew this game, I had played it with both sides, the more open-handed the host appeared, the more he had to hide. He held out his hand to me and led me into a long low room containing tables, we walked down the narrow corridor between the tables, past a notice for 'Silence', readers intent on newspapers, forty readers to a table. I tried to make out the foreign titles of the papers. He took my arm. 'There's nothing here, we'll go into the schoolroom and you'll know where you are.' My glance returned to the page. 'Do you not want to go?' 'I'm in no hurry, I'll come soon.' Four young men got up from one of the tables and came smiling and mumbling towards me, I found myself nudged and bundled towards the door. 'Where are we going?' More and more of them followed me into the next room, and before I could quite tell how I had got there, I heard the door shut behind me. A young soldier was teaching arithmetic to a class of about fifty older men, they were learning Roman numerals, each in turn went to the blackboard to write a date in Roman figures. The teacher asked: 'What was the date of the great battle?' Came a prompt reply from the massed troops. Questions and answers about the battle occupied a few minutes, the writing of the date was a matter of seconds, and then on to the next historical date. No doubt it was a lesson in arithmetic but to a casual observer it seemed to consist mostly of history. The class by their replies showed that they had a remarkable knowledge of recent history. The young teacher told me that only combatants were taught history, the difference between their education and that of others was that they were made to realise the importance of history. I said that this could mean anything. The teaching of history depended on the teacher. One would explain events as he saw them, another would teach otherwise. 'Oh yes.' I asked him whether he himself received instruction on methods or approach. 'I teach as I please. But mine is a unique position. It was my father's intention that it should be so.'

While the father had been uniformed, with medals, buttons, epaulettes, a ring on his forefinger, a tough old man, his son was of another type, he had a gloomy smile, a subdued expression which marked a face not yet crushed, a moral agnosticism different from anything I had seen. Yet the only blood was the blood of the father, the son had to fight him with the hope of a wild animal, with a cold bare silence which could not be beaten, with an obedience which accused. While he taught, the son was on his own: 'In the occupied areas the population slowly but steadily decreases while in the liberated territories it as inevitably expands.' He pointed to a map, a large space containing gold, enclosed by forts, squares of black. In moments of seriousness, in the tone of his voice and the words used there was always the same line, a pathway to the dead. He was in pain, but would have no doctor, doctors were 'dull and pointless'. The revolutionary troops sang songs together with clapping hands and dancing, and the whole point was something of love, with allusions to their life in the town. 'My father objects to the dancing, though dancing is our only amusement. He has a conviction that nothing can be clean.'

When he looked past his father towards me, the expected cold was felt, the air was as if it had passed over ice. He was young, he had seen the world, the blue line in the distance, his eyes bold, well-shaped, deep blue, startling pieces of ice floated in the blue. Half the face looked straight over the sea, he was tall, not ugly, yet confined and bound, cut by the river itself. The father said his son would not stand the cold, and it was true. He cracked to pieces, was half-destroyed, there appeared a break in the old shape, he faced me, taller and thinner. This deterioration was to be observed. Rouge was used. His cheeks painted to imitate youth, his origin lost as it stretched out, his neck the beak of a duck. In the shadow of his father he failed. He was no longer remarkable. The absence of concentration, it was the first time I had noticed it. I had never known a father who killed. He continued to teach the history of the party, and of his father's role: 'Full of courage he assumed power. He destroyed the organisation and divided the party.' His father stood at the back of the crowded room. He nodded to his son, who went with him to the adjoining room, the son's voice, higher pitched than the older man's, could be heard through the board partition. 'I am tired and would like to go to bed. When the sun rose I was so tired that I could not enjoy anything. The rush of water coming over showed itself, I would not make the colours so rich, twenty feet of water rushed over in a column.'

The white beds and the delicate white curtains, no flowers, no books, no work but mental death. The faces were happy. The lack of hope brought calm. The windows were never opened. The rules, dress, system of life, were those of the army. Side by side with the doctor, stalked the father with all the knowledge. I noticed the names, some familiar, some foreign, written over the beds. I was a man who had been sent to study documents, yet they did not accuse me of indifference. The punishments were the same as in the army. They were denied the little food, made to kneel, allowed to talk only in echoes. The father visited the dying, gave them water, touched their foreheads and noted them down in the records, which they did not see. The son remembered and spoke of his death which he did not know of. He saw a shabby monument which marked the spot. The land belonged to the people. He told me his dream of his death. He was three men. The weather was cold. The three looked small on the battlefield. Straight under the steep rock, coloured brown and yellow, the untidy town, full of colour, was reflected in the water. The season was over, the boats no longer ran, the river fell straight over the cliff, there was no decline, you saw no rocks, they were hidden by water which rushed with violence, it was not a fall like other falls, it was not what it was, it had been diverted to make electric light. 'I did not realise it was my last chance of seeing lights, I saw nothing but small white wreaths for the dead, the trees had been cut down, there were no trees in the place, no gardens, the land not built upon was covered with rubbish. The last man missed his footing and fell. He was already fifty yards away, he threw his arms into the air, the fatal instinct, the body was not recovered, though it may have been. The life was over. Can anything be more logical?' I tried to understand the sequence of events. He was ill, but still seemed to want to know more, spoke with an odd pride, grinned with pleasure when I told him that though I was a foreigner I believed that sooner or later some form of victory must come. He let me see then that he knew something of the struggle that was going on. I would not soon forget the intelligent face. He had not spoken of his sister. I asked him to write her a note. He said he was incapable of writing, he could not remember her name, he could not write a single word. It was not writing but real work that was required of him. As soon as he was well, he would ask to be transferred to the fighting front.

In his private room, the father gave me fried eggs and bread. He played the violin. He was drunk. We played cards, each trying to cheat, he distracted me with his talk. 'I have seen the destruction of the best men.

One wife would not allow her husband to be buried, she gave us the name and his body was sent by car, concealed under my coat, a hat over his face. We told her he had escaped by aeroplane, I remember the streaming from her eyes, he had died defeated, in the corridor, killed. How she suffered. And the lips of some agonised mother I will never know, her son among the missing. He had left that day, before lunch. No return. He had disappeared without reason. Yet I am not worried, I don't feel.' I threw my cards down. 'I must find the girl. I am not interested in anything else.' 'First we must eat. You must stay, we'll have a party.' He gave me his son's room. Two wooden chairs and a table, the essentials. He pushed open the door without knocking, stood in his military greatcoat, his face had a hard, obstinate look that had not been there before. He sat down opposite me, offered me a cigarette, and began a drunken monologue. 'My teeth are bad and so is the life I have to lead.' He fell asleep in the chair, I took the lighted cigarette from between his fingers. As I had been told that I would not be able to buy any food on my journey, I stole from his cupboard the rest of the bread, some tea, and a few eggs. Before I left I noticed with pleasure the trembling of his legs. We were both foreigners.

4

I REJOINED the regular troops. They talked of bandits and mass slaughter, but I knew they were deceiving themselves, it was the new human mind. I saw signs of recent battles, I noted them particularly.

The sky was usually grey, yet I could see the road for miles, every object was distinct: piles of stones, gravel, a steam roller, axes in use, logs, small bridges. We drove along red roads, between trees sunk into soaking fields. We reached the forest, and from then on it was never out of sight, even from the suburbs of the town, house after house, people walking, carrying, bundled up, human beings. It was cold, we lost the way, it rained when it should have been fine.

My reckless driver handled his car, he put on the brakes to avoid a collision, I was frantic, the powerful car spun round twice before overturning, I sprang from the car. He remained calm. The car righted itself, he gave a contemptuous flap of his hand, indifferent to my shouted protest. The road was metalled, the earth had frozen, the forest was not far away, the land was derelict. 'Now we have lost contact with our escort,' the driver said. 'We don't need an escort.' 'Impossible. We cannot go on,' with fear in his eyes, 'there are bandits, the roads are too dangerous.' 'We are going on.' 'I have other things to do, important duties, I cannot go any further.' 'You must go on, it is an order.' 'No.' 'Stay where you are.' I had no alternative. I depended on him, not least because I could not drive the car.

'The road is not really so bad.' He did not reply. We were in the front seats of the car, by the side of the road, just within the forest. He did not say 'this is the forest', he did not speak, he had other things on his mind. He studied an instruction booklet which seemed to relate to the revolver which he had taken from its holster and laid across his knees. A farm to our left had, or had not, a patch of birch trees growing close to the walls of the farmhouse, I was not certain about it. A family was being taken from the house and loaded on to a lorry, together with their belongings. The driver noticed my concern. 'Do you want to see them taken away? It's only half a mile.' 'What is there to see?' 'Nothing. It's just a place like this.' He said that to intrigue me, to interest me in something else. I replied: 'Then there is no point in wasting time over it.' The map he showed me, on which was marked the place to which the people were to be taken, showed clearly that to have followed them would have taken me in the wrong direction, back towards the troops' headquarters. I could see also that his map did not correspond with the map I had made, nor did it bear any relation to the map the girl had given me. 'By the way,' I asked him, 'will the family be loaded from one lorry on to another? Or will they stay on the same lorry?' 'They change at a small town thirty miles away, I hear that they are going to be allowed to stay in that place. It is a pity there is no road to it, you ought to see it, it's a beautiful town.' 'I'm afraid there is not enough daylight left.' 'You should see it. The fountains are famous.' 'Wasn't the town destroyed?' 'No, the inhabitants were cleared out and it was preserved for hunting. The army was sent round it, not through it, so it did not suffer. It still contains rare specimens of wild animals.' He showed me a newspaper photograph of a young man in a light grey uniform similar to his own, though his was darker. He laughed: 'A boy. A bandit killed in a raid, he was thirteen years old.' I said that this was a surprise to me, I had not realised that these gangsters were so young. 'Are there many left?' I asked. 'Perhaps eight or ten. Far too many, they must be shot down.' I was winning his confidence. He talked seriously, with terrific enthusiasm. 'They are a pest. Their stupidities and brutalities no longer trouble us, but they attack farms and kill the animals. They drink the blood and leave the carcases.' 'Blood?' 'They get desperate and kill sheep. They had all been driven back across the frontier, until one of their old leaders escaped from prison and built them up again.' He showed me another photograph, of a naked man crawling between ranks of soldiers, like a dog, a small tough dog roaming the ruins. 'We have a battalion competition,' he said, 'there is a money prize for any man who can capture two bandits on the same day. This one was caught in a pit. A hole was dug, the top covered, mud and grass scattered over it. We left some food, he was starving and made a rush for it. The earth collapsed under him. It was cruel. Imagine the weight, the earth fell on top of him as he crashed down.' His face was sweating with excitement, I had a sudden glimpse of what it must have been like. 'We pulled him out the next day, he was alive, but with badly broken limbs, we chased him, you can see, hemmed him in, after I managed to get a rope round his legs he couldn't resist, once the noose was pulled tightly we dragged him in the desired direction. The others struggled to get their ropes round him, they leaned on him with all their weight, even that was not the end of it.' 'You seem to have enjoyed yourselves.' He pulled back the sleeve of his shirt. His upper arm was contained in a plaster cast, his finger went along the surface of the stuff, which cut his arm almost into equal parts. He wanted to talk freely. I knew that the way to get him to tell me what had become of the girl, was to ask him about himself. He told me about his family, the war, and in a gesture of friendship he said that I must sign his autograph book. 'You must start a fresh page.' 'I am in a special category,' I remarked, as I wrote my name on a blank page at the back of the instruction booklet. As I wrote I lifted the corner of the preceding page, to try to read the other names. He snatched the book away. 'Tell me,' I asked in a friendly tone, 'how were you taken into the army?' 'When I got to the camp I was told what would happen if I didn't join up, they told us again and again. Then the war ended and they said we were no longer required, that we could return home. I refused. They sent me away, I picked up some food from the floor and was sent to prison for stealing.' 'When did you learn that you were wanted again?' 'They never told me, but I knew it would happen, and I started off. The nearest railway station was two hundred miles away, I walked from one place to the other.' 'How did you manage to live?'

'I did some work, serving my country, then went on.' He was under twenty. He had an amused look on his face. 'I was joking,' he said, 'I was not taken, I went by myself.' 'You must have been taken,' I protested. 'I am telling the truth.' 'Did you have to prove who you were before they would take you back?' He laughed: 'No, they knew.'

While waiting in the car we had eaten the remains of our food. It was still light, I could still see the trees, I wanted to see them. I said to him: 'You know that I am trying to trace a girl. Have you any information as to where she may be?' 'She's in a room.' He was joking. I would get nothing from him. I needed to speak to her. I was exhausted and lay on the ground, it was frozen, there was no light or water, she lived in a destroyed town, she could only hope to get one kind of work. The bridges were down, nothing would be done, it was impossible, there was no point in looking for the girl, the town was erased, nothing remained, she had been killed, people lived in holes, nothing lived above the ground.

The lorry returned, filled with soldiers armed with sub-machine guns. The commander was in civilian clothes. He had heard of my change in plans and he made it clear that he and his men would accompany me. 'I have come to offer you an escort for your journey.' 'That is most thoughtful of you,' I replied, but there is no need for me to take advantage of your generosity. I came this far without an escort and I think I can manage the rest alone.' 'Then I shall follow you.' 'In that case I shall be delighted to have your company. I shall be leaving immediately.' We shook hands, and he walked back to the lorry. My driver mumbled: 'I don't like it. That's bad.' He studied his map: 'Don't you think it would be better if we went through the forest tomorrow rather than tonight?' I agreed. I had had enough. I told him to inform the commander. 'From now on he must be advised of my plans or change of plans.' We could not take the route by which we had come. The temporary wooden bridge had been swept away by the spring floods.

White clouds and sunlight: the winter had gone. Spring revealed the tears in our clothes. The troops put up a prefabricated shed. The length of the pieces varied but the thickness was five inches by five inches, tongued on one side, grooved on the opposite edge, one piece slotted into the other. The commander shouted orders: 'We need twelve hundred blocks to build a house. Work with fury. March. March. A town can be built in this way.' It was for my benefit. They cemented the floor and the walls, the long process ended, the floor soon spoiled, the whitened stone got coated with mud. I asked why they were building a house so isolated in the forest. They blew up the house, and burned the greater part of the two remaining walls. Under the open sky they assembled the planks and wooden frames to construct the wooden shed which was to serve as a temporary shelter until the house could be rebuilt in a proper manner, and they slung petrol over the wood and fired bullets into the pile.

It was near the end of the steady plodding slaughter. They were shooting from the upper storeys of gutted houses, they hurled down bricks, bricks blocked the streets.

By myself, without a guide, I didn't know where to go next, I wondered how she was earning her living. It looked like being a filthy business. I was tired of trying to keep warm, tired of the tedious task of rebuilding. 'When do we return?' No answer.

The escort was ready. We drove at seventy miles an hour. We were in control, flying from town to town. The people were aware of our presence, they went about in threes, they whispered as we passed, when we were close they preferred not to speak, it was too risky. We passed an openwork stone wall. 'What is that?' 'Our monument to the men who died fighting.' 'How many men?' 'Eight.' 'How did they die?' 'They were tried and shot.' From their precious supply of petrol they gave us enough for the journey back to town. There were not many hours of daylight left. The driver mumbled: 'I think the light will last. We shall make it.' He tried, furiously. One hour's light still in hand, a bare arm stopped the car, the door opened, he had half clambered in when he cried: 'Who is in there?' and fell back on to the road. The driver went to him but returned alone. Ahead was a cart loaded with hay, it kept to the middle of the road in spite of our violent hooting, we fired shots in the air and it still kept to the middle of the road, the cart had a front axle and a rear axle, the rebel farmer was a careful driver, we were hundreds of miles from the town painted on the back of the cart. The road was bad, anything might be in store for us. We forced the cart into the ditch at the side of the road, the horse tangled with the harness lay on its back in the ditch, the hooves in the air reminded me of a scene in a film. We heard the man calling out, we found the body gleaming yellow, he wiped the tears from his face, rushed forward and demanded, was silent when the driver told him, then went over to look at the body and walked on towards the village. A couple of men walked about the village, no effort had been made to repair the doors of the houses. 'It is difficult to get anyone interested. They have no civic pride,' the commander informed me, 'they are not progressive, they have a school but not one student. The hens lay small eggs and the hogs don't fatten. What can we do? They are like insects, they store small things they have made, they have gold hidden in the earth or under the roof. It's been a bad season, they have become victims and left their houses. Or they have stayed inside and starved. They need money, only money would protect them against the bandits and the havoc that follows the spring floods. The forests could have been exploited, the railways put in order, three hundred ton barges could have sailed up that river and passed below the bridge.'

We tore through the town. We wrecked like fury. The public baths had been only partly destroyed, they had begun to repair the doors. 'We have a powerful new light, it was installed the other day, and we have painted the doors.' We wrenched the handles off the doors, shot to pieces the apparatus, slit the padding in the soundproof room. We crowded into the room. We ate bread and ham. 'What do you want?' Silence. A boy in a light grey jacket, with a sub-machine gun: 'Get out or I shoot.' He stared round at us, his fear shown by his grip on the butt, he was trying to work out what to do next. 'We'll never give up. We'll fight. We don't need tractors, we want horses, we want bread.' Some drunken soldiers had shot one of the horses. The commander spoke quietly: 'Look at this.' He took a wrapped toffee from his pocket and threw it on the floor a couple of feet in front of the boy. The young soldier, awkwardly, transferring the heavy gun from his right hand to his left, bent forward to pick up the sweet. A shot sounded but made no echo in the sound-proof room. The commander continued: 'As for horses, only the collective has the right to own them, if one or a dozen horses die, the individual has no cause to fear.'

We had breakfast of white rolls and butter, two eggs and coffee. I was accustomed to destruction, there were standards of destruction, the little town had been destroyed. There was nothing. The thing had disappeared. Not a brick visible. A man appeared out of the ground, a boy from a hole stood beside the man. 'What do you live on?' 'Potatoes.' 'No corn?' 'I can plant only potatoes.' The commander indicated that things were not so bad now that the land had been cleared of mines, animals were no longer injured by exploding shells. 'Not long ago any one of these people would have lost his own son or his wife in exchange for a sound calf or a pig.' He had seen cattle caught in minefields, whole collections of the feet of animals, legs severed at the knee, bones sprouting from bushes, and in cottages, collections of hooves, fossilised, kept.

I changed my plans. I told the commander that I intended to stop at the next large town. 'As you please.' Racing through the rain, the driver accelerated, the heavy tyres skidded sideways across the metalled road. I looked back: 'Where is the escort?' He seemed indifferent, increased his speed, the rain smashed against the windscreen. 'Stop. We must wait for them.' They soon discovered their mistake, and a minute or two later we saw them behind us, as I intended. We drove on towards the town, a few lights miles ahead across the bare land uninterrupted by any tree or building, no traffic, no noise, we travelled slowly. Under waiting clouds we entered the darkened town. The headlights of the lorries flashed on blank spaces, remains of houses, flat ground where shops had stood. 'You won't be able to go any further.' I got out and walked towards the seven-storeyed silent blaze from the lighted windows of the new hotel. Behind me the driver worked in the rain, mending a punctured tyre.

5

OOKING ACROSS the town from the marble steps of the hotel, if I did
not lift my eyes beyond the ground floor, I could believe I was at
home, in the shopping centre of a normal town, but above the ground
floor there was nothing. The upper windows had nested snipers, the walls
around them had been smashed by shells. The hotel was empty, half-built,
it had electricity but no carpets, no glass to the windows. The few
undamaged houses were used as barracks, more than five thousand
troops garrisoned the town, but they were kept apart, and were often
difficult to find. One large old building near the town centre was reserved
for officers, the ground floor used as a restaurant, the upper floors for
private parties.

Though I knew the answer to the question, I asked the commander
whether anyone lived in the rooms upstairs. He said that the rooms were
occupied from time to time. From my seat in the car I could see curtains
in one of the upper windows. It was her room. I said I was hungry and
asked the commander to take me into the restaurant. 'The food is poor,'
he replied, 'the whole house is badly built. The foundations are shifting,
only the ground floor is habitable. The central heating does not work
properly, it is always cold and depressing.' He clutched the top of the seat
of the car alongside me. I was alone with a fanatic. He tried to get me into
an argument, but it was futile, I was ready for him. I kept quiet. I had the
information I needed. It was only my need of his help to get into the
heavily guarded building that caused me to remain polite to him.

Two soldiers waited for permission to speak to the commander. They were talking together, there was a laugh and it had something sly in it. The commander said to me suddenly: 'I presume it is still your intention to help us obtain medical supplies?' I answered vaguely: 'I'm sorry, it was not possible—' He interrupted: 'You were followed. Our information is that the person you visited is in no position to assist us.' I said nothing. 'You led us to him. Although he had fled before we were able to check with certainty his identity and role, we were able to learn something from the documents left behind, among them photographs of the girl in whom you show such interest.' I replied: 'She can't help you. Why do you continue to suspect her?' He held the car door open, but prevented me from getting out. 'We have to be careful. She is confused, she has a natural reluctance to discuss her father's whereabouts, but we are confident that a period of re-education will change her attitude. It would be in your interests to persuade her to co-operate.' I looked at my watch, it was five o'clock. I made no comment. I had not changed my plans. 'The driver needs food,' I said, 'he cannot leave the car unattended.' 'We can provide an armed guard for the car.' The commander smiled and went up the steps into the building.

I got out of the car and spoke to a child who was sitting on the steps. 'How old are you?' 'Eight.' 'Who lives in that big house?' She would not speak again, she had seen the armoured car.

The commander reappeared at the top of the steps, with two armed soldiers. He beckoned me up. When I reached him he took a sheet of paper from his pocket and handed it to me. It was a list of names. I said simply: 'There are hundreds of names here.' He replied: 'Very few. Practically none.' But that is impossible.' 'We have had dreadful losses.' He spoke hurriedly as he took me past the guards, through the crowded restaurant, swing doors, kitchens, up two flights of stairs. 'Now I tell you. I cannot tell you. It is nothing new.' He ran up the stairs ahead of me, laughing in an unexpected way. His military training and his supple leather boots made this kind of game easier for him than for me. Outside a newly-painted door he stopped and waited. He took the list from my hand. I said: 'These names mean nothing to me.' The door was not opened.

Then it was slightly opened. Fear and pleasure in half a face: 'Why bring him here?'

A table. A floor. We faced each other under the glare of the light. Her body rigid, she faced us. We waited. 'You work together,' she said defiantly. 'Nonsense.' She persisted: 'He knew what I had said to you.' The commander moved towards her: 'Let's talk about something more cheerful, about the old days.' He dominated. We had met, but we had met in a fog. Troops marched in the streets, she heard them below, her hand went to the light. She hesitated. The commander took off his spectacles and wiped the dust from them, his eyes were dark blurs. She swiftly looked towards me and managed to convey that she could not speak now. I stared at her. She seemed to shiver. I would have to wait. I asked the commander: 'Has she all the things she needs?' He seemed to realise that he had missed something, and answered irritably: 'They are on their way.' I had had similar replies before. I said: 'Excellent. When precisely may they be expected to arrive?' There was a silence. He said: 'Some parcels have been delayed. Your people at a meeting prevented them from being sent.' 'So that is the story.' 'It is true.' I looked round the room: a long gilt mirror, a lamp, two herrings, a pair of stockings over the sink. 'What is her attitude generally?' I asked. 'She will not co-operate. She was asked her father's name; she gave her mother's maiden name.' A kind of sunlight shone into the room, blue without any trace of red in it, so blue as to be harsh. I knew I would get nothing done. I left the room and waited in the corridor. I heard him ask her: 'Where is your father?' 'I don't know.' 'And your mother?' 'She is at home ill.' A lie. 'Why are you not working?' 'I am not allowed to work.' 'How many are there at home?' 'The baby and my brother.' 'How old is your brother?' 'Thirteen.' 'What does he do?' 'He carries water.' 'Has he a work permit?' 'He does not get paid, only tips, it is no life here, he wants to go to America, he would get tips besides his wages . . .'

I walked down the corridor, it was full of dust and rubbish, the floor had not been cleaned. In the restaurant I sat at the long table, it was crowded, as I sat down they stopped their conversation to watch me. I walked over to the window and looked out. They lost interest in me and continued talking in low tones. 'Things are getting worse.' 'He did not come home.' 'His wife has gone to look for him, she has not yet returned.' They were everywhere, I could hear nothing but their insistent conversations.

I moved towards the door. The driver stopped me and told me in the friendliest way that I had 'taken the wrong road'. With a grin he showed me what he called his 'old autograph book.' My name had been carefully inked out. He closed the book. I knew my luck had come to an end. I tried to regain his friendship, I asked him where his next job would take him. He said he was driving north to search for some pieces of machinery, he had already located some crates thanks to information given him by a workman who had assisted in the packing. I said I was sorry I had not the time to get from him more details of what would normally have interested me as a commercial operation. I asked him how he acquired machinery and got it transported without cash or credit. 'Well, the bits and pieces arrive.' 'Who pays the workmen for setting them up?' 'They get paid cash for work done.' I could see that he would not disclose more than this.

I joined a group of young officers, I got them to talk. They had no suspicions, they thought they were telling me secrets, though they knew nothing, they had no idea of the work being done, I could not hint at what I knew. Even here I heard her father's name, the name that was disturbing the country. In this garrison town, his friends had gathered others who shared his views. I thought of the girl in the room, she was sitting on the bed, she had guessed something. I felt I had left her a mile behind.

The crowd packed itself tightly round me, I heard the commander mutter to the driver: 'This fellow is a foreigner, get more out of him for his fare.' 'No use, he asked the price before starting.' The crowd split into two, leaving a corridor along which the commander walked, he called me to come with him. He went to his chair at the head of the table. I was given, as a place of honour, the seat next to his. My elevated position soon became one of isolation. The rest of the company began to ignore my presence. The commander did not speak to me. For some time, I was not able to order a meal, and when I tried to find out what I could get to eat the host became rather embarrassed. It was evident that there was not enough food for such a large party. He did not wish to abandon the banquet, he imagined it was an event in his life. From what I could gather, he insisted that he could provide us with veal cutlets, but naturally it would take time for the meal to be prepared. I could hear the commander making polite conversation to people opposite and on either side of me, but he did not mention or speak to me.

Someone came in from the street and made some kind of signal to the commander. He came up and stood between us. There was a quiet but agitated discussion. The commander turned to me: 'There has been a mistake. This man and his wife were expecting me to have dinner with them, and everything is prepared. But I have, as you see, ordered dinner here and I cannot cancel it. What should I do?' It was seven-thirty in the evening, there was still an hour's daylight and dusk. 'We can have a hurried meal here,' I said, 'and then go on to the other house for dinner.' He looked surprised, but made no comment. I seemed to have created a bad impression. I had assumed that I was included in the invitation, but from the way in which the stranger looked at me it appeared that I was mistaken. I decided that it would merely magnify the error if I were to make any kind of explanation or apology. 'There is nothing to be done,' the commander said at last. I sensed the unspoken protest. He refused the invitation to dinner.

To make matters worse, we had nearly an hour to wait before the cutlets arrived. The food was almost uneatable. The meat and soup were served together, the meat was over-cooked, the soup tasted sweet, like ink.

I was relegated to my aloof place of honour as the rest settled down to their food. Now and again I caught odd scraps of conversation. Once the subject was myself, who, it appeared, had had the audacity to go into the town on market day in an attempt to meet people from the surrounding countryside. But 'they trust the police', one of them said, and turning to me: 'Nothing you can say will alter their opinions. If you try to find things out, they will say they know nothing.'

Silence descended on the company as a second huge dish of cutlets was placed on the table. The commander spoke to me: 'I advise you to pack up the remains of the food. You never know when you will get your next meal, or you may know someone who would enjoy the scraps.' I noticed that he hardly touched the food. Encouraged by his new friendliness, I asked him his opinion of the girl, and I was surprised to discover that he was quite willing to talk about her: 'She is no more brutal than the rest, she is not wilfully cruel. Only by practical experiment can the truth be learned: before condemning her, take her place, pay her that compliment.' 'She has no energy,' I said cautiously, 'she seems to be thinking of something else most of the time.' 'She needs more intelligent training,' he replied, 'a hand laid on her side would have been enough, there should have been no need to rely on the sudden pain of the whip. Enough for the hand to have been raised as if to strike, though in moments of excitement—' Through the windows I could see the river. I was suffering from a curious sort of fever, as if I inhabited another body. He continued talking quietly to me: 'These bandits are becoming a problem. They are tough, otherwise they would not be alive. They have lost the habits of civilised life. These filthy people are driving us out of this decent town which we have made. They are a lower order of human beings, they are not like the ordinary decent individual, they are not willing to obey orders, so their decency is gone.' 'They need care.' 'I'll give them care. I shall examine them all. If I find one case of disease I shall destroy every one of them. It will be in the national interest, I shall make them see that. I will talk to their representatives.' 'Representatives?' 'Worms. I shall convince them. I shall arrange joint control to avoid delays. It is grand work. It is full of difficulties, but we shall get over them. Were you able to talk to the girl alone? Did you discuss our policies?' 'She was told "no work, no food".' 'She should have come to me.' 'Your clerk told her that you were busy and that she was to return in the afternoon.' 'Sheer incompetence. I shall be ruthless.' 'When she arrived in the town she went without food or water for twenty-four hours.' 'I am investigating that.' He dashed across the room and picked up a telephone receiver. 'What is the latest news you can give me about the progress of the investigations?' The girl at the central telephone exchange did not know the part she was meant to play. He slammed down the receiver. 'They are following the matter up. We are going to stamp it out. Any bandit found escaping over the frontier is to be brought before the court, dragged in front of a judge. He is to be tried by special tribunal. The minimum sentence is ten years.' I said that she had no wish to escape, she planned to settle in the district. He replied: 'Do you happen to know whether she intends to settle here because of the climate, or is she merely trying to get as near the frontier as possible?' 'She would like to buy a shop and remain.' 'I shall help her. Not only has she suffered terribly, she is also a most valuable asset to the state. You must see her again, once more before you go.' He wrote out an order for me to be allowed to visit her. The order was in the form of a travel permit, we were to be taken together to a certain destination, the name of the town was then unknown. I understood what had happened, what arrangements had been made, while I had been entertained with food and friendly conversation.

6

WE DROVE THROUGH the sunset over miles of new roads towards a chain of hills in red stone, through stone quarries which provided the stone for the great stadium, the modern hospital, for constructing the aerodrome. Ruins, alternately red and grey, were splashed with red, the red grew from inside the ruins. Without moving, the earth shaped, the red persisted as we drove, at dusk a crown of domed red blown away into water, red arches opened straight on to water on either side.

All morning we drove slowly, I was thirsty, there was no water. We stopped, we had an excellent meal, seven or eight courses, I should have liked to stay but the car was waiting.

A coat was thrown over her. She stared stupidly. No one spoke. No one told her where she was being taken. I leaned forward to ask the driver. He nodded. 'We're almost there.' With a quick movement he inserted a rod between her legs, her strength drained away.

Surrounded by wide grounds, by a high wall, I stayed silent. I heard a faint jangling from the bracelets she wore on her wrists. Doors were unlocked and locked, she walked forward dragging the rings with her down the corridor, through doors which were unlocked and locked, down the continuing corridor, each door noisily slammed behind her. She touched the rings. Then she forgot them. They were no longer important. If there had been others willing to take her, none of this would have happened.

From the outside the main building had the appearance of a mansion: marble pillars, ornate gilt, complex decorations. The building, though dilapidated, was not in ruins, the upper floors were kept from crushing the lower, by steel struts placed upright and threaded into the walls of the corridors and rooms. A wooden barrier topped by a low steel rail extended the length of the entrance hall, separating a crowd of women and children from the administration. Here, parents searched for their children, children for their parents. I inquired about her and was told that she had been asking for news of me. Her block number indicated that she was in the central block.

In the courtyard through which I walked to reach the central block, two girls in protective clothing, wearing masks, were examining the contents extracted from the pockets of the dead. If positive identification resulted, the news was passed to those waiting, and the contents of the pockets given to the nearest relative.

The central block composed forty rooms, each with a grated hole as a window. It was the store that interested me, a cupboard crammed with clothes, medicines, soap and food. The heavy sliding doors to each room had been pushed back and I had the impression that the occupants had retreated to the wall furthest from the door and in each case were crouched under the window round a small iron stove. One room was empty except for a table covered with a brown sheet, a stretcher blocked the corridor outside, we stepped over it, and walked on down the wide corridor with rooms opening on either side, the commander first, then myself, the driver trotting behind. In spite of the open doors, there was not enough air. The commander said that normally the double doors were kept closed.

I wanted to see the girl at once, but the commander insisted that I talk to the people in the rooms, implying that they would be disappointed if I walked by without greeting them. He stood back, and allowed the driver to assume the part of a guide: 'Each room contains two families.' In five rooms I counted maybe thirty women and children, with perhaps two or three men. I asked where the people slept. 'They have bundles of clothes. They sleep on them. Those who have nothing sleep on boards.'

They squatted silently, keeping back from the heavy doors, only the children crept closer, peering curiously at us. I spoke to one of the women crouched at the other end of the room. She shouted back in a harsh unpleasant voice: 'They took them. They sent them back.' 'What do you mean?' 'My husband and my two children.' 'Where are they now?' 'They sent them back.' She would not come nearer. I asked one of the children who had poked her head round the door and was looking down the corridor, whether she went to school. 'We work in the factory, making bricks.' 'Do you get paid?' She shook her head. The commander said curtly: 'They had time to find normal work.' A boy pushed through the crowd of women and came up to me. I thought I remembered him, he resembled the boy with the sub-machine gun. He made me feel his ragged grey jacket. 'I cannot get more because it is written on my identity card, one jacket, one pullover, one pair of shoes, and nothing is said about them being old clothes.' I was wearing a new suit of greenish-yellow tweed, and my heavy overcoat. The commander had on his fur-lined waterproof and military boots. There was nothing I could say. I was wasting my time, I knew that. I was not thinking clearly, I was not asking the right questions, nor taking proper note of the answers. The commander had given me a bar of chocolate, I broke off two squares and offered them to the boy. 'Why don't we get new things?' the boy asked. The driver interrupted him: 'I work. Why don't you work? No work, no clothes.' The women came forward and pressed round us: 'They won't give us food. If we can't eat, we can't work.' My guide repeated: 'Those who won't work shall not eat.' 'They won't let us work.' 'That's a lie. I'll get you work,' the commander shouted back at them, and bending his head close to mine said quietly: 'If you wish to see her tonight, we should leave now.'

'They treat us like bandits,' the crowd followed us down the corridor. 'We fought. They disarmed us. We worked in the forests. Those who were ill were left to die. They deported us, then took us back and jailed us, now they call us bandits. They won't give us work, they won't give us food.' The driver took a whistle from his pocket and blew several sharp blasts. Guards came thundering down the corridor. The prisoners' lives were spent in terror, they rushed back into their rooms, they tried to close the sliding doors but the locks were electrically controlled, the children banged tins, they threw stones into the corridor. The guards forced their way into the rooms, four guards to a room, the doors slid shut behind them.

We were in normal surroundings. We walked along grated steel floors to the dining hall. The commander had tickets which gave the number of our table. Small tables were set along three walls leaving the centre clear for dancing. At the far end a jazz band played. The driver sat alone at the next table. There were few women, the place was full of thick-necked business men. 'They made their money,' the commander explained, 'and they like to spend it. They don't have to tell me where they got their money from.' It was incongruous, in that room, where each piece of furniture spoke of former owners. We talked of difficulties, lack of this, lack of that. Food was scarce, food was a constant theme. He would not say much about his work. 'Large packages, they send us the dead, discs, portraits, paper soaked in blood. We are obliged to sort them, handling each object with care, repacking and redirecting sealed boxes in thousands.'

I asked him which room had been used for the children. He said: 'This room.' He described the six hundred children packed into the darkened room, the marks of their fingers could be seen on the walls. 'They must have known what was to happen.' 'We told them it was to be a concert, we provided music, from a violin and a piano, until a woman stepped in front of the curtain and called for silence.'

I was being diverted from my object. I asked him directly: 'When may I speak to the girl?' 'You may see her. A meeting has been arranged.' 'Where is she now?' 'In my room,' he paused and added pointedly: 'She is resting.' I was holding a glass of wine to my mouth, I felt my hand tremble to the point of insanity, I dropped the glass on to the table, it smashed and sent the wine over the cloth. He said calmly: 'I took you for a friend. I see I was mistaken.' I had begun to apologise, but before I could say more than a few words, he left the table, and after speaking to the driver for a moment, went out of the room. The driver came over to me with a supercilious smile: 'I am asked to inform you that the question of the permit to visit a person charged with a crime against the state can only be dealt with through official channels.' 'What does that mean?' 'You'll have to apply through the office like everyone else.'

After I had waited an hour in the outer office, the commander came in but did not appear to notice me. He whispered something to a secretary and they left the room together. Within a few moments she returned carrying a length of dress material. While she was handling the material and draping it about herself, she turned to me and said irritably: 'There's no point in you waiting here.' But she merely glanced at me in an impersonal way when I walked past her into the private office.

The commander was alone in his office, with books, a man with a history, his head square and large in bone, his coat black or brown, his well-made boots climbing a steep slope of work. Steel blinds protected his head from the sun, he was aware of the threats which shadowed his life. He got up from his chair and shook hands formally. 'You have come at an awkward time,' he said, 'I received orders to bring you here and answer your questions. I obeyed. That is all.' He had an easy manner. I was an official guest. I was offered a seat but declined it. 'I regret I cannot receive you in our senate room, but it is undergoing repair after damage during the war. In what way can I be of service to you?' He looked beyond me at the charts on the walls. I was not deceived. I said: 'I don't wish to cause any trouble. I want things to go on as they are, I want to keep the wheels turning.' He made a sign, picked up his coat which had lain neatly across the back of his chair, and walked towards the door. I respected him. I stood aside. He passed close to me. I felt his breath on my face. The light was terribly bright. I watched his face, his mouth moved: 'A mistake may have been made.' I tried to touch his hand. I asked: 'Why do you speak in this way?' His expression changed. 'I will make further inquiries. Should I receive a favourable report, arrangements will be made for the transfer of population. In any event I shall show you everything, the bad as well as the good. And afterwards perhaps you will not be so anxious to see her.' He waited for me to go. 'I hope she will be released.' 'She will get out, but only to some other place.'

7

I CHANGED MY LIFE. I went among the prisoners taken to the camp for labour purposes. I wanted to make certain, I wanted to get inside, I knew the language. I wanted to learn more, suddenly. Where I might not have understood two words, I got used to their slang and abbreviations. My work was in that place. I began to study murder. I made plans. A few feet between us, the open country beyond. Success depended on whether I could reach the open country afterwards. I studied maps. The plan was complicated, there were roads to be watched, speed was essential, there were two main roads leading to the town, they formed a junction a mile north of the camp.

I watched the driver, his hair was white, he was my man. All the rest were prisoners, he was not. The others wrote to their families, he did not. I examined the identity of this man, I lived with him. He talked, he had no suspicions, he talked about his family, he discussed his girl, showed me her photograph, there was little I did not know about him. He was very particular about his food, he spent hours planning meals, he had trained to be a cook. 'I got work which entitled me to a room with furniture, and then I sold the furniture. I bought these trousers, and a fur-lined coat. That's how I got this job. I looked the part.'

I was no longer myself, but him. I wore his best black trousers, I squeezed into his coat. I could not bring my arms to my sides, my head was too large for the cap, it was hot, the sun hit my head, I was not good-looking enough. I met the commander walking along, I never showed my face, he did not know I had passed. I noted the shape of the commander's thin fingers, felt the texture of his palm. His palm smelled of sweet gas. I knew the time for his death. He was to follow those who had disappeared at his word. I was the person in the crowded courtyard who knew the date of his death. I did not tell him anything. I often walked close to him with my gun, there would have been time, he was in easy range. This time he was larger, bolder, more conspicuous, I happened to catch sight of him crossing the road, I had a dear view of the small person, a fleeting glimpse, he was a tremendously fast walker, always in a hurry, he preferred the open roads to the densely crowded courtyard, he was most careful where he walked.

I did not know that I was being watched. I was stopped by police, a bomb had been thrown. The police closed in. Their caps made them taller, guns on either side, their hands held sticks. I was knocked down by a sergeant of police, my arm crushed by his boots against the walk. He ordered me out of the camp within one hour. A lorry was leaving in forty minutes.

I gave up my plan. I needed to know him better. I threw away my loaded gun, the barrel was hot, it was painful to touch the metal. Then came shots. The pain from my arm underlined the reality of what was happening. The sound of the clump of metal on the floor, a man without legs, false legs and metal feet, carried on a wooden board, I heard a clatter, the driver lit his pipe, he fell dead, I could not prevent the blunder, he was hit by five bullets. The driver, not the commander, a mistake had been made, I learnt the meaning of a gun. He stumbled, he didn't move, figures came towards us loudly calling his name, they wandered aimlessly, they didn't expect to find him in the mist, they were a long way away, he was beyond reach. Not hearing anything I thought of wild plans, the gun I had hidden, I wasn't sure, I got up and brushed my clothes, tired, uncertain. In the shouting and panic I dragged the body through a doorway, carried the load up two flights of steps. Every door was locked.

I was overtaken by medical officers. 'You should not have touched the body.' 'I could not find anyone to help. I've been wounded.' My arm was soaked with blood. The officer insisted that I cease work, led me away, ordered me to hospital. 'This man has worked well.' He demanded my name which I had to give, he promised me a decoration, I was to be taken to hospital for treatment for shock. I had been an idiot, I had not followed the agreed plan, now I was being taken to hospital.

The doctor treated my arm. I had done useful work. I was put to bed. I slept for an hour. I woke, stared at the man standing over me, it was the sergeant of police. I had to think of some excuse. He wanted to know why I had not done as he had ordered. I told him I had lost my way, the lorry had left without me. There would have to be a fuller explanation, he was obviously suspicious. Maybe he was waiting for my brain to clear. He waited too long. The doctor returned, I showed him my letter of recommendation, he allowed me to go. There may have been suspicion, but the disaster had been an accident. At that moment a telegram was handed to me inviting me to attend the funeral of a man cruelly assassinated by a fanatic. I was still wearing the uniform of the tall handsome man. The trousers were stained with blood, I had to wear my own trousers, they squeezed me into the coat which gaped wide open in front, the hat would not stay on, I had to carry it under my arm.

In the morning the lines formed in the streets leading to the ground, the approach to the lines of cars led past houses, we were watched from the gardens, the people watched in long lines behind the gates of their houses. He had been a young man, greatly liked. Protected by the neutral flag flying before it, my car drove with the others, surrounded by mourning crowds, to the desolate gardens. The commander was attended by men in magnificent uniform, they wore gorgeous dark blue and gold. I was introduced to the presence, he shook hands and talked with me. Encircled by death, walking the path between the stones, a long walk in a lovely forest, the daughter passed walking slowly, at the sound of my voice she tipped the funeral flowers she carried to one side using the leaves to screen her face so that I saw the thick plaits but not her face. I went on as if I did not know she had passed. Opposite the wall the tall pine stood, the shooting had dealt a blow, he had fallen victim, the bullet had been wasted, the bullet had waited from the hour of his birth, he had been unable to protect himself.

A crowd had gathered to read the funeral notice posted in the entrance hall. I felt her hand. 'Lean against me, it's cool.' I want to tell you—' She spoke in slow carefully articulated words: 'A mistake. The wrong man. You find it strange?' She said her father's men had fired the shots at random, part of their war of nerves, they were not concerned with whom they killed as long as they killed. Her father had his own methods, the assassination was meaningful, the work of his brain, an excuse to wage sensational war. But she was trusted by the commander and she would deal with him in her own way. 'Get him in bed and stick scissors in his back. That's the method. We shall make sure of him this time.' She took me to his room, she knew her way about, she showed me where they slept, she behaved like a wife, she said I could stay, I would not have to hide, I could sleep in their room.

8

HOLDING HIMSELF ABOVE her, moving neither forwards nor backwards, the commander allowed her to survive, he turned with ease, mounted, just as he reached her she shifted away, he pursued her, she shielded herself with her arms, facing him and crouching, she tried to escape, suddenly she turned towards him, hopeless, it was over. Failed, beaten, he continued in hope, really tired, not persevering, he did not share her panic, his exhaustion made it easy. As he woke she prepared for a long fight, she was persistent, she stuck to her hate until it happened, but she was thrown off by his remaining motionless, by his motionless power. She endeavoured to close with him while she was strong, an amazing exhibition, she furiously hunted, grasped him, he flicked aside, he saved himself, she shifted to avoid the agony, it was driven home, there was no agony, he seized her neck and gave her a sharp hit at the base of the skull, it was over, swinging, no sound, she was overwhelmed, silence followed, clapping, whiplike, in the dense atmosphere.

With his height and weight he knelt on her spine, they fell with violence, her shocked face and flapping hands, her wrists against the wood, discoloured eyes, stains of earth and tears, bruised lips, cheeks splashed with tears, his dog between her feet, her feet in its belly, streaks of black across his face, his fingers. The short whip with a pellet of lead at the end of its lash, the hairs in his nostrils, the gaze of pleasure. The fourth stroke tore her skin, the patches of suffused blood were at first dark red, sharply defined injuries produced by blows, rupture, the skin dragged in a particular direction. She was aware only of some dazzling, some flattening, very slight, her red reflection, I could see the folded skin, the muscle dislocated, the normal state interfered with, altogether lost. Her body shook with frightened movements, the movements in her chamber, unusually deep, complicated, dragging. She fell downwards and inwards, it occurred several times, her body was dragged back, the nature of the pain was not understood, the pain in the stretched membrane remained, portions of the membrane stretched in fine threads, detached by a blow, the blood lay red and fresh then black, a fly moved slowly across and came to rest, glittering spots, small particles of white, appeared in the blood and danced about with slightest tremor of the skin, lasted for several minutes and disappeared, leaving the surface wet.

No feet or stones, some soft thing, her head twisted sideways towards a basin of water. 'Lie still.' A fat face, poor child, a smell of onions, the marks of his teeth on her shoulders. She tried to stand up. He threw a handful of sweets towards her. 'No.' I saw her struggling, I touched her skirt. His fingers held her head, reached her elbows. I watched the pointed bones move, leaned forward and picked up her hand. I saw her teeth grinning, dim squared shapes with a side still grey. I touched her mouth, he moved her arms and hands. I tried to help her, I saw her in the centre of the room, her throat, hair. 'Her arm is broken,' I said. 'Very well, strap it to her side.' He lifted her on to the bed, I watched the touching of the two of them, the specks on her fingernails, her white skin, freckled, reddened. They had both been hurt. He seemed taller, older. He set her arm in splints, bathed her mouth, brought a scarf for a sling. She bent down in front of him and rather than look at her breasts he turned his head away and examined the ironwork on the door. By their references to their childhood both seemed to have come from the same town. This irritated and depressed me. She ate from his hand, the feeding was done in silence, in his fingers the food became toys, coloured string, painted wood. He looked at her, they whispered, he kissed her face. No one spoke. He changed her bandages, trimmed the edges with her scissors. I handed her the scissors. She looked at me coldly: 'You said?' 'I? Nothing.' He bathed the wound, touched her body, humming. He took the bandages from her arm. 'There may be a scar.' 'Are you sure?' Her smooth face, pale mouth, thick hair. The ape was on her, I trained myself to watch.

When she was bitten by his dog, she welcomed it with a bowl of milk, she put in some sugar, the dog ate from her hand saturated with cream. She hung like a black thread round its neck, her hair round the roots of its ears, she spoke to it, confidently. Her sharpened scissors were three-quarters of an inch long, longer and sharper than they ought to have been, for needless pain was inflicted. She sat low so that she could stab freely, she stabbed hard, seized the dog's legs and twisted them so that they were dislocated, and it lost the lower joints as a result of this trick.

I did nothing at all. I avoided killing the minutest insect. I walked carefully, examined every seat before sitting on it. I wore muslin across my mouth. I counted fifty insects lying on the ground. I scrutinised every bit of dirt lest I should tread on and crush something.

I received word from her father, of the plans being made outside. The advancing troops had surrounded an important town, and new attacks were planned.

She stood still in the centre of the room. We waited, I by the door, the commander asleep on the bed. She would not cut his throat with the scissors straight away, though nothing would have been easier. She said she preferred the continuous presence of death, the long sickness. She went to him like a dog a hundred yards away from a building, she sniffed the walls, then went away without eating. He placed ice in a bucket, she licked the frozen cubes. I reminded her of the plan we had made, I described the state of the war outside, the changing fortunes, I hinted at the prospect of revenge. She showed no response, concealed the scissors, while he watched, listened, watched the other, ready to dodge violent attack.

I went outside and started walking. I did not choose a direction, I could think only of what had happened to her, unable to believe that she had changed. I avoided the prisoners, I knew no one. I walked out of the camp without any idea where to go.

9

HER FATHER'S MEN had taken half the country, they had moved from the hills towards the town, so it was easy to make contact with them. I was stopped and threatened by their frontier police. I waited until the son came to me in uniform to thank me for what I done for him during his illness. He was especially grateful that I had not betrayed him to his father, he distrusted me, but recognised my good qualities nonetheless. He was still a sick man. He told me his father had refused his request to serve with a fighting unit, instead he had been required to broadcast propaganda speeches to the other side. I remarked that this was responsible work, a compliment to his abilities, it would give him scope to speak and write. He said he was incapable of writing, he had never written a single word, he 'spouted' what others composed.

The father received me in his spacious and magnificent apartment, there I found him, sitting in one corner, near a window. I had remembered a more impressive figure, he was not good-looking as in his photographs. He wore the blue coat and darker blue trousers, his well-worn clothes contrasted with those of his handsome son, an imposing figure in rich uniform, whose hair grew low on his forehead, who wore armbands and epaulettes each with a knot of gold. I paid attention to what the older man said while he listened to me closely, his penetrating mind at once absorbed the essence of each question, his answers were as sharp as a command. The son impatiently shuffled his typewritten script as he prepared to rehearse before his father the speech he was to make later in the day. In accordance with custom, he began with compliments: 'Within three months our leader will revolutionise the country, restoring it to its former high position among the nations. But if conditions are allowed to worsen, three years may be necessary for this task . . . Wounded in the trenches, oblivious to personal advantage, our leader has succeeded in creating a powerful party, but has remained a man of simple tastes. He is generous and warmhearted. If he chooses to live austerely it is to devote all his energies to his great work, he lives in a modest palace, the only diversion he permits himself is playing the violin, he does not drink wine, nor does he smoke, he never laughs, he entirely prohibits any projection of his own personality, he is not only a clever but also a goodhearted man, here is a man who resolutely puts the futilities out of his life to leave place for nothing but work. A perfect gentleman, his charming wife, a clever son and pretty daughter complete the family group. His photograph, sent to all who apply, will be valued the more in the knowledge of how rarely he allows himself so personal a gesture. He is unfailingly kind to visitors, he receives them in the spacious and magnificent state apartment, there they find him, sitting in one corner, near a window, paying close attention to what is said, his penetrating mind at once absorbs, his answers sharp as a command . .

I saw the son each day, it was a privilege to be his friend. He never failed to run after me in the street, calling a greeting until he attracted my attention. The father resented my close friendship with his son. He explained that there were those at that time who were in the highest positions, who had access to state secrets, and yet were known for their sympathies with certain persons. The son's high station made him difficult to deal with. An order was made that all letters were to be left open except those addressed to the leader himself. The repeated leakage of news to the commander, made them suspicious and wary.

They accused me of failing to comply with certain regulations, though I performed my duties with straightforwardness and strictest impartiality, whatever my sympathies. When they tried to prevent my reporting interviews if these were unfavourable, I pointed out that this prohibition constituted a breach of international law. They replied that they were not a party to these laws. Such lack of understanding I found disturbing.

Certain messages related to the manufacture of munitions. Finding that the son was anxious to earn large sums of money, I arranged transmission of these messages through him. When he insisted that no message sent with his assistance should be against the interests of the country, I said that such requests confused the issue. He replied that though he was and wished to remain a good friend of mine, he could not be a party to treason and consequently it would be necessary to replace him. My conscience would not permit me to agree to this, my mission demanded his co-operation. I tried to persuade him that his work for me need not affect his other duties. I pointed out that he needed the money, which was his by right. I said to him: 'I admire your character.' I told him what he already knew, that this work was being done in other capitals by other envoys. I increased the sums allotted to him, and he was finally convinced by this argument. But there were further complications.

It was my custom to bring the morning papers to the father's office. I knocked on the door at the appointed time. The son was there. The storm was raging. 'What do you want?' the old man demanded. 'To give you these papers,' I said, closing the door, never to open it again. I saw that nothing would change. For myself, I asked and received attention, I was promoted, but I realised that it was unwise to remain too long in foreign lands. The father was growing senile, one obtained favours only through his son, with whom one had to deal. Friends warned me that these were difficult and dangerous superiors to serve under, but for the time being I remained with them.

When a serious dispute arose between the father and the party, he let it be known that if his son was raised in rank, the matter would be settled in an acceptable manner. So it was done, although raising a young man to high rank was contrary to all custom. The father was old and unattractive and his lack of success in war worsened his chronic bad temper.

It was impossible to rely on the son's loyalty. There were many who sold information. They knew no side but their own. I discovered that while he was taking money from me for disclosing secrets, the son was at the same time gathering information on my movements. I was cautious, my first duty was to preserve strict neutrality during those difficult days. When he asked me to work with him on a film he was to produce, I did not accept at once. I began to make inquiries. I found that both brother and sister were in the pay of both sides, that they exchanged secrets impartially. They had associates on the border, and messages were smuggled through several times before they were discovered.

The son should have paid with his life. He was jailed for fifty days, on suspicion. Then it was proved that he had been falsely accused by a real spy, a deserter taking his revenge when the son said he would not take part in his treasonable schemes, and had flatly refused to provide certain information. The son was released, to continue his criminal, dangerous work.

The son came to me, with a woman he called his nurse. He had been ordered to pay certain restaurant bills, but had left without paying. He had given my name and had been told that the man was unknown. I was annoyed by this feeble swindle. He then said he needed money to send to his sister. I promised to help. He returned within minutes to say that his sister had not received the money. I said it was impossible in so short a time. He said the money had been mislaid and produced a record of the correct sum sent. I said I would straighten the matter out by finding the money and repaying him. He would not accept this. I reasoned with him. He began to shout. I was obliged to call the police. He was furious. I could not understand him. He was one of the few I had trouble in dealing with.

He was accused of supplying troops with cocaine and he was detained on this charge. He requested help, through friends. But justice could not be interfered with. At that time no one cared or dared to tamper with the law. However, the accusations were proved false, by other events which later transpired. After he was caught and jailed, he dared to telephone me begging me to pay his bills, which of course I could not do.

The police planned his execution with unusual strategy. A senior detective was entrusted with the case. A friendship sprang up between them. They decided to escape to the frontier, police followed, they arrived, he grasped him by the throat: 'You are detained as a spy. I am an agent of the political police.' He was brought home, and judged, expelled from the party, and shot, protesting that he was a friend of mine.

His father announced that 'the heroic defender had been taken prisoner after the demolition of the fort, after he himself had twice been wounded.' I was there when the father learned of the son's execution. He began to shout. 'And they call it war!' It was a bad sign. I tried to interest him in the plans he had formed, the tactics he had originated. 'What do we want maps for?' he snatched the maps from me. 'We'll want maps. You'll see!' He unfolded the maps, replaced them on the table so that the battlegrounds lay face down, uppermost were the gentle hills, and the sea a fresh unused blue. 'I need a rest from this war. It's peaceful there.' His finger pointed to a seaside town famous for its boredom and its waste. I said he should go there, the war would continue without him. His mood changed, to loud laughter and wild behaviour, I could see his son in him. A young soldier came in, from the son's detachment. He stood waiting. 'Have you news?' 'There's nothing left. No one.' 'What do you mean?' 'The situation has not improved.' He turned in military fashion, saluted, and left. The father mumbled to himself. 'These are details, details. He saw nothing, but that is not to say there was nothing. The man showed his blindness, that is all.' I pointed out that the 'skirmish' took place close to the frontier, his son could have escaped, though nothing would be heard for months, he could be posted missing, this was the normal procedure, he could be alive, in another country. I was relieved when he interrupted me rudely: 'That's nothing. I know that. You tell me nothing I do not already know.' He continued talking to himself. 'I used to shave every morning, now see what I will do. I used to eat meat, and fish. I cannot be the lover of another man, even my son.' He staggered round the room, I insisted on helping him into his chair. I pushed towards him the model of the new piece of artillery with which his men were to be equipped, but he was not interested. He showed me again the photograph of his son in uniform. 'Take a look at this. So you see. Better for him to have been shot, than to be kept forever in prison without trial. What could I have done to prevent it?' He stood beside the table, memorials of battles, tattered flags, hung over the table. I spoke about his son's desire to go to the front. He answered: 'He's disappeared. Finished.' He went on to discuss tactics. 'The strength of their artillery, and for defence we use sheets of tin! Tin is useless in modern warfare! We must improve our supplies of steel or we'll all be blown to pieces! The leader must be cheered when he meets his troops, they attack with bayonets and are killed, the artillery goes on firing, they fight and are killed, hand to hand. The battle comes to an end. They cannot understand why it has taken so long, but if I have learned the name of a village, it has been a necessary battle. I dream of the battle of annihilation. Kill them all, so there shall be none. Annihilation does not mean physical annihilation, annihilation means surrender, demoralisation. A battle which goes on, is not annihilation, annihilation means surrender. But these fellows fight. We must have artillery, the concentration of forces on one front, the direct blow against the enemy's decisive forces, tactics face to face with tactics, tactics orientated towards the offensive, tactics adapted to defence, to terrain and climate, based on the simultaneous use of weapons for defence and attack, in the pursuit of the enemy. Activity which knows no seasons gives an absolute tactical advantage over the enemy, the enemy is to be misled about our positions and dispositions, our defence in depth, our tank defence zones. Night will cease to be a time for rest, we shall break through at night over frozen lakes and rivers, we shall overcome by force as the result of superior tactics systematically applied.'

My courage was upheld. I organised an office 'to help the victims of war'. A few friends assembled in my room. Hundreds of persons worked together, the organisation was perfect, daily it dealt with missing soldiers, money matters, food, every detail of everyday life. We were in touch with both sides. We forced the belligerents to respect our neutrality. We gave of our resources, with punctillious impartiality, most lavish generosity. Wounded soldiers were met by ladies with drinks and cigarettes when their train stopped. So long as they travelled behind the lines, they were attended by ladies who served as nurses.

At a luncheon for sixty or seventy people to support the hospital for severe surgical cases, for the sick who could not be cured, I was the guest of honour. I could not speak. I attempted without the aid of grammar. 'What is he saying?' 'You should be able to understand. I am endeavouring to speak your language.'

A fine-looking man, the son transformed, doomed to meet his death, stopped to talk to me, on his way back. He had been dying on the battlefields. I invited him to lunch. I was filled with admiration for what he had seen. He ruined my velvet-covered furniture by scraping his greased boots over it. The incident gave rise to satirical verses. He was a trouble-maker who tried to kidnap and kill, but the plan was found out, troops were summoned, with instructions to shoot on sight. So order was restored. A strike was called, no papers were printed, the town was still. I could not find out, men and women were falling, soldiers caught the disease, the schools were turned into hospitals, thousands died. Bread was sold by card. A relative sent me all I needed from home, but I could not cook the food, the people's police were free to enter. The drenching rain followed us everywhere. I found a room unoccupied, and there I sat on a chair. It was raining on the bright uniforms. Shivering, weary, unable to walk, ill and tired, I discussed plans for my return, and for the return of those who planned the commander's fall. They were willing to help me return, to simplify their own problem; they took care to protect their own. I was ordered to keep watch on the daughter, they suspected her. I waited for the long train carrying soldiers from one part of the country to another, men without boots, with no food, crowds waited for the train, they had to make sure of their places. I slept on the platform with a block of wood for a pillow. I could not sleep. The others slept and could not wake, and when they woke they shouted or wept. Because they could hate, apathy in death was easy. Indifferent, they celebrated hysterically, which intensified their indifference. They had worked but not owned, they had had no chance and no choice, no ration of life, no notion of danger, the threat to life, to their own. A mobile kitchen arrived, with soup and potatoes. After the crowd had had their food, they sang. I travelled with blinds drawn against all contact en route.

10

I ARRIVED BACK without disaster. An hour later and I would have been caught in a storm. As it was, I was her guest. She was well clothed and well fed. She said she had been attacked: 'He came in the night, the commander tried to set fire to my room.' She was talking in an even more excited manner than usual. 'He came last night and dragged me from my bed. I had to make room for some other women.' Then came a long involved story. At first she said three women were brought into the room, then it was five, then ten. I doubted whether any figure was the true one, it was not possible, it was not reasonable to suppose it had happened.

She knew she was watched, she felt the breath on her neck, but she was ignorant of what was going on, she did not know she had been cruelly treated. I told her nothing, I left her alone on the other side of the room. She asked for my opinion, I gravely replied, going through the farce. She had suffered, she told me quietly about being in prison with dangerous neighbours mysteriously dying, the walled darkness, the sound of sighing, intricate and jealous people inserting poison under her skin. I smiled at her grotesque accumulation of horrors. She said: 'It's true.' She knew her father no longer trusted her, but she felt she had done all she had been asked to do. She would not believe her brother had died. She belonged to nobody, but she was under the control of two masters, imbeciles and idiots. I made attempts to help her, I brought her parcels of sweets and chocolates, cakes, and all kinds of confectionery. Suddenly the gifts were stopped.

A picnic had been arranged. The weather was very cold. I received from the commander a box and a letter, a glittering gift. He was old and ill, hobbling on one leg, there was a wound in his foot which would not heal. 'You must stay,' he said, 'we'll have a party.' I noted his defeat, his age. No one enjoyed the party, we stayed indoors and played cards. He no longer had any hope, but he heroically went through the ordeal, although hatred had marked his face, his eyes showed no sign. He did not shake hands, he thought only about war, he did not want anyone, he did not want us to leave, he was helpless, he himself had to go, he wanted to shake hands with everyone, to remain part of things. He talked endlessly of his dogs: 'I had the last one shot. He killed a prisoner, he pulled down an old woman, I had to have him shot. I am training his successor, I hope to get better results, but he is putting on weight.' There was a note of insanity in his uniform, rich garments blazing with jewels, and the girl, who accompanied him, was gorgeously dressed. 'The girl is my mascot, if I cannot bring her where I please, I will leave.' There was a gasp. She was slow-moving and short-sighted, she found it difficult to see in the crowd, she followed him with grim persistence. The commander led us outside, we danced in the garden, from the camp hundreds of voices lifted, he urged us to enjoy ourselves. 'You can go hunting. The organisation is superb. The guests can choose. The shooting is done from the tower.' 'Kill for fun?' one of the guests asked. The commander did not reply, he blinked. I had an impression of yellow fire, the explosions of battle, as his troops retreated towards the camp.

He brought us indoors, we talked for hours in the great hall, the yellow-tiled roof supported by pillars, the darkened room lit by candles, the wax dripped over the gold. Each of us was presented with a medal with a piece of silk or skin attached to it, supposedly a ribbon. We were entertained by women playing music, keeping time with their bare toes. As there were no men one woman played the part of a man. They looked like mushrooms, each mushroom a girl crouched under a hat, bending so they touched the ground. It was amusing to watch their backs, one lost her footing and rolled over, she was seized by the legs and pulled along. Divided from the women by the width of the room the guards watched in silence. Two girls carried fire from behind a screen in iron dishes as tall as themselves, suffering magnified their limbs, no greetings, no word, the wind rising, their voices lamented, I could not distinguish one from the other, we went on eating, their breasts hanging over us like long potatoes. The sound of drums on stage confused with exploding shells outside, the building was roofed with tiles, the pillars painted, the walls streaked with lime. She was seated in shadow, her face oval in the dim room, she carried an umbrella which she twirled to prevent any man staring at her, she offered me a bowl of milk, placing it on the ground at my feet, it was not necessary to know what she meant by the movement, there was no mystery, she used a poem to kill. The troops were outside, there was no time for marriage, I gave her some clothes but she would not put them on, she sent them out of the room. Because she had been bitten by one of the dogs she kept her face half-hidden. I had only to wait, the idea was to do nothing at all. The stage was a fortress surrounded by a wall, loopholed, on either side were piles of grenades for the last troops who kept guard. The crumbling of the place brought out the rats and other vermin, circus dogs dressed in yellow, wearing caps, trotted on money. Her hunger was so strong her flesh was like earth that disappears, with her skirt held up she ran with the spotlight, she scrambled for paper and rubber, there was no space, she had no form, she drifted in the strong light, in the haze of dust her face was white, her body bare, she wore no jewels, I had no desire at all. She was ashamed of the ugliness of her legs, a feather had been tied to each ankle, her head swung from left to right, she pretended to be absorbed, staggered round. The commander said: 'Duties are taught to the girls. They used to live by making mats, now they are kept alive and not ill-treated.' Her answer was a smile, indifferent, divine as an almond. An explosion shattered the lights, brought tiles and plaster crashing on to the stage, the commander brought torches and placed them near her, her legs with gestures invited me to enter. I put on my coat. She sang a song, waved a flag, advanced, stumbled against the dark walls, I could see her feet in the rubble and dust, the two legs blazed white, the heavy head hung on the long neck inconceivably slender.

In silver, infinitely high, the commander raced by in one of his great cars. White cloths were spread on the ground, women shouted, they were forced into doorways, women made themselves into wheels. She ran with them, stones swinging above her lips, she threw flowers through the windows. The commander stopped for her, rode with her, a rug around his shoulders as big as a town and tipped with metal. They walked across the wide plain, a wind blowing vast blue, his gigantic forehead, her eyes splashed with gold, dogs in a gale, lost in its sugared darkness. Her hair was unclipped, touched with dyes, decorated with blue beads, she wore a collar loosely round her neck, on her back embroidered stripes of yellow and blue, a cap on her head, her long hair parted in the middle, scented and sleek.

He allowed her to search the mouths of the dead, the gold in their mouths was increasing in value. She brought her dead to the river where they were torn by fishes, perhaps I had never seen them seven feet away, I saw each move, I watched, during all that eventful time I saw nothing impossible. He had to train her in the work. She came to deliver his share, he tried to take one from her, she refused to part with it, there was noise, face to face, each grasping the dead, with feet fixed, to get more. He took it, she got away with the gold from the teeth, she hid the bits of gold in her own mouth, this annoyed him, he grabbed at her mouth, got a hold on the tongue, she shrieked, dragging, at last she freed herself, she dragged herself away. He went on as if nothing had happened. She was left wandering, unable to feed herself, away from the others, her mouth a mass of cotton wool, oblivious to what was happening, they sat close together again and watched the flies round the bodies. The food cry was heard and the heads went up, the cry repeated time after time. Disturbed, she gave the cry, went up to the body and touched it, dragged it down as the others crowded round, clamoured for it, each one desperate for it. She wrenched off the leg, jabbed it, thick end first, into her mouth, tried hard to swallow it, could not get it down, the thicker part became less visible, there was nothing but the foot, she twisted off the protruding foot. Holding the body, she twisted it, with a cutting and pulling action, with a final twist the limb was removed. She knew how to do it. The limbs were small, then they increased in size, and became too large, then only the rats dared to go, the rest were left starving. The commander's voice was heard, she crept into a sheltered corner, close to him.

The cages were broken, the crowd had got loose and invaded the shops. Though they picked up weapons, they remained victims, blind, breaking down, drowning. They were driven out between the roofs, the crowd cried slaughter, they had a passion for picking things to pieces, they found crowbars, they moved with plunder, grew to great size, fought for a place of power, they had no leader, were angry, with a new kind of headlong terror, a clumsy plunging and bounding. The old man's face was red, over-fed. One hand hung, his face terrible. They watched his face in order to defeat his plan. He had failed to find others to carry him. He threw them bread, but they did not run for scraps. He went into the street and stood whining, spent time sitting and looking at the rain. They rushed at him from opposite points, two or three at a time. He was not allowed to reach home. He dashed back between walls, in sweeps and curves and rushing and collision he shook them off. He used his nails, a stone. They circled round, five yards from the walls. His favourite dog had gone, I had seen him tormenting the dog who hated him, the dog had learned to watch. He peered in at windows, at the heat, longing for the fire. Someone threw a stone, and in a minute a dozen others followed. They chased him with shouting, they tried to kill him by grinding his head on a stone, rubbed it on the ground, split the skin of his forehead and crushed one of his ears. Without her help he could not reach home. She sprang on him, opened his mouth, scooped out the spit while he chattered. He had to wait till she had finished or went mad. She put on prisoners' clothes, mounted the goat, they came closer, he glanced at her with begging eyes. She threw him backwards, leaping, he struck the hot embers piled together, dropped, received in the face the hot coal. She started laughing, he filled his fist full of clear glass, passed a slow hand down, lost interest, waited. He would kill himself. She slit his nostrils. The final sound when they slit. And when they slit it was impossible. He received blows from thick sticks, he staggered round, blind with blood, exhausted, he fell against a cage, dragged himself through the electric wires, for a moment he was confined in a dome with an iron floor, it was painful to touch the electrified metal, he crashed through the glass and was seized on the other side. They put sticks into his mouth, little by little he died, disfigured. He was tied to a post, sticks were thrown at him, they would kill him in the end, he was not left to bleed to death, he was maimed, spreadeagled on his back, forked pegs held down his hands and feet, he cried slaughter, others attacked him and held him down, he cried slaughter, their cry, he was beaten to death in the dark, given the name of stone, shaved and blackened, hung by his feet from the branch of a tree.

This punishment was inflicted, that is how he was treated when he was too old to be of any use. His foot may have been cut off with a heavy knife and put into his mouth. Presumably it would cause his death. If not, the throat was cut.

A horse galloped in the street, the hall collapsed, the walls were not intact, the old walls had fallen, there was nothing left. There were the feet of two stone monuments, the left inscribed, the right without writing, the central block had a square of iron remaining, the rest had disintegrated, there would be no restoration. The old man and the old woman were no longer in existence, those old people found on the corners of streets, they were too frail, they were wiped out when disaster came.

I concealed myself close by, cut off from the crowd. Nothing happened. He remained motionless, his brains had probably, without warning, dropped to the ground. He remained, stillness maintained, there was no cause to walk across the intervening inches, stillness maintained for hours, except for slight alterations of the eyes. The eyes were closed at times. I saw his head, long, rounded, the trunk projecting beyond, the grey head, finely lined, bristles around the mouth, the outer bristles tipped with white, the effect extraordinarily twisted, serrated like the teeth of an iron comb, the comb used to clean the bristles around the mouth. We stayed close for hours, two enemies, my eyes passed over the bits of twisted wood the edges of which, little bits of brown and grey bark, represented discovery through half-closed eyes. He was not far away, wounded, crouched, sinking, he could have stood up. I saw him laid on the stones like a bit of stick, bare earth underneath, some kind of resting place, leaf mould, bracken crushed flat by the weight. His skin was dull grey turning white, barred and streaked, pencilled with grey. Our two bodies placed side by side were small, hardly to be seen, bits of stone or grit which the eye passed over.

11

PEOPLE PUT ON their best clothes and went into the streets, they put on fancy dress, they wore head-dresses and capes and came and went offering congratulations to one another. People like roaming dragons, people in furs like flowing water, their noisy shouts filled the streets, they opened shops and began business. Their lights were lighted, scattering lantern flowers, scattering customers, a hundred thousand lamps were lit at night, scattered on stoves, the gates, the doors, convenient blocks of stone. Like fireflies, stars, to the sound of drums they were put out under silk coverings with floating banners and small objects carried in front: artificial flowers specially made, flowers of all seasons, with painted scenes moulded out of ice and from cheap tin imported from abroad, and from shoots of wheat by order, symbolic figures of men and animals. All shops displayed her father's face, each window larger than twelve by twelve held a photo of his face, her father's face in every street in frames of wood, in frames of silk and glass with small pieces of silver and gold secretly put inside. The night was filled officially, with official fireworks of every variety imported from the east, three hundred small boxes, a thousand flower pots, fifteen fire and smoke pools, twenty-two thousand rockets, ten peonies strung on a thread, forty plates sprinkled with water, twenty golden plates, thirty pinwheels, thirty falling moons, dozens of flags of fire, fifteen hundred double-kicking feet, a thousand fire crackers which exploded on the ground and then again in the air, ten explosions flying to heaven, five devils noisily splitting apart, ten bombs for attacking the city, eight eight-cornered rockets, a hundred lanterns of heaven and earth, twelve silver flowers, twelve trees of fire, the sounds dinned the ears, the flashes darkened the eyes, the dust from the feet gradually lessened, the shadows fell stretched on the ground.

She cut out coloured materials and put them on her head, she ran through hoops to the sound of a gong, she made small cakes for her father. He made her stop her needlework for fear that it might injure her eyes, she made umbrellas out of coloured paper. She sat talking to me, her hand on an animal, she had a dog of her own, when she had pains in her ears she touched the dog's ears, when she could not see she touched his eyes, when she had broken bones in her feet she stroked his feet. She cut out of stone a channel for running water in the form of the face of a dog, and she floated cups down the stream to other children waiting below.

Her father took charge. He ordered the commander's death to be marked by two stone monuments, a stone platform, a stone column eight feet high surmounted by four banners inscribed in four languages, iron coloured tiles, an iron covering. A bell was cast. It was fifteen feet high and fourteen in diameter, the knob of the bell by which it was suspended was seven feet high, the thickness of the iron was seven inches. It weighed twelve tons. It was carved with characters inside and outside, the characters were each an inch in size, and close together like the teeth of a comb, they were written by a scholar, they echoed the words written on the banners. One banner asked: 'What is religion?' Three banners answered: 'Fear.' The bell was suspended. The tower was levelled and the bell buried in the ground. The bell was removed. A second tower was constructed fifty feet in height, it was square below and round above, there were windows on all sides, a circular staircase ascended on the left and descended on the right, each stair was carved, above the bell sprawled a bronze dog being knifed by a man, the bell hung in the centre, pure bronze, exactly upright, with a fine sheen. I never heard it sound. It was the year of hope not to be realised, not for years, not in the way expected.

Her father ordered the completion of the bridge, the bridge that had been begun before, the bridge that had been talked about, the link between the old town and the new. It was nothing unusual. The bridge crossed the river, it passed the town, there was nothing, then it ran, it was impossible to prevent. There were tunnels, a strip of metal, it carried, it was built, rocks were moved and heaped up under mountains, the bridge was built in terror, the work was finished with songs, she sang, the earth was moved, step by step, filling bags with earth, she worked. Other hands attempted, failed, she stayed there, bending. She longed for a jug of milk, a drink of water was the taste of apple in her mouth, a touch on the shoulder, a smile. She picked up a piece of sacking to wipe her hands, it was soaked in oil, it made her hands glisten. She worked for thirty hours, alternately lashed and praised. Her brain was nailed in a box.

Her father shouted, his voice against the noise, boastful of the labour and colossal expense, the cubic yards and thousand tons. She struggled, a patch of sweat under her lip.

She slept close to his animals, his valuable hounds. In the corner of her room she kept a dog, kissed his teeth, she adored his sharp teeth, clinging to his teeth she turned, falling on to a sloping table. I said: 'Something of yourself.' And so?' she replied, 'was it not you?' Her face began to speak of home. She had returned to her family, waving her hand, then a piece of lead replaced her slow hand, her lips moving, she came towards me. We did not meet, she had no reason to tell the truth. She left, motioning with her hand towards my cool recess, a table placed between columns, pieces of furniture within an archway, musical instruments, elegant clothing, gentlemen gazing at lakes.

She worked on the line. She took the risk, by regulation forbidden, when the smoke came, to leap off the line. She came to me. A sinister fact. It was the rule to choose to do without. She jumped and clung to her need for the new. There was no wall, no wire, but terror was their weapon, there were all the signs, the blocks were kept ready in huts. The rest were imprisoned by the familiar, the family wall.

I was not bound by their regulations. I asked for information. I was told that the work could be seen in steel. I measured the steel and asked again. I was referred to the inspectors, I saw none.

She lifted the wheel, walked in a circle, prevented the wheel from slipping back. She worked on the hardest roads, her skin a blanket, a leather bag, she could not drink water, her comfort lessened, she scraped the hillside, she was thrown, slipped down, her feet caught, she lay like a stick on the ground. Drivers passed in rock-filled trucks, lines of trucks on the roads, the rock-path, rock-blast, engineering to the end that two towns should be joined by a bridge, a railway track, a great high road. Watchmen guarded the iron, they did not notice her, while the trains were in motion with a wild air, brass encased in patterns of brick red and black with pieces of mirror, crowned with iron and patterns of red, with a high front, brass lower down, tints of bright lights and wide areas of iron clapping against metal or wall, rock, iron held in fire, wheels working, streaks daubed on cement walls and the name branded on stone, her family name, slate-tinted, slab-sided, gaunt and hideous beacons of usefulness hurling themselves over walls.

I heard her breathing. She refused my help. I could not protest or protect as she scuffled past, hollow, narrow, unknown. She had shaved her head, she was dry earth, burnt grass, blackened wire, torn and scrubbed, she worked on uneven ground, crawled, moved, marched, portrayed the work, a show of work. She led the shouting, all messages and questions sounded sinister and shouting was greeted with cheers and shouting. She carried her shoes round her neck, she would not wear shoes, her yellow shirt was red with sweat because of rage, her sweat stinging, her skin dotted with a fine white growth, she alternately drooped and shouted. On a platform a propaganda man, plump, with white teeth, his full mouth quivered with laughter, beneath the poster the torn remains of an early proclamation . . . inviolability of person and dwelling, unlimited freedom of religion, speech, press, assembly, strikes and unions, freedom of movement and occupation, election by the people of army officers and recall of any of them, at any time, by the will of the majority of the electors, replacement of the police and the standing army by a general arming of the people, eight-hour workday for all hired labour, allowing, in case the work is continuous, for not less than one hour's time for eating, complete prohibition of overtime work . . . She threw away her shoes, unwilling to be the one with shoes, she was sweating, her body closely covered with grey cloth. The bones of her face were still good. I had eyes. 'When I leave, will you come with me?' I was about to say more, but that was sufficient. Slowly she began to lose control. 'I've had enough,' her eyes inflamed. There seemed to be no danger, calm was a sign of strength. 'I could not do so, I might want to, the frontier's closed.' I pulled her down in the heat, there was no room, the roof moved, the ground was forced up, her knees touched the ground, the skin was hurt by the stones, she was forced to stay in that low place, she tried to get away but was jerked under.

Friendship was survival in the face, the rock foundations of the bridge and the songs moved forward slowly. She organised the dance, they followed her, shouting in time, circled the fire, died down, sat and slept by the fire. Some were accused of sabotaging labour discipline. They were expelled by soldiers with bayonets drawn, piled into lorries and driven off at top speed. We built brick structures, the earth was loaded, the rock tipped, the earth rose up, compressed by stamping. The towers of bricks held the weight of the bridge which would open by swinging or lifting, a counterpoise bridge supported by beams resting on abutments on either side, having lattice girders, a hanging scaffold, a railed plank extending. She wheeled a load of stones along a path of planks, her feet were bandaged, the bandages on her crippled feet were tied with cords. I observed her straining her legs forward, stumbling over the wheelbarrow, her movements as she practised moving forward in bounds, her convulsive grip and struggling climb, the proud look on her father's face, he appeared at ease on the observation platform, but wanting nerve. For the first time he climbed down, his clean shoes sank in the clay, he held her arm firmly, he was in a good temper, she had to climb the slope at speed, he helped her up. He was sixty-eight years old, short and stout, with a round flushed face, with a pipe the feature of his dress in all his portraits, the hand covered the pipe. The detective who always stood behind, turned hastily. Entangled his sleeve in the sleeve of the leader, the pipe fell to the ground, those surrounding him formed a close circle, and the damage was repaired. She was not trying. She kicked at the loose stones, she struggled up the floor of rock, a long slope with sides of stone, stones pulled off a wall, a new wall built over the mountains, a line across a map.

I walked carefully along the track, made a map of the new line where it paralleled the frontier for twenty miles and branched south-west a few miles from the town. The workers were sent in trucks from the town to the camp, they crossed the track at two points. Heavy supplies in armoured trains travelled at dusk or at night. I hid at night and watched the guard through a window in order to note when he left his post. The door opened, he looked in my direction, walked back towards the bridge, the man failed, his back was turned when he was meant to guard.

The skilled dynamiters split the rock more slowly in the last hour of work. The great rock shook. A ruined engine with roaring coals crashed into the shattered trucks, twisted metals flung the trucks with violence on their sides, an ammunition truck loaded with shells exploded, in two places the track was obliterated by splintered rock. I saw her running in the middle of the track, she escaped a collapsing wall, two others were killed. One armoured train had been derailed, twenty-three trucks turned over by the explosion. My job was done. I should have cleared out at once and returned home, but I could not leave the dozens of men on the ground, foolishly I went to help the dead, I worked at speed, rounded up rescuers and cranes. I opened the gates, held them open, cut the ropes across the road, as they fought to get free of the wreckage, they threw themselves over the rubble. The wind raised clouds of dust from the rubble, then the dust was laid by rain. I was not wearing shoes, my bare feet slipped on the moistened dust on the rotten planks which led to the bridge. The bridge was cut in two, half lay in water, half on land. I leapt across a strip of water, I tried to reach her, it was dangerous, water was already flowing between my feet. I was sixty yards away, it was unsafe, water ran down the wall, the roof started to give way, I was forced against the wall, it was useless to try, I turned back, I was trapped by a rush of water, it was hard to keep my balance, I steadied myself and waded through, I pushed against water up to my mouth, I felt her with my hand, I leaned against her, I could not keep awake. I saw furniture, the room was mine, the front room, the living room, words could be heard, someone was walking, there was only one, the wind blowing the dust. I went through rooms, to go to the lavatory, I knocked the light over, I could not put my foot on the ground, I could not open the door, I lit the lamp, the glass was broken, it was not safe, the light went out, the glass fell to pieces. No light showed the way, lamps would not keep alight in water. Listening to the water rush, I felt for the plank, crossed the darkness. Stones fell from the roof, I heard the stretcher crack, it made no difference. I was careful to crouch. The others were hurrying back to warn us, they delayed us. Her desperate face: 'I have no pay. I have not worked a full week. I have made a bad start.'

12

S HE WAS an asset to the state. If they discovered her attempt to escape, she would be taken back immediately, and I would be carrying dynamite if a shot should strike my back. There was a safe area a mile to the south of the town well away from view at night, from there it would be easy. There was a moon. I was confident. The guard was lying dead, I would be him returning home, my papers in order. I carried the actual papers of a real man, including the photographs of his girl. Silently we crouched by the side of the road, the broken moon gave light, there was nothing, a whisper. I could explain everything to everybody. I was complete. We lay down by the hedge until it was light. The weather was very cold. They would not know where to look.

The straight white road, the trees by the side of the road, the man mending the wall, the narrow poles with white faces turned backwards and forwards from the town, we left the road to see the slabs of rock.

On a ridge of boulders, a but of boulders frozen over, we set about building a shelter, we made a tent by drawing together the edges of a piece of cardboard, with a slanting roof as a precaution against falling stones, we worked together to weave a tent to shelter a whole family. Drawn together, essential to each other, we slept covered by tough sheeting to keep out the cold and preserve the warmth generated by our bodies.

I returned home with food. We sat and repaired our home. I was putting on my boots when men approached us and asked us what we were doing there. They could not understand our language. We had to wait while they checked our papers. I said we were there to admire the palaces and see the fortress pulled down.

She knew she was threatened with capture. She had been given her freedom after being kept locked in for years, and in the end liberty would lead again to capture. Some troops approached, a company of fifteen, part of a regimental band, whose music we had heard before, not far away. One of them played the clarinet, the wood shone black in the sunlight. She kept apart from them, I diverted their attention from her by conversing with them. I learned that in the plains below for some days there had been heavy rains, the floods were out, with the result that some troops had been drowned, valuable equipment had been abandoned, one of their dogs could not be found, the families of some of the men had lost their homes. Their senses were dulled, their powers reduced, they stood on the ground trying to practise the same tune. Two young drummers sat on the stone wall a few yards away, demoralised, helpless. They tapped out the same rhythm over and over again. One of them undid the heavy leather harness and placed his drum beside him on the wall. He was warned by an officer: 'You could be shot.'

A yellow bar of light dissolved, we lay on the rough sand, the last light of the sun in her mouth. A footstep warned. We retired quietly into the depth of our home, to lie low. She would have run, flown. But her injured, tired body was incapable, due to her slight build, her habit of running, the painful shocks she had had. I told her it would be better, more effective, to hide. We enclosed an area on which she could lie flat on her back, an area protected on all sides by a series of stones raised to form a sort of diamond, irregular but strong, with a vein of stone running across obliquely to the outer edge. She lay back safe and smiled with her fine teeth. Her head lay in a small clear area where the sand was a dark colour and the stones made a straight edge, hard and sharp. With flint I entirely removed the roughness where the grains projected. We were not alone in bed. Built around us in successive layers, were old patterns fixed in design, immovable without breaking the body.

I used my hands to alter the ground, the patterns, until we reached perfection, giving complete smoothness around us both, to our eyes an indescribable beauty, magnificent, costly. The strength of each stroke was the slow and careful elaboration, the only style which had success. My hands used her like an object, carried her forward. She judged my caresses by their weight, the lightest being the best. I felt a vibration between us, we communicated, and though we no longer completely overlapped, a space was formed, enclosed, the outer surface formed a box. I moved slightly in, tentative, intermittent, then more restrained. Suspicious, she appeared to recede. Then the two were exactly symmetrical, in our peculiar bends and convolutions we corresponded perfectly. I left her easily, attempted again without success, certain muscles hardened in that position, then attained the perfect state. With unusual patience, without injury to the delicate structure, we found the desired position. She seemed not quite happy, to be making a conscious effort, by crossing one leg over the other so that the position became unintelligible. Then everything, the sand, the rocks, the structure of the building enclosing us, everything was used, until that time, and another time, became equally perfect. If a part went dead and had to be moved, the suggestion was reversed, and the same seemed the same. She was quite silent. Her love came from joy. She invited me to come to her, expected me to come and join her. I was unable to discover any fault. I remained quiet, carefully, she saw me retreat quietly, she remained quiet. I went towards her again merely for my own pleasure, for the pure joy of life. It was interesting to attempt to force her to retreat into her own dwelling, and find both of us in one home.

Hearing songs I thought they were being broadcast, but the band was being drilled, marching and countermarching into itself. We were near the end, the outside was closing in on us. She covered her legs. We could both appreciate the music, the band was making itself a life, we were swamped by the big sound of the band. She was seen, she wanted to sit in the sunshine to hear the music and watch them exercise their dogs. She had grown young, she was not lined in any way, her skin had been carefully smoothed. We had only just room to turn round, our building, commenced at the beginning of winter was merely a winter shelter, not right for the spring, though I could have enlarged it, perfected the smoothness of its walls, it was still not a home, merely a shelter. The whole of the labour had been performed, but the place must now be left and the labour wasted. I knew that, though she did not. We were really in the earth, simply lying on the surface of the earth. She pushed off the roof, like a lid. It was not a question of escape, but of moving.

She listened to the cries of the dogs stretched after us, moving in leaps. Fleeing from the dogs with the speed of a greyhound, her life a struggle against attack, she knew how to reserve her strength when running. She kept ahead just enough to avoid being caught. Occasionally dodging to one side or turning suddenly, she changed her direction and followed their steps, jumped a gate, forced through a hole in a fence, leapt five feet running at full speed. She escaped by mingling with them.

We climbed a higher, far higher rock, more dangerous, falls of a hundred feet led down to ledges of terrifying steepness. We stood on the edge of a chasm. A gun was fired at the foot, at the legs. With bewildering sounds of thunder and splashes of blood on the rocks, they left a dog dead on the ground. Like a ship covered with hair, the teeth quite small, the eyes large, the inner surface blank. It appeared blind, the power drawn from its eyes, facing a storm of rain. I used a handkerchief to clean its eyes. We made a grave in the shelter of a bush. She scratched away the earth.

She did not feel sorry for herself, she did not care. She dug a hole and knelt in it. She waited for hours, she did not know whether she was falling asleep or dying, then an inner change occurred, she began to murmur. She underwent a peculiar transformation, dashed about in fits of wildness in the middle of the afternoon. She made a sudden rush down the hillside, about a quarter of a mile away from me she turned towards the guns, they came out to meet her before she had a chance to turn. 'Best to hide! Don't risk being killed!' she shouted to me as she ran.

Cleverly she crossed swampy ground and doubled back towards the town. She taught me the art of lying motionless on the ground to avoid being seen. She showed me how to feed on milk sucked from a feeding bottle, we stole a few garden vegetables and scraps of meat left lying on the ground.

We were challenged by a guard. I heard her inward grunt, pathetic scream. 'The only way, the open fields.' I held her arm. I showed my papers, told my story. The hour was marked on the papers, two or three of them, each with a different date. The guard was in a hurry, he had no time to investigate. I considered this man. He was not satisfied. I had made a mistake, I had hesitated to declare myself. I said we were returning to the town. We walked around, uncertain of our direction.

13

IT COULD HAVE been any town, on either side. Squads of soldiers marched the streets in rapid time, drilled, disciplined, yet at moments, where the road divided, uncertain which way to march. The way back to the bridge was barred by a lorry loaded with coiled barbed wire. We went to the nearest cafe, moving in the direction indicated by the police. We were trying to reach her father's house by a roundabout route, we were disturbed, and everyone knew it. I thought we had found the house. I saw no sign, maybe we were too late. Information about the escape would by now have reached her father. I had been too talkative.

The front door of one house was slightly open. I had no hesitation in entering. Her father was at home, eating. I asked the old man whether we might stay for the night. I said I wanted to return home, I wanted peace and quiet. I whispered to him that I did not wish the police to know, they might ask questions, although I had a proper explanation. He said he wished to talk to his daughter alone, but I remained. They, on the other side of the room, sat and talked in his bedroom, she sat on the edge of his bed. 'I want to speak to you,' he said. I could not hear the reply, only the sound of his feet shuffling on the floorboards. His low voice: 'I knew he was not what he appeared to be. You should have come to me.' She asked him: 'What has happened? Why are you living here?' The shuffling stopped. I looked at the door. Then a slurred sound, not like speech, a different sound, his voice, but his voice changed, high-pitched, almost singing. The building was in perfect condition, as my official residence it belonged to the people, not to me, yet heavy bills for furnishing and repairs were presented. I sent them back, they were returned for signature, I refused to sign. I knew nothing about repairs, there had been no repairs. Every pressure was brought on me, they begged me to talk to the press, I allowed myself to be persuaded, but after one tumultous interview I knew I had made a mistake, the reporter had been carefully chosen, as one who could be made to serve their purpose. I signed a joint statement for our mutual protection, setting out the facts of the matter, but after his article had been published, he disappeared. Then one day, smiling his vacant smile, my deputy handed me a copy of the paper. I glanced at the paragraph, I understood I was to be accused of a crime against the state. Anger is no weapon against power. I consulted old friends, well-known men, but control lay in other hands. I learned that my removal was the price for the setting aside of a menace to the party's power. So I was involved in the party feud, my career was of no importance, the matter was to be arranged between them. I was advised to tell my story, and I did so. But unrest was increasing and personal problems faded before the emergency. I was promised that as soon as I resigned, the wrong would be righted. I submitted. I went to them and was welcomed, but one of those men warned me. I knew his advice was wise, I had not yet heard the end. I came to rid myself of my power. My old friend was asked for an explanation, he attempted to defend himself, saying I had been ungrateful, he had loaned me sums of money and had not been repaid. I could not answer. I wrote a letter. Fear of the new man was so great. I was tried for treason. My opponents were powerful, connected by family with other politicians, they were feared by many, it was useless and dangerous to fight them. I would lose my case. I was avoided, followed by spies, a prisoner in my house. I still believed I could win. I had cheques proving it was I who had loaned the money. I was acquitted. I won my last victory there. I had been persecuted, a letter had been written to the judge by the Ministry of Justice, he was "interested in the maintenance of judicial dignity." My adversaries sought a sentence condemning me to exile, if only for one day, it would have been sufficient to break my power. On the day for the trial of the prosecutor's appeal the court was ready. I called my lawyer. He was not in court! A search was ordered. I could not understand his failure to appear at the last moment, before the court of last resort. I demanded that they acquit me, I was obliged to do so, I demanded payment of my costs. Each spoke in turn. The prosecutor said he would take my argument for his own, he would not speak of costs, I had borrowed from the people, and their debt demanded to be repaid. I became ill, I asked to be allowed to speak, I repeated my request. My lawyer had had in his possession a slip of paper containing conclusive evidence, the full explanation of all questionable transactions, the paper was delivered to him so that it could be examined. The usual procedure had been followed, but the clerk entrusted with the work had apparently overlooked an important item, he had abstracted the slip from the file and kept it. With this conclusive evidence in his hands he had sent word to the lawyer on the other side and had said that he would without hesitation publish this overwhelming proof of the injustice of the accusations and appear as witness for the defence. I had asked him to show me the precious document, he had done so but had not allowed me to take a copy of it. I had set down our entire conversation on the back of a letter which my lawyer had kept among his papers. This trial has meant the loss of my home. I have been obliged to remain here under police surveillance, they made it easy for me to go elsewhere, but the dense bureaucracy prevented this, and anyway I knew it was better to remain. This was the result desired by my adversaries and their tactics may keep me here for years, my agony is due to my own actions, I have tried, wanted, my years are clouded, but I have kept alive.

Voices outside, voices gave instructions concerning luggage for despatch by train, the handing over of letters for personal delivery. 'Give . . . immediately you . . . ocean . . . funds.' One foot across the step, I heard her shout, I twisted to look across. 'Thank you for choosing me to be the one to come with you.' I saw that same individual, criminally stupid. 'Good-bye.' Her fingers digging into my arm. 'The wheels won't go round.' The words in her throat, staring at a lunatic. Her face did not even know the essentials. She laughed. Her manner became quite different. I remembered that I was not supposed to know the meaning of the journey. A word, a look, a kiss, a scarf, a sleeve, those white arms, thick red hair, her father, his crushed face, he grinned as he watched, he had trapped wolves and buried them. I saw his face twitch. 'She has disappeared.' 'You mean she flew.' Alone in his room her hands seemed helpless, fingering ribbons, her wet eyes singing of murder, her body among red and green embroidered cushions, a wasp sting on her cheek, a pity, sad. Bending forward, I kissed her hair, her voice was cut off, she fell, I held her.

Sixteen miles from the town I lifted her on to the train. We travelled together towards the frontier. She became violent. 'Never again abuse those who welcome you, or judge when you have shown yourself ignorant. When you get home, find that out for yourself.' Anger in her eyes. 'We shall continue the life we are used to. We feel free. Look at the map, and try to understand why.' An underlying layer of jealousy. 'I don't see.' I pushed the girl towards the train, climbed on to the leather seat, we flew towards the gates, the cracked light, brass, blood. We drove, continuously changing, with hollow trees, drowned in rivers, one hand to shade her head, with the other testing the balance of a whip.

There were no cars waiting outside the station. 'It is too cold. You can't expect them to wait.' Another train, this time unheated. There was no light in the coach nor in the whole length of the train, though the windows were intact. We sat on wooden seats in the dark, in the cold. She showed a knowledge of politics far in excess of mine. We discussed her father's programme, a subject about which I had the haziest ideas. Three hours later they managed to get the steam working. We slept: a triumph.

Fresh coffee and bread were provided at the frontier town. There were two stalls for coffee, so that when one was handing out hot drinks, the other was boiling a fresh supply. Once more we heard the commander's name, the name that was disturbing the country. His friends had gathered others who shared his views.

Hours to wait for the night train, we explored the lovely town, streets shaded, iron walls, the superstructure of a sunken ship caught lengthways across the mouth of the harbour, the coal-dark sea, silent, alert, the coming night, change of light, the night filled with basketwork chairs. Our argument about wealth. Her small fist on the book, splitting the pages. 'For the last five years we have been very orderly and well disciplined. We have become organised. The only bridge across the river is a temporary construction. Everyone wonders whether it will stand the rush of ice in the spring. Work on the other, partly demolished bridge, is planned to be completed in July.' In comparison with the harbour, the town had not suffered much, houses were still windowless, bookshelves bare, laboratories devoid of apparatus, but this was to be expected. She stepped on to the street, sucking an ice cream. 'I assume you are interested, though I know you are from a wealthy land.' She persisted in continuing the conversation. I said: 'I'm starting home tonight. If you agree, I should like to photograph the spot where the commander was killed.' The scene of the crime was pointed out, with her customary charm, politeness and generosity. This sort of reaction made it difficult to hit out. He was dead, a sore on his mouth, no mark on the pavement in the peaceful street. Meanwhile several iron-hooped packing cases on which there were many curious marks and growths attracted her attention. She examined a length of brown paper which she pulled out through a gap in the sewing by slitting the tightly stretched canvas with the sharpened blade of a pair of scissors. A rolled rectangular piece of brown paper; she told me she could tell its origin: 'The place from which you come.'

We ate a cheerful supper in a brightly lit restaurant. Bells rang and were answered by bells. We strolled about, her hand on my sleeve. She stared at a shabby monument, the statue of a soldier, a brother, a kneeling man. There was an inscription, it was impossible to read. We wasted the day, though we had been warned not to. The trams were running, people walked to work in lighted streets, they looked at their wrist watches by the light from shop windows. She liked whatever I gave her, a length of steel, a leather case. She stood in the doorway and tested the instrument. Free to make the most of the minute, I hoped I might be delayed. 'I'm leaving tomorrow morning. Write a letter to me and give it to me before eight o'clock tonight.' I presented her with the package, and some tea and sugar. I understood her hatred, I saw failure ahead. But the partial concession succeeded. She puzzled over my speech. With arrogance, soundlessly, her eyes rested, the gloom, the light, close to my hand. She pulled my coat, her breath dry, rapid. 'You often said you would leave. I accept it. I want you to stay. I cannot force you.'

With pellets of light thudding overhead, she held a needle, we were huddled in a shelter, wet planks, rope, the copper light beat high above, which the eyes, the smoke, the wind, glimpsed above, we ducked for shelter. 'You'll be glad to get home.' I steered her away from the track with my hand, it was impossible. 'You tell me how much, what power the state has.' 'I wouldn't know.' 'Have you thought about it?' 'It's different now. Of course I'm against war, genuine war.' Smoke flew past with a white hand, distinguishing marks, white numbers painted large. Empty huts, long hills shone with oil. Her glance went to the town with its menacing platforms, barracks, roofs, furnaces. I planned that she should. Without a smile, she shifted her position, leaned towards the curved and slatted sun, completed her turn back to the walls of red stone, the sun now behind low cloud, through smoke, lines of streets, lines of trees, a spire hidden by smoke. I was home. My luggage would be taken down by car, unless I neglected altogether . . . 'I can collect the stuff tomorrow.' Her hand clutched. The smell of oil and smoke. A woman walked along the gutter, her grey face bleeding from scratches. A statue, her silence blocked the exit, there was no room. Flags, letters, I hoped to be home, the sky filled with familiar buildings, this visit would be made. There were two trains leaving at about the same time. I made sure that the luggage was sent on the first, it would be well looked after. Of course this visit had to be made. I had two hours, and during the whole of that time it would be necessary for me to shave and dress. My luggage contained my notes. When I unpacked, these were not to be found, they had been mislaid en route.

14

S HE LIVED CLOSE BY. A green painted lamp with rust on it, a dozen narrow steps, zinc handrails either side, a table, steaming food, a dark place, bright metal and white plates, the staircase leading away. I turned my back. 'Eat in this place?' I said loudly, stopped suddenly, interrupted. 'It is, is it? Terrible?' Then her terror disappeared, she behaved as though she were welcoming me home, she referred to the food: 'When did you last eat?' 'I haven't eaten. I'm not hungry.' To save trouble, she said, I should take my meals in the restaurant, set out on a cloth. I guessed why. I nodded towards the stairway. 'Is there anyone here tonight?' 'The person who has been sharing the room left yesterday.' It would be possible for me to have my old room back, but I must understand why, and on what conditions. I said I had hoped to return home with her, after what I had seen. 'It's late in the month,' she sniffed, 'one returning after so long should expect this particular difficulty. Everybody comes, and stays for days, a whole week at a time, you should see the crowds we have in this house.' I picked up my possessions and began to climb the stairs. 'You can have half then.' 'A man doesn't come back for half.'

The door was open, light filtered through dirty windows. The room was adequate. Fireplace, table facing windows, against the wall by the door, a side table with necessities on it. Four chairs. Beyond the small table, a cupboard in which, among rubbish stuffed away, were two painted jugs, a cup decorated with the figure of Frederick the Great, a plate with a ship painted on it, a note found in a drawer, a bundle of papers written in order to be left behind. I examined the windows of the room, the lamp on which green letters were painted, attachments decorated with imitation leaves.

Staring idiotically at the closed door, I listened to two conversations continuing simultaneously. A man saying: 'Not like you. The injustices, the iniquities of the system.' Her soft reply: 'I'm not saying which one I would choose.' She sounded frightened, the door crashed open, her face showed in the doorway, she lost her balance, her shoulder fall was broken by the room, her face on the floor, flushed to the forehead. Light, bright light, yellow in the dark-looking burdened home. I followed, rested my knee on the curved window-seat, ugly foundations of the old house, a tombstone from the old building. 'We should celebrate my return.' Tell me, what do you think of yourself?' My reputation for being uncommunicative about either my movements or my amusements would not let me reply. Illuminated by the moon, she smiled. I held a fold of her skirt. 'Leave me alone.' I held a fold of sacking, looked down at the face of a child, ghastly with life, strong, violent. Betrayed, I sharply instructed her, she became frozen, I lost patience, I became an actor, she quiet, simple, cruel, an unhappy child shaped by the shape of a fall. You killed! She went for my cheeks with her nails, I tried to grab her, she got to the window, tried to leap out. 'Murderer!' I dragged her back, put my hand over her mouth. I turned off the light.

Next morning she had a scab on her wrist, she stared in surprise, she was sick. The house was bright with daylight. She was unable to move, she said her back was broken, she lay with wide face asleep, without a word. I understood what had happened.

After three days I called the state doctor. He came gorgeously in gold buttons. He was worse than a priest. He wrapped her in sheets, sheets soaked in icy water. He made her stand, he ordered pills and massage. She wanted me to nurse her. She was choking to the point of suffocation. The heart was bad. She feared the knife. I rushed out of the room, listened through the half-open door. It was too late. He wrapped a blanket round the child to save its life. I banged the door shut. I remained by the side of the bed watching the terror. The operation would help. She nodded. An envelope on the table under the lamp told me that she had received that morning . . . there was no time for discussion. He decided to inject. The reaction was terrific. The body sprang up in a violent fit, bleeding from the nose. The condition improved. It was intensely interesting to watch the case. The child must be removed or the mother would die. I knew of no suitable place. The arrangements were inadequate. The doctor ordered it to be removed. In the morning it had gone. I dared not tell her, I decided to wait. The body was taken and buried. I nearly fell. It must be buried. It was impossible, it was forbidden by law. The body must be burnt. I asked what would be the price for a first class funeral and grave. Times were hard, there had been a rise in the price of coffins. Ten thousand would cover everything, flowers would be extra. I arranged to have the body burnt, it was against the law to embalm or otherwise preserve the body. The certificate was signed, the cause of death was the heart. The sum paid in advance would have saved its life. I visited it, I had reasons. The night was dark with rain, my foot against the soft earth, I fell. Neither wanted to tell her. She knew. She had been sitting up in bed, she thought she was dead, and said she had died, looked straight and knew. She wanted to write a letter to her father accusing herself, I told her such a letter might make her father crazy. The next morning she was carried down and taken home. She presented the nurse with two big trunks full of clothes, and a hat. I persuaded her to keep the hat. I spent an hour on my knees in the room, on the floor in a spare room, I can still see the carpet. I told her I was all right. I wanted sleep. My brain dropped. I was asleep. The bell rang. I heard her voice. She was standing on the table in her short white skirt and embroidered bolero, painting her eyes and her mouth. She asked me how much money there was in my wallet, she needed some of the cash at once as she had come to the end of her savings. I told her the wallet was empty, but I offered to loan her some money if she wished, and gave her my personal cheque. She borrowed from me several times, and I was told she borrowed from others. She developed a mania for economy, forbade the lighting of fires, and at each purchase of food she complained bitterly. I entrusted her with the despatch of my reports, but rather than spend money on telegrams she sent them by ordinary post, though she knew that the messages were for immediate publication. I was accustomed to cigars of the highest quality, but she bought the cheapest and wrapped them in silver paper. I threw them on to the fire.

She had been years in the grave. I remembered her long curls but now they were faded. She could not live again. But she found friends. Two middle-aged ladies began to take an interest in her. They took her out for walks with them. It became an unnatural thing. She fell in love with them. Then she sent them flowers, and they were returned burnt, and with them, her note torn in pieces. With her memories of the dead she caused bitter suffering, she had no friends, in the night she cried terribly. She offended many people. She told them too plainly what she saw.

Only her father continued to welcome her. He gave her a job to do. Her duty was to read him the papers. She concentrated on the press reports of crime and scandal, these were the matters, rather than the famine which had set in, which interested him. He demanded her constant presence throughout the day and refused to allow her time to prepare my meals. She grew tired of the work and became devoted to little dogs and to plants. She brought home an object found in the street, a puppy sewn up in the skin of an animal. When he met her carrying two plants she had bought in the town, her father startled her by calling out: 'Two lovers in her arms!' Their arguments grew, and they turned to me for an opinion, which I declined to give.

I climbed the hill towards the bridge, aware of the threats which shadowed my life. She refused to join me. I ate solitary, extravagantly, pouring on my plate the remains of her food, three large spoonsful. I stopped at two o'clock, torn between knowledge. My work to do. Her desire to sleep. I left the decision to her. 'Do as you please. If you go out, do not come back a minute later than half past two.' 'I shan't go far. I'll take a walk to the bridge.'

The bridge had a but by the entrance. The wooden-sided structure was divided into three, one part waited with benches, the other shivered and muttered, the other was interesting with coloured bottles. I took the key from a hook near the door. One corner of the but fulfilled many purposes. Its outer part, where the wall projected, served as a store for board and pegs. Coal was stored there. Beneath three windows, a carpenter's bench. I touched the teeth of the saw, the cutting edge of a chisel. Her father had spent hundreds of hours working in wood and the lighter forms of iron. I pressed my face against the chisel. She looked away. 'Enjoying yourself?' The voice came from her lean face. 'Haven't you had enough?' I ignored this attempt at humour. Her trembling increased. Her face shook. She said she had been on her way to see me but had decided to keep away. 'You said you wouldn't mind.' 'I never said that.' 'What have you been doing?' I asked her, for something to say. 'Nothing much.' With her head level with the second window, frightened of losing her balance, she started to look over her shoulder. She tried to stop in the right position, began to walk towards the mechanism, she tried to run but was unable to. 'Funny way of running.' 'I suppose it is.' 'Are you coming?' I knew the signs. 'Will you come, for an hour?' 'Longer than that.'

I went down the hill, unsmiling. I could see the bridge, I gazed down at the sides of the deep water, I had seen the road beyond, the new road did not go forward. Higher on this side of the bridge, level with the tank from which water was piped to the town, the road approached from the far side, the wide road, its animal feet moving, pulling, it died away in the reeds along the banks.

I waited for her. She appeared from the bridge. We went through the old pantomime, I behaving as though my purpose was to caress, her insistence that more was needed, until despite denials and protests, she found the hidden gifts. We decided to return. She accepted the invitation, said that the evenings were usually empty, and that evening she had wanted me to come. We agreed on a meeting place, at the foot of the slope as we came off the bridge. 'Will we need to repair the house?' 'See for yourself, when you get into the place,' she said serenely. I knew that, to begin with, new timber was needed. As the subject was of interest, before continuing to speak to her about it, I demanded an account of where she had been and whom she had seen. I could hear my voice thundering. My attitude terrified her. 'I have been preparing for that question from the first. You know the story, the pattern, my family.' She began to turn the handle of the mechanism. She went back towards the bridge, pulling me with her, climbing the hill until we were high above and then down till we were exactly level with the door of her house. The road ended, we had gone through a narrow tunnel, and so into the yard. We walked up a path, and here was a waterway, the river grew wider. Reaching ground level after slithering down a grassy slope, she turned back to look at the chimney on the roof of her house. Guided by an unknown law, she defined her need and the way of satisfying it. In a recess about a yard deep, on the left side, up three stone steps, was the doorway to her house. Opposite was another door. Inside, a flight of wooden steps led down to the stone floor, a small compartment shuttered on two sides, one shutter facing the bank, another being used for ashes. 'You're lucky,' I said. 'Our levels are now equal,' she began. Her speech became less precise every minute she remained inside the house. It was hot. 'I cannot stay long. I have jobs to do. I wanted to go across the road for a chat.' She was wiping her hands on her dress. 'I've finished.' She went, I was by myself. I wondered whether or not I should have spoken, in confidence. I didn't know. Indecisive, I stared up at the lines which crossed to connect the two buildings. The cellar had been long unused. It was not likely that she would come back.

15

I PASSED OVER the plank spanning the brook, a tributary of the river, skirted the swampy ground, climbed down to avoid a gang of boys playing a dangerous game, a suicidal game. I climbed over a gate. Rows of gardens, rows of houses faced the lane. I knocked on the lowest door. Her father. Strong, bare arms. He was not pleased. He saw me. He looked at me and thought nothing.

'Her things are stored in her room.' He sent me into her room. I found the things there. As I collected her clothes, he followed me about the room. He wandered into a long discourse which I had some difficulty in following. 'You work, perhaps I too will work. I'm not unhappy. Soon we will all think of nothing, there will be a new world. She had a mother, she tried to talk. She said, don't judge, don't experience, don't try to get away, only doctors know the causes of diseases. Now this girl, she's a child, don't deny it, like it. I don't think there will be a war, but it may all end.' He looked suddenly old. 'We did not know how to live. We fought, we had to fight, it was simple, that was all there was. That's not true, appearances lie, it was for nothing, our revolution was one of the most insignificant, we used big words. My useful time was when I lived with my wife, we had a small flat, ordinary chairs, played hide and seek with work, there was dust over everything soon enough. Her eyes were always tired, she knew what she was. I heard it said "your wife seems tired," and my reply, "not really." Her womb twisted over, choked by work. She used to listen to the wireless. I was too busy, she was old and leading an empty life, she never had the windows open, she begged me not to open them. No basin, no proper clothes, she was lying on the bed covered by a coat. She was in pain, she needed medicine, she couldn't eat. I was very, very tired. We could not afford a doctor. When the ulcers burst, I was bathing the baby. In those days I could do a lot, now I haven't the patience, I am unable to move or think. We never went out. She had kidney trouble. Two children died. Three children, two died. And the girl, you know, has been operated on.' 'I didn't know.' 'My wife would have looked after you. She had to do all the lifting, she had to shovel, carry coke, those were the hardest days. I blame myself. Because of my work, nights and days of fighting and planning, she had to lift things. She injured her spine, it gave her pains in her shoulders, she should have stayed in bed but she would not do so. She felt acute pain, but her horror of hospitals was stronger than the pain. There was no remedy, only stupidity and ignorance. I am damp and old. There was no one to lead them, no one who would die. My son fought and was killed. I saw him fall. All he could do was die. In those few hours, I hope he was suitably drugged, probably not, now there is nothing, no one stays alive, he has died, his house is in ruins because of the chains on his legs. He was made to run over loose flints during great heat, allowed to fetch water but forbidden to drink it. He was isolated, the windows of his but were nailed up and painted over. He was made to lie inside on his plank bed all day and all night, except for one hour when he was taken out for their pleasure. It was not possible for him to keep his own cup and plate. There were no bedclothes on his bed. There was no gas stove or oven, no meat safe. His room had bare boards, little warmth, the bed was badly broken, very damp and cold. The floor was earth, the plaster had fallen from the walls, vermin nested there. The opening to the air was on one side only, so narrow that ventilation was impossible. In front of the opening, sewage stood, and a pit over which the air that entered the room had to pass. The liquid which drained from the pit seeped through the earth and lay in pools by the walls of the room. The surface of the water was polluted, the ground saturated with the foul liquid which darkened the walls and ran beneath the floor, soaking the boards. There was no stove, no decent cupboards, a kettle with a broken spout, two bowls with holes stopped up with rags. The floor was bare stone. The mattress was broken. The room had no furniture besides the bed. The room was empty. No gas stove or oven. We had two lead spoons, fingers were used for eating, no basins, we could not drink tea. Inside the air was bad and he became unconscious. He was strapped down to a block, his head muffled in blankets. He was given twenty-five lashes with a whip which had been left soaking in water for the purpose since the preceding day. They took it in turns to beat him. He was hung up on a post with his hands tied behind his back so that with his toes he could just touch the ground. He was sent to a dark cell and given fifty lashes, he was forced to run with his barrow full of stones. He was not allowed to move. He was told he could not be free for twenty years. You will never come out. Coloured stripes were sewn on his clothes for shame, red bands perpendicular on the back, yellow stripes with red circles, red bands crossed, red bands with yellow circles, red bands with blue circles, blue bands, perpendicular yellow stripes striped on his back. They got tired of tormenting him. He was made to work in a water-filled ditch, forced with blows beneath the surface. When he crawled out he was forced back, forced to crawl on his knees, made to stand while others ate, given twenty strokes of the lash, a tapering thong of cowhide. He was strapped to a trestle. He seized a hammer and tried to brain himself, but was stopped. He tried to hang himself, but they saw it and he was saved. He sharpened a piece of tin and opened the arteries in both arms. A load of stones was tipped over him.'

I walked back towards the house. I paused to lean over the wall where the camp had been. Building was in progress. I continued to the bridge, where, on turning, I saw her, far away, approaching. Fifty yards further on, we met. 'I saw your father this morning.' 'I know. He told me you would go there. He's hardly a father. A friend. But a friend for years.' Slow speaking, slow thinking. 'I wish he could have more fresh air. He works long hours, he needs more air than his long days permit.' 'He's by himself at home, like you.' 'The same. Yet he's a man, a man whom a woman could desire for a husband.'

We went home, to the cutting of wood, the laying and lighting of the fire, smoke from the fire, amused manoeuvrings, her pulse beating in her neck, though she was conscious only that the hours were wasted.

CELEBRATIONS

1

Certain accidents had culminated in the wash-out of the year. Williams was well equipped in the tone of his impersonal voice, he polished the surface of the desk, nursed his torn arm like a broken engine, prepared for disaster. He was dominated by a mood of simple dread, yet since the machine could be repaired, stored for a year, kept in a shed, his urgency had no meaning. The break-up of his team of men worried him too, he was a gambler waiting for something to snap, for success or failure, it was a matter of routine. A diffident, unimaginative man, he disliked the phenomenal, moved more deliberately now, walked down to the factory with his hands behind his back.

'The excess oil disappeared quicker, just over seven hours, fine, fine thank you.' The covers were lifted off, Williams stood by the machine, not an ounce of excess flesh on him, the sun gleamed on the heavy oil. He turned the wheel slowly, his temperature and the machine's were taken, his serious brown eyes apart, reading the faintest movement of the quivering needle. The cloud of noise subdued, he had no choice, his two assistants noted the start and finish. 'What do you think of her?' At seven fifteen he disconnected the inlet tubes. After the faulty decision to start the power, the man was a stone lighter. For the third time the hammering had been due to human error. 'These machines are all the same. I will build another.'

'He was a jaunty man, I remember,' they said when he died at sixty-four, his appearance dry and crumbling, his face grey from contusion in the brain.

His buttons still glinted in a neat row, his eyes very blue, there was no point in measuring them, the ruptured middle ear caused tears to run down the cheeks, crystals on wheels. After months of useless work, the most unsuccessful of all time, he lost his nerve. The loss in reputation cost thousands, it was all over. The photographers took pictures, Williams wore one of those shirts made specially for him, the blazer made of blue, his elder son Michael in a suede jacket at his side. Williams described the difficulties, the personal sacrifice, then tendons in his neck, he would end with nothing.

The power was on, Williams turned and grinned. He fixed a baffle plate to prevent buckling, the medallion round his neck swung as he swung the handle, he liked to work in the open air. 'Better take a look at that.' The opinionated extrovert man had no worry and no doubts; all he said, he was. He averted his eyes from his two sons who were standing by, fiddling with the wiring inside a home-made slot machine.

Most workers owned motor cars and at weekends they journeyed to admire the surrounding countryside. Those who stayed behind spent their time playing with the slot machines they had built in their spare time. While they played they had the illusion of travelling abroad, to the tropics and the Arctic, even to Mars. Williams had a sense of humour and when he saw the men wasting time on these toys he did not register it as a breach of discipline, since it could do no harm for them to play to their hearts' content. As long as they were back by Monday they were free to travel hundreds of miles, to foreign countries, to the planets. They were not asked where they had been. Such nostalgic links with the exploring tradition were recognised as natural.

Williams took his time. After a last check, the way a mother would look at her child, he walked away, aware not of his technological achievement but of the need for a show of confidence in his calculations. There was a flaw in the manufacturing process, he thought about it as he walked away, the thought cut him off completely. He went back, to test his sons' reactions, to understand their relationship. He decided to complete the job, he needed a new approach, he began to form a series of ideas beyond his control. A plane flew overhead and plane and man were remote from time and impossible to track.

In the factory forecourt a metal pylon was planted, with a flag at the top. A new piece was added every day, to counteract the feeling that 'nothing is reproduced', to help combat nervous strain. Indeed, it became difficult to think of the place without the growing pylon with the flag at the top.

Despite the heat and the cloud-cover lowered over, Williams wore his coat. While he strove to create the perfect rhythm of work to be done in any weather, the skilled men considered that their work was produced more by their imagination than by practical effort; if there was any muscular exertion it was not apparent, there was a tendency for sweat to be regarded as an anachronism now, production was becoming no more than a branch of the mathematical sciences. Already the beginnings of unfriendliness appeared everywhere, morale became a substance with a practical use, it was tracked and weighed and reduced to a mark on a graph.

'Do you realise what it means to be involved, responsible for this work?' Williams asked his sons. As far as the elder, Michael, was concerned, it was a bloody place, filthy, something unearthly about it. His brother Phillip crouched over the pinball machine: 'I've beaten the record! A hundred and eight!' 'Possibly, but what do you think you're doing?' Williams switched off the power, the light was poor and the dim outline of his young son's face winced as Williams held his breath and slammed a steel bar against the glass top of the box. 'Will the new prototype be ready on time?' Phillip asked. 'It's not my concern, you must see to it,' Williams spat the words out. It was more than a matter of time, his was the controlling personality, apart from him there was no point, when he was away the place collapsed. As the bar hit the glass with a crash, Williams muttered 'It's good to see some action.' The father smashed up the machine which his sons had taken months to build. 'We all had fun with it,' Michael said, 'there'll be hell to pay from the men.' 'No doubt, but the thing was a disgrace. It had to be destroyed.'

Williams was a man of character. He spun a wheel, then was swallowed up by the machine as he bent over and examined the damage. He stayed there an hour. When he looked up, no one was waiting. He jerked a lever forward and down. Here the individual could look through his own small window, he could come and go. Williams pondered whether he should show any sign of bitterness, in any event his feelings would count for little. He had worked through the night, the sky was brightening, he seemed to be changing his mind, he went to inspect his son Michael's work. Williams was in the centre of the main assembly room, the size and shape of an aircraft hangar, glass roof let the daylight in, floors connected by metal stairs like fire escapes inside the building, rows of tables beside quiet conveyor belts. One moment Williams was sitting opposite a new machine, then it was a heap of junk. He thought of his sons, Michael and Phillip, and he knew he could work harder than either of them. His responsibilities had held him for twenty-four years, now there was no one waiting.

He took the grey car with the new tyres, drove towards his large green armchair, thinking about the horizon and the glaring parallel along the wall of the eternal, Williams saw the bright circle of the luminous watch made specially for him. On his journey towards the mantelpiece he sang 'Sun and Sky above', he reached the arterial road, turned right, towards home, the job complete. He drove down the blue road to the waking town. The factory had once been sited in town, then new buildings had been erected in the fields, now again they were being encroached upon by the expanding town. 'That damned man works like a maniac,' Michael said in his sleep. The ritual remained unchanged, Williams drove with elation, from the road came the sound, the faint whimper, whistle of poured salt, it will finish.

Williams required total loyalty from his sons. They were his pets, he called them his animals. They answered to his call with grunts or with effortless gliding according to his will. He never stopped talking about them. They stayed with him. 'This is my family,' puffing his pipe and keeping his secret, a suffocating man who knew where to find oxygen.

'Well, what do you think of them?' he stopped in mid-sentence, the linen shirt flapping in the wind.

'A five pound note to the one who climbs the mast.' The two young men raced to the mast, while their father retreated inside the dim green room . . .

The wind and the sky, these had been the events of the day, there had been no others. When Williams and his wife had arrived in the town, he had not been able to find the street on the map. Ten houses on either side, the houses had three floors, the rooms small. The iron foundry still stood and dominated the street. From the railway the sounds of the trains were part of their dreams. Their neighbours were poor people, five in a room, who watched through windows. Williams at thirty had an ordinary name; tall, with few interests, he worked hard. The mother was a woman who died. They had always lived in even-numbered houses. Michael was a good boy, he enjoyed games, he sang in the choir. Phillip was frailer than his fellows, he swung his arms, the presence of others did not help; smothered, he lacked vitality. Phillip developed a horror of dirt, people noticed it, he felt free when he played in the grave, there were things to see, he feared female magic, photography was Phillip's hobby, and the church, he learnt to dance, a joke he kept to himself. On the right upper arm, five bruises; right buttock raw; true I beat my son; he broke dishes and stole money. The child under the stairs, his arm up to protect his face, Phillip did not understand the pattern, he kept quiet, he had small feet, his hair was ginger. The house was too small, soft earth outside, the stairs faced the door at right angles to the bedroom, a room above a room, a man of sixty whose eyes were about to fail, who left his room unfurnished . . .

Williams had started his elder son as a methods engineer. Michael was responsible for the complete free flow along the line, he was father of the product completely. Michael was a man whose eyes missed nothing, nothing which had not already been announced.

Phillip volunteered to work at a great height, in excess of nine thousand feet, attached to his ankle was a meter which gauged his preoccupation with his work, a chronometer recorded the time. During this period, of all the work done in the factory none was as methodical as his. Then the boy complained that the plastic coat was not thick enough, he felt cold, though his heart thumped with the effort of work. Phillip was removed back to his normal workplace and was seen to benefit from the reassurance of a definite routine. Michael was taken to the centre of the factory and told to avoid exertion. It was noted that between these two extremes a comradeship sprang up, this made for a poor standard of work, the experiment was abandoned.

The main transmission belts and fifty superbly complex machines, if not more, were in Michael's care. At a comparatively low cost he had constructed, to judge by the framework, one of the most hideous gantries in the world. Rust was beginning to erode the base. Michael, who never drank anything, suddenly ordered a beer. His brother brought him a glass of water. The younger brother had always had difficulty in learning obedience. When empty wage packets had been distributed, their contents confiscated by the management, Phillip had been sent to spy on the men's secret meetings in their houses, but had reported back to his father, merely 'It needed nerve.' Phillip knew he had made another mistake. Michael recognised the strain across the throat, the neck, the face stiff with ugliness, the mouth hidden behind obscure houses. The boy experienced a sharp pain in his eyes when he was sent again with the order written out and the key words underlined. Phillip came back to say he could not find the right room, but his words were cancelled before he had finished speaking when his brother pointed with his foot at the door. In dealing with a younger brother Michael felt that a hint should be given; a hint was frequently needed.

'This is a significant achievement. I ask for a drink and you bring me nonsense,' Michael said, as Phillip arranged the glasses. Michael pointed at his brother, and said loudly 'Now who's that chap? Does he work here?'

The younger brother bent his head. The attitude demanded paralysis, a blow on the back of the neck, but it would have been too costly, the move would have taken up too much time, dislocated work schedules, added unduly to the engineer's excessive responsibilities.

Phillip was trapped by his machine. 'You could crush me with a single turn of that wheel,' he said to his brother. Then an accident crushed the apathetic boy; he jerked; only the head could move. 'What happened?' Blood and the usual gash in the face. 'It hurts.'

Williams was called, he walked unhurriedly across to his son, busy with his notebook. He leafed through the book, glanced over it and asked Phillip if he would like a game of golf. The boy gave a short laugh, crinkled his eyes with pain. 'No, not just now.' With his hand Phillip made a gesture to cut his throat: 'All I'm fit for.' He continued sawing the air with his hand, then his hand slipped to his side. He held a sheaf of papers in a blue folder which he laid across his face to shield himself from the light Williams played on his eyes, with a torch shaped like a pencil. The boy closed his eyes.

Phillip ate and slept clutching a letter from his wife. Although the factory radio broadcast only music, he listened perpetually for news from her. In bed he wore the little conical hat his wife had knitted for him; though it was three years since he had seen her, the network of esoteric memories persisted. He had left her for three months to join a geological expedition and had not returned; every month he applied for his release, and a day later requested that his application be cancelled. Phillip did not take the old letter from its envelope, but spent hours examining the postmark. During a regular monthly period he slept out in the open and doctors noted that his reactions revealed a clear pattern. He would walk as far as he could in temperatures below zero, then dash back into the warmest part of the factory, trembling. He repeated this game twelve times a year; it became a cliché.

'What are you doing now? Do you want to get me the sack? Would you behave like this at home?' his father asked, pretending to be annoyed, then he moved the folder to one side and the light darted into the pupil of the left eye. Phillip's expression now showed he was startled, his face twitched, the movement spread to his arms, he jerked the folder out of reach: 'Mustn't touch!' Williams played his waiting game while his son held him with his gaze. 'Live and let live, dad. You two go off and play golf or whatever it is.'

Except for one or two disconcerting psychiatrists who visited the factory and answered 'Yes' to every question, no reference was made to the past and everyone agreed that life was so much more lively now. The new motor cars were seen to be racing about, emphasising the sterility of the place. Little was said about children: 'These matters do come up in discussion, but not often. The men are more spiritual than their fathers ever were.'

Then silence, five seconds of it. Williams licked his lips, his tongue slid along the thin dry lips while he watched Phillip fiddle with the buttons of his untidy smelly little jacket. 'This is riddle talk, you don't appreciate that I'm merely checking your reflexes, pure routine,' Williams said. His eyes probed into the boy. 'You have your trade and I have mine, or so I like to think.' He tightened his son's tie, forcing the collar close to the chin. 'Must be thorough, can't afford to miss anything, understand?' 'This file is full of notes,' Phillip said, 'if anything happens to me it goes to my wife. I've got witnesses and everything.' 'Exactly sir,' from his place at his father's side, Michael bent down to assist his brother hunched in a chair before him, 'now is there anything you need, or would you prefer to be left alone?' Phillip sighed and surrendered and an hour passed.

Towards March the sun began to shine, those who normally wore coats began to appear without them, there were no other signs of spring to be seen, no birds, no cockroach on the floor. Apart from a couple of mice kept illegally in one of the storage dumps, the men had no pets, neither dogs nor cats. Soon the sun became fainter each day.

Phillip's strained eyes moved slowly and read a word, he looked beyond his brother, the workshop seemed longer than a train, darker, more dramatic. He wanted to dream peacefully, for hours, before it became too cold. He tried to speak, his throat caught on a note. The workshop was startled, conversation ceased with a click. From the floor, the menace of a lunatic. Outside, flowers in an oval bed. 'There's been a mistake!' From the foot of his machine Phillip looked up at his father. 'We pay for a doctor to protect us, why doesn't he come?' 'What's wrong now?' Williams asked. The response was a struggle of laughter, Phillip's eyes lowered, the silence held steady. 'It's against your interests to make a fuss,' Williams said. With a sharp and urgent insult to his father's intelligence, the boy coughed and slid to the floor. He was lifted on to a bench. Williams picked him up and cradled him to his shoulder, the swift professional movement was set and held for the men gathered round. 'See that?' one said. 'That's enough. There's nothing to see.' Michael overheard his father mumble to himself, 'I said one was enough' and Michael's quick eyes caught the look of help, but he would not chance getting involved by kneeling down and helping to carry Phillip, nor did anyone take the slightest risk of losing a day's pay by being called away altogether.

'It was a hundred to one, sir,' the doctor held Phillip's legs to stop him injuring himself. 'On the right there is no movement in the lower limb. The leg, or part of it, needs blood. Tomorrow he can have a transfusion, we will have a sample from the wife.' The doctor would not use the father's blood without testing it, he could not be sure, he thought the blood groups differed. 'We've enough on our plates without taking unnecessary risks,' he fiddled with his stethoscope, whistling mournfully, thoughtfully. 'Time is short. It would be a pity to waste too much time,' Williams said. The doctor said it was a calculated risk, 'Something should be done to simplify procedure—' 'Save your breath,' Williams said, 'we'll have plenty of questions now. Don't worry. I'll deal with them.'

The doctor was due for his annual holiday, he thought he would profit from the extended leisure, in the daytime anyway. There was a pause, slowly the medical man reckoned on his fingers the vacant days. Like the rest of the factory workers the doctor contented himself with the usual distractions, good food, nightly movies, the photographs of last summer. Sealed off by routine, two at a time, the men remained at their machines. Family groups, personal messages, helped to sustain morale. Their relationships generally were good, more grown up. None of the men were normally permitted to marry while they worked at the factory, so they thought not of production norms but of fertility figures, they dreamed of the red-haired girl swimming naked in the sea.

In the white room where Phillip was taken, polished and shining, divided into squares, the amputated leg had nothing to hope for. 'It is sad, it is the law, it is punishment.' The yellow chair with the high back stood as in the family home. The table was built into the wall, the electric door led to the telephone, the plug pulled out. The room was an achievement. Phillip was carried in on a door, the quiet room filled with flowers, he looked triumphant, his legs and hands could not rest, he wanted to touch, to do, everything. Michael returned to the factory cinema where the latest film was being shown. Alone in the electric room the boy was teased with needles. The door opened and the flowers were taken away.

About forty of the skilled workers, those in excellent physical condition, took to sleeping in those parts of the building that were constructed underground. They gave as their reason the need to check that no rats got among the stores.

Phillip developed an obsession with the radio, spending hours at a time hugging it to his body, listening to the everlasting canned music in the hope of hearing his wife's voice, though he knew that the music was broadcast from a stock of tapes in his father's office and that the radio was incapable of picking up anything else. The facts were patiently explained to him, yet he would be found by the radio each day. Only after some time did Phillip's understanding return, and he was amused by his elder brother's description of his behaviour. While others took to excessive drinking or smoking and barely noticed the food brought to them, Phillip gradually became more isolated. He lived for days in the most savage of all climates: his own imagination. His brother Michael behaved in a subtle manner, he avoided any human gathering, he made his journeys alone. At this stage Phillip appeared so well that the doctors thought they had found the recipe for rude health; then he began to speak about the factory in a distant, disconnected away, that it 'had the merit of simple living', he asked to be moved to where the surveyors were said to have discovered rare minerals beneath the ground.

Phillip's mouth slobbered all the time he was feeding it, the thick acute eyes were pale underneath. The boy continued his bowel movements and the doctor said, coming in after a few minutes, after beaming a bit, 'A few glasses of sherry will restore his confidence.' Then, 'He's going,' and called in Phillip's wife Jacqueline who roused him and fumbled about at his side for twenty-four hours. 'I'll get it,' she said, when the young head raised and asked for water. So he prepared for the end in pain and isolation, his wife was brought in as witness to it. Phillip said in a joke that he wanted her to go first, for someone to go ahead and prepare the way for him.

Phillip's wife was at his side, she held his arm. 'I forget the time,' her voice as smooth as her face. 'Phillip's shoes are missing, I saw them in his father's room, they are canvas and very light.' Jacqueline stayed by the bed. For an hour the blue eyes remained as he had been for days, nil movement, nothing to see, neither moved, the smile swinging through her lips became her language. The light was cut from under the door. The night slipped out of the sky into her neck, she felt the curtains, the room absorbed her skin with the hopeless sky and the bluish light of morning. She was afraid of her own breath as she crept towards sleep.

Jacqueline woke with the clash of clattering buckets and asked the cause of her husband's accident. On Williams' orders the files were sealed so her questions could not be answered. She was given a large pile of reports, the relevant papers were mixed with others to lose their meaning. Her urgent questions were stopped by an anxious gesture of the doctor's fat red hand.

Intermittently Jacqueline slipped her hand under the warm bedclothes, dying to go downstairs where the windows were open and air blew in. Phillip's mouth stiffened with sweat, she held him till he slept. Under his pillow she found a cigarette, she looked at it faintly in the light that leaked in through the curtains. Her hand was trapped by his arm, it was not hers unless he told her. Phillip lay shivering, she knew what her husband wanted, open and shut, opening herself brought a smile as she kissed his eyes. She put her hand on his mouth, rehearsed the cause of the accident, rubbed hot coins against his legs. 'Can't you tell me, how did it happen, were you drunk?' 'There's nothing to tell, ill as I am.' The questions led home to his brother. Phillip refused to answer. Her hand rested on the counterpane, it was not important. She touched his check and he promised to help, saying her name, Jacqueline, as though it had been water. She said he must pretend to be dazed. 'Confuse them. That is the impression you need to make at the inquiry.' She stroked his hair. 'The lawyers will need your cooperation.' 'I must sleep.' 'There's the question of compensation. I have to live.' 'On my word of honour there is no more I can say. I'll do what you wish, but put this bad boy straight back in his warm blankets as soon as you can.' This was Phillip's pretence at being dazed and it failed. 'I'll leave for court tomorrow if that is required. I saw Michael an hour ago. At the moment that the soul of your brother is real to you, leave him, not in your arms but in a place of danger. Give others the burden of his life. When I'm through, it might be today, you can try to blame the guilty person.' Phillip refused to name his brother, the cruel renegade, the hard kind. Michael thought he was safe, his younger brother had fallen. Phillip had to be moved, together with the equipment which preserved his life. The machine and the boy were taken to a room, his wife with him, he was bombarded slowly, there was plenty of time.

In the hospital there was nothing to do. 'I've been after a job,' Jacqueline said. 'You've a job here, with me,' Phillip pulled her hand, his reaction was to kiss, he persisted. 'The interview is tomorrow, I'll leave on the early train,' she said. 'Don't try to be smart,' he said, sinking his teeth in. 'I have my reasons, you'll see, there'll be jobs for both of us, two newcomers. You'll get on well.' 'I need you here. Everyone is being moved into the corridor.' 'I am not afraid to leave you.' Phillip's hair, forehead and lips were quite strange. Jacqueline felt drawn to men who looked sleek and who wore boots. She smiled 'I have the job, I've been accepted, there's no point in discussing it, there is nothing more I can do here. I have seen your father, I spent the whole day with him. Everything you need is on the way.' Phillip said 'All I ask is that we start off as soon as possible. We'll say our goodbyes to the family, go straight there. It won't be easy, it will require all our energy and skill to get away, if you mean to take me with you.' 'Your father doesn't want you to go.' Jacqueline said nothing about herself. 'Talk it over, persuade him to let me go. I'll be better off with you.' 'It's no use, he won't let you go. It's late,' she said, 'trust me.' 'I waited for you, you didn't come, we said Sunday the fifteenth of June.' 'Believe me, there's no more to say, I must go alone this time.' Phillip's face had gone dark. 'Go home and stay. I'll come.' Tired of the patternless walls in the middle of the afternoon, the husband and wife could not find anything to say.

'Who's paying for this thing?' Phillip prodded the bandage lying at his feet, he was in pain. The laser aimed a beam of light to cut a millimetre deep, a weapon from space to earth, the secret rescue squad, the critical attempt. 'The plan may be abandoned if problems arise.' The air held death lined up and waiting for him, he saw no sense in delay. Phillip pulled back his sleeve to look at his watch, he did it well, with confidence, his eyes on the other. His wife's mouth was an absent guest.

'Nothing but bad dreams.' Whatever he was made of fell to pieces. He felt cold. The end of the life was the sound of yellow, rattling across the floor. Williams looked at the woman in the chair, her expression unchanged. Michael in a coat waited across the corridor, near the lavatory bowl, the dark nostril, he began to walk to reach the bowl, he looked down, his face lifted suddenly, he felt the weight of the dead when time will not come. When Phillip died his agony was equal to those fierce expressions flying over the surface of water, with a stroke in which neuter light and black were mixed in equal parts.

Phillip was pulled from the bed, his body opened and the parts numbered. It was impossible to make a mistake: it was efficient and peaceful. Two parts became one, then five, seven, ten together, the quantity of numbers grew, two hundred bones, three hundred muscles, the signs were placed on a chart, the mysterious blue in the red, a sign in the brain for hours.

2

The factory management undertook the funeral arrangements. Morale demanded that they be magnificent. Phillip's corpse would travel alone. If the multitude of mourners pressed too close the coffin horses would presumably bolt. The family mourners followed the plumes. They were proud that death should be so popular. The purple drapes in the parks attracted crowds, mobs stood about in the streets to watch the ceremony in the cheerful place. The charming hats stalked the dignitaries who came for the kill, when it rained they slipped rapidly away. Williams mixed with the crowd, he talked to their children. It was an agonising experience to attend the drama, the top hats hot and loudly ran from the rain and from the drums and other guns going off. The music and commentaries slid easily on, nothing had changed for the corpse, perhaps the coffin was carried a hundred feet or so from the cathedral, it was all very bizarre as the coffin crossed the circle, the lieutenant and the cortège fused, the candles died in hundreds, the crowds strained to view the sleek heads of the managers, the lucky ones watched from windows. It was like centuries ago, the men remained midgets and they trod the cathedral floor as the coffin cruised back and forth, and all were informed by radio about what was going on in the vast desert of stone. The skeletal saints combined with the choir around the altar, crosses of gold, heavy with thousands of forlorn candles. It was difficult to imagine when the first sadness began in the gunmetal gloom deposited year after year as the priestly voice intoned: 'This man was outstanding in his field and a great loss to our work. Today the techniques and knowledge of conditions reduce the hazards of the past but sometimes tragedy strikes and a new name is added to the roll of honour.' Organ music porpoised from the Norman doors, squads of police created panic around them, it seemed that the fanfares with the gunfire had scared the police horses and the crowd began to surge. Williams was safe in his car, cars had been reserved for the departmental managers who took their wives and endured the long day, cars with black ribbons contained the widow and the rest of the mourning family, the desired result was achieved, the assembled boots and smells did not come over the radio, the guests strained forward to the moderate feast, the ham and pork and German wine were flavoured in their imagination. Jacqueline fingered the family necklace as an onlooker climbed a lamppost and focused his camera, slipped, hung by the strap, cheering the last of the uniforms. Men sold matches and apologised for doing so, acrobats swept the streets, soldiers wore their medals and stars. Williams had the uneasy feeling that he was not looking his best, as he waddled away to the beginning of the home-bound procession. The father of the dead boy had arrived and had to return, he was committed by the one to the other. Williams poised at the top of the high steps, ready to dive into the crowd, an arrow from a cliff shot into the incomprehensible sea, ready to take part in the mass celebration that was basically meaningless, yet it was impossible not to be moved by the sight and size of the idiot crowd. Michael's beard battled and leapt to be seen before he fell back, wedged against Jacqueline, she slipped away, a flare of white thigh, a glacier surrounded by feathers, her skirt soiled and black, Michael followed, he was as fast. The great battalions marched the route commemorating the military and terrible death, the bearded boy surfaced brilliantly, his hand on the curve, then Jacqueline knifed through the sweat-filled crowd, lost in the depths by twisting quicker than the little stubborn maniac in love with the shrimp he chased, she heard him cry as exhausted he clambered away and Williams came up, saying 'I'm a man, can I help?' as Michael returned and moved with the procession, encumbered by three parcels, the wooden troops stood still, the lines of diplomatic penguins froze, Michael said 'I live close by' disentangled himself from the column, scrambled back for his coat preserved for a century in cathedral stone, he dug it out in the manner of an archaeologist, emerged a clad and decent man, a formal male.

Phillip's body was buried, it turned to earth. In the end he could not omit his bones from the new experience. He lost his appetites, he had no further interest in science, in new ideas or violent action, he was incapable of the sudden jerk into responsiveness, he was dead to the act of love.

Michael sat for an hour over a cup of coffee. 'It's like a war and he's lost.' A girl in high-heeled shoes offered a cigarette in passing. He did not blame her but she was too fat, he went to an amusement arcade to pass the time.

On his way home Williams passed a wall. He was silent. He watched a boy sink into the earth, a man stamped his foot. He would find the windows of his home hidden by curtains. Williams opened the door of Jacqueline's room, the woman had not heard him. He had a view of her face. She was his son Phillip's wife, he remembered the picture. Williams went in and she offered him food. He went for a walk in the park for lack of anywhere else to go. His son was dead but the widow was alive and Williams was afraid she would make trouble. The park was no man's land, he was on his own, thinking. Williams' father had been a war hero, the monument to the fallen still bore his name, his father had been an engineer and a good man, Williams had been the eldest child, ugly and subdued, his parents had not known what to make of him. As the eldest son he had joined the firm, the second son had stayed at home, the third would have been a doctor. It was his parents' dream. Williams' father had devoted himself to the education of his son, he had given him books to read, his eyes became nervous, his forehead marked with misery. In this park Williams' own boys had played under the ash tree, the game had depended on the number of boys, three, five, or seven, the lot of them chasing butterflies under the ash tree and their colours were the same as those on the holy medallions with symbols and ornaments in the form of men and animals. An egg had been found by Phillip, first a white one, their value was small, then a speckled. The blue had been incomparable. The boys had kept green sticks which had flourished throughout winter throwing flowers from leafless stalks in old age. No further mistake would occur if he fixed his mind on the green.

3

There was a somewhat austere reaction in Williams' home to anything that disturbed the routine. He was a man in a suit with heavy eyes and fingers waiting for breakfast. He was sorry about the death, his friends knew why, there had been too much delay, Williams had had a good night's sleep, he doubted if the inquest were desirable, the difficulty would be in dealing with questions, there were those who died, his son, himself too, no point in fighting the custom, we all had our customs, they were hygienic, there was no necessity for an inquiry but in the event he would do what he could. Williams had not been given the co-operation he was entitled to but he completed his complicated arrangements. He had to change his suit, he had agreed to attend the inquest, his head down before the open window, snatching at fresh air, his teeth chattering.

The inquest was to be conducted by one of those institutions under managerial control and meticulous supervision staffed exclusively by lawyers. The two judges resembled each other and all lawyers resembled them, they were dressed alike, without charm, no love on their faces which showed two black curves on the head, imitation eyebrows, a nose and lips, apparently a face, which could be studied, the neck of each different when examined closely. One found differences in the wigs which curved backwards and were arranged between the ears, the artificial hair passed under a comb and appeared as string. A number of long pins served to secure the hair, some of the pins could be removed and the hair tied with a ribbon. No name was understood. To mention a name was to cause uneasy smiles. The lawyers made no errors as to dress, wore black gowns and white cravats, the badges of their profession. 'In a strange country, be prepared for surprises' they would say, if they found a colleague taking the first meal of the day without wig and gown, they would call him mad. 'And the gown should lap from left to right, not from right to left, or there is no equity.' The right wing of the judges' gowns overlapped and left and almost completely covered it, except for the hidden fold which encased the flank. The reverse arrangement was adopted by junior lawyers and their clerks. The judges were invariably right-handed, the others left-handed. To know the one was to know the other. As for justice, they understood well enough how that should be arranged.

'Certainly not!' Williams dealt with their preliminary questions. They knew or would know everything. There had been no delay in treating the unfortunate person, no suspicion of unpunctuality. 'Sauce!' he said, as his ill-adjusted magnificence sat himself down as if to dinner. 'Unpunctual? Never. We eat at seven. To the dot. With my work it is the same. I arrive at eight. And at eight I begin.'

The presiding judge had some doubts as to which of the lawyers should be recognised as the deceased's accredited representative. While each of the five lawyers addressed the court, Williams' attitude was one of injured pride. He doodled on blotting paper, fiercely scribbling semi-circles as if he had given a lifetime to their study.

The poisonous face of the widow was in the court. Jacqueline took the oath, she spoke perfectly, a flute learning the alphabet, no letter forgotten. The senior judge was unfriendly, his eyes unhappy as he glanced at her. The court was cold, it believed in reason.

'He was my husband. He died alone. I went for a walk. I did not know it would happen.' Jacqueline wanted to know why he had died. It was the doctor's fault, people did not call in the doctor to die but to be cured. She had been shopping when the news came, she had bought a thin linen dress suitable for the spring, they had been married at Easter, but the day his coffin was driven to church it had rained. She apologised: 'It's nothing,' blinking in the smoke-filled room, dangerous fatigue in the narrow face, trying for most of the day, for four or five hours, to remember what had happened, there was little to remember, the weather had been fine. 'On the eighth day Mr Williams came to see me and wished to tell me something. I met him in my room and he spoke to me again but I did not understand. I thought he was lying.' 'Then what do you claim you did?' 'I was going to see my husband when I came home from work. I said goodnight and went upstairs. When I returned on Tuesday evening they told me about him being dead. I went into the room and put on the lights, Phillip appeared dead, he was lying on his side, that is all I know.' 'Did you notice any blood?' 'There was blood on his shirt.' 'There is not a scrap of evidence that he was wearing a shirt.' 'There was no fire in the room. He had his woollen pyjamas over his shirt, he needed the warmth. I can't remember more. The floor was uneven, it was dangerous, the boards were noisy when I carried the body to the bed. I don't remember more.' 'You said you saw blood on the shirt. Was that true?' 'No, not true. My memory was bad. The lie was about the shirt. It was his pyjama jacket over his shirt.' The false statement about the shirt took several minutes to sort out. Jacqueline said she understood that someone had panicked when he applied the tourniquet a second time, and she looked at him. Williams traced thoughts in her eyes, they were triangles, not pure, there was a hint of shame, and abruptly he withdrew to the furthest corner of the table away from his son. 'You persist in allegations against a perfectly innocent man?' She answered no. 'My learned friend reminds me, I will tell you what is in my mind, your husband is the victim, you are his wife, along you come and say whatever is most profitable, you carry it further, tell a dozen lies, begin lying about a shirt, you cannot extricate yourself, lies are added to lies, you end by admitting you tore the shirt with your hands.' 'What is the question?' 'Answer the question.' 'The answer is yes.' She might have answered him, but he had reached the end of his cross-examination, more or less, and he sat down. 'No further questions thank you.' The woman held her handbag: 'He was all I had, my lord.'

A splendid oak beam supported the circular roof, the bench of green chairs, the senior judge sat alone on the central chair, behind the chair was an arch, the coat of arms, the sword, benches for students, seats for distinguished spectators, incomparable libraries, a box, a jail. The octagonal ceiling surmounted the glass wood frame, the place was an exception, it measured the rare occasion, it may have done so ten or twenty times.

Guarded, Michael went to the box, his face matched his careful hair, the elder brother took the book and swore to God and his life depended on it. The professional man with years to live, he took his degree, the son of a celebrated man. The lawyers rose and charged and pleaded and sat. Michael was required to speak in detail and he complied. The court was concerned with the brothers and with the wife, they were regarded as one, was it impossible to separate the brothers or the man from his wife? Michael answered yes. To separate even the days was hopeless, he picked his words, determined to exonerate himself. He came near to the truth, the evidence emerged, then he almost lost by trying. There was a gap of two hours, he could not explain it. Yet this is not to say 'this is the man who got on badly, this is the one who lied.' He went through that day. He was brought to court where he confessed himself. His was an expert art. He would be impossible to answer. The one who might have helped was not called. Asked about the accident, Michael told God the truth and gave minute thought to the effect. The Lawyers demanded it, they demanded justice. The trouble was the wife. Her suspicions could not be hushed up. Michael described the circumstances. 'I am sure you will be most careful,' his lawyer said, when he mentioned the blood on the wheel, though the two acts were part of one, done by a man in a state of mind, they were regarded as one, impossible to separate. When questioned about the transfusions Michael said he had not noticed the label on the bottle, and then the young man's voice altered, it was noted the way it changed. 'His voice tends to fall.' 'I have a quiet voice, it is the result of the war, my lord,' Michael explained. It was nothing of the kind. Yet the man had lost his voice. They knew nothing of his life, but the judges were waiting. 'Will you take a glass of water?' 'It doesn't matter, I can manage.' A decent sort. 'And you go to your father and confess and follow it up with a speech about what you are alleged to have found, yet you knew perfectly well that Mr Williams was in no ways involved?' 'Yes.' Had he made a statement? He had done that too. Yes. Hour after hour. Wisely he stuck to what he knew. 'I had to live.' It sounded sweet. He said he was tired. He was nothing of the kind.

The judges retired to consider their verdict. The two drank the thin white wine, the green and tasty stomachs stood on the polished table, their wigs and hats on the convenient shelf, each day a brandy in a balloon. And to follow? They pushed their stomachs close, each had a slit for dropping in pieces of pie, each a toothpick in a pocket, they picked their teeth and drew blood, it took ten minutes. The judge's clerk, a clean and handsome man, said the veal was good. It was blind white bread from the slaughterhouse, meat in frozen form. The tribunal announced: 'The only comment we can make is that he killed himself by smashing his head repeatedly against a wall.'

As he left the court Williams murmured to his son 'It was your last blunder.' Michael pulled back his sleeve to look at his watch, he did it well, with confidence, his eyes on the other. 'Never mind, nothing but bad dreams.' Michael walked away from the man in the black suit, remembered something and turned. 'I don't know, it was not too bad. I thought she might bring up the question of compensation.' He caught sight of the widow across the room, she shyly recognised him, walked up to him, Michael shook hands, said 'I'll be back in a minute' and hurried away.

4

Working with the two others, in a closed room, Williams was led away by the world of astrology and knock-about spiritualism. Spanning two wings of tragedy, brother and widow, he postponed his final condition, their support was seen by his friends, he was judged a success, yet an abyss divided him from them. The last moments recurred, the spiral of ideas which stood for time, as if he had died at the same time. Michael and Jacqueline were a constant relief, being young, it was they who catalysed the revelation. Worship of life was proclaimed, that which commenced and closed, proceeded, reiterated its appeal. Williams' apocalyptic visions were cries of hope in a form which contained his age. The man of humanity was approaching, he was coming, belief was imminent, they would be believers among themselves in the rigmarole of faith. Williams had a new birth at sixty-eight, he declared he heralded new ideas, they would appear to him in a room very similar to this, with startling and precise details. When he felt the storm preceding the advent Williams walked rapidly from West to East, declared the date of the clouds, clothed in glory he would reveal his ideas surrounded by his sons, they would sit on thrones, the thing he most anxiously awaited was that the judges would reappear, he constantly awaited their judgement, he would be caught off his guard, as in the times of Noah, and judged according to his deeds. Ready for sentence, as the elder, Williams kept watch, he prepared for the day when he would come to the feast like a thief in the night and run from one end of the crowded hall to the other, making declarations of friendship with all.

Sprawled on the couch pretending to read important documents, Michael listened to his father on the telephone for half an hour, lying opposite, feet against the wall, hands in pockets, legs stretched out, periodically contradicting some assertion of the speaker, ridiculing his virtues, bored, almost ill, Michael appeared to be listening carefully, but the young widow by his desk was his primary interest. It was Jacqueline's first visit to the burly man on the top floor of the building, Williams had not avoided her, he had made himself accessible, he had nothing to hide. Michael had warned her that she would find his father charming, he would pour tea, they would drink great quantities, he would discuss her problems and say 'You will find out one day, my dear, it is not easy to deal with colleagues.'

Michael glanced warily at his father before walking over to Jacqueline, he sat on the edge of the desk, played with an indiarubber. The two men were on their feet as tea was brought in and Michael was in his corner making himself obscure, checking figures connected with the payment of staff, he concentrated steadily, stood by the girl, Williams inserted himself between them, taller by inches, with greater dignity. The younger man tried to copy the expression and style of the older but could not manage the eyebrows. Jacqueline flicked the rubber to the floor, Michael was expected to retrieve it, he knelt, looked up at her, Williams' forehead frowned in protest, he had recently started frowning, this nervous twitching was unprecedented, it intensified until the face reddened, but it did not affect his position. Jacqueline anxiously motioned the son to sit down and he obeyed. Each glance indicated mutual observation, the quarrel had grown quiet, but any chance of compromise, avoiding a scene, taking no risks and getting into bed and sleeping quietly, were barred. Williams studied the list of men to be sacked but did not see his son's name. The dazzling white of murder steamed into his mind, the strap on his wrist, his coat was soft, he had stepped into the rain with the wind blowing, a hat on the grey hair. Williams heard the insolent voice, passed over it twice, his concentration interrupted by laughter, Michael's face would tell him nothing, the sniggering stopped. Michael explained that the inquiry would have to be re-opened, an arrangement which corresponded perfectly with the requirements of the situation, in future the firm would not be troubled by claims for workmen's compensation, widows' benefits would figure in company policy and 'thank heaven for it, if one may make so bold.' Williams' answer to these proposals was clear, he put his hand to his spectacles, 'Some form of legal affidavit will normally be required, on the simple condition . . . that, in a case like this, would not be unreasonable, though it might be disagreeable for those concerned. My dear Michael, you fail to understand, the uncertainty will make matters worse, in so far as . . . Everyone has noticed that . . . . the most acceptable solution . . .' Williams was beginning to sound as if his mouth would remain open until it was time for him to die. 'The question of whether the idea has got about that the stage has been reached at which the question would become other than academic . . .' 'What's that he's saying?' Jacqueline whispered to Michael. 'Are you sufficiently aware of your own position?' Williams continued, 'I suppose you realise that not one of those fellows had my permission—' 'To be a nuisance?' Not that it worried Williams unduly, he remembered now, the affair was well in hand, he had seen the certificate, the widow had signed, the other documents would he in his hands within the week. He had yet to produce a firsthand witness to the accident, but he was not obliged to do so. 'If I had your nostrils, Michael, I would smell him out.' Williams was a poet who found excitement in realising he could do anything. 'The lawyers have investigated the position, the books can be verified, any irregularities occurred long ago, if they did find anyone who took part in the so-called conspiracy it would be too late now to re-open the matter.' 'Don't worry, that conclusion is fairly obvious,' Michael's tone was routine, it was not intended to be reassuring. Though he lacked that period of undisturbed contemplation necessary before taking a filial decision, Williams knew that when they searched his desk they would find old newspapers and leaves of vegetables and scraps of blanket and it would be for them to insinuate their relevance . . .

The interminable feud continued. The worm of guilt produced a stifled silence. Short of breath and of time, as if his life had been in danger, Williams went towards the door. There was too much light coming through the windows, he stood in the middle of the room, the sunlight hit him like the beam of an arc lamp. 'I humbly apologise for my little joke, my dear.' Passing Jacqueline he felt her breasts brush against his arm. 'I appreciate your point of view,' she said coldly. Williams would have the pleasure of seeing her again. He crossed the room, lit a cigarette and talked of business affairs. She sucked her finger with unconcern. Williams moved without faltering, his shoes in the pile carpet, the flow of 'their common sentences joined in understanding.' 'Am I a bad boy?' She had her hand in front of her mouth as she shut the door. 'I am sorry if I made a mistake,' she said. 'It will have to be corrected.' Her black dress had gone violet, the mourning had ended. 'You have been kind to me,' she said. 'What's that?' Jacqueline's sharp nails searched for a match. Williams handed her his lighter. 'Quite wonderful,' she said. 'Well, I don't know,' Williams considered the course of events, he had discharged his duty, he was curious to know if she were living alone. Worried by the delay in payment of her compensation, Jacqueline asked how she was meant to pay the rent. 'I'm afraid I'm not exactly sure where the petty cash is kept,' he said, 'and you know that cheques must be countersigned by a fellow director.' 'I understand.'

Williams showed no surprise when Jacqueline applied for a job as his secretary. She was concerned to know what the wages were, the training she would be given. 'You will be taken care of, with cheaper lunches in the canteen than you can find outside.' She would have to be vetted for her tact in shutting doors and her shining religious convictions. Fortunately she had been seen coming out of chapel, and her references contained the necessary information. It could have been worse, she might have been less attractive. Women did not have the same feelings as men, they were equally insufferable, with their childish faith and hatreds. Williams could not put up with it any longer, he was a 'man of culture', an 'individual in a hostile world'.

With Jacqueline, Williams visited the men's quarters and questioned them about their work: 'How do you spend your time?' 'We spend our time working, naturally.' 'Have you any complaints?' 'Our main difficulty is in getting backwards and forwards to work, but we manage.' The men helped each other cheerfully when the sun shone and concentrated on evading the innumerable regulations. Williams had ordered that no variation in working conditions be permitted, the windows were to remain shut in winter and summer except for a period of six minutes at noon of each day. At first the men found it a little difficult to acclimatise themselves to the new routine, but soon it became a pleasant thing for them to look forward to the noon and the entry into their rooms of what looked like breath. Sexual satisfaction was as far away as the moon and the moon was always high. Their notion of the idea of a woman was that she would come in a plane 'out of the cloudless sky' and they would recognise her at a glance, though she would tend to relate the whole experience to the everyday life of a normal person. If there were a female visitor, the men would pick her up, children, dogs and all, and carry her into the main workshop. They would call it the miraculous visitation and think of it in terms of the mental strain in the isolated place. Most of the men were satisfied by a few pin-ups on the walls, a red-haired naked girl swimming in the sea, a figure of a blond languidly reclining with sea shells and sunbursts, dark girls half asleep against crescent moons with ragged drapery caught (inevitably) by the wind, an amusing dragonfly in purple, white and puce, a woman in an ornamental garden feeding peacocks, a naked girl embracing a bull between pillars, a real girl with real rain shining on her yellow plastic mac, the form of an American dancer called Loie Fuller whipping up the train of her dress into a billowing hood and beneath the billows was concealed a light bulb advertising the fame of the Folies Bergere. In their cramped dormitories lit only by a Primus, they lived like dogs without yelping. Their remoteness became less noticeable, except for a certain giantism, as they crouched over their cooking stoves forty or fifty feet high. 'It is good business to watch over the welfare of employees, they work harder,' Williams said. The men fed like starving dogs in their eagerness to be away, they were harnessed to their work, they experienced a more intense loathing for the factory than for any other point on earth. 'Each man has a set target, a comfortable day's work. If you work harder the bonus increases. To a large extent it's up to you.' The unskilled workers were transferred from place to place like units of frozen meat. When each man was at his accustomed place, painting the girders, or repairing the massive concrete huts, all thinking of women, the same sort of women, when the work was done and they had assembled the machines, produced two thousand one hundred and ninety units per day, the atmosphere became gay, everybody talking to his neighbour, they drove off at speed across the countryside, stocked with tons of food and fuel, with the intention of travelling hundreds of miles without pause, knowing that at any time they could be picked up, precisely and securely, removed back to their place of work and anchored there so that they could not move.

'And now?' Jacqueline asked. 'Now you will settle down and find suitable friends. No pressure will be brought to bear on you, the unhappy past will be forgotten,' Williams said. An official statement had been issued, but the smell would not disappear, not that anyone was to blame, the problem had been inherited, the case had been handled beautifully, but rumours that facts had been suppressed were too widespread to be contained. Michael had been no help. 'These young chaps, I'd have fired them like that, slapdash, no respect, feeble, don't give a damn.' 'Michael has taken to wearing a bow tie,' Jacqueline said, 'he puts his arm round me and calls me darling. He's joined the golf club.' Phillip had had such long curly hair, remarkable hair, he had played the piano, he was marvellous. Williams said he would have a talk with his son, but not for several days. Jacqueline had come prepared with the draft Williams had asked her to type, with red ink decorations under the word, as the singular was corrected to the plural. 'There's an odd paragraph here, I don't understand it at all.' She looked annoyed. Williams said she should not pay too much attention to his corrections, suggestions, it was merely an informal report, a preliminary to action. 'Know what that means?' The arc of her eyebrows framed her reply. Williams asked her if she knew

Michael well. She said he was 'rather boyish, desperately provincial, though always very sweet to me, especially when he plays his practical jokes.' 'Are you fond of him?' 'I find him interesting.' Michael overheard this tribute, as he raised again the men's demands that the inquiry be reconvened. 'Do you not share their concern at the possibility of further similar accidents?' 'No one's really thought about where this agitation can lead. We've not heard yet from those directly involved,' Williams said. 'Some of the machinery is dangerous.' 'If it is dangerous of course it has a guard round it. Our workers wear protective clothing, including rubber overshoes. They are not allowed to eat sweets, they may lot sleep at the bench, they are forbidden to set the building on fire. Their names are included on the roll of honour. If there's a war they're busy with that,' Williams said. 'We play for time while the men become impatient,' Michael said, generally speaking there was no order, irregularities continued, something on more military lines was required. When he was warned that he could be replaced 'by someone a little older, more mature,' Michael said the board must decide, only they could dismiss him, but he had reason to believe that they were not out of sympathy with progressive views.

Williams intended to avoid any dispute with his son, he sent him as his deputy to key meetings and inquests. 'They say I am prejudicing my position, but I have no intention of doing so. If there is a conflict, those who remain loyal will gain and deserve my support. Confidence is a weapon. My word goes while I am in command.'

It was not yet September, preparations for winter had not begun. An excited yapping and barking and shouting was heard from the stores. Williams investigated immediately but could find nothing, no animal was unearthed, no woman discovered. From then on every incoming and outgoing vehicle was checked thoroughly. On Sunday evenings when the men invariably tumbled out of their cars, drunk and exhausted, they were taken to the medical wing and meticulously examined. They were given weights to carry the equivalent of enormous distances and the question posed: 'What keeps them going? Why do they have no desire to return to civilisation?' Their skin was microscopically examined for boils and particular attention was paid to the smallest protuberance above the surface of the skin. It appeared to the doctors that certain men benefited from exertion, those with the weakest constitutions, and they were made to wear special overalls made from non-porous plastic, as thick as a normal overcoat but infinitely hotter.

Williams continued his superficial but gracious tour of inspection. For an hour he timed the builders' labourers slinging bricks. Presently he saw his name chalked on a wall, the letters over eleven feet high, the edges deeply chiselled out along the sides. The offensive slogan could be seen from his office window, he asked Michael to investigate but his son ignored him. Williams could not find the right words, the right approach, when he spoke to the men. The best workers remained slumped on the ground, the cackling high spirits of the others offended him. But these men were useful, they would not have been employed otherwise. Their wild habits were tolerated though they made the site a jungle at night. In one place, two or three times a night there would be a fight, they did not hide it, they announced the fact. The victim could be recognised from the running and shouting, when one shouted the others joined in, their purpose was to announce the existence of one individual to another. Williams walked as far from them as he could, heard his telephone ring and raced back to his office. 'It's all right,' Jacqueline said, 'Michael has dealt with it.'

Williams worked late that night, the building was in darkness except for his office. Jacqueline normally went home at six but she waited with him. Williams called her his confidential secretary. A secretary? Behind the name was a woman. He found this touching. She wished to be found attractive. She patted the hands of the old man who waited for her, he showed his teeth and gums, his arms out to embrace he pinned her close in her chair, his lips tight against her blouse, she put an arm around his shoulders and enjoyed the desire and embarrassment moving in the recesses of the old man's body. Then she looked at his watch and said it was time for her to go.

Williams stood against the wall, a man watching the night, he heard nothing. He waited until three in the morning, staring at the wall opposite. He knew that the responsibility for keeping intruders away was not his, it was in good hands, yet he kept watch until he fell asleep. He was woken by a tapping on the side of his head. The person must have the key to the office, the door was open. Williams turned off the lights, no sign of anyone, a man's form behind the curtains, the shape might have been a shadow. He crossed to the window in a business-like way, the two were separated by a shadow, the man held a spanner. The high wall was impossible to climb. The intruder held a spanner level with his head, the room gleamed with the varnished surfaces of desk and chairs, soft glowing on sheets of paper, the rest dark. Standing still, the man adjusted his mask, the face remained hidden, Williams knew who it was, he was certain. He would deal with this himself, he would not want it to get about. It was probably someone with permission to enter the building at odd times, perhaps to clean, or check for security. His senses caught the sounds of the night, lie had not yet made up his mind, there was something he could not account for, when daylight came he would investigate thoroughly. He was stopped by a patch of damp on the carpet, a rumpling of the pile as if somebody had lain there. Williams was no fool, he knew what that meant: a person had passed close enough to touch yet he had not seen him. He experienced the fear of one who knows he has only just escaped.

When Williams left the building in the dawn light five men stood where they could not be seen, below the half-completed stairs. An obstruction on the stairs was held by a piece of rope, cunning move. These men were unknown, Williams had seen only one of them before. A man stepped close, a hand limbed and crept over the soft clothes and held his mouth. The hand was removed from the mouth, a man struck him, one laughed, one whistled, one gripped his head and told him to behave himself. One spoke a warning and forced him to the ground. The act of sudden violence when it came. This thug knew the texture of a truncheon. The blow must be directed upwards, with force to meet force. A dictatorial note: 'Get out of my way.' There was no way of saying thank you. This specimen should be isolated, for psychological and physical reasons. Note the shape of the back, the height of the head. The blow on the left side of the jaw. Effect of judicial hanging. Instantaneous. A jarring motion was abruptly and very rapidly repeated through the limited space. The design of the body had one function only: the crack on the jaw. Sticking plaster was used as a gag, and to secure the wrists to the leg of the table. A nose was picked before the application of the plaster. A person under the influence of fear shivers, as the flesh under the surgeon's knife, though more fundamental and enduring. Contortions in the face, like a fit. Drowning. Keep on, keep on. Pronounced dead. Throw him back. He would not cry for help. He began to judge the time, to get on top of it. Williams did not ask what had happened, he strained to hear their talk. 'I was fixed on this job at the start. Once I make a start I like a tremendous amount of thinking before I start.' A sheet of newspaper on the floor divided Williams from his attackers, a photograph from the jungle war helped to calm him. 'I was always keen on animals, especially leopards.' 'Time has run out.' Williams knew how to fight: if attacked, hold height. He stayed on the floor until they had gone, the newspaper in fragments.

There had been no disturbance and the shadows collapsed across the lawn, the flower beds, the ground beyond the factory. Five men vaulted a low fence, merged with the unimportant surface and the hard marks of darkness.

5

Williams could not reach the house in which to fall, his eyes hurt through the darkness towards home. Some came and carried him, searched and found sticks and fingerprints. The place was like an air raid with smashed machines on the pavement, iron shapes of every kind. Here was his strength, in his suit he returned to the place where the men had broken in. His friends restrained him, his back against the breach in the wall. Williams crawled over to meet those who were travelling east and found a body across a gate, lying flat. The electrified fencing was reinforced, traffic halted, there were no expresses, speed was a rarity, a ray of the past, as guards checked countless strangers until they disappeared, cluttered with luggage and fears. The young men travelled to work in the form of an arrow flashing in phase, they came in cars and often with hope, they worked in groups, while the aged were pushed in flat trucks with machinery and equipment open to the weather. At the congested turning Williams saw life sometimes at the end of the street, scrutinising the eastbound lorries, the intruders might come again from there. He crossed the park, intent on discovering the link between his crime and theirs, climbing every day more fences as he found them, he studied the ergonomic solution under crash conditions, the work done by unit force on a body which moved in the direction of the action of the force.

The morning broke across the workshop with the warmth of an engine. A new person, a different man, Williams ventured into the main assembly room to supervise the mechanics testing a new machine. Two men stared down at the coils of copper, one shook his head, fiddled in the dust with his boot, their faces lit from below by the light from their inspection lamps. Williams walked backwards and forwards, clinking coins in his pocket. The dynamo alone, though incomplete, was bigger than a tank, it came near to scraping the galvanised roof. Williams seemed to have forgotten the previous night, he enjoyed the tension, his eyes joined, he looked fixedly at their feet, working on a plan like a watch, caressing the polished chrome. He had returned to his rightful function, he advanced on his own. In front of these men Williams' face developed, reached perfection, his mind became specialised, the lines on his face travelled pre-determined tracks, said things he would have preferred to hide. He would have sacrificed his right arm, the stump casually dipped in creosote. He wondered whether the oil was properly lubricating the soft bed of brass.

On Sunday Williams walked down to the empty workshop wearing a pair of old tennis shoes. It was difficult to know what to make of him, staring down at the still machine, holding one of his two teddy bear mascots. By the light of the weekend emergency lamps he plugged the cable into position, fixed the wires on to the switching block and carefully checked the criss-crossed multi-coloured electrical connections. A globe revolved, there were three in a row. The dominant eyes became less assertive. Williams enjoyed the theories as to how and when his power would end, everyone knew it, but he intended the lonely role to continue for years, flashing messages to unseen people across the world, turning his back on those he wished to avoid.

With a few friends Michael sat in a room thick with smoke, beginning a movement which would have been successful if the old man had allowed it to get under way. Their conversations had hardly started when the inherent danger of factions was pointed out. They suspended discussion until the formal company meeting opened; while they waited they ate fruit.

Williams hurriedly presented his new plan: an elaboration and specialisation of previous plans, it transposed all departments of given size into bodies of a higher type, each would acquire a new structure and function. The organisation was an organism composed of cells, each fulfilled a distinct function. 'Some will be concerned with the outer fabric of the building, some with work discipline, others with safety, the rest with administration, in no case will an inferior department be permitted to function as efficiently as its superior. Those responsible for outer coverings will defer to those producing complex surfaces who will in turn be supervised by appropriate functionaries.' It was due to his profound understanding of the wider context of the theory of organisation that Williams achieved success. Flexibility was his characteristic, while his colleagues hardened with age Williams retained contact with unorthodox methods, allowed himself to be infiltrated by new ideas, thus he retained overall control without question and without difficulty. Michael termed the new plan 'a tribute to ingenuity and extraordinary resilience'. But Williams had got into his stride. He recalled that it was he who had developed the process by which tokens were accepted as money. 'I asked all my employees, on my birthday, to bring me their wages in exchange for tokens. I would reward them for their long and hazardous lives. I acquired the capital to buy machinery, became a director, and ceased to live among the poor. I was enterprising and spent long hours improving my original process, a good head, I knew the value of my own invention, I liked it, I tried it, I had good fortune. The first factory was built by the river where the vessels came from the north. They came to me for a design that had strength, I showed them the frame, I eliminated dangerous bends and projections. Harness in front, unconscious analysis behind. The single stroke from door to floor. I placed a mirror to satisfy the vanity the image was upside-down, corrected by a suitable lens. I would not have my customers moved sharply, I protected them like eggs, I strapped them in against flexible shelves that folded upwards. In their view, in the window, the display was always lit, always visible. I took care that they remembered my name. I invited them to come to me; I kept them by force. Till now I have not been concerned with prestige. I have moved over the world uncared for, searching out new methods and markets, sleeping in trains, seeking the most modern, the ultra-progressive. I received an historic award which I disregarded, it had no relevance to my work. And still the telephone rings around the world!' The last words were lost in the scrape of chairs as Michael indicated that it was time for the luncheon adjournment.

Lunch lasted two hours, it did not matter what was eaten. A speech was made, it did not matter what was said. A decoration was hung round the neck of a guest, a necklace round the neck of a girl. A speech was read from a sheet of paper, the speaker drank cold water, he was a government official, he scratched his head and wasted time, he spoke vaguely, he had 'come to learn', Williams did not hear a word, his eyes concealed his thoughts, the brief applause ended in silence. Williams spoke shortly : 'My business is the world, I am a company director, I retain my convictions, all are welcome, I even employ the man who killed my son, it is all the same to me.' He held his cup of coffee, the saucer sloped, it was small and white. Michael watched his father pick it up, with palms open, Williams shook the saucer to demonstrate the hold, feeling its lower surface he rolled it sideways. As he leaned forward the chair legs shifted under him, he tilted sharply, his feet pressed to the cross-bar, he lost his balance, grabbed his son's shoulders before he crashed with the chair to the floor. Michael helped him up. Williams began to hum a tune, he had succeeded in becoming a millionaire, he would cheat them in the end. At the mention of Jacqueline's name the stormy and aggressive man was diverted by his own thoughts. Michael said she was proving invaluable, she was a trained nurse as well as the perfect secretary. 'We need a stenographer to take the minutes—' 'I'm busy. Don't interrupt.' Michael waited till the mood passed, he knew his father's mind. Williams studied his official portrait on the wall, the sense of disturbance made the features incomprehensible, he tapped his fingernail impatiently against the heavy gilt frame, his thoughts poured grey tape through a wind machine, little scrabblings, symptoms of restlessness. 'Can't lounge around like this,' Michael turned abruptly, 'I said—someone—' Williams opened the window behind him, nodded twice as his son spoke, beat twice with his hand, walked across the room, returned and stood listening to the rain by the open window raining eighteen inches away and tentatively spilling from the gutter to the car park below. Michael closed the window, he wore a youthful smile above the unlit passage and into the collar, his face took on a tanned healthy look from the crowded furniture, he appeared as cool as before lunch, except that the eyes were watchful. 'Wotcher, soldier,' Michael joked, handing over the slips of paper, or money. Williams received them slowly, looked angry. 'Lunch is over, have to get back now, understand?' the father said sullenly from his chair, 'and don't forget to take your umbrella along.' Michael put on his raincoat, buttons on the shoulders, he hovered in front of the old man. 'Did you wish to see me?' he asked. Williams turned away from him. Michael came forward and went past, saying 'Shall I lead the way?' to Jacqueline, as she slipped by, trying not to be seen. She was wearing a man's shirt and trousers, which Williams appeared to find amusing. 'I still feel an attraction for any passing woman that comes along, I should be past all that nonsense now but just the other day—' 'You make him nervous,' Michael said to Jacqueline, he held her hand as they walked from the room.

One curl of the match occupied the room, lit his throat, his match with the cigarette close, and on that the cigarette stuck. Williams gave the waitress half a crown and placed his cup on the table. He was absorbed by it, the smoke in silence slipped to his shoulder. A passing touch jogged the table on which he was writing. In the yard below a car drowned itself in the empty cup.

When the meeting resumed, for two hours Williams' voice made the room vibrate. 'How do you feel?' He did not know what was wrong. 'When it comes to the point at which we can decide the manner in which we can achieve the object in view it became apparent that it cannot be perpetrated in the manner intended. We cannot do as we wish. That may seem a fundamental objection . . .' He rested a moment, recovered, coughed, turned a stream of phlegm over his suit. 'I propose . . . I apologise.'

'Maybe,' drawled Michael, fingering his clean shirt, studying the agenda. 'We might now turn to the next item. I am pleased to be able to inform you, gentlemen, that the turnover for the first four months of the current financial year has increased by practically the total increase in turnover for the whole of the last year. We shall repeat our interim dividend at 71 per cent and promise a second interim payment before the end of March. It is not practicable at this stage to forecast the amount, but coupled with the fall in profit from £1.06 millions to £816,000 in the first half of the current year the prospect is not inspiring. The Company has problems, sales at home have fallen, the outlook is uncertain in spite of recent improvement. Exceptional rain has affected production, but the backlog should be made up in the latter part of the year. Sales and profits from July to December should exceed those for the first half of the year, suggesting a total before tax of over £1.6 millions against last year's total of £2.1 millions.' Michael was loudly cheered when he concluded: 'If it is said we have to pay the price for efficiency in organisation then I say we have paid that price and we are not going to pay more. We have suffered enough.' Michael added that the new plan sounded 'marvellous and very intricate, but we need to know the facts, not merely an idea without details.'

Williams got to his feet and said 'We have a plan, but we can only know the beginning, the end no man can know, we must accept that. We will retain the same two thousand men, three thousand machines, but new buildings and new management. I will intensify my study of organisation. My mind has been working on problems of past and place, each connected with the plan and integrated with the overall scheme. My son is ignorant of the elementary truths I have tried to teach him, he thinks a skilled worker is indifferent, indistinguishable from a machine, one among ten million. But he will learn that from a lifetime's study a pattern appears, man resembles the ape, but the human form emerges and closes the series, man is an animal, nothing more wonderful.'

Michael proposed a committee to explore the problem. 'But meanwhile we might do something about these chairs. For too long we have suffered considerable discomfort on account of the boardroom chairs and the generally poor standard of seating at these meetings. I for one do not intend to tolerate discomfort. We shall rise for a period each morning and each afternoon. The chairman's throne is upholstered in leather, but I daresay even he is feeling the strain.'

The telephone rang. Williams held the receiver awkwardly. It took him an hour to complete a sentence, he stopped several times, Michael looked at his watch. Williams continued slowly to make the words fit his face.

With the meeting adjourned, Jacqueline remained a familiar point in the room. Williams turned to her, her simplicity pleased him. She was replacing a potted plant in the centre of the boardroom table, the broad leaves filled the room, the magenta buds were just opening, their hearts were broken. Williams wanted to speak about his son, he said he had just buried him, Phillip was the one on whom the stones had fallen, his head had been crushed, his mouth filled. Exhaustion held Williams' lips together, his body slumped in the swivel chair, he remembered the years abandoned, without air, under the ground. Jacqueline's mouth drooped in silence. 'They put him away,' she said, 'I am the one left above ground.' Williams addressed Michael: 'We committed a crime.' 'A crime? Even if it were.' Michael's lips were evasive as a game, he put his hand up to conceal a yawn: 'You consider it a crime? And if it were?' Williams was a tall man, the expressionless face was the same, the beauty of those fat hands, the stale face red with eating, little eyes able to measure strangers, he could not keep his hands still, the face with fever hunted for shade. At eight thirty, half an hour later, Williams should have been prepared, the first weeks were for waking and prayers, he was covered with turf, with two stones a length apart, they will be praying again, now, one at each end, the land was quiet, little prayer herself, Williams saw Jacqueline's eyes on him, it seemed to him as if she looked down on him, the expression set in hostility. She asked if he was needed further, she understood their moods. Williams maid he did not mind if she stayed, in a voice worn out with politeness. 'What do you mean to do?' Michael asked his father. 'Nothing.' Jacqueline transcribed her shorthand notes, her mouth cut a line in three. Williams sat beside her on the couch. Michael said he was wanted in his office and must go at once.

Williams tried to talk to the girl, it was hopeless, he had forgotten her name. He handed her a note, she said he could not ask that of her, she would read the note, she accepted it, but she would not reply. Williams did not care whether his few lines offered her everything now, or nothing, year after year, for he had money, and when his pockets were pouring with money she would follow the scent of it home.

Jacqueline stood in the passageway where Williams could see her, he waited, in repetition of his first mistake. He talked about love and honour while the messengers and other authorities pushed by. He spoke to her as to a familiar, she sighed she went on exactly as before, busy with envelopes, her expression pleasant enough.

Williams was unwilling to meet his son, he had said what he had to say, he was business-like, he did not refer to the matter again. When Williams' telephone rang, a recording replied: 'He is not here now. I cannot say when he will be back.' Williams sat on the floor, he was in unknown territory, he talked to himself: 'I ask you—seriously—'

'That's bad,' Michael said in the night air, and waited below the windows. Williams' position was weakening, his opponents were closing in, they threatened him. The glow of sunset was getting no nearer, a moment later the red turned black, then stopped. Two men turned up, Michael went towards them, they had come to see the old man shouting. The hair on Michael's head was angry, then he forgot about it. He thought as hard as he could: all that would come to mind was his brother and a dog sniffing his tie.

Respect for Michael increased, the men began to associate him with authority. Though Williams remained the father and the most famous, the founder of the firm, Michael raged more frequently and in their homes his voice was heard. When banknotes rustled or furniture crashed, the son's voice continued to exhort and instruct while the father stayed in the gloomy room. Michael relieved the image of the stern and barren man by promoting a rumour that he was planning to get married, his charm emerged clearly when he was seen practising dipping his finger into a ring, nothing could have been more natural. Michael even began to express concern at the half a million social casualties, the chronic sick, long unemployed, the widows, the separated wives. 'We must rehabilitate the homeless, visit them in their homes.' Williams attended meetings less frequently, as his troubles gathered and prepared for him. His portrait remained on the wall and at times, hard times, men glanced at the face, the heavy head and shoulders on the wall. But Michael wielded power, old loyalties shifted to keep pace with latest developments. Michael signed letters and documents in his father's name 'to ensure continuity of policy', the younger man impersonated the older for as long as he was allowed, then the business and the family split. Each required the other to give way, one could not avoid humiliation. Each was obeyed in the absence of the other, all remembered the good old times when nobody doubted who was boss or gave a damn about respect or what to say on formal occasions and no one walked with care. 'Nowadays we watch our step, we prefer not to become involved.'

6

The mirrored steel of the new building shone in the sun, noticeable from thirty miles away. Williams shut his eyes against the glare, it was a question of technique. According to plan the factory was being transformed. Thermo-plastic strips coalesced into the new symbol: an arrow wavering close to the head, the head protected by a helmet. The gaily-striped workers revolved in cylinders, the appalling millions struggled for money. Accountants checked each operation, there was nil extravagance, no one walked in or out without cunning machines counting the cost. The new towers were cleaned and stripped, display windows wiped with a rag, glass doors opened without fuss, information was accurate and up to date, electronic minds worked ideally in the future. Bulldozers turned large stones over and sucked pebbles into themselves, the operators turned and talked in their sleep. Hundreds were killed, dressed, displayed: yellowish fat and lilac hair, crosses placed on the breast. The management celebrated their memory, proclaimed a holiday. The operation was organised to maintain profit margins, goods were sold for weeks at higher prices.

Williams escaped from the din. He drove to the river. The long machine flew soundlessly over the flowing lights.

In the centre of the arcade strong lights blazed, the rest dark. A rectangle enclosed a circle, chairs were placed in a ring. The bingo cries resounded through the hall, Williams looked bored, the look of a man who knows his name will not be called. The flying lights and clinking noise were entertainment for the people. He shot a steel ball, spent hours playing games, with fifty others sat in a semi-circle, a head nodded, an arm froze. The band played The Blue Danube. He joylessly clicked billiards, the game of boredom. He sat for an hour with a cup of coffee, he tried to get up, he put his hand out for a moment, his neighbours could not see his suffering. Promptly at two, Williams met Jacqueline sitting there, as arranged. She stuffed a chocolate cake into her mouth as if she was pushing in a handkerchief, she wiped her fingers, she was brought a bowl of water to clean her fingers, she dropped silver paper on the floor, rubbed the crumbs from her fingers. Williams put on his glasses to read the bill. Her nail rested on her cheek, Jacqueline scratched her neck under her scarf, she made washing movements with her hands, prayed with them, clasped them together. Williams thought 'What that girl does with her hands is a complete ballet.' The position of her fingers, the forefinger tapping. Williams leaned forward and said something. 'Hmmmm.' She could not hear what he said. He studied the bill. 'I'll settle it.' 'Thank you.' They got up together, faced each other, she turned and went back into the crowded arcade, and he followed.

He bought violets for her lapel. She knew how to thank him, his generosity entitled him to thanks, but she did not have to smile, she was no film star, she knew he had come for a reason. Williams asked her what religion meant. God was God he said. He had spoken to Jesus Christ once, in the street, He had said He was born in Aberdeen. Jacqueline said she gave money to her mother, they lived as best they could. 'You don't need much money to live. I wasn't born yesterday, I've done all the things there are to do, I mean I've had all the night life, not recently, but before. I've done the lot. Now it doesn't interest me.' She was attractive, dark-haired, compact, quiet, dressed in a black wool dress with red trimmings. Her father was nearly seventy-six, he was what was termed an old man. He used to have a shop at the corner of Union Street, it had been three storeys high. She used words used in the street, hard or soft, she was not a woman but a thing sold in the street.

The arcade was crowded with meaningless machines. Jacqueline said if she had her way she would break up and destroy all machines. Williams said 'If money is needed, we'll give a million.' 'A billion is better than a million.' She was not interested, her mouth full of biscuits, she leaned against him while he rambled on about his past. 'My fingers were burnt, I lost money, three thousand at the races, I lost a packet, I quarrelled with them all,' he lit a cigar, the smoke spread up to the canvas ceiling. 'Wait, I'll show you a trick,' he held her hand tightly, 'I'll bet you a fiver.' He spun a penny, threw another into the air. 'See, it slips from the top, the finger in the centre of the change.' He spoke of money with affection. 'I swallow money. I play the fool but I work the better for it.' His face was lined with money, his business talent was remarkable. 'The street was my home,' Jacqueline said, 'I stayed with my father till he failed. Then five pounds a night. I've tried to get out of that line. It's not easy to quit the business. I have travelled, I've been all over, I kept my family for years. I feel at home in the street, I've danced and sung in the street.' 'You're a funny girl.' 'My dress was dotted red and black. I greased my skin and dabbed on my war paint, there was good money around.' Her short coat showed off the shape of her legs. Williams put a penny in a slot, a wire horse lit up, its eyes inspired with slow poison, the horse danced with two penguins on a chromium highway. At the moment the horse was reduced to ashes, fireworks went off. He did not know whether the coincidence was intentional but the effect was 'quite delightful', stars shot up, spun about, shrieked and died away above their heads. 'Green is the colour for stars, the manufacture is dangerous, chlorate provides the colour, sulphur the risk.' The horse was an elaborate structure of wires which passed and crossed, life was the result, a small green blob, a load of damned rubbish masquerading as a miracle.

He took her back to the chauffeured car, determined to go anywhere at all, the glass wheels burst in the form of grey flowers. 'You don't have any fun, that's your trouble,' Jacqueline said as the old man climbed slowly from the car, the ground was further than it looked. Williams felt the nervous build-up for the prize, all the paraphernalia, her shrouded look, distant shouts, phrases repeated for effect. His mauve-lensed spectacles looked puzzled as the car was driven off, turned around, swept away and headed north-west, leaving him alone with the great assurance of her heavy hair, his shaky legs in the endless land, to kick a hole in the night. He could not show her moonlight: there was no moon. He showed her a tray of rings like bits of machinery, co-ordinated rings worn on the finger. She said 'It makes me nervous to think of rings. Hell to be seen with a ring.' At five o'clock he pushed her to the ground and managed to kiss her. His attention was diverted by the calm with which she looked back at him, got up and rubbed her bruised arm. She stepped over him, she said she was hungry, she asked for fried fish and tea. 'This is not a hotel.' Then he put the questions, she gave the answers, she got bored, he began to enjoy himself. Her skirt had embroidered seams, one cheekbone was scratched, her hat lay on the ground, she held it for a moment, then walked away from the useless decoration.

When Jacqueline returned her eyes trembled with pity, she leaned forward, displaying her bosom in her blouse. She offered her cheek, she pleaded with him to make love to her. He apologised for what had occurred. 'Unable to comply with my bargains, bang, bang, bang.' She said 'It's not your fault, you're worried.' 'There's a sort of ache in my back.' 'Why didn't you say? I can't guess these things.' 'I didn't tell you, but that's what is making me irritable.' 'I'll get you a cushion.' 'I don't need a cushion.' She let him lie with his head in her lap. She located the pain and rubbed the small of his back.

Williams' earlier search for her had been successful, now she was disappearing, now she talked about her father. 'Sad, white-haired and living at Teignmouth, he looks normal enough, at least he can walk quite well, it is slow, it is costly.' Now a smaller bungalow, a small lawn, you can get a girl to do the cooking. Williams remembered her naked skin, her legs, the breasts pointed, her skin had a shine, a smoothness when wet. Her eyes were not simple, Jacqueline had reason to suspect his motives, evidence from her husband. Williams had not known Jacqueline in the remote past, she did not speak of Phillip and say 'I miss him', the memory of her marriage must have died.

Her name meant she was his child, her first name came from her grandmother. Her generation and his were different, she was less sophisticated, the differences created barriers. The problem had been complicated by placing her next to Michael and allowing the two to touch. Now Michael maintained that he owned her, his claim was inadmissible. Williams and Jacqueline had contrived what they called their 'connecting link', but it had become modified by time. When Jacqueline said she now wished to go back to Michael's house, Williams knew that she was closed to any other man by his son's hold on her, the old man knew that the younger occupied first place.

7

Williams changed his mind about visiting his son, he drove alone towards Michael's house, he had to turn right, his shirt was sweating under the armpits, it was too early, he would call in for drinks at ten, perhaps he would walk, walking was better for the health, but it would be foolish not to drive. The man from the lower ranks was staying put, the chief was coming to him, it was shameful.

The father arrived, ruffled, blustering, reluctant. He walked into the room which was warm, there were two chairs, curtains, a carpet. Jacqueline was sitting on the floor near the fire, staring at the flames, her hair was hot, she wore a ring, Michael was beside her. It was the turn of the elderly man to be helped and held in a chair. Williams said to his son 'Like other relatives of the same species, we cannot be kept separate, you understand?' 'I'm afraid I don't follow.' 'Can't you see it?' Their friendship was buried in irrelevant formality. Williams' fierce face, set and bleak, betrayed the division. He ought not to feel ill at ease in his son's house, this was not his son and never would be, the young man's eyes were his own, he must learn to understand, no one could be trusted. Michael turned towards the array of glasses and busied himself. Williams attempted to control the dual picture of the two sons, the lively and the vegetable death, the fighting boys. He took off his coat and went nearer to the fire. Williams said 'I will have a glass,' his cold tone regarded the other man. 'Shall I help myself?'

The whisky spread into the old man's neck and percolated down, warmth gradually returned. Williams needed to talk, the heavy shoes rested on the floor, the best thing he could do was keep talking without moving. He talked like a sickness, the cough came back to the bitter throat, he forgot there were things he should not have said. 'Well, I'm glad I came,' looking round their room he had been in many times before, though without the light-backed woman, erect, seated at his table among the faces he had known. The young couple were discussing the different ways of making a good Martini, and Williams sat down again and listened to the benevolent game, he said he had once been a bartender and had devised a means of increasing the profit on each drink, he would give them a demonstration of how to make a real gin sling. Michael produced a pack of cards, laid them face down and said they represented the letters of a name. He was beginning a line of seven letters on the table and saying they went like this when Williams got up and sat beside him, his black shoes next to the brown. 'I can't sit on that chair,' Williams said. Jacqueline's light lipstick made her lips look bare in the brightness which bisected the silver lining the mantelpiece, her bare brown legs half smiling in white linen shorts. Williams touched her knees and said 'They constitute temptation to the aged, a resting place for the fallen.' They felt their intestines contract, the conversation halted. Williams bit the inside of his thumb, he made peace with laughter.

Williams mumbled out the cards with a bottle of whisky. 'I'm a professional,' he said, in the same tone he went on repeating the names of the cards with fury, they shot from the pack. 'Let's get it over quickly.' Michael felt a touch of shame, 'Sorry, I'm dreaming.' Williams held the cards with the broad, tough hands of an engineer, he sat low over the edge of the table, while they waited for a sign that he would get up and go. But he said he would show them a trick or two worth knowing. 'Mark one side of the card with a dot or a pip. A chalk-mark will serve.' He said he would read Jacqueline's palm, his eyes scoured the hand for the lines of her past. 'I haven't the secret. So there we are.' Williams caught her glance at Michael and avoided the implied invitation for him to go. 'I can read the face but not the palm,' he said, 'well, I'll try, but you must co-operate. I want to see your mouths cancelling the words I pronounce:

father or brother or husband might do it.' Williams longed for some reaction or other, to bring the war into the open, in the family, individuals in the heat of conflict, like the leaves on a tree variously tinted by the hot edge of summer.

From indecision Williams stayed. The role of the eldest living child was played as Michael stared down at his drink, into his own palm. 'A man is no more than a bag of bones,' Michael spoke without motive, 'as a father perhaps you can cure this yearning for power, and the consequent pain in the kidneys?' Picking the hearts on the cards between his finger and thumb, tracing the squares on the table as if the missing cards were still set out, Michael said solemnly 'There are possibilities and probabilities as to the disappearance of the table and the disintegration of the family, and the table hath disappeared.'

Williams looked through the misted windows at the lights of the town spread out in the night, he shared the stump of a cigar with his son and after two or three false starts talked sensibly about the rebuilding of the factory. Then his words slowed, he played with two coloured pencils, making marks on their score-cards, either red or blue. 'My temperament, no, my life doesn't matter, but I thought I could squeeze a living,' Williams said. 'In business you ease out slowly, waiting for your sons to take over. I must go away and think, thirty years' work have been enough.'

An old man with his hat in his hand, the hands in black string driving gloves, Williams was in the position of kneeling in his son's room, in his son's house, the charming house looking onto the river. The contest would last for years, for longer than that.

The billowing cloud of memory Michael held for her as he held her hand, her sad eyes, the young skull on her lap, the floating skirt of sand, the arm growing from the sky, the pyjama jacket, bow tie at the neck, as Michael looked forward and she looked back.

'Grant me one gift,' Williams had begun his fall, he stumbled on the skull, he would try again when she felt hungry. The peacocks screamed in his dream: I knew you would come. The wreckage of the garden, the curtains of the house. He would end, moving on a few steps.

'Not long ago,' Williams said, 'I went to Michael's room when he was asleep. I leaned over him and took a key from his pocket. I opened his desk and found hundreds of love letters. I could hardly believe it, what did they mean to him? After reading for hours by torch-light I found what I was looking for, I knew it was time to change my plans.' They stared at him, saying nothing. 'Do you wonder, Michael, why Jacqueline here sobbed on my shoulder after the funeral? She was practically unconscious after the long nightmare, she fell on the floor, I put my arms around her and offered her a cigarette: 'I don't want to worry you, father, she said, with a look of true contentment. I could see the fear slip from her as if I were turning the pages of a book and the grey print brightened with colour. The life came back into her body, she looked as if she had attended not a funeral but a feast.'

The angled light cut her shoulder and connected her with the young man's hand, demonstrated the isolation of the pair before the impending storm. The young couple held hands, they were celebrating, they went together, they announced their intention to marry. Each, ready for duty, supported the other, the man in front and prepared to deal quickly with trouble, while she walked in the garden following the wall close to the house, for her dress to be seen in a crescent, the pace was slow and the white flowers twined in her romantic hair and she was so happy and cared almost nothing for the crowd's chatter or the father's disapproval.

'Can we go out tomorrow?' Jacqueline asked, and Michael thought, take her out, now, immediately, manage it, be with her, whatever she wants to, make up to her with gratitude and kisses. 'I've got a surprise for you.' She looked up eagerly. 'It's beautiful, this moment, to uncover happiness. We'll have a good time today,' she said, 'you can stay till morning.' He wagged his finger at the laughing face, the swinging lines of her hair.

Williams turned into the wind, with hat and coat, it made him more set on getting away this week, a tremendous joy it used to be, no, he was playing with pictures. Alone this evening, perhaps yes, but of course she would want his congratulations. His age and eyes could not possess or be possessive, as he went out of the gate, he had lost her looking at him. 'I'd like you to approve,' she had said. 'Well, well, we shall see.'

In his office Williams sat in his chair, his unhappiness alarmed him. He was impatient, his hands merged in a spire, cuffs shabby, spotted with acid, he examined his hands without realising whose they were, thinking he should be kind to them, as he received a message that could not be forwarded in a voice that would not come back. His sight grew better, he could see the clock on the wall. He said to Jacqueline, 'You'll marry him?' She joked 'Who can have told you?' Then, after she had looked at him for a moment, he said 'I'll help you both.'

Williams could manage the stairs without her help but the boots were too large, or the laces broken. He needed to ask certain questions. The descending shiny stairs at the same pace turned left through a door, there was not a room, only a region smelling of acid. The floor regarded him, Jacqueline left him with the door painted green, the hot wood smoking. Williams could have opened the door and gone outside, the door remained open with hinges on red and green and the ends of iron smiled as at a party, he could see the wide open smile in which teeth glistened after rain, the slack muscles of his mouth were the texture of melting ice, he felt the warm fluid running over his cheeks. When Jacqueline came back through the door she could not recognise his eyes which had changed colour and changed shape. She brought him a glass of boiled water, he drank to move the muscles of his mouth, he could speak more easily, the thick lips pushed between her hands. 'This is the last outpost of civilisation. I'll hold you here with my teeth,' he split matches lengthwise, swearing slowly. She said he was expected to give away the bride, she asked him his full name and wrote it down, she told him where the ceremony was to be held, and when, and gave him the ring to hold.

Williams watched the needle waver uncertainly, Jacqueline was trying to steady the details, her mirror constantly with her, the scent of powder, he felt her nerves contract, death between them, probing the sullen fire. He said it was stupid and pointless, he was more than sixty years old, she was less than half his age, he talked about the distance kicking the edge of the day, the edge of change. She said 'I haven't got all day.' He replied 'I'm staying here till—' Jacqueline detested his hands fidgeting in his pockets. Williams said 'I'd like some hot milk.' She heard him talking to his imaginary companion, the sound that came from his chest: 'I cannot for the life of me remember, it's gone, the trouble is. Look at this, an axe head found in a field, before history, all these things remind you of the olden days.' 'I'd like to have seen that. Are you sure it is stone, not bone?' 'I've thought that before. I like that thing, the way it catches the light, I've been wanting you to see it for so long,' Williams said. 'You know, you don't need to wear that suit all day,' she said, 'I don't like it, you look funny in it.' He had been trying to describe the axe head, he stopped talking about it. 'I feel like some fresh air, it's very bad to be cooped up, I've got too many clothes on, I'm used to being out in all weathers. If I go to sleep again I'm bound not to sleep at night,' he said. 'You would sleep better in the evening, you pack too much sleeping in during the day.' 'I need to keep occupied. I'm getting too much sleep during the day. I've got to learn to sit in that chair without dreaming. You should not have left me for an hour with the fire on. You look nice in that dress, refreshing to the eye. You help me up now.' 'Heavy, aren't you.' 'Quite heavy.' 'What are you up to now? What's going on?' Williams lay a long time in the same position on the couch, one leg extended towards the wall, the head craned back, staring at the ceiling. Her pleasure came from seeing him asleep with his lips bent in a curve of loneliness, it was the only time she was not afraid of him. She wanted to put her arm round him but did not wish to wake him, she raised his head and he did not wake and she was able to crouch there watching him. Jacqueline moved her head so that her hair touched his face and he woke. He bent over and enclosed the part below, simple, soft part, the inside of a fish, later and lower, the cave in the wall, discovery. 'If he asks me to marry him I shall.' She lay on her side while he pierced the wall that separated them, there was a division of labour, they were both important and remarkable, they formed a pair. In his mouth lay her ear, he shifted and she could see the nostril, a pit above the mouth. Williams felt a pain at the side of his head, Jacqueline a sense of pity, depression, it was dark, she could feel his face, the parts of her body seemed separate. Jacqueline thought she slept. Williams heard her talking about him like a ship sinking. 'I'm staying with you.' She got up and went to the lavatory and washed herself. When she came back he was sitting in his chair, his feet on the rungs, in the middle of the room on his own. 'What are you doing here? You must have something better to do?' he said. She looked away, while he went through the mechanical motions of work with all the excitement of his body, one shoulder forward, he spoke of a house and wife and his sons and from the tension in the fat face he might have been back at work, except for the eyes which were not fully open. His mind was held by some inward strain from the past, but he liked his belly full: this amused her, he kept on asking for more food and however much she gave him his plate was returned empty. The office was barely lit, for Williams' commanding presence demanded drawn curtains, the gloom began to affect her nerves. He insisted on the windows remaining closed. In the summer he had seen a bluebottle beating against the glass and had fallen badly in his efforts to let it out. He said 'If you had valued my son Phillip's memory you would not have married again.' She was too secretive to answer, she merely nodded.

The stroke of seven died. Williams saw the watch fixed to her wrist, she had been looking out at the yellow fog slipping, her face was so nearly fine, the narrow lights appeared to plan the colours of the pavement, the hurried railings, the slam of temper at the door, her feet sensed a reluctant animal, a man's grip in every direction. Michael said 'I'm glad I was in time.' Jacqueline felt her face tighten, the scrape of her chair. 'I want I to tell you —' her voice died, the sound of the fog beyond the walls. 'I must tell you. I do not wish to come here again.'

When Michael said he would go home alone, Jacqueline asked to go with him. She dabbed her face with powder, she was still a woman. 'It's nice to get out of this place.' Her lips apart, a pair of dirty yellow gloves squeezed together between houses and covered with rubbish.

From the window Williams watched them down the street, he gave them time. In the open air he remembered her toneless voice in the closed room. The works of a pavement artist were lined up against a wall, now it was quite possible he didn't paint them himself, ye glens and lochs with the most ghastly lurid lights. Williams wondered, did anyone buy them? He supposed so, simple souls. It was winter, cold air covered the sides of cars and low buildings, street-lights lit the wide road, the dry pavement with its coating of dust a few millimetres high, the quiet buildings lined the road, the objects, telephone kiosk, pillar-box, were touched by the cold. At one point the monotony was broken. In the centre of the road a heap of stones were piled one on another, a few tufts of grass grew among the stones. In the square brick house, on a bed, the girl slept in her clothes.

8

The cathedral had the walk of a woman in love. Their alcoholic wedding flowed jubilant and huge down the turbulent aisle. The scarlet carpet led Michael and Jacqueline to the altar of gold, the shining cross rose and wavered and fell, the desperate choir rose painfully, their treble soft and soundless, the vaulted ceiling thin with song. The broad columns ruled the building, the nave had windows, walls and chairs. Even a telephone. The storm outside swept the slates loose from the ancient roof, the guests in the graveyard shouted 'Goodbye!' Williams in a milk hat, a beard on his chin: they left him alone. His great coat was covered in fur, the sad beard shielded his eyes, there was no room for him, he was covered in fur, like a kitten, his beard covered a mole, the mole was a novelty at the corner of his mouth, he stood in the corner and they bid him goodbye. They put on lights, the building was lit on three sides and surrounded by fairy lights, the wind blew, the roof shook, the priest intoned and the choir sang, the building trembled and the stained glass shone onto the stone floors and the unseen waves of the sun made the ancient slates vibrate as the thoughtful faces broke against the floor.

The verger put up the metal shutters to stop the panes from falling out, they had closed the windows in the morning to keep the cool air in. The nervous groom hiccuped in the morning, for five minutes Michael jerked at speed, Jacqueline was miserable and slapped his back, the contest between them continued, he jerked, she slapped, till the force of the woman won. The famous bride with the pretty ears, her breasts bulged under her wedding gown, a drop of saliva dripped from her mouth, her chin in her palm, eyes on the cross.

The bride and groom ate the bread and wine, the warm wind made them belch, the chalice kept sliding off the cloth, the bread was made to be eaten. The bride hung over the altar rail, she belched, the choir waited and were quiet, they were not allowed to sing. In the chancel the fat little boys sat on pillows stuffed with hair, they sat with straight backs, playing with marbles at their feet, furtively rolling the marbles about. The congregation waited in rows of pews divided by pillars from the main nave, while the bride cried before the cross. As best man, Williams slipped in to flourish the ring, his technique was bold, the slim lines of his body swung, as he faultlessly executed the necessary bow. He had known better days, much wealth, little art, more's the pity. His fingers flicked at the ring, he added 'the ghost of a smile', just right. The clergy wore hats and badges, waited with folded arms. The groom flopped on his knees, the bride stopped slapping his back, the best man gave the groom gave the bride the ring, Williams rehearsed his bow, the window panes smashed by the wind on the floor, the congregation was overjoyed with its toys.

Jacqueline opened the book while the silk light touched her fingers with a slight sound. Her hand and purpose was to convince Michael that the man who had died was nothing to her, because when death came it stayed. Kneeling side by side, their faces in the shadow cast by the cross, they could not move from their place. Michael closed his mind. Jacqueline attempted to edge away from the smell of sour meat pies. Williams stared at the strip of silk that edged the bodice of her wedding dress, shifted his religious glance to her face. Her hands on her lap, she waited, it was a waste of time, the priestly voice was lost in space, mildew clung to the ancient ceiling, the stone gave no warmth. Michael bent over his bride's face and wiped the eyes with his handkerchief. The thought hung in the face, she heard his voice answer against the steady hum compounded of vague, curious noises, two voices heard, one deep, one high. Jacqueline watched Michael speak to the priest, question and answer went outside and merged with a girl passing. The bride's body was trembling, her eyes fluttered like pet mice, she loosened her silvery dress. 'It's terribly bright, too bright for the occasion.' 'It suits you, it's lovely, you're so dark.' Williams smiled encouragingly, the bride answered the marriage lines, she hid her mouth with her hand, she had not been heard by a soul.

The congregation held on to their hats and picked up their wives from the floor, they peered at the cross with hope, the incense left a pillar of smoke in the vacant church in the world. The steel seagulls turned, the steeple pushed into the sky, a small green tree emerged in a cloud on the right, the cathedral stopped in its tracks, stealthy, incomprehensible, huge.

The wooden pews contained the wooden men, each was examined by all, each tapped on the chest, resounded like a bell, a coin, hollow, perfect, sold. The bride stuck out her ordinary tongue, wet her lips, pink and gleaming, worrying the anxious priest. Because of his inexperience, he glanced at the silly girl, her breasts swinging, and the incense swung back and forth till he quieted down a little. Not so noticeable, she knelt before the altar, examining her nails. Her attempt to make him look had failed. Sex between a priest and lady, grace before the feast. The choir sang their songs, played their ancient game, from time to time they stopped, a dog barked, a coin clinked, one rubbed his foot, or something hindered them. Whenever they stopped, she smiled.

As Michael knelt by the flat-topped block for offerings to the deity, the long music resounded and the older man had been beaten by the younger. Williams knelt as the white arms were raised, the father murmured as he fell, he behaved as if the issue of the fight had not been determined, he grumbled constantly through the service, they thought it was prayer. Williams swung his arms, clasped his hands together, knelt on the cushion, while the priest continued his beautiful monotone according to the order of the service and the rules for making his living. The praying man shoved his fingers into his mouth, scratched the wood with his nails, this was not permitted, the congregation took an interest in it, Williams was a sinner in hell. He tried to break his nail by jamming it in the spokes of the chair in front, no harm was done, the chair was moved away. There were no chairs left near him, they laid clean sand on the floor. The old man sat on the sand and blew his fingers, he raised his hat in greeting, he waved with incredible persistence, he lay on his back as long as possible, he did not want to disgrace his name, he crawled round in a circle, lay still on the stone floor. Michael put down his little book and hurried to his father with a speed one would not have expected from a man in formal dress, he spotted the miserable sinner and came down in a flash, he grabbed the older man and forced him off the ground: after ten minutes hidden struggle he succeeded. Michael pulled a small crucifix from his pocket and presented it to the mournful man as he led him to the harrier so that the father was forgotten and put in a room beneath the stairs where he could not be seen. Michael's brilliant gesture with the cross made the congregation forget the tear-smeared face and the bruised lip and eyes.

The bride stood lovingly over the cross. Round her neck hung a cross. She looked young and cheap. She knelt on the stone floor which was covered with patterned carpet. The carpet over the mosaic floor weighed half a ton. Jacqueline prayed for the first time in her life: it was significant, a great event.

After the service the transparent light hung over her. A short distance away the waiting priests played chess, one read the day's papers, the other bent down, placed a captured knight beside a bible on the floor. An elbow knocked a bowl of wine which spilled on the stone. Above, the stained glass glowed with sun, a red light shone on the floor, the set faces turned towards the eventful spot. Jacqueline thought she should walk to the altar to study, observe, take note. She ran there at speed, she stepped in the wine on the floor. Blue eyes, pretty ears, pink lips, the priests regarded her suspiciously, their joyless eyes gazed not at her but at Him. 'By suffering, how else communicate faith?' the bishop intoned. He studied the list of the rich, the twelve richest, God was a wealthy man, he sang on the radio. The portly bishop in the grey suit, his head was grey, his hands small and smooth, he held an object made of plastic: the pornographic bosom of a star. He said nothing had changed. He wished the couple every happiness. He seemed anxious to get away, the pews were empty, it was the end of his day. But the bride and groom would see him again, he decided to use those last minutes, he picked a last remark. 'I am not too well. It was the war.' Their answers were not much help, he was trying to show that Christ was up to date, He read the papers but he could not decide which side He was on. On contraception he was cagey, he stood up and said otherwise, the panel of experts was now examining the problem. 'My position on the bomb, inclined against the pill,' waiting for the holy father in charming fashion, carried a ciné-camera slung beneath his lace. Christ had allowed a man to walk, the plank had reached the door, the noisy boards had masked the door, along the passage in the dark, the day trip in the dark, something moved across the floor, the movements stopped when Christ said stop. The priest with kindly eyes, Michael's elbow in his hand, his hand on Jacqueline straying, he steered them to the door, he warned that the future might be hard. The couple posed for the customary photograph, the two looked straight at the camera, and Williams in the photo had his hands up.

9

Shaped by the rosy affirmation natural to people who own new cars, the happy couple were shown to the crowd but the trick did not work. The steel sun covered herself with snow, the workers barely raised their heads, it was a matter of fatigue. This slackness lasted an hour, it divided the men from their work, it reduced their value. To Michael this was a sign that it was a time for culture and for art. A holiday would release the men, they would dance round a tree. When the novelty wore off the taxes could be increased, the law would remain in force, the people would be sheltered from the blast of peace.

Not a twitch on the face of the bored constable whose deadpan expression turned towards the crowd that was egging him on. Beneath the intractable gaze a woman patted her headscarf with white gloves, a hard-faced man with regimental tie said he did not intend to be home till two. There were well-wishers too. At five o'clock the joyful couple were asked to step outside. To fusillades of flashbulbs and shouts of 'God Bless you sir' and 'We're with you Mr Williams', like stars ducking, Michael and Jacqueline turned their backs as the crowds swarmed, and their car revved up and swirled off towards the square. In the public gardens at nine in the morning before the pubs opened the crowds arrived to drink the nourishing beer. The men took off their jackets, they had come from their different jobs, and at seven forty-five they disturbed the district with the purposeful rattle of railings. There was fun in their faces, a thirsty queue formed round the garden, the gardeners looked in envy, the head gardener closed the gates and soon the plush and straining ropes held in the crowd's common determination, they were not all young, the coaches kept rolling up to discharge their loads over the hedges, they were going to have a wonderful time, the pace of the early hours would make climbing the stairs hell by evening, still more honest workers arrived, to hell with the licensing laws, and so to pleasure. There was another reason for the general gaiety, they seemed almost grim as with determined step, hell-bent on this hilarious morning, with added mateyness they thrilled with the sense of sin. There were few lone children at play or pleasure, naturally there was one huge insistent party as the trains put down their passengers and the coaches collected the crates of beer. Williams and Michael drank large whiskies with beer as a cleansing chaser, Michael brought his bride and sat her in the corner of the garden. On every chair was a can of beer and as the morning went on the garden became barricaded with crate after crate, barrels were opened and emptied and used as seats. At the centre of the alcoholic typhoon the tempo warmed as they piled themselves on tables and the stomachs heavy with beer turned towards the afternoon sun. Out came swarms of bees and the lovers liked it hot and were found in corners with their passionate sandwiches wrapped in greaseproof paper. Someone said Now and off came their skirts with the sun, the embarrassed gleam of white skin was hidden by hills of bottles as the music took possession of them all with the whole range of Spanish vibrations and clever guitar strings. Williams' jacket was off and his tartan braces down, before the afternoon was over the garden gates were open to the town, everybody brought tomato sandwiches and a hundred pairs of welcoming arms embraced and carried on drinking. By nine thirty the queues wound round the garden before every barrel of beer, whole families came with great weights of potato crisps and everyman had a pickled onion belching out his past. Hairy-chested Williams proudly showed his chest. Those not in the family on the hot and Sunday morning, with a potent bottle in each hand, joined the club and brought along the bottles and shook hands with friends. Jacqueline joined some jolly girls bobbing up and down, and there were people who came to the party who had not previously had the pleasure, jerking and bending with greetings and singing, standing hour after hour. The family included outsiders and other congenial companions. Jacqueline was up again in a white frill of cotton, and she knew a trick worth two of that in the widening circle, she was dressed to kill, and for this came the crackle of the loudspeaker, Attention Please! And she was awarded the prize and she said she was pleased, and they were twelve marvellous hours.

At Michael's home the fashionable party proceeded. Jacqueline's two pink shoes danced with Michael's two black shoes, hers followed his, side by side, like a child clinging to its parents. When he mistimed the beat and led her impatiently to the exit, he received her opaque eye, her short questing nose pointed at his as they took turns showing each other the steps, she swept him back in a tumble of words and gestures, explaining the steps and the rhythm. Clumsily handsome, Michael stretched that elegant neck like a chick breaking through its shell. He put his hand in hers, 'I'll soon get the hang of this.' Jacqueline pretended to be fluffy, helpless, and her inert little body darted away as though with his mistakes he had ruined the intimate party. Williams flung his cocktail exultantly into the air in order to know the glass at the moment of crisis, regarded the girl, her slim arms almost as light as her stockings, he did not shrink in the anonymity of the music when a circle of trumpet expanded across the room. Williams and Jacqueline were on their own, apart from the watching guests. Each glance remained a character, the moth-eaten appearance of a kiss. Then, her lips waves, she came to him and he to her. The extraordinary kiss was seen, the explosion was unquestionable. She tried to eject the tongue, it would become embarrassing. His tongue was short, then elongated, no explanation was offered. The tongue did not return, it was dispersed in space, grown and lost, like eight million tongues, wasted. This theory was offered: if they are wasted their numbers must diminish, they must be preserved, remain in the family, members one of another. Once a tongue moves outside the family, it dies. She felt the tongue had a stony shell, the inner composition was not known. The presence of fluid could be explained, the deep mouth contained life, microscopic animals, one upon another. The probing of his tongue was hard, she wished it to become fluid, why is not known. When the skulls of men are found there is only bone. Ideas were offered, guesses made. Some supposed the son allowed the father at different times. Others conjectured tension in limited space, war in the home, or agreed definitions of warmer and cooler areas. No physical explanation could be found for these hypotheses. Michael was rigid, his tense axis could not be shifted. If he had been elastic he could have been shifted, by means of a very slow process. The true cause was seen by few, the increase of love, the love set free, the action of family love was not considered. Ancient relationships both expanded and hindered, the myth created and obstructed, the contradiction would cause the fall.

Jacqueline was stopped by a man with a camera and a man with a notebook, they came to her for titbits, she was asked her story. 'My father was a famous pianist, I was the daughter in his house.' 'Your father was a famous pianist, your background —' 'Well, it must have been musical — I was five years old. Like nothing in the world. I was born. My father was. I had a governess who. She said well don't you think you'll ever be as great as your father? Well. But I went to the pictures, and liked them very much.' 'Was it a career for you?' 'Oh I enjoyed it yes.' 'Will you make a success of your marriage?' 'Oh if this is success I will go on for ever doing the same thing.' 'Is this wickedness entirely assumed?' 'Oh.' 'What is the essential quality of the excitement you wish to enjoy?' 'Oh, I don't know. I am very happy because I do not have to. So full of enthusiasm, more or less. In the beginning I was too young.' 'Your friends, are they amusing in themselves?' 'Not all.' 'Did anyone influence you greatly?' 'No, no. One was dark and one was old. When he was smoking a cigarette he said, Kill it. It was his idea of power.' 'Do you think this quality, this ability — ?' 'He always loved to bring people together, the day I saw J. P. Macavoy the writer. The most colourful personality in the world. It is necessary to be ruthless in any walk of life. Yes. I'm only interested in winning. That's the only way you're going to do it. I don't know whether anyone can say how far you can go really.' 'Would it be fair to say you enjoy fighting?' 'Oh yes I love a fight. Get in. That's what I feel. At least you've got some satisfaction.'

She did not think of Michael again in the midst of the hullabaloo of the curtains falling, the young body at the end of the party, the thighs were sweet as Williams moved the skirt away, close to his suit. Despite the fact that the time was wrong, she was very active and demanding. Meanwhile with a face of ice Michael waited by the door, he maintained his dignity while guests fought for their coats. Her hectic breasts trembled as Williams' fingers folded over them for six minutes standing there in the tremendous commotion.

10

The wife's life changed. Instead of an artist working alone Jacqueline was continually asked what she was thinking. 'Why do you stand around talking? The film starts in an hour.' Or, in relation to friends or patrons, the design of the furniture in her home, her worship of God or was it stone, Jacqueline was asked to hurry and was invariably late. She discovered that her husband was a small man with fair hair. She became one of the trend-setting gossips. Whom she worshipped or why she worshipped him, everyone asked. Sometimes she said it was the way he put on his glasses, the way he moved. She was haunted by hangers-on in a search for originality, she soon found she could answer those fashionable questions, those that were taboo she discussed slowly and talked quietly, so that it was difficult to hear, and this, combined with the in-group fighting made things meaningless to her. Jacqueline was still not clear what was being done. She asked 'If a thing is made in half an hour, why is it bought and sold as if it took a year?' She wished to know why one person had a replica of himself in continuous huge close-up installed in his lounge, as if it were man-magic, as if to touch the cardboard made one well. Why did he live with himself? Why not a woman? If a product was supposed to sell for three hundred pounds why could it not be sold for three hundred? After ten minutes' discussion of this point with a man who had made four fortunes, and an argument with a few people who could not answer her, it was this metaphysical girl arranging hairpins in her hair who decided in a voice flushed with failure that it all seemed to depend not so much on manufacture and other creative activities as on supporting a sound system which told her she was to be given success. Privately she acquired the legendary phrases like 'I have just strangled my pet Duchamp.'

Jacqueline spent her time picking up objects from shops. She bought her dolls from a man who made figures of wax. Their heads were small, with coloured faces decorated with elastic threads of glue. She picked up a doll and put her thumb to its nose: 'The thing is a stick and a piece of leather, and this is a ball of putty. Does it looks like a man? Where's its head and nose?' Michael said the heads were made in Hamburg, many were sad rubbish. She said she loved these ancient toys, she adored the feel of dolls in her arms, armless dolls with pretty faces, in lace jackets and velvet boots, the hats painted blue.

Jacqueline achieved the personality of a star rather than the reputation she deserved, that of a person of common quality. Occasionally she startled her guests by singing, and once she sang a man to sleep for hours, this was such a success that she did it again and again. She was reported as saying that she preferred quite ordinary objects, eating a banana for instance, the papers took an interest in her performance, she became the mediator between the 'strange' and the 'hostile', she was said, if you please, to be 'imbued with wit and magic', she called it 'magicalicity'. She kept bowls of sand and empty shells in her room, and a bleak humped photograph of Jackie in a tribal village dance. There were her bracelets, and the ceiling covered with purple stars, thirty reporters were waiting for her, she pulled off her dress and allowed herself to be loved by people who did not exist, as the young woman brushed her hair, this was fashion not publicity, her uncreative mind fluttered her nipples and pouted her hair.

In the front garden of their home, Michael faced away from the front door, towards the iron gate set in the hedge. He carried a suitcase filled with Phillip's clothes. One hand held the case, the other empty. He put the case down and took a newspaper from his raincoat pocket. He kissed his wife and asked how he should dispose of the clothes. Jacqueline gave him aspirins, made him gargle, to hear the sound in his throat. They could not live with the boy who died. Michael took sleeping pills, talked about himself and the size of the world. He said she should have burned the clothes. 'It's nothing, his hat or gloves are nothing to me,' she said. 'I never thought,' Michael went to the head of the stairs, 'it is so long since there was a sound from below. Shall we talk about him?' 'I think you ought to,' Jacqueline said, 'I'll be back soon, you stay, I'll be all right, we have so much time.' Michael pulled another chair to the table. 'You mean he—?' as she placed a jar of potted meat beside him, she would have a good hunt for some salad. Michael hurried his food. She took his plate before he was finished. 'I can't tell you how nice the meal was,' he said. 'All right! If you don't like it. You've waited for something to happen. I can't keep you here. There's no sense. Does anyone care what happens in doctors' surgeries?' Michael went towards her, eyes puckered, the light was too bright, she ran forward, he did what he could, at least, she said no, kept turning her head round. They were silent for an hour in memory of Phillip's long-playing records, a description of the smile he wore, that kind of thing, he kept the records in a case, not on the table, he entered the numbers in a book, careful, remember he had certain qualities, the game with the radio, long solitude, things of that sort, they had lived together. 'I wrote him letters, you heard about them I suppose?'

Fumbling for himself, Williams ate lunch alone. He could not remember where his overcoat was. Machinery roared, his spoon scratched the plate, the contrast stared at the clock, a perpetual light illuminated the whirling hands. Williams had his office separated from the others by a partition, in his room the stubborn man, he tried not to sleep, to avoid growing old, lest he be caught off his guard. He kept Jacqueline's photograph on his desk and pointed with a pencil when anyone called, they were made uncomfortable, his predicament could not be explained, no one thought aloud. Engrossed in his own health, Williams could spare little time for work.

Michael kept sane, ate cakes and told marvellous stories. The men respected him because he grew rich, thus he increased his fortune, he was tenth on the list of the rich. Michael's name was justly celebrated, his style advanced, his teeth had a vivacity of their own, hugely successful teeth, sales half a million.

Williams conceived crazy ideas: to train the workers by electricity. They were to be ordered to move and they would move, to stop and they would stop. They might play dead. Then like small white animals they would run away, squeeze into their tiny cells, impossible to feed them, no room for the scrap of food, they would complain persistently.

The old man became a memory, a name without distinction. He gained a reputation for being unhappy, he made his friends unhappy, apart from that he was unknown. Williams tried to keep his name alive, maintained the cult, his notepaper printed at the firm's expense, the concrete plate in the floor, the print of feet. He was the same man, with fur on the outside. He rolled along the road he could not see, across the dirt, to resurrect the old times, the poverty and absurdity. On his head was a cap, he began to shout he was old, age was nothing to youth, the bald head fell across the chair. He recalled when he had demonstrated the first lamp of the new type that burned around the world, the thread that would not break, he attached the lamp, he could not speak, he whistled, he spoke like a child and ended in laughter. He cursed work, the times had not been right, he had not had a chance. 'I'll show you, you don't know a thing.'

For a long time Williams could not find his way among the constellation of unknown corridors, he seemed stationary, wandered around, played with matches, he felt his way as an automobile drives down a street of closed windows. He noticed there were no lights from the old factory, when he looked up the lights on his side went out. Someone had operated the master switch. He remembered when nearby every lamp hung a chain, to turn off the light you held the end of the chain, a pull on the little chain and the light was pulled out. When the last workers had gone home Williams began looking for the button that controlled the lights, and at that moment there was no button. In his old office Williams found the furniture and the old-fashioned lamps guarding it, a brown-looking scarcely visible light trickily painted the old portable chair. He sat in his chair, a fat old woman whose time was limited, yet comfortable.

Williams feared that when he breathed so deeply that he sat bolt upright, his chin would spring out of control. The machine had been tested and gone badly, the neck tendons showed the strain, his breath drawn in, he gripped the handle in his attack on the world. The maximum had been reached, exceeded. He talked to two men within five feet of him, someone provided a chair, his red hands gripped the white chair, the weather was bad, it was not fair. 'I'll give her eighty-five, watch the dial.' One of those grey-haired men with a serious face said success depended on numbers and power, the temperature was too low. 'Switch on the radio and forget it, pack it in.' Williams bent closer to the set, waltz time, his long black coat like an undertaker, he suggested they run the machine more slowly, to magnify each fault and make analysis possible. 'It can be done,' furiously digging his toes in the rubble, rubbing the back of his neck, the sound grew, his heavy breath dug furrows in it, made a dent an inch deep, but the wheel had no intention of moving. 'I was born to succeed, a successful man makes a track like a meteor,' Williams said. It sounded easy, the opening and closing of the valves of the heart. As the machine shuddered, Williams looked as if he would shake to pieces. 'What I would say to you, gentlemen . . . officially I would say to you men . . .' the formalities continued, at slow speed, forty words an hour, he would go on '. . . my opponents use consistent tactics, it is war, all weapons against me. I too use tactics. They anticipate feeble resistance but we shall turn the tables. We have had ill-luck from the start, our opponent has no scruples, a man who crosses the room to avoid a meeting. But I am determined, if it is said that murder would have a frightful effect, none the less, in the course of time . . .'

Rubbing the flask against his cheek, Williams coaxed a drop into his mouth, heaven, shut the door behind. He pulled his pockets inside out, the last drops hazed his being, swarms of flies darkened the corners of the windows, he threw the bottle among a clutter of others. 'There's no money in it,' his eyes fixed. From outside the door: 'That you?' Head slumped onto the desk, he hurried into sleep, his nose twitched with pleasure. He rubbed his nose, a clucking sound. 'I'm sorry to wake you dear,' Jacqueline's voice. He was glad of it. 'I reported you ill, I had to think quickly. You might have warned me Jacqueline's clean hands smelled of surgical spirit, soft lips folded over. 'I've forgotten something,' he said. 'I'm here to help,' she whispered.

Sunlight hit the corner of Williams' desk on time, reached over it inch by inch, spoke softly of brown butter, swung across Michael's voice on the phone: 'I'm not concerned with details, perhaps you should be more careful, move a trifle closer to the community, what do you think?' Williams tried to frame the reply to his son, but the film of whisky stayed like rain he studied his fingernails, heard a bus in the street below. '. . . must not impede the spring production drive . . .' The faint sound of a pressed bell, reluctant answers touched upon his crimes, stolen money lay across his face.

'I would not go down yet, the panic is still on,' Michael said, from his father's chair. Something like pain became the tight pulse in the centre of the room. Each sat in his place. Father and son 'filled identical habitations', the one confined in his place, the other held him there. 'Children must be stopped from stoning dogs, and vermin washed from their hair,' Williams said. 'I do not accept instruction from one who knows less than myself,' Michael replied.

His handkerchief stained red, Williams' voice tapped on the clean floor which his cold eyes suppressed, his fingers jerked into Jacqueline's face, she was not beautiful, she had let go, 'desperate for love' from whatever motive. Williams promised her a car, on one condition, she must not tell Michael. Jacqueline wondered why she bargained with her lover over what she should say to her husband. She appeared excited at the prospect of a row, this angered Williams, yet money for the car was deliberately put into her pocket. She regretted the joy in her reply, she would not bother to tell Michael. 'Do you mean that?' She would probably tell him sometime, she could not conceal it. Williams said he would throw her out of his room, settle with her that night. He realised what day it was, Tuesday, what had happened that day, his promise of money, the six thousand pounds, his arms stretched and made an arc of importance, he said he understood her curiosity, her anxiety, her desire to make trouble. The slammed door cut out the light, the yellow wood edged with black.

Jacqueline remembered the tear in Williams' shirt. Thick tufts of hair stuck out of his nose as she sat on a stool mending his shirt. The young woman in the wide straw hat decorated with daisies, the white-lipped woman, beltless and shivering, the years abandoned in the place without air between the floor and the ground. Williams said 'First: my work is no good. I make a profit from men. The crime is recorded, our profits have risen ten per cent. I buy a man for less and sell him for more, that is a cheat, that is all. Second: does not arise.' Jacqueline understood that Williams was in love with her and disgusted with himself. 'Michael gives me terrible little presents for Christmas,' she said, 'all that sort of thing, I wouldn't care if, but, I went out for the day and was not back the following night and he was just, you know, very curt, I mean am I supposed, he said, oh, you were away for the week? I said, oh, I come and go.'

Jacqueline became younger and noisier, Williams' handkerchiefs were her home, unhurriedly, on holiday and walking at home in the hottest summer, her limbs in an indolent pattern, she assisted the old man in his work. 'I will give what help, as I have said.' Jacqueline's presence distracted him, Williams looked older, stooped, he said he had never intended taking her into his office, he could not concentrate, he blamed her. She offered him coffee every thirty minutes from a device which sent a column of water into the air. For a minute he waited for the necessary response: it would not be recalled.

Jacqueline spoke to her husband. 'I thought let's contact your father again and see. I had this idea which might be acceptable, but no. Not that I like him, but he lives on his own. I thought I might, he might be rather stimulating, but he's like a sensitive child, you don't see him, you don't know how your father's changed. Almost tearful. I speak to him, he likes listening, understanding smiles come to his face. But I would not have him back if he were dying.' 'You're not keen to become involved,' Michael said. 'It's not that.'

Michael sacked several key men. 'I was born with an unlucky face,' one said. Michael bent down, examined the nose and cheek bone, the eyes came round large without speaking. The factory was an excellent place, a welcoming place, in the circumstances, very fine. The man would be pleased if they would let him stay. Two others were sacked, they started a business, raising hamsters for medical research. One was permitted to stay. He underwent the routine checks, the blood count was normal. A wonderful place. The lucky man said it was wonderful, an island with a corrugated roof, plenty to eat, a family of lovely people.

11

Williams came in answer to Michael's bell. 'Do sit down.' The chair was deep, soft, easily adjustable, to suit people of different shapes, heavy lobes of foam rubber, strengthened internally with pliable steel. 'There's nothing wrong with my work?' 'I had to be sure,' Michael said, 'I did not want to trouble you.' The vacant face had not heard. 'In a few years perhaps . . .' Williams began. 'I'll hear no more of that.' The son's eyes were empty. 'Well, well, it's time for my nap.' Williams went to his room and lay down, the blankets stretched the length of the body, from the scraps of hair to the wrists, his head bent as Jacqueline tucked in another strip of blanket, his son said nothing, Michael watched his wife's hands from a distance while the operation was completed.

The morning rains were green across the hills, the trees would begin to bloom in five minutes. Williams could see one quarter of the black door at the end of the corridor. Michael began his tour of other men's work, he conferred with managers, was absent to all of inferior rank. Williams became concerned lest he be shifted from his office. 'The size of a man's desk can be crucial.' He arranged to eat and sleep in his office and moved in the necessary furniture, he called it 'the cage', or 'my fourteen by twelve'. Sometimes Williams talked with intelligence, but most of his time was spent in his little room, dressing and undressing with care, bustling about with fantastic energy, folding his elegant possessions, arranging and re-arranging his collections of private papers, his memoirs, his revelations, slowly perfecting his life.

Each morning Jacqueline tidied Williams' papers and cleaned his room, he would allow no one else to do it. He talked to her as she swept the small moist room. 'It's got the length but I need it about four feet wider. I keep forgetting as I go in the door, the cooker is at the side. There's grooves to fit the table in, if you want. Last night I had to move to one of the bunks, I had pains in my back the whole night, it wasn't a soft joint, it was a spine. So here I am lying down, exactly this width, and on that side I've got the built-in cupboard, I should think it's about five foot six, I slid, I banged my feet against it, it's only plywood, I tucked everything in all along the bottom, my son says two people could sleep here, but that's the double one with the joint, this is the single, I've had to move from the double to the single. I've not measured the ceiling height, I should think it's four or five inches above my head, it makes the whole place steaming, all the moisture you see, it steams up as soon as you have the heat on, it's shocking. My bed's too warm, so you know what I do? I put my damp things on the pipes. And this miserable business of water, I can't have my breakfast in peace, in my dressing gown, I have to get all dressed up and walk and get the water, you bring this lot here, you wash yourself, you bring all this lot back again, you need a huge kettle really, one of those enormous things. All I do in the morning is, I do some toast.' Jacqueline was required to listen and nod, then to stand by the window, look down at the beds of flowers and admire the view.

Williams clung tenaciously to his remaining privileges, his unique uniform. To his father's complaints of neglect, Michael replied 'It seems to me that you have not lost but gained a family,' indicating himself, Jacqueline, the managers who accompanied him on his morning tour. Williams said he was stiff from lying around, rusty, the food was too rich, the day's work too short to justify keeping in trim, he was unused to the day without work. He complained of sounds in the ceiling, tramping feet, furniture being moved. Williams had his room sound-proofed, with padded walls and ceiling. 'Thwack!' a wet mop threw a stream of dirty water under the door. 'More than I can bear,' staring in the mirror at his great thick face.

The firm's name was changed, coinciding with fresh activity, from side to side with constant increase in intensity when attempts were made in certain directions, usually upwards, success was achieved. There was always some movement forcibly in one direction and an attempt to maintain it for a length of time in what corresponded to the boundaries of action. It paralysed when driven in the wrong direction at a time when it would otherwise be strong. The growth was imperfect, centres of power appeared but of them little was known, there were changes in these centres, altered states brought about by abnormal conditions, their course was not clear.

From this point a growing rebellion was observed in Williams. He lay awake till after midnight, pencilling notes on scraps of paper. He was found with confidential memoranda in his possession. These were the early signs. Michael followed these symptoms which closely concerned him. Papers which fell on the floor or were found in Williams' wastepaper basket were taken secretly by Jacqueline to Michael's office where he laid them on his desk and tried to piece them together. Michael noted the times his name occurred, invariably the only name was Williams, the notes consisted mainly of reports on the alleged inadequacies of the junior clerical staff.

Michael talked of 'mischief makers in our ranks' and advocated 'measures to counteract the spread of misinformation'. 'We all know,' he said, 'those noisy types, full of complaints but short of solutions, who think that what they lack in force of argument can be made good by the cunning of its presentation. It will pay dividends to combat subversive influences who thrive in times of difficulty and make the task of their superiors immeasurably more anxious, but who would not survive for a moment if the real truth were known.' Michael's intelligence was plain, but his arrogance began to defeat him. His position was precarious, at any time the board could demand his resignation. Michael was not unaware of this possibility, nor was it intended that he should be. It was impossible to remove all traces of the old ways and the old name, on the other hand 'It must be done.'

On transfer from the executive to the clerical department it was customary to take leave of one's chief before the removal of desk and papers, but Williams omitted this ritual. He said he had called on Michael but had found him out. This deceived no one, the protest achieved its purpose. Williams left his papers with Jacqueline, the notes and reports filled thirty boxes. The form of Williams' new work was decided for him. He would not take a clerical job until he was assured that he would be awarded a substantial pension, then he accepted without question. Jacqueline accompanied him to the lift, he waved goodbye, he went down to the basement where the typists worked. A woman took him in charge and entered his name, one among four hundred. There were seven to a room, he had his own table and chair.

'I was away from the office for six months. When I returned there was no suitable opening, so I came here,' Williams talked to the man laying carpet in his room, he knew how to handle him. He boasted of the position he had once enjoyed, he had no need to keep up appearances, he drank and sang, he acted freely, only his notes remained secret. Michael let things take their course, then a stop was put to the private writings. Williams' pencils and paper were confiscated. The old man had difficulty in becoming obedient, he was discovered scribbling secretly at night: 'This needs nerve.' Williams confided in Jacqueline his method of concealing his 'last words', he pointed with his foot at the floorboard under which his papers were hidden. She knew the strain across his throat, the neck, his face stiff with ugliness, the mouth hidden behind obscure papers. She agreed to supply Williams with the firm's headed notepaper, she left him a message to this effect, the vital words underlined. She could not give him all the details, but a hint would be given if a hint were needed. 'I talk to Michael maybe twice a week, he'll never tell me anything now. I know there are several deals pending but I don't really know, his office is a difficult place for me to go to now. There's been all sorts of troubles, actually I'll tell you a secret, not about me, about Michael, ha ha, very funny, he meets a girl, in a hotel actually, just round the corner, they have terrific rows actually.' 'Where?' 'Round the corner, now don't spoil it, you know what he's like. I used to complain in my childish way but everything was so hopeless, I suppose certain types shut out the external world completely,' Jacqueline said. 'I should have thought there were two kinds,' Williams said. 'I was thinking of really crazy old men.'

Williams asked for a private room where he could write, but however hard he worked, he failed, he was no worker. He was moved by love of the absurd, in order to justify and preserve his individuality, this taste became a disease, it took root, he could not disregard it.

Again Williams was transferred, the policy was to keep him on the move, stop him settling down and learning enough to make himself useful, to prevent him influencing others. He ignored the fresh instructions, they did not concern him. Another clerk took over Williams' vacated table as the old man was given nothing to do. 'I came here to do a job,' Williams said. 'You've got the job.' Then Jacqueline came to tell him 'Everyone is being moved from here, from this corridor.' Williams grabbed her hard, his reaction was to kiss, he began to, persisted. 'Now don't try that. This moving around will be finished in time. Michael has his reasons for his decisions. He's sending you and two others, the three of you, back to the old building. It will be more convenient, more spacious, everything will be easier, more familiar, there's nothing for you to do here. You need not see Michael, I spent the whole night arguing with him. Everything you need is on the way. All he asks is that you go with as little fuss as possible,' she said. 'Michael told you to tell me, to persuade me to go. It's no use, I won't go,' Williams said. 'It's too late to object now.'

When he was taken in to the new department, Williams had a different table, it was a change, he and the change embraced, there was no proof of victimisation. Yet as he unpacked his things the mouth drooped, the same shade of brown as the boots and trousers. Williams' mood would not change, he drank the last of the flask of whisky. It was good, nothing so good. He had now to sign the deed of transfer. 'We need your signature on this line, right here.' 'What is the sense? I can sign ten thousand lines.' Jacqueline smiled. 'Calm down. Have a drink.' Williams began to peel the label off the whisky bottle, he said he felt fine. 'Oh yes, it's funny, because this new chief clerk, I'd heard a lot about him from the others but I didn't know what to expect. I didn't go straight into his office which was just as well because I walked into him, it was rather a shock. I've never known an office like this, it's the worst ever, it's never light is it? Yesterday was worse, it was dull, admittedly it was raining, but it was dull. You know the funny thing is, this is strange now, when I was on the road and slept in my car I didn't feel shut in, I could sit in the dark in my car and feel all right, but in this place I feel shut in. It would be nice to do something about it, but what can you do?'

Williams took his transfer form to the personnel office where deeds of transfer converged and were registered. The form made the move official if it was brought by hand with the transferee's signature affixed. The typewriters took over in a frenzy of activity, what little time remained was concentrated in the typists' room. They raised the question of Williams' table. 'Who usually supplies the table?' They looked to him, it was responsibility. Williams had played this game before, as accomplice rather than victim. The cleaners were dusting and blowing the dust around him as the paper was angled at a dozen different angles past three. After an hour's probe into the form's validity, the cleaners were assembled outside, they looked embarrassed, each suggested an experience he had been denied. The matter was to be decided. Williams sighed like a man turning over in bed and he said he hoped his judges would not prove amateurs. His mind diagnosed a burst of sound, the clerk stared from his chair: 'Who said that? Was it you? Are you mad?' Gagged by the other's voice, Williams' eyes blinked in his head: 'Hard to say, no, I don't think so,' a small dry voice, not his own, 'I might have been in error.' The clerk with the pen said 'There may be a short delay, no more.' They blindfolded him and turned him round many times, lay him across a desk, in a room on his own.

The dullness in the new room, the tortured boredom. Williams examined his pencil on the desk, held it up in the air, fingered it, ran his nail halfway down, picked at the soft wood. 'Jacqueline said I should calm down, well it's calm enough here.' It was quiet. 'I'm a fighter by nature, I've always had to fight, mind you it's not been easy. I'm an incurable optimist. I don't like planning too far ahead.' Clustered around the small window were a dozen birds, someone had thrown bread on the sill. The birds tried to get into the room, one flew at the window and tapped its beak against the glass. The voice of a stranger told him to sit down and the excitement ended. 'Time to get out, fast.' Williams closed his eyes and turned crafty with a thought a thousand miles away. 'Pull yourself together.' He crossed to the door where someone waited curiously with a sharp push to return him to his room.

12

Though his muscles informed him of life like a vice Williams was not sure, he became aware of a deterioration, he had learned the latin name but everyone explained the thing differently, confused him to the point of exasperation, one said the word referred to one thing, another to another, the contradictions drove him mad. On his own, the high ceiling was silent, the mind wandered, he felt easier. They were discussing him again, they had a taste for disease, whose names slipped in from the remote land of Rome, these names were men in his room. Williams' son had scrubbed hands, Michael's hand against the desk, the desk had nothing to complain of, the nails were clean. Michael's tie was grey but the eyes talked, it was unnatural, the curious eyes were unhappy, neither gold nor blue, but grey, an extinction of colour like a long day of rain.

The pains in his body compelled Williams to seek an explanation of their different causes. He enjoyed the pain's intensity but asked for pills to kill his will to struggle for the remnants of his life. His son insisted he maintain the fight, warned him against the crime against oneself. In the battle between them the stronger supported the weaker, one lay still on a narrow shelf, the other held him there. The son attempted to exchanges roles, to submit. Michael never appreciated the older man, nor approached the person. The weak body of the infirm man was his weapon. Instead of widening, Williams narrowed, reduced to the strictest limits, the son was forced to submit under the threat of the father's succumbing. Their existence remained based on mutual extermination, the son supported by fact, the father by his primitive spirit, the one dominated by intelligence but of greater importance were Williams' habits and character, his enjoyment of life against Michael's wasting energy. The old man developed his ideas, and a few months before his death Michael placed a bandage over his mouth, telling him that it was Williams himself who had insisted on the pitiless struggle and that it was in his father's own interests that he should attempt to forget his existence.

Instantly, Williams recalled his function and became part of it. He dumped his case on the desk. He looked from the window at the few trees that still grew on the bar of green, his serenity returned. He read the papers and thought: 'If I had not read that before, it would be interesting.' He grew fussy about his food: 'I will not eat another meat pie.' He stepped out of the front door to meet the sun, he took off his coat and was blown over by the wind. He had his monthly medical examination and made a note: in fine shape. Old age was a trick after too many drinks. 'It's ridiculous,' he said next morning when he was refused a second helping, the food was good, he had bathed before breakfast, he was enjoying himself. Up and looking for love, there had never been a more heated eye, none more magnificent than the moment he said 'Look at that girl!', walked into town and sat through the nightly movie, found himself a girl nearly twice life-size, bestowed on her the favours of an emperor.

With work a necessity, the night filled with thick writing, the accusations accumulated, the result compressed into a line. These were Williams' best hours, the cracks in the wall blew warmth into the room, he sat at his desk, papers on a tray, tapping the tray with a pencil, 'It will mean power,' he smiled through the smoke at the bottle of ink which would not keep quiet. His final report was to be complete, the last draft done in the course of the summer. A thorough examination of work methods would be ordered, certain facts would emerge the existence of which had not been suspected. The board would learn the name of the author of the third anonymous report, it had been kept from them, now they would meet face to face. As Williams prepared for the crucial meeting, Jacqueline stood by the door staring at water trickling over the wooden desk, he had knocked over a glass of water. He whipped his papers out of the way and lay them on blotting paper. Her face had the appearance of wax. His fifty boxes of notes were wheeled away on a trolley. He put on his best clothes and asked her if he was 'fit to be seen by people who had ceased to exist.' She said she would wait for him, he must remember who he was, he had a good memory. She would stay and look after his papers, she sorted them into neat piles.

The tea-break hooter sounded, the scramble for cups and biscuits began. A woman wheeling a tea-trolley barged into Williams scurrying down the corridor, he apologised and offered her a cigarette. A nose was picked before the pouring of tea, two packets of tea were stuck together by chewing gum. Some tea spilled over his shoes, he bent down to wipe them with his handkerchief.

'How did you get on?' Jacqueline asked. 'You know,' Williams said, 'I'm better off here. I could not face the winter in your place, the size of the electric bill, me, I don't mind where I am, I must say there's something I like about this little room, cosy, the construction is warmer in winter.' It's a war and you've lost,' she said. 'I've a good mind to invite myself over to your place for the warmth, just call round and say I'm freezing could you spare some fire.' 'Did you speak to Michael?' 'I had nothing to say to him,' Williams replied. 'I must get home and prepare his meal,' she said. 'You could stay here, sleep in this room, if you don't mind getting up in the dark and leaving before morning.' Jacqueline did not blame him, but it was too depressing.

By winter Williams realised that the length of his report was inconvenient, he could not complete the work, it capsized, it was a mass of blots, lack of time was the reason. He studied the single sheet of paper, the parallel lines had a subtle meaning. The twelve involved paragraphs had marked his face, the muddled sentences revealed the strain. 'Come along now, time to stop,' Jacqueline tidied his papers. 'What of my research? I need to question Michael, to know what was in his mind.' 'Don't worry him, he's busy.' 'I don't need him, there are others, I have often talked with angels on the subject.' 'Oh . . . how dreadful.' She was crying, with triumph. Williams remembered each detail, papers lost, pages re-written. The day he had had it right, there had been an outburst from her. 'That day I was inspired,' he said. 'What an amateur you were! And every year you celebrate the anniversary!' 'I am writing the history of the world. A new Bible.' 'I'm not a complete fool.' She had whispered like a murderer: 'The words are in disorder, there is no sense, you are not in the mood.' She had not come out with it, she had hinted, spoken without vibration, with the intention of being inaudible, 'No, that is not it, it needs to be changed.' When the work had gone well she had looked unhappy, shown alarm, it had been a revelation, her reaction, her face, all those years, three years at least, like the smell of his mother's arms, he'd been a fool, he could not hold that against her.

Jacqueline blushed when Williams asked her if she had arrived by car, he said he did not need her to wipe the sweat off his face, her hands were clammy, he had seen the lights of their car, the glints of sequins on her dress, the full skirt sweeping the floor. She would not take off her coat, she chatted about the crash, the front wing dented by a bus, the silk-dressed Daimler smiled politely, the driver would not let them go, he had grabbed the wheel, Michael had called the police, that had calmed them down soon enough. Between them the narrow gap, a sleeping bird disclosed, desk of wood, a filthy comb. 'Well?' Jacqueline asked. Around her lurked the smell of dignity as she crossed the room to ask questions, she had married a kidney-shaped object, the shops were full of good things, forty million shopkeepers were short of silver, their appeal for funds must not go unanswered. Jacqueline made allowances, disregarded the dirt, there was no call to be rude. She asked the name of the nurse who had let her in. Williams' mouth stretched over the question. 'What was wrong with that girl, she was so rude?' Jacqueline asked. His lips rubbed slowly against each other. 'Nothing wrong with her, she was in trouble in the factory. I have tried to help her, she was badly treated. I help all I can.' 'You're not well. I have discussed it with Michael, you must take care, try to forget what you were, spend more time in sleep, a small thing can knock you off balance.' Jacqueline continued with a detective's calm, Williams looked impatiently from the powder on her nose to the hands tied together in prayer. 'I could order you out.' Jacqueline opened the door to go, the nurse bustled in with three cups of tea on a tray. 'Now what's going on? This won't do. He must not get over-excited.' The two women looked at the sweating face above the piles of papers. He had two nurses, a girl and a woman, both angry because he could not hold the cup steady, it had something to do with the central nervous system, shouting at the sick man who spilt the hot tea. Williams asked what had become of the parcels sent by his son, the sugar had been 'mislaid', there was no sugar for his tea. Jacqueline said he should not complain, he was living in comparative comfort, she wondered why he chose this of all times to worry about food. His sores were spreading, he was dying, drinking the bitter tea.

'Nice legs,' he said of the nurse, when she had taken the cups back to the kitchens. They heard the sound of smashed dishes. 'How are you getting on down there?' he called after her. She had held him all morning; when she had gone, with force detached from the desk, she had held out her hand to him. 'Would you have done the same?' he asked Jacqueline. He pulled some folders from a drawer, the girl bent over him to shift some books to make room for the folders, soft contours, two low hills in her blouse. 'Thank you, my dear.' Jacqueline pulled a crumpled piece of paper from one of the files. 'With your permission,' she smoothed the paper on her lap to decipher the hurried writing. 'Will you come tomorrow?' he asked her. 'I couldn't say.' The drawn curtain sighed with rain, Jacqueline patted the back of his chair, her clean hands close to his face.

'I offer you freedom, why not take it?' Williams spoke to the lamp on his desk. Jacqueline's high voice passed over. 'You stay because you hate,' he said, 'of the three, perhaps four of us, you are the one who knows what to do.' Williams sniffed the tea, gave the biscuits to the nurse who ate anything, he was tempted by the smell of chocolate but he deprived himself, he watched the girl eat. In a corner of his room he found a spider for company and fell in love with it, he confided the story of his life. Now he owned his home, he had it from God, whose face was cleaner than a clock. The radio instructed the people: Follow my leader! He sang submissively.

A man in a hat walked into the room, his fashionable cigar floated in front like a gun, Michael, and with him the inevitable lady moving like a man. Williams was caught; in place of a meal gladly offered, his son had dragged him away from the food. Williams spilt soup over his desk, he touched the bread with his fingers, his back pressed against the chair to prevent himself from being taken. Outside, winter froze to death in the street, it broke the windows, thirty frozen people were produced in evidence, smashed machines lay instead of food upon the tables. The colour of Williams' clothes remained unchanged, his report was not complete. His son Michael had read the first part, he had said the humour was splendid but apart from that he did not like it, his son had passed him in the corridor. The dud torch and the homeless girl coughed behind the screen, it was the fog, a space filled with ersatz lavender, while thieves made easy money in the south.

The nurse smiled at Jacqueline. 'May I treat you as a friend?' This attitude the older woman found disturbing, the rare word 'friend' used as a greeting by this young woman of inferior rank, no more than a servant, it was annoying. 'I have nothing to say to you.' Jacqueline was exquisitely dressed, her blouse in fashionable scarlet. 'My time is taken up with this poor invalid,' Jacqueline spoke grandly, proud and rich, her husband a person of importance. Her politeness appeared as disguise for her suffering, her calmness impressed for a time. Sharing the tiny room, she seated herself on Williams' lap, an excuse for a flickering line, he described his gift for catching fish at sea, the fire blazed through force of habit, it could not be pretended, they let it burn itself out: the stale old man and the overflowering wife, the handling of meat and money. Williams smiled like a child, Jacqueline drank her cup of tea, as she named God her face became sad. Williams asked 'How do I know I have not died in the night, been reborn and given a history and previous life and set of memories to complete the new life given? Do I die each night, and born again by morning?' She did not respond, sat as if she could not hear him. She turned to the girl, white socks and red hair, her factory uniform had her badge of rank on the breast. 'Do you know that you are beautiful?' Jacqueline said. 'I can't help it,' the girl replied. 'I am serious.' 'It's all the same to me.' 'My husband could help you transform your life.' 'He's your husband, not mine, it can't be helped.' The woman inclined her head, considered. The girl asked 'Is he really all that rich?' 'I would prefer not to discuss it.' It had been a wooing across the valley. 'Since you give me no sign I shall not try again,' the girl understood that her chance had come and gone, she got up and behaved as if she had not heard the curt reply. Jacqueline spoke to Williams about his health, and her impatience showed. The nurse sat by herself in the corner of the small room, she knew the man would die, the plump young girl sat crying. Jacqueline glanced at the sobbing nurse: her shortness and peculiar mouth did not become her. 'It was good of you to come, but you cannot help, leave now, he is tired.'

When Williams said he must do something useful, they gave him work, it was good for him. It was cardboard laid flat and on one side he stuck cellophane. It was not easy, sometimes he bent the cardboard back to make a box.

Michael and Jacqueline discussed the family problem. 'It seems he was transferred to a smaller room,' Jacqueline said, 'some people said he rather resented it, they just automatically it seems, made a decision, to make feeding him easier you see, he didn't want that, none of us wanted it, but what can you do?' 'It's in your hands entirely,' Michael said. 'He's still very shaky, very much so, but improving. I'll always remember him he had a man's face, then he was broken up, one moment he was a man, then a heap of junk. He was someone I thought I knew, and then, absolutely mad, he is, they say he is, and he's not terribly good at tests, the record shows. It's amazing how a person can influence you, I used to respect him immensely, and when I got to know him he was already ill, you know?' 'Embarrassing,' Michael said. 'Well, I didn't let myself be embarrassed, so it wasn't too bad. I had to meet this new female, you know, you get the type, a girl who knows what's what,' Jacqueline said. 'I don't know much about her.' 'He had a sort of magic,' she said. 'Yes,'

Michael agreed, 'he could be most exciting.' 'Well, I saw him with this new girl in his room, and then, most extraordinary thing, they were kissing. She had a shock of auburn hair down here which didn't look too terribly dyed. Your father has changed, he might have been a Swiss from the sort of restraint,' she said. 'I'll go down and see him. It is only a question of finding the time,' Michael said. 'The last time I saw him,' Jacqueline said, 'as soon as I arrived he said I had to divorce my husband for him, leave your flat and God knows what, he had his reasons, he talked at great length you know, about me, and you, and his life and how it all happened, he talked and talked and I couldn't say a word, he was half manic.' 'Using the word in the sense of the manic side of the depressive state?' This voice came from the chair, I mean, honestly, when you talk about mad, that man was. He once had all sorts of abilities, he's the kind of person who never stops for a minute, you can never kind of, I was impressed far beyond, one minute absolute bursting and floods of tears.' 'I had a dose of that,' Michael said. 'And the next minute there was very little wrong with him.' 'You mean there was very little visibly wrong with him?' 'But I couldn't stay, it's natural I couldn't,' Jacqueline said. 'Now you can get back on your feet again,' Michael said. 'I write to him every day, he said he was going to send all letters back, so I went on just the same, there's nothing to write, I can't lie, but I write.' 'One part of him is irrational, nothing can break through,' Michael said. 'There's no argument. I always said it was on purpose, that side of him is completely, you can't break through, have you noticed how much I am affected? It affects me, you can't expect anything else,' she said. 'My feeling is forget the whole thing,' Michael said. 'That's right, I keep telling myself, there are signs, in the whole face, there is something, I don't know.'

13

The food trolley was pushed from Williams' room, an untouched chicken on a plate, narrow and breathless, a piece of grey cheese with a thumbprint on it. Jacqueline was nice and clean, she pushed the trolley smoothly over the rubberised floor to the room where Michael, his tweed coat flecked with green, held the door by its chromium ring. He said she had kept him hanging around for twenty minutes. She stared and said nothing. Michael winked and said 'Which meal is this?' 'I don't know.' 'You'll have to take it back. We can't afford to waste good food.'

Jacqueline shuffled her feet constantly at night, Williams thought her feet had a life independent from her body. In the corner a pointed cross, she stood in front of it. The doctor walked in unhurriedly, balanced himself easily, halted. Their palms touched in a universal gesture of 'You know what I want.' Jacqueline glanced down, he pushed her lightly, her eyes clicked shut, the second step back, soft-footed against the wall, again the click of empty eyes, Williams heard loud, indifferently. The doctor walked back to the door. 'Go home and wait, I'll come.' Williams looked from his bed at the snakes in her hair, the eyes harsh, different from home, walls made of bricks topped by whitened wood, beneath the wall a path of earth and stones, the blankets were yellow, the beds low, he leaned away to avoid seeing them. Cautiously he felt the outlines of his face. He had a body, with appendages, legs, a convenient if simplified form of locomotion. One appendage was the head; the function of this organ had yet to be determined; it was decorated with bristles.

'I missed it in the dark. They're trying to make me miss the best meal of the day,' Williams said. 'They say it's best to stop all food,' Jacqueline replied. A hot spider landed on his eye. It was two paces to the door and Williams started towards it, he came up fast from the floor in a panic, he knew where he was, he was here for a short stay. He lifted himself and pushed out, turning his head for help, the narrow wrist hesitated a yard away. His midday meal in a swinging pot was bobbing towards him, held on a string by someone laughing, fiddling with a wireless set.

'I enjoy all the crazy things I used to do,' Williams talked to Michael, 'I've got the same energy I always had. People are so kind, that's why I want to get back and meet more people, I like people, I'm always doing something, I come and go, that's what is so wonderful. I am going on, oh dear, some people get like that, I should be settling down but I still enjoy myself, I can go all old school tie, it puts the gleam back into any woman's eye.' He was out of bed and talking to himself, his body hidden by the open door. By craning her head round the door Jacqueline got sight of him, she grabbed his legs and tugged him towards the bed, he seemed to shrink, a moment later the kneeling woman got up, she smiled, the grey man was in bed.

Williams had no more worry, he leaned towards sleep, preferred to be cared for, they were not murderers, nor would they let him go. The light steadied, died. Moving without friction, without anger, the big-wheeled trolley whizzed easily enough, lifted, clanged, went whistling over the floor. A bandage was taken away, dropped in a bin. The bruise in the centre of the sky formed and spread, the night without being told that it must be quiet was quiet, the furious and mortified blaming monkeys slept. The first Williams had known of heavy sleep was ushered in, his body hung from poles, he was unable to plan, it was no one's fault. An unlit globe hung over him till the night ended. Nurse checked the window, the lock was intact, she walked from window to window.

Woken by a sharp light impossible to avoid, he waited for nurse who moved ahead of him a distance of inches. The trees outside were the things he had failed to do. Confined in bed, Jacqueline held him there to stop him injuring himself. Like others in beds below, Williams had begun the year with his mouth on hers, taken his life from her. She had improved as a killer, inventive, meticulous, systematic, painstaking, capable of thought, she could sneak and shoot in the back. She was a lethal play-thing, religious violinist, destroyer. He spoke to her. 'It's lovely here, you get used to it, persuade Michael to come down, turn the mattress, just get me the papers, get Michael to come, ask him by letter, he must have a holiday too, lovely here isn't it, phone him, otherwise he will be too late.' 'Goodnight,' she said. 'Goodnight. It's warm.' 'Hm?' 'Warm. When you come in. I mean I'd like to go to London with you. Like. Might. Do. What you do. Listen I bought these pyjamas for a fiver listen and when they wear out I throw them away and buy another pair.'

In bed, the perfect place of ambush, between restless neighbours who tempted him into uncomplicated suicide, Williams acknowledged flickered visions of expert self-slaughter. He considered the problem. He lived in exile, in the bowels of another creature. He had food. He could not eat, he did not need to eat. He had no means. There was no development, nothing startling in his life. Though he was cooped up he led a complete life, he was capable of limited movement. He could anchor himself in position. He had weight, which protected him from being dislodged. He was bathed in soup. He breathed by habit. He possessed a mouth, the centre of alarm, close to the spine and the stomach, the mouth moved, fingers across the lips, steady, tired at last, the fascination of the thin strands of pain still held him, relaxed, compelled to give in and wrap his arms around his body.

Williams was recovering on schedule, he had had a comfortable night, the mild sedation had been dispensed with, he had walked round his room, taking several steps unaided. He had taken small amounts of soft food by mouth. His family had visited him and they had discussed a wide range of subjects of mutual interest.

With her mouth Jacqueline covered the sore on his neck, no smile, a cool animal with soothing pastes, her face bound with strips of cotton.

He wanted no food but sleep, he slept like a sickness, the heaviness rested on the floor, the best he could do was sleep, the mouth full of water, better off in every way. The sea of gravel moved and swelled without water and was never still, a marvellous sea of stones and trees that no man could cross.

He could see the car racing past the scene, it was effective, it was likely to be seen, and the fatal accident, the marks on the road where the wheels would come off. The technique they planned to use in that particular case included radio contact between driver and police to let them know what was going on. It was simple for the driver to operate: 'We live with what can be used in evidence, and we have for years.' The elderly body with the big stomach was found in the stationary car: knees apart, holding on to himself. It was frightful. It had given him no pleasure to watch the passers by. It was necessary to tow away the car, put out its lights, it had been left in a precarious place. Everything had to be taken from it, the key, the licence, the luggage. The body, which had squeezed itself into the small car, had to be watched for hours so that no one should steal it, while the flesh was softening. The man had no money. He had been preoccupied with business. On his seventieth birthday he had found a way out. Came the evening when he carelessly left himself out in the cold, he was quite chilled, he crouched in the back of the empty car. In the street there were few people, he had not begun, it was unfair, life had gone badly, he had begun and ended.

14

The third day of hot water admitted a remote possibility, the quiet was a holiday in a garden, the body of the father was in the quiet house three times a day, the physical family disappearing. The collapse of the lips, fumes from the cracks in the walls, the head of ice in the fatal air, the green watch stopped at one.

Michael took the gas-mask form of public transport, the horse on the point of collapse, the frightening white cotton, a series of paralytic gutters, crosses across the world, the stretched arms of women, the precipice across her shoulders, the lush women swaying on bare feet, the hard remote region, sacking placed over the land, thighs raw in the wooden box, the tall thin man became aggressive, the neck swollen and dangerous, the drunken heads in the wild country, the white mud became slow, the shirt at one o'clock was sixty-five years old, with only an hour of daylight left for the unconvicted murderer.

The question staggered under the weight of the question. Michael was asked for half an hour. The queues of flowers moved towards the day. How much would he pay for a single chair? The day for ten days consisted of a box on a table. The rubber boots were lost. The crying blowing kisses booming, the foretaste of bruises and bitterness, continually bombarded by bombs the size and shape of God, the taste of earth tomorrow.

The worldly estate had been divided: there was some suspicion that Williams had planned to donate everything to a foundation to benefit every person continuously employed in the factory during a period of five years before his death. Fifty boxes of bank notes were said to have been found in his room, concealed by timber, the paper money wrapped in cloth. These rumours, in an hour, brought two hundred to his bed, then eleven hundred workers gathered below the windows, with Michael's permission, to witness the dispositions. Michael and his wife Jacqueline were neutral, neither could be regarded as belonging to any faction or being interested in the outcome of any dispute about the will. They had hardly known the old chap, they had kept in touch, they were three who met at Christmas. The old man had apparently wished to draw attention to the family situation; the frustration of this posthumous desire, however, was the purpose of Michael's presence, he was tense and watchful, it was, after all, a pitiful, curious business, and Michael on his voyage through the world would have avoided this chair most gratefully, not that, in some measure he would not have appreciated a small present. Michael had been in a similar situation before: he had had a present from his wife's father, who had had a certain dream, and again, as the one who attended the dying, Michael had taken the customary gift from a boy who had passed away some years ago, his young companion, there had been a watch in his pocket and a wallet now empty, nothing dishonest about emptying the pockets of the dead, robbing the coffin before the body was cold. Michael hoped the sequence would not be repeated, nor the dreams from his unconscious in which he walked close to a man in a shower of stones, each held a net and a sack. For two days Michael remained in his room listening, waving his arms above his head. He had proved that he had not profited from the dying sense of gratitude, he had not wanted survival for himself, it was like food pushed down the throat.

Michael was compelled to retain in his office the official portrait of the founder of the firm. He wanted to take it off its hook. He touched his father's painted face, it had been struck by lightning. He changed the position of his desk, the portrait remained for a purpose. The image was visual. Hard to explain the memory of the old man holding a bottle, the cold from the broken window, someone wrapping him up. Jacqueline's high voice stretched from the window to the street. Michael returned to the portrait, the painter had been poor in terms of line and tone, the background was white to suggest light. From Michael's window: the glass-covered yellowish day, sheep floated down-river, a thousand priests sold shaving soap, a ship glided down a filmed canal, two men stood by a lamp, the street came to an end. His father had been a difficult subject, the smell of oil paint had offended him: 'You know me well enough,' he had said, too tired to lose his temper.

Michael wrapped his night blanket tight again. He had to be sure, he had been sure last Sunday at the death. Go back there again? His hands clenched in the corridor incredulously. Then, 'For Christ's sake!' at something on the pavement.

Michael attended to money matters, he studied the glass box of copper coin, the marble cheeks of the girl cashier, a cigarette in the thick moustache, the cigarette irritated her, he strolled back to the bank notes lying on the counter like herrings on a slab, the cold finger along the cigarette into the mess as the hard boy went forward. She watched the shillings and pence. 'Come downstairs,' the heavy cash register strained at the implications. 'And supposing someone comes along?' The second death made the same story, the man in the cafe, the woman sweeping crumbs from the table.

The second shock helped to pinpoint the happy pair, to make their life appear lucky. The public pressure of malicious gossip increased. The accuser rose from his place. Michael had mentioned the will five times to five persons and what had that to do with it? The formal plea was heard. 'Let us look at those occasions, the previous lies exposed.' It was not yet time for the truth. 'I'm sorry you must wait.' While they waited the corpse went by in a box, originally painted white, now overlaid with various colours, the black and gold moved down and staggered away. Michael whistled through the gap in his teeth, he was honest, sincere, liberal, he knew enough about history: Here Is A Message booming through the more than that.

'A split family liberates energy like a split atom,' Michael said he could make no progress, he would leave, go North. He made his statement to the press, with black coffee, black tie. 'After the funeral I'll leave town, I'll take nothing, a man on a donkey, a thousand miles with a piece of string, I'll set up as a monk.' No newspaper gave a fair account of what he had said: 'Son leaves business. He gets out on his own'.

Michael crossed the street, the railings, the drop to the basement. The street paused, the eye was painted on the wall of the house. A gate in a green light, the ground sloped upwards, the main road smelled of mud, the steady road curved towards a new element of power. The sky was crowded with stars unrolling, hunted, agitated. Going to his retreat in the country, Michael made to lie there. Who may sleep here? Anyone. No one is asked his name. No one is asked his occupation or his past. Night lodgers are given bed, coffee, free of charge. In the morning they receive coffee and bread. They are then free to go away. The sole condition is that they take part in evening and morning prayers and make a contribution of twenty guineas a week. Michael said his Father was rich, they thought he was talking about some other. The next day he left, the thing was over, he began to cover his tracks. A red flag signalled the train out, chaos splashed from the jungle: apocalypse, mysticism, prophecy, blood in enamel bowls. He turned for a last look. The wall below the cemetery was blotted from sight by the cold wind. The moon was surprised at nothing, she thought the earth was one of her puppies.

A prominent business man affected by travelling overnight, broke his journey in bizarre circumstances during his tour of the north yesterday . . . while his wife today in his home . . . the couple were on their way . . . his sacrifice outside Perth in the line of duty, to attend the funeral of his father, the christening of fame and medals. Michael became confused by the twisting bends, and part of a bridge collapsed onto a hospital. His wife assisted, she went with him, 'I gave what help as I have said', their Jaguar lay out of action for an hour because the suitcase failed, the coffee in flasks was kept in evidence, there was only one driver.

Michael waved and wept in a hotel room, lolling about on a low-level lie down for extra comfort, the guests in open-necked shirts sat next to the hot water pipes, responded to the tension he generated. He was himself on the bonfire, he kissed God's sinewy arse, his ankles felt the cat.

His father's hands showed brick red beneath the white cane chair, the portrayed line across the eyes, the blanket over the glass table, as if a child had given the table a kick and gone to sleep. The room put a bullet through him, the young man's teeth counted the years, the confusion of a choice to be made by the one who survived, climbed, recognised time written on; walls, accounts for the eye to study. A collector of art, Michael was struck by the sinister implications of a message which described an event which had not yet taken place, he caught sight of someone across the room and remained quiet, arms folded.

15

Recovered from being attacked by bees, Michael arrived back from his country home in time for the funeral. He was told that everyone was talking, Williams' trouble had been his sons, the factory, the brothels, like a huge Italian drowned in wine, the tall, tangled man had fallen through burning floors, stunned by the loss of his child. Jacqueline said she was 'dried up', she 'felt no sense of victory'.

Michael was taken on a tour of the funeral route, the splendid monuments were pointed out, no less than two hundred possibilities as to the place where his father might be buried, he could be laid in the earth or burned, drowned or lost. The fact that the destiny of the world was involved, and that in defeat a body was dumped in a public pit, was stated and noted: death seemed better for the rich. Michael wept in his father's room, he was waiting for something he called the next world, brooding on the ruins of the arch tyrant. The shock remained in his memory of the time when the old man left and took with him the message of Jesus, he had been a bright island in a grey sea, he had governed the waves, his humming spirit had dominated, his tyranny derived from love. It was not clear what Michael was doing in his father's office. He said he was checking the stocks of cosmetics and cameras his father had stored for use in a novel free-gift scheme. The board stated that this was routine procedure, that Michael liked to take a walk after a heavy meal. The newspapers scented a story: they tracked him down and found him as he lay, with a woman's handbag in a hot bath, a remote expression of calm indifference. After two hours' interview he had sold the reporters a case of French novelty lipsticks, some perky umbrella shaped salt cellars of German origin, and a chess set made from poker chips.

Michael could not get back far enough from the shout of life, he was a guest in another man's club, he had not expected so many mourners, he had thought there would be a male figure issuing orders. There were guarantees of safety on the cloudless day of Saturday or Sunday and all were guests of the management. Michael told reporters that during the war he could never remember being frightened when his father was there. 'And this has remained with me, it is part of my life, my daily routine. I can relax, get away from it all. I have a thing which I call time. A limit on these things. Sometimes it's longer, sometimes shorter. In one's mind. The other experience. Have I managed to convey my meaning? I want to put a time limit on it. Ten minutes a day for charging batteries. It is important. Right the way through childhood and one's adolescence. The pressures. I don't do anything else. I don't drink. Sometimes I think about the day I've just had. This is one of the subjects I meditate on. I am lucky. I prefer to think I have attained a sort of philosophy of life.'

Neither Michael nor Jacqueline slept without mentally marching the ordained miles of the funeral route, stiff as guardsmen prepared for the hours beside the coffin. The crowds collected like mosquitoes expectantly around the cathedral, they were a pest, daily they concentrated more heavily. As from Monday the guards would use force to clear them away.

Jacqueline insisted on visiting the hairdresser before the coffin arrived. The plague of mosquitoes grew, the visiting dignitaries were to be supplied with nylon netting, there was not enough for all. The cause of the plague was found: drains along the route had broken down and could not be repaired before the day, the stuff exploded in the streets, people complained of the shortage of netting. The corpse had taken on an unfashionable pallor and a smudge of rouge was provided to relieve the gloom. The catafalque was decorated with bits of green carpet, taken, at the request of the deceased, from the room where he had been born, and bits of the same carpet were placed around the plinth to protect the stone. Meanwhile the women complained about the inadequacy of the nylon netting, a wife had been attacked while crossing the street, had collapsed and died. Foreign visitors were returning home before the ceremony had begun, in a short time the oriental section would represent nowhere nearer the east than Marseilles.

Obstacles punctuated the route, straw was down on the wide roads. They came in cars. The guards' guns swung on a spring, the police used dogs, a sharp order shouted once or twice. Carry the dead gently, it rains and rains. Slowly the line moved, the coffin, the conference table, a man took his nameplate off the door. The road was made of rubber, the bowler hats were grey. In the huge hall for an hour, money turned pink, there were great men in the hall. Then came tea and beer. What class are you? The loudspeaker found the stunned mark. Stomachs full of Guinness, to face the dawn in alphabetical order. Girls handed round baked potatoes, 'You give me two dollars. I give you change.' A procession of black castles slowly through the suburbs, patience on the dead face, his clothes taken from him, his feet buried in nettles, there was no significance. Black walnut, brick wall. Michael asked for a carton of coffee, it was water heated up. A brick wall advocated huge white letters hidden by coal. A seizure. Vegetable houses. A grubby bird, fancy-dress Spaniard, did not stay long. The living were talking. 'Settle for a whisky.' 'How long will it last?' An hour and twenty minutes. Pitch the load generously among buildings not quite gleaming. Walk across the road. Transferred from one department to the next merely by passing through a gate. Grey endless girl in his grip. Follow the coffin along the road, ignore the face of another, come through the confusion threateningly, obediently. Put the boxed body on the floor.

Prompt. Within the hour. Jacqueline waved and wept. Six minutes to go. The sun fell under a sooty bridge, the flat river close, there were signs of cranes, epitome of beer, mud under bridge, twenty miles of tunnels, growing old among piles of improbable telephones and objects lying with feeling of abandonment, a mess of weeds and washing, dismal dumping ground, this time there were no flowers. Michael expected to see his brother, ceased to care, the long delay, convolvulus in the afternoon.

When they covered Williams with earth, the best parts of him, the relatives stood by. They each waited for the thing to be over, for the happy time to come, they had plenty of years before they died. They were satisfied until their signal came, they were insolent until then. The women wore pearls, pearls for years. It was called the system: each one's terror gave the system weight. The fifty-fives guarded the sixty-fives, guided their feet with a stick while the man with the spade stood by ready to strike or to push. The corpse was held in a harness. Splash of paint looked green on the wood, cut and polished, sides bevelled, chiselled, finished with sandpaper. Something more was expected of the witnesses. 'Whom do you represent?' Michael counted his way forward. 'I emphasise, it's unofficial, round the grave introducing a piece of thin typing, he offered a salmon sandwich. Jacqueline laughing away as if she was having a really good time: 'That stone, why does it face that way and not that way? Those birds, where are they flying? That lady, what is her name? Why doesn't she wear a hat?' In the old man's time her voice would not work until his word, an electric current ran through her. Now: 'Who are you? You spoil my enjoyment of the view.' Michael allowed her to use his name, he would take his time.

Family after family wrapped in moleskins loaded their pockets with the remains of breakfast and shortly before nine the young ones became members of a matey group. Two of the boys had six beers each, they behaved like their fathers, typical lads with fish and chips, two thousand and twenty four in the dreary queue, larking about to relieve the sufferings of others. Michael in black shoes asked why they were allowed more than one portion for each person, why they queued in groups and not in ones and twos, why that loud-mouthed youth and his twenty companions had been invited to the celebrations? For most it was a matter of taking off their jackets and grabbing what girl and food they could, more than one girl for each when they began to take things easy. They'd been easing up since six o'clock, they had taken, for obvious reasons, the cheapest coach to the party and here they were. No need to watch the kiddies, the thoughtful management had provided instruction booklets on how to make a baby harness from a pair of braces, a blonde woman settled down to the homely game. She said how it made her tummy turn up with all the laughing, mockery on a giddy Monday morning. The girls played solo on the whirligigs on Tuesday, swinging low at first so as not to disturb the normal grave and probable melancholy, they did not understand except to swing, wider and higher, swinging their legs in cotton skirts, the shortest was cheapest, swinging and singing at the tops of their voices, and as each girl swung she sang, 'Why am I on the way to heaven?'

16

Jacqueline had removed her black when Michael arrived home. The kisses he tried to force on her at one thirty-five in the morning, the maroon towel smiling, she took a bath and was in the steam when he came in, he held her in the water with wrists together, his face over hers, over the rail a belt and two stockings, he grey-haired and wearing grey. He wanted comfort. He found her on the floor, in the effort to speak she lost consciousness. Without consent and wearing white she woke late in her bed. She rang the bell: 'My head aches lately.' He knocked on the door, 'I am sorry. I was violent.' 'I remember running away. I am to blame. I drove you to it.' They had made love where they stood, he and his wife. They had been shown death. This was new, it could not be maintained. The father became a highway, a frontier preserved by memory and physical tensions.

Their new home was a lawn and a bursting tree telling tale: of chippendale beauty. The house was hidden away, well protected. Two sets of doors and long grass around a water tank led to the head of a flight of steps, with barbed wire edging the stone steps which dropped in rows to the end of the long gallery where there were three buildings. Coiled miles of wires reinforced rock doors of steel. Michael liked to live in safety, unlikely to be hurt in war, ample protection against an enemy, even bombing would not affect him. 'Loss of the chairman can finish a firm completely.' His father's records and notes filled a dozen four-drawer filing cabinets, space was limitless, the papers filled a forty yard tunnel, precautions were intensive, he said surprise was on his side. 'If my men can use a knife, they use a knife.' Jacqueline complained that the house faced the wrong way, the floor was squares of white cement. 'I did not care to move, to choose. A house, a fort, safety, a dull, feeble way to spend money.' 'An intruder's reception would be a rough one, he'd be thrown down a stone staircase, kicked or knifed in the back.'

Then their garden became his hobby. He planted a new hedge, inserted stakes and posts, with heavy-duty mesh, proof against invaders but almost invisible. The garden was overtaken by a cloud of bitter spray, the fruit trees died, roses got the spray in the face, the poison was unknown, a side product of war studies. 'Folly and madness to scatter them around. My wife and I suffer blinding headaches.' According to law he had failed to take reasonable care.

That summer they found carcases of small animals enveloped in furry growth of minute fungi, as though the skin and hair had lain for a long time in moist warm air. The animals had not been killed, they had been seized. They could not have lived covered with mould. No sudden catastrophe had annihilated them, but infinitesimal change, as slow tides, gradual sinking. They did not die of starvation, in their stomachs undigested scraps were found. They died from change a thousand miles distant, the flesh preserved, the change in temperature followed death, it did not cause it. The meat was still fresh. Michael held the small head, shook the body, the neck was torn apart, the corpse lost its form, a spark flew between the separated parts like a furious animal, disturbed, distorted. Defeated by the shaking hand, releasing gases, the flesh did not break away, it diminished, fell apart.

Celebrating his fiftieth birthday, Michael was a curiosity among his guests. Led forward to claim his drink, he said he had lost his reason for his existence: 'Fifty years of rainy weather — you're only as good as you last, the tough ones last longer.' Jacqueline treated him normally, the rest turned away. 'Not his father's son anyway.' The father's death had done for him. Michael complained of blurred vision caused by the heat. The ice in his shaking glass betrayed him, Jacqueline pushed her way towards him, the sound stopped at once, it was the effect of shock. 'I need to change my direction,' Michael said, 'pull myself round, squeeze my body into a new shape. A drink might help.' The heat in the room said 'pray', Michael was confused by the crowded room. 'Another drink before I go,' he was given a glass from a tray, the tray turned over, his wife helped him off with his stained jacket, he knelt to pick up the broken glass and bottle, picked up two pieces of glass and pointed them at one another. The large dark spots on his balding head were depressions, black discolorations, the depression detached itself and landed in the room, the distance to the lavatory was approximately one mile. 'Sadly,' Michael said, 'my father's good intentions were not always marked by results. Apparently he was skilful in handling dual bank accounts. He allegedly managed to bank £17,000 during February of last year alone, the total unaccounted for is in excess of one million.' Three unidentified guests appeared to note these words but their reaction was difficult to assess. Michael continued 'We've always worked hard here but it is satisfying work. This is an interesting place. There have been rumours recently. I sometimes think. If only.' Jacqueline helped him into his chair, the diseased hip welcomed the warm cave, fragments of bone were soft as soil. Most of the guests were blatantly drunk, the heavy drinkers were comatose. A solitary entertainer played the saxophone in an empty room, he appeared with a lettered board around his neck to indicate his lack of practice in communication, he played, then vanished, it was unreal. The drink induced a feeling of communal warmth, it swelled the blood, gave a sense of thickening unity, hastened prayer.

Michael preferred to drink alone, or with Jacqueline. After the party he would need a nap, genuine sleep, in pyjamas and under covers, he would ask for a packet of biscuits. His chair was made of springy steel covered with thick rubber, his unconscious mind was safe, the demand for whatever joy there was. To the kindly guests around his chair, he said he would demonstrate a game, he needed three cards below the value of three, the apparatus was a low table, he instructed them how to play, made appropriate noises, started his watch and noted the time of the first collision. In the surrounding circle of desire, the room full of guests who admired chaos, the clever kept at a distance, saying 'We've won!' if the odds were right. Michael passed through darkness, the escalation of protest, sensed a whisper, lowered the window. 'Get some air.' He heard grunts from the ground, from a pig as big as a church, while in the room the guests watched commercials. Jacqueline bit her fingernails as her friends admired her pink silk dresses. 'This is beautiful and unusual and rather costly.' 'Simple, chunky, geometric.' 'Attitudes are changing, people are beginning to realise.' They questioned Michael about the doctor who had attended his father: 'I know nothing of his name or any other. If he was here he has left now. He was not invited. I have heard rumours. Found battered to death in a house. I cannot say for sure. He has not been seen for a fortnight.' Jacqueline offered wine for thirty minutes from a device which sent a column of water into the air. Michael mumbled and searched behind his chair for the plastic bag which contained his cheese sandwich. 'Father always said he hated me. Fathers are apt to say that. He presided over all but had no more than a useful talent for publicity. He scarcely needed knowledge. He was a showman. The key to my present position is that I intend to retain my desk at the new establishment. This is the big, almost obvious thing. The chart showing losses scheduled is small beer. After all, for example, we suffered a series of fires. I am still somewhat apprehensive about unsuspected difficulties. And everyone behaves nicely, in spite of what some pessimists say.' His glass of whisky glistened with sweat and talk. 'Tell the girls how gorgeous they look tonight.' Michael carried a canvas angling stool for anyone who wanted to sit beside him. Half a doughnut circled the back of his head. He said 'I'm a family man and don't go out much at night. If they don't like me they can go hang,' as he pored over entertaining photographs: a file of girls with yellow hair and cotton clothes, a lady made of cushions bathed in the sea. 'Why do they need this rubbish?' he asked. 'It's not their fault,' Jacqueline said, 'the trouble is with the schools. When people are sick they should turn to prayer.' She collected pottery fragments, bones and hooks; she had a cardboard box full of prayer.

Michael concerned himself with significant matters. He conducted inquiries and frequently published the results. He remained at his desk. His voice was heard. An intensive investigation did not normally reveal complete information even on important accidents, yet Michael's confidential reports circulated all departments, and he went into minute detail. He discovered that for the past twelve years not one accident had been reported to the safety inspector. No one would have believed this had Michael not unearthed the yearly digest of accident reports: 'Here is the so-called sacred report on my brother's accident. It states clearly that I was abroad at the time. But memories are frozen at the moment it happened. Distortions occur. After his series of misfortunes my brother could be said to have been in the accident business.' The first curve in the red graph rose over this thought. 'Well, here I am,' Michael went on, 'some years after the occurrence, still somewhat disturbed after discovering unsuspected difficulties; certain men are accident prone; and so we elaborate our precautions. It turns out that just what happened to whom and where cannot always be determined. Until these new machines settle down we might as well stay put. Call a halt.' 'At least the dumping of fuel from an open pipe cannot be allowed to continue. This step could be taken without offending anyone,' the safety officer said. 'Now, you can say that. But overemphasis on safety creates anxiety and defeats its object. The investigation may be said to be levelling off. There is no more we can do.' 'The doctors will not be short of work. Phillip's belly was only ten paces from the thing when it happened.' 'We are definitely getting on top of the problem. One can only assume that the heat intake is safer. Six hundred killed each year represents a statistical average of nought point four. The story is typical of modern high speed production methods. Machines cannot be developed in a year. All you need is common sense, in triplicate.' 'Will the men accept that?' 'I am convinced they will. Until their oxygen is used.'

The speed-up in the assembly room was under way. No fewer than seventeen workmen had 'died of heart attack', recorded by a woman doctor who missed the marks of suffocation, she failed to turn the body over, it needed imagination. Michael gave money for a new machine, for electron probe analysis, twenty thousand pounds. An idiot child was born with too many toes. The new factory measured seven miles from east to west, three from north to south. It was in this context that production records were broken.

The new machines were excellent. Michael was impressed, to each he gave a box of rivets and a little silver medal. Thirty workers died in their homes. Michael presented their wives with 'as new' washing machines. He had the machines dug out of the mud, trucked back and cleaned with compressed air and oil. 'They'll run for ever. Re-set those switches.' Michael put on his overalls and examined them all. 'Notice in this case how the seal has been broken. A fancy prototype. There was nothing to prevent the intrusion of a fragment of dirt. All the coils were there but the wires were broken. What strikes me about those men is their thousand a year. Less than twenty years ago I thought only of the romantic and artistic, then I was kicked around. This gave me a balanced view. My father was a man, now, and damned good years he might have had. I became, alas, the sole survivor on the side of the ideal. Life is not a romantic and stationary object, it is like a pier which the indoor brain with authority and purpose moves with the times. And that was money then, a thousand a year. Every man I have known has learned to gauge his strength and power. I can now never enjoy. Take my father, everything he said, he did, and now he's gone, though he went in for modern ideas. He disowned the socialistic tag, the group horse. Your friends will not feed you. They are few and far between, men like him, you will not meet another. I revel in such skill as I have acquired. I am an idealist with a sound sense of philosophy. My father had courage. He took them all on. He could deal with the different sorts you have to meet. And I take after him, eighteen stone and a half of muscle and an electrically-heated telephone.'

Life was still surprisingly good when Michael collapsed in a London street. He lingered for an hour. The constable pressed the telephone to the heart. The nurse had her eyes on the watch. She opened the airway to the lungs before she was told No. She would have circulated blood to the brain. She put electrodes over the chest to shock the heart. The biggest surprise to the young nurse was the sharp blow when the body reacted. She got up to help, not fast enough. 'I'm glad of that.' A cloud grew from his lips. Much was vague and left behind. The electricity exploded an impulse into the body. The passers-by turned to look at the man who had died, his neck on the pavement, wheels rolled across the road, he stared upwards, feet in the gutter. The nurse put her mouth to the mouth. There was time to waste. They searched the pockets.

17

Jacqueline's hair was the subject of an experiment that turned it blue. 'Just as well,' she said, 'if it turns red it means the change of life.' She mixed between six and ten shampoos in a bowl which flushed into a dirty crimson, and soaked her hair. The scalp and the hair turned different colours, she became a mixture of two different people. It had taken her fifteen years to achieve the desired result. 'Identical patterns are out of date. Most people have different fingerprints, why not different hair?' With the aid of a computer the precise shade was determined. She was recognised by her remarkable hair, blue tissues dyed to a tone of green, thus she advanced science. Then her tests and experiments were discredited. The papers followed a new lead: 'Polaroid microscopes are easier, thanks to the method of Barbara Dodds. Small spots of dried blood can be useful, neutron analysis is today's most fashionable technique.' Jacqueline's attempt to use seminal fluid failed, stains were found on a policeman's uniform, her claim that the stains were caused by his saliva was not accepted. The ensuing case caused her breakdown of confidence, whether deserved or not. Dandruff was found on the adhesive tape she had used to repair her comb, her hair absorbed some slight impurity from the damaged comb and the dirt on the surface became distinguishable. She could not explain what had occurred. She had the stuff washed from her hair, a white-coated girl bathed the scalp and wrapped the head in a piece of cloth. Jacqueline had the hair cut off, the edge of the blade showed stains. The man with the scissors denied negligence, he denied cutting the hair, the man behind the wheel had not been driving. He was accused of assault and not permitted to contradict. Evidence was collected by private detectives, the remains of the hairs preserved in a plastic bucket. The exhibit was shown in court. 'Don't touch anything!' The penetration of dyes was analysed, dandruff in particular was noticed because it was not expected, otherwise the case was straightforward, obvious enough. 'I am utterly and totally extravagant,' she said, 'I love having guests. I'm neither mean nor extravagant, I like to think I am generous. I have to address twenty women's clubs, I have to open several shows. One lesson I have learned, I have no real advice for young people. I like to cook. My mother was a cook. I try to start my day right.' It all depended on electronics, and electronics were liable to bugs. The lawyers lived in rooms and wrote reports, they had powers to confiscate equipment, they made evident their nervous intelligence, they confiscated a box of soaps and a little silver comb.

The disastrous case compelled a change of setting, her flamboyant public image had somehow become confused with her actual personality, there was a harshness that did not suit her.

Life was now mostly by telephone several times a year, she tended the flowers in beds, she treasured her youth, the deepest friendships went into too much detail. She had been offered lots of love affairs but forty years was old, she did not believe in friendship, a man might make her leave her flat and she would not have liked that. A friend in her flat was a man who left her or vice versa. The road home was blue roses on wallpaper, the impression of rare speed equated with happiness, the perfect day spoke Scottish poetry, her cigarettes had her name engraved on them. In the constant state of something like tension, the dust in the fridge exploded, the dangerous woman got pleasure from eating, in the dazed heat she planned meals lavishly, the whole mess was dumped on the table, nobody had bothered with the layers of dust for months after breakfast, they were more or less necessary. Jacqueline was always sitting there in that chair because she was immune to control, crippled by the difficult situation. The morning dark was a good life, vacancy a word for morning. On account of allergy she had lost track for two years, she had friends who died, 'You don't see many people in the dark.' She was contented religiously, able to follow the big dogs, sex was her husband in the ground, that side of things was going to fall from the sky when she had mapped it out, but the good life lived a long time and married somebody else.

In a leopard skin coat with a pattern of microbes floating in it, Jacqueline went away for six months to a great silencescape of white mountains and pale blue time of danger for the not so young. She met a man who had made his way, he carried a briefcase. He was a regular man, he had never had information laid against him. A native of the north, he traded in chocolate and biscuits, his sport was parachuting, she thought his courage distinguished him from all others.

Their meeting was celebrated, they attended an air display. Half a dozen light planes, nine cameramen, a hundred and twenty-five reporters, thirty hundred-foot radio towers, a thousand spectators, the loudspeakers announced the warmest, calmest, clearest day. The loud clouds opened over white buildings, white planes flew, a choir sang, rows of competitors were adorned with decorations. The parachutist unplugged a cardboard telephone, relaxed for a keen look, jumped with the hook, lost height, he clapped his hands to attract attention: he advertised a chocolate product, displayed a packet of biscuits. There were cries as he fell, turning in effort, head clamped down, the staccato cry descended. Officials interrupted the show to adjust the synchronising gear, to protect the man, he could not stop now, he was falling, he would be better off from every point of view. His parachute filled the world, he said he was dumb, he made his name by floating, the net supported by a hoop, he was drawn along, he waved at the crowd as if it had been an enormous serpent and he born along on its back. He could move forwards and backwards like a king in draughts. In the crowd were huge numbers of flowers, gorilla-like jewels, the women's hats led the cheers. He could not fall without laughing, as the men ran beside the women who led them in time to military music, the trap was sprung, the white parachute with its damp burden, a man pointed, the white flower turned over all the time, the giant waved to the people, the body was now on its way, to speak when the time came, he knew how to fall, he knew the qualities, the weight, the starting point, part of technique, whatever it was, however he came, married to energy, that was why the thrust, the compulsion, was the outcome of desire. A rope hit the wires, the act of sudden violence when it came, it sizzled and fell away. Terrified of failure he took refuge in history, sick with the smell of death he prepared his gift. A doctor rode a bicycle across a field.

Jacqueline watched from a high window. She had not expected so many mountains, she had thought there would be a cabaret and hundreds of sun worshippers who would strip like in France, and curious dancing, and continental sandwiches which would make it still more continental, though she was glad there were none of those tongue-twisting words, nor was she asked to peel off her clothes and show her white skin.

BABEL

THE LONG-DISTANCE WAITRESS SNIFFS THE COUNTER, she keeps glancing at the sandwiches two miles away. The drunks that pass in the night should not be there, the eighty-year-old waitress fusses over vegetables, busy with fresh paper, painfully working alone at midnight, travelling her years on the street because anyone has to have money at the end of the week and a bed to lie on. The brilliant chef is made of pastry, he is said to make people cheerful at the end of the long restaurant, wading across raw people of the pie and sausage-roll variety, screaming for a great sauce. His curry is bland, it tastes of the mudflats behind the railway station. The beer is pepperless, there's not enough splash in it. Our Father with the flask is a gambler between prostitutes, his home is the Savoy in the evening. The coffee attracted him, the human cannot stand exposure. The bacon and egg pours out, cooling him, he last washed his haddock three years ago, things are better every day. The mistaken impressions of the few people who are still such nice people are those of well-dressed queers on the watch. Father starts the heater and of course the blue steam starts a person thinking. Some who say they love the night cannot get anywhere in the day. Women look old at five in the morning, the skin business drags on, the young man livens up, actors think it exciting in Earl's Court, the Italian waiter could be brilliant frequently. It's energy takes the money in the gambling business. Here you find friends, good friends arrive for fifteen shillings, a small crowd stays the night. The American woman grows stronger and stronger, a young couple spoke to a chap in a woolly jumper, when people said they were hungry the silk spaghetti was slung at them, the place made money somehow, each hand was a hand on a quid. During the night the mood shuffled and the changes entered quietly. 'I won't drink watered wine.' A body is sixty per cent water, sixty in the room are nude, none knowing what would emerge, sitting back or sleeping, though Frank proposed to stay warm this winter. Because of the shape and weight of their bodies the liveliest women undressed for easy money, the daughter kept naked and drunk for half an hour.

THE FATHER RAPES HIS DAUGHTER, which is something she shouldn't see. The fellow is knuckling down and getting in further. It is hard behaviour from a man with religious grounding. And he expects his son to turn out really bad. The long-haired boy should marry his own, loose skin-colour conventions corrupt the people. The boy with freckles has breakfast, then a long talk, he is worried about Vietnam and insists on having an open discussion on the decent life. The hard father will pass him in his car. The thing about his manner is that the pivot of him is claustrophobic. The constant contact with children has not brought a sympathetic manner during twelve years of family. His minicar is more important. The muscular man in the football club is ready for jokes about sex. Like the painted angels he renounces the world, except for sex and money. With his ironic neighbours he gives money to the priest and tells his son to learn good manners and agree with Eamonn Andrews.

THE FLORID ADOLESCENT FINALLY BURST OUT, the lid flew off the saintly parent, the hysterical war of nerves more powerfully restless concentrated on total inessentials. Studying the dress of love the biblical teenager sheared his locks, sex was the worst thing really, poking his thumb in Miss Hueth, (but it was an idealistic thumb).

THE PALE BRITISH CITIZEN AND HIS CHARMING FAMILY, family of killers.

WIFE WOULD BE HIS TO HATE. The disappointed love was tears on her cheeks. Her house was unlucky, her child had no money, there was nothing careful in her marriage. She stopped at the end of a sigh. She told her husband to accept it for the moment. He patted the scared girl.

AFTER A TIME HE KNIFED HER IN THE KITCHEN, between the counter and the machine, as the fork water turned dreadful, the noise from the machine as from eight women, trays of dregs of purplish colour full of the whirring fan continually in fever. 'It is the blackcurrant jam which makes a noise five feet wide, it is that which does this, with the little glass of laughter.' The tall woman with the washed-out metal features loved like a knife, the shaped and sloping waitress was peculiarly vicious, her legs got trodden on three times a day. She said she would not sing, but she refilled her lungs 'just in case', her plate of hot water beside her, her sterilised eyes filled with singing, but very softly, with long apprehension. Fatness is like her husband, all his fat had died, her bosom huge, her arms, four of them, were good, elegantly tapered, and she scrubbed floors for friends, ponderously for a penny. She fell in love with ham and flowers, he would slip notes into her salad, she turned her head in regret. Her deep-sea face was too shy to speak in a public park, before the vibrations of summer in fruit dishes replied. The tea is sugared in the lavatory where sexual women slip off for a cigarette on Thursdays, the plate of cakes left on the stairs. Sex behind their hands, deposited in dirty cups, the English elemental, talking tea, all they talk is tea, her voice is dissolving sugar into which she laughs so soft it is difficult to hear or understand.

THE SPRAY OF GRAVEL was delicate to anticipate. The car would not return.

FROM A CRIMINAL LUNATIC SOMEWHERE IN EDINBURGH there are signs that his survey of sexual development in the female knows what it means and determines the sex acts of two thousand people: some of these are symbolic; some make abnormal arrangements; something is wrong with the symbols used by some of them.

YOU CAN MAKE MORE MONEY FROM A GIRL WHO'S IRREPLACEABLE. Twiddle the cumbersome girl and make her spin on a rod. It is easy to make her happy with bits of varnished wood. Most girls leave home shiny and clean, then the fear is melted in, the hellish environment makes them mad. They are quite good looking, endlessly smearing handfuls of clay over their legs till they're black from top to bottom. The bright manager examines seventy-two girls for three weeks and there's no complaint. The red hot girls have gone to America, two thousand are in demand, northern novelties come in teams of four, they can be bought in antique shapes, globular brown, and crumbling tan. The froth flies off into the foreseeable future, silence waits for an answer. Future advance depends on America.

HOUSEWIVES COMPLAIN THROUGHOUT THE UNITED STATES, they can't see the cream in the carton, and the boutiques in New York say the customer's attitude changes. The milk bottle is likely to remain the drab sign, the economic stamp of the machine aesthetic. Resistance is expected to be wiped off in the tragic-looking disposable early stages, but the spread of cups and plates is considered inevitable.

MUCH OF THIS MEAT IS DOG EXCRETA. The housewife puts her fingers in her mouth. This way may end in blindness.

THE DEADLY PURITANISM OF THE CITY OF NEW YORK IS ENRICHED BY TECHNOLOGICAL INTELLECTUALS COMPILING A HISTORY OF LOVE. The architecture was harder to define: spindly forests muffled in snow.

IN THE UNITED STATES, WHEN A MAN HAS COMMITTED HIS FIRST CRIME HE IS MOVED TWO BLOCKS, TO PROTECT SOCIETY. That means that they have left technology and gone human, and these men have been sent into the state of being XYY.

DON'T FORGET YOUR GENES FOR DARK EYES.

You HAVE TO HAVE YOUR FACE PANELS PRESSED, and you learn what shape your face is from the point of view.

WITH POINTED KNIFE CUT MOUTH HALF-WAYS AS SHOWN: open for use: closed for protection.

EACH FACE IS DIVIDED INTO OBLONG PANELS which give an impression that the outer plastic panel belongs to an effeminate male. One of the panels lets down like a trap-door and in a maximum security hospital anything can be inscribed on the outer panel, a circle or a square. The panels arrive with an additional hinge and often an immediate change is made. Like a card-house they are assembled, less than one in two thousand is collapsible. The men and women lie side by side, concealing their physical differences, their behavioural prohibitions. As soon as it is light they display their most striking characteristics and other secrets, faster and faster they move, the old men competing with those of much younger age, and the sort of thing for which they are punished is genetic crime. Jokes are made about the link between brain abnormality and style, and some of the style is very white indeed. It must be done by drugs or something self-exploratory, that is quite clear. As far as we can tell they can never control the symbol, so the treatment is a total waste. After a time there is evident a slight loss of gloss in the personality, from his environment in fact, and various drugs are added. The doctors make various predictions, you can buy their words, they change the signs, fifty guineas is best, it is possible that cash is important, its function is found in the bank, where they keep the best symbols.

WE ARE OFFERING CATS TO EVERYONE TO RELIEVE TENSION, a little bit of button is homosexual and happy, happiness is a very good product, the law should be nationalised now and then, pancakes at breakfast remind people of the underground, start the day with urine distilled from tea, it will save you from the liberal arts.

another month gone, you know

THE FADED PEOPLE SPECULATE IN THE COMPLICATED SITUATION FOLLOWING THE DEATH OF RELIGION. Divine possibilities follow death: though the bishop burns with death, the urgent martyr is not persecuted. Nothing is happening for a thousand years. Superb communications go straight to heaven, the neon makes a taller cross in the sky, sixty feet high to gape at for hours. Love your intellect, is practised by the archdeacon. Personality is really Christian, shabby clothes are not baptised, Jesus was crucified and humiliated, as was customary.

THE LOCAL CHURCH WAS ASKING FOR SUBSCRIPTIONS to cut the parish in half. The danger of crossing the road would prevent the people from coming to church. The petitioners have since collected even more solicitors. The old people seemed doubtful, everyone lacked faith in the winter evenings. But the Duke knew exactly, he went back again and again, he was furious. The marvellous man was enormous, he wanted to look at the coats and raincoats, he had the fabulous idea of shopping in shops, he drove down the straight road north. Meanwhile the retired chief constable was more sensible, and the actual committee of powerful names . . .

THE DUKE IS A GOOD SINGER, he plays childish games. He agrees to sing a verse with his tongue, as proof of his sincerity. He's not exactly musical but he's fond of maids listening at the keyhole. Only recently he had been excited. When you're young you need Don Carlos, you've so much energy in the voice. And this maid pouring the yellow wine which she served her master, he knew to be his. Then the unmusical man is buried in the sand. His hands are presented to the wives of committee members to grasp for a secret purpose. The royal family is a new name for God. The allegory costs JJ5o. Not surprisingly they like to get a member of the royal family in dishevelled state of undress, they press a thumb against the stranger's ear. The glass tongue in the royal throat is involved in the ordeal, they add a bite to give more pain over the face, banging the head with a stick, the knock makes contact eight times a year. There is nothing after dinner: a drawn sword dance is given with musical swallowing, the law keeps the ritual going, the dance with daggers is magical, the enthusiastic Duke repels intruders, his hand on the towering masonry gives the sign that is sometimes used as a satisfactory answer, he prepares his equipment to photograph the alcoholic festivities. The distressed widow waits outside with the coffin, her hand closed on the plastic skull. Boys and girls are asked to help by being murdered.

THE SIGNIFICANCE OF THEIR SACRIFICE he saw, as his forefathers did in their time. He visited the town when a boy went to war, and photographed his history. When a girl married, he made the boys march round. There were some who claimed they had seen him running in a circle and saluting, and the girls recalled the inflicted shame as they curtseyed. He recorded these events which are visible today and still surviving. The war was remembered in church on Sundays although it was not pleasant. It seemed to be a town where everybody was as servile as the stabilising mechanism built into them, the population appeared to possess a surface which forbade collapse by refusing to be cut off from the surrounding area. The Duke would not permit any rapid movement from the rural areas, because of the atrocious roads. The one woman who used to delight him, was gone, turning her bottom towards the dead. And now the war had started, the infants were thrown in the river. These bereavements were described in words and pictures for ever. One mother made the photographic detail extremely difficult because her child had drowned in the pond and she never turned her head without bitterness.

THE FILM is balanced into the sun of course, the tricky picture is useful to lighten the day. The pleasant shadows speed around the sun, the royal face is made very gentle as the colours change. The bright rim is slow round the auburn outline, the rich colour tends to blue failure, the artificial day gives orange shoulders, the yellow film creates cold eyes, the sunset is for future use as the tree moves further away before the flash reaches it.

THE YOUNG HAVE BEEN EATING HIM for thirty-seven years. Gazing through binoculars at girls in big beach clothes, the brightest beach of red women, the red globe golden love, the female slap across the face, as the man in the brass cage took pictures.

HIS BEAUTIFUL CANVAS YACHTS are involved in the texture of royal living, the sloping line of a boat against a wind that has come wandering from America and the Cape. The concept of an hour, a gale. (The high wind chasing the miles of sea, blowing the Atlantic into a hole, a murdered man on a windwrecked ship, under the water of the smashed ocean, the slashed cap turns green.) But I never saw these craft in vicious waters. He is lucky to have money. Sometimes he collects eggs, or the birds themselves.

HE PHOTOGRAPHED THE QUEEN, sitting astride her horse by moonlight, standing in a crater on her personal birthday. There had been an emergency on the recommendation of the Prime Minister. The Household Cavalry were to be activated immediately, the armoured brigade took readings from strained gauges as she went on: 'My troops were pleasing from the start . . .' Isn't she elderly? You know that she is. She appeared to be affected by the glare of sunlight, she came to rest gently and did not tilt, she was laying the firm foundations for sound, permanent improvement. She had been in Hansard several times. She slithered four hundred yards on her belly before walking into a trap set by security police. 'Who suffers during a period of inflation? Isn't it the Queen? You know that it is.' Owing to the weakening influence of radical politics poverty no longer ranked for tax relief. From tax surplus the twenty-five killed in India's cyclone were to be equipped with new clothing and a plastic digging device. The emergency resolution swept the Eastern states. Asked if she would take into her home two boys trying on new jackets, she replied: 'It is a matter of fear. I am married, with a daughter and a son, I live in St Paul's Road, Staines. Should I fear Allah? I phone the police. I phone for the ambulance. I cover the face with my handkerchief.' Eight men, protesting that they were 'cooped up', (their identity was known), had helped to murder with a 0.22 rifle. And cash had been taken from the royal house. Thus the boiled housewife watched her darker masters. She knew she would get food, in case of Russian attack. And when the boy's imprisonment was signalled from across the river, and his green pullover disappeared in Vietnam, she was found, passionately lying in her walled garden.

THE END OF NATURE IS IN ENGLAND, the innocent magazines are faded, drowned in money in two years' time.

THE LEADER OF THE HOUSE OF LORDS IS happy and fulfilled, he doesn't like plain girls, he has six children, 'I feel everyone can become beautiful. The truth is I'm tied to the physical life like Barbra Streisand. I have a mental picture of dolls at the age of seventeen. I don't have to feel them. I know what they're like. Fulfilled or unfulfilled I find some people terribly romantic. Mrs Kennedy is exactly the same. You should do something creative to express your fantasy. I fix my mind on the plump seventeen, the wicked idea of women. I just sit back happy I'm not married. I imagine myself close to my three daughters, looking at them being born, the eldest is growing old, I see wrinkles, the feminine thing is terribly pretty, I keep thinking actually that the world is frightfully important. One of the nicest things in the dark is someone to love at a party.'

NINETY YEARS AFTER, the statue of Victoria outside the Empire, bears no insignia of her own.

THE SCENERY IN LONDON will lead to the glorious society, but saddened by the disembowelled future a hundred gathered for trouble outside a church. A man is placed in front of the world. A loud-speaker released energy. The honoured heroes stood in a circle, anyone can join the nonsense. The sparrow had heard it before. The paper slogan is revolutionary. People dislike the nose and coat, a finger points at something. The answer is faith-healing every Saturday morning. The speaker receives a directive issued by God, but he cannot face ridicule. Jesus travelled overnight to Maida Vale, spent some nights in Fulham. He wanted to know the way to become the most loved person on earth.

THE SUBURBAN CINEMA CHRIST WAS THERE, spending a week in Britain, preaching at the Albert Hall because Billy Graham was in bed with 'flu. They were boys together, they fell in love, pointing his finger at Mary, going bang bang, it's war. The spiritual scum lead others to the Lord while Billy and Mary spent six months in the States. Then he rang up from Birmingham and asked the people to go on a crusade. He decided he needed an organisation in October, professionals to work at it. Billy was looking for businessmen, (his chunky cardigan cost four hundred pounds), his relations were scattered round the country working for the Lord at reduced rate. The Lord told him to marry a young American girl, and he went away on a youth night with Betty Lou and her psychedelic rhythm while his transcendental wife was missing.

THE PARSON IS SPECTACULAR at the age of twenty-five, feeling unconventional, different from other people because there are books in his house, roaring loudly round the whole town most Saturday afternoons passionately during the period of self-doubt. 'It's worthwhile once a year keeping in touch with people. Mrs Davey helped me come to Christ.' He had a nice car, a wonderful gift. He looks like a lady from the Church. 'A man dies and the funeral at home is handsome, rather a delicate service, a friend and I barge into the room with various people, the wife's face prematurely frightened white, I think that's marvellous. You pray to God for the novelist's ideal, and that includes sex if you want a bit of ass, that's the advantage of being a bishop.'

DOWN IN THE GARDEN THE BISHOP IS FEEDING THE RADICAL THINKING EMANATING FROM HIS FAN-TAIL DOVES. He admires the gardener bent with the courage of the people, trying to make the flower-beds into the gospel. Digging it up, people can understand, the work of some remains in the field, with the muted elegance of a barrister. 'Rich people do the best work, the early Victorians knew where they stood.' Despite the growth of creeper inside his house, the walls are hung with new opportunities. 3,000 for the reform of gambling, an undisclosed figure for the treatment of alcoholics and miscellaneous repairs. All the influences make the bishopric sound. His two uncles think he is a good bishop. 'I think my father was at Eton.' With parish tins of Coca-Cola he is repairing lives. There is no more room for improvement. Both daughters are pleased. His wife pays the price.

THE BEAUTIFUL BISHOP WAS ONE OF THE FIRST PEOPLE TO CRAM THREE SECRETARIES INTO ONE DAY, he showed me two himself, he had one every hour on the half-hour, his day off each week is spent at the House of Lords. His taste shows right through the red ceiling, his Persian girl is speaking: 'What's the use of passionate Christians? Very effective, bare against a wall.' 'One has a desire for love like raw meat. In the Christian face the missing teeth are symbols of privilege.'

TOTAL STRANGERS PLAY THE PIANO TO MAKE HIM SMILE. He glanced down, embarrassed by it. 'This bit of upbringing of mine.' The munch menu sounded awful if you put it into words. The bishop's lobster was uninhibited, he had a capacity for close-knit camaraderie. 'Swiss trains are clean like good church people.' He was preaching something cheaper, he took the service of England. 'It's not just a matter of talking to the wife, you know,' discussing a clergyman tortured by the people.

MOST PEOPLE WILL CLAIM TO BE PEOPLE, USUALLY.

THE CHOIR SINGS OF COMMUNISM, half a lovely hymn about a Rumanian Dean who speaks the language of theological literature. The priests are rational enough, but what they said turned out inconvenient while the political climate is changing.

reason for change	this is bad luck
Britain in front	swop roles
how long?	in Greece
I understand	and now in Zanzibar

THE BRITISH COUNCIL IS A REMARKABLE SURVIVAL OF INTELLIGENT EYES, their action is prescribed by the trim beard. The classical voice knows how many booklets we sell to the gorgeous children of believing families, and the number placed out of sight behind the screen.

AFRICA IS OUT OF LAWFUL REASON. The jungle is allowed to the inhabitants. It offers the maximum wind which blows and gathers the immense momentum of the years across hundreds of slow and hesitant tortures. There are reasons for the action, and for the reactions to it. Careful information is collected from the muddled nations. Nationalism is advertised under pressure, the sunless hothouse of separate slogans. The motor vehicle is put in prison. The flag flies over the trees.

THE PRIME MINISTER IS UNCERTAIN IN THE SENSE THAT HE WAS TAKEN OVER BY THE ARMY TODAY. The police and terrorists are forming a government. Independence is what you want, in January the war is on here, the liberation will be three weeks ago. Lady reporters patrol the streets, the radio men moved in, neither group wishes to fear the other, the reputation for being terrorist does not last long. 'We don't demand release of prisoners.' The troops help the existing government to resign for a fortnight. No return to rule is planned.

ECONOMIC OBSCENITY WAS SUPPORTED BY THE PEOPLE, the aim was a few dollars' worth of inflation. The police were certain to win, the army occupied the streets in total silence and steadiness, the minority died of cold.

THE OPPOSITION SUPPORTS THE MOVE. 'That's the guy to shoot from the top.' His ambition worried them. Everyone was shot on schedule, for successive numbers of hours, with white face staring in the evening, the daylight smashing into the face suffocated with tremendous energy. The brown prime minister stoops in spectacles, shoulders point straight at his rival, now they can see his voice is not questioned. With multi-technical tricks of tightness he survives the battle, he controls the road himself, he bellows his word, he cows the complicated men with his energy and presence.

WITH BLISSFUL SUB-MACHINE GUNS DRAWN IN FREEDOM, seven ministers stood in dreadful white paper. The fortress was fitted with nails, the dungeon sound of public occasion, the trumpets dripping and flat, fireworks floundering. The casualties were promoted too, by ladies in mournful gaiters, five women specimens of monster, their length and breadth offended. Coloured ribbons were used for decoration by the heroes marching past, the grey-green distant future overhead.

MILITARY AIRCRAFT EMBRACE EACH OTHER. The war dead do not hit back, they are received in soil, riddled with hail.

CAN WE SALVAGE ANYTHING? Is there anything to be learnt?

ROMANTIC MUDDLE, ROMANTIC CREATIVITY. Are we going to survive in some way? Numbers increasing steadily, decade by decade, people are leaking, these are crises. Forgive me, but I do not think that this is even half true, even of the smallest of them, the vehicle of community: the family. Some sort of social and political fragmentation, some sort of dissolution sooner than you anticipate. Families are falling apart, falling away from the natural pattern, the intimate parental relationship.

CHILDREN ARE NOT SUPPOSED TO POSSESS SOULS. Nonetheless, their fondness for someone's face can be unpleasant.

INVITED TO LUNCH WITH HER FATHER. On the day of the fresh start, the girl in the home, surrounded by babies, waiting, like the end of a term. On the other hand, when the father of the girl said, 'What do you do, then?', surprisingly, she said she liked knitting. She talked like a girl, that is to say. She said she was studying for her 0-levels, when he gave her a good talking to. She had one eye on the television set and one on the baby. And when her father arrived to see his grand-daughter he waited for his baby to explain exactly what the position was, her ear cocked for the telephone ring. As he asked her if she was glad the child had been born, he was naturally apprehensive when she said, 'Could be,' and how could he be informed on what concerned her? When he asked to see the baby, she retorted: 'Her first sight shall be her own home.' Her expression most serious, she could not change as he could not, and most of the time she did not know who he was. They could not meet. 'Would you expect me to look agreeably surprised?' he asked her. In the home he would not leave her alone, she was one of his girls, one of three. She did not like to be called his baby, she wanted to be out, like an appendix is out. He had been using her for a purpose, four weeks ago he had invited her back to his house, she had promised to come at the end of the week because she knew this would shock him. For a year now she had lived in town, she had taken her stand. Though she missed her favourite pop programmes, she confessed that there were three men involved. 'Unfortunately,' she added on a rare occasion, 'I'll be away for much longer than that,' when her father charged her with having intercourse with them and they were sent to prison. Yet she was not the first girl to have a baby standing in the park, and equally it was not her fault they were sent to prison.

THE GREY LIGHT ON THE LAWN, her relations dreaming in the afternoon, her friends slowly and happily following what was happening to her baby.

THE BABY WAS SICK IN THE GLASS, the awful young was sturdy, pale-coloured, concerned about her teeth she was. Her hand grins and folds her lip, she can't say sorry, her top teeth stuck in food.

PEOPLE LOVE A BABY. Little babies are most painful, they have to be looked at all the time. The woman-child in her behaviour developed despairs, the mother underlies her silence, sitting and stroking her, the exact opposite of her sexual feelings, a highly unpleasant physical sensation.

THE BABY-SITTING BISHOP HAS A FUR HAT, he coughs in the face of the baby, he is working for the first time in his life, blowing the layer of dirt from the wall. 'I don't know how people can live in this way,' he says hungrily. Holy men must eat. He is plumper than the child.

THE PREGNANT THREE-YEAR-OLD IS HURLED AGAINST THE WALL, a baboon is strapped in a bus, the corpse of a small child shows restraint. A different type of injury is sustained. An unborn baby is better than nothing. The impact breaks a bone. According to the sex of foam rubber the fair passenger with the firm moulding of her outer skin reproduces what happens every night, the flesh is needed for discovering why.

HER BOYFRIEND'S HEART WAS GOING BLUE, he couldn't stop smiling, dieting on fruit in Woolworths. Two policemen in pink shirts sat together, asked him how he'd saved £15. 'It's nice to have some guineas around.' 'We only want to talk to you.' With lots of love and other things in his pockets.

A COMPLETELY NEW THEORY OF BREEDING AND IMPROVING CHILDREN: a prototype of the high-speed youngster, avoiding the discomfort of a failed education. Radically new humanity needs a four-wheeled drive, a youth-control system with the zig-zag child encased in plastic. We should not underrate them. The lateral oscillations, the minimal aspirations of children at high speed, should improve the youngsters early in their lives. The soup served in schools is stagnant and ineffective, the signal received by the school which has lost its vital tension is proportional to its failure and social inferiority. Machines shorten the future. He talks of libraries in supermarkets presenting information on cuts of meat. Living industrial processes which customers can cash, the electronic transfer of the child by qualified technicians. Transfer should be orientated towards group acceptability, developed in the future to give fully automatic control. This would need entirely new suburbs with good domestic managers who would be kept largely separate from the existing system, with jazzed up hoverpads supported by middle-class invention, with mothers and fathers of similar shape becoming less motivated but inherently capable when told the state of the signals ahead where there might be advantages in individual success.

BOYHOOD IS SPENT WITH CONSENTING ADULTS IN PRIVATE IN THE WEST END ON SUNDAY. Life changed at the fall of night, the ugly suits transformed each time, red sweat men, small boys happening.

THE TALL AND SLENDER FORMER NAVAL PERSON, friend of the Duke of Windsor, belies his years. An enthusiast, he sends a cheerful message to his shareholders this morning.

UNTIL THE CORONATION EGG IS KILLED BY WORKMEN, THE GREEN AND GOLD SOCIETY WILL SURVIVE. The Vice-Admiral likes boiled sweets, the Duke and Duchess give each other presents, the medieval icon is sold in a shop, the Bond Street shop is closed to the Bolshevik revolution, the ladies of the family look delicious, art has peculiar virtue, the simpler objects are moved about, an ornament costs six shillings.

BLACK SEASCAPE TWELVE THOUSAND POUNDS.

A REPROACH TO ABSTRACT EXPRESSIONISM, Euclidian abyss, I move to the edge, and the edge has a yellow edge. It should have ended where the dark part comes.

HER INTEREST IN ART IS GOING BADLY. She makes visits to London with her brother. 'I am always on the look-out for a genius, and in London we found, in fact, a pretty painter in a fashionable jacket.'

UNUSED TO WORK, HE WAS SHORT OF TIME. A painter over thirty, he had moved in circles for years. He looked at his brushes and they did not speak, he embraced the sea-mask of the young. He was not prepared to dirty his hands after lunch. At the back of the white canvas the trickle of oil showed like a bomb. His iniquity is in the top price bracket. 'Dylan Thomas was an especially close friend, but business is more my thing.' He knew lots of lovely people with very blue eyes bounding everywhere. The soft arms and chest greet everybody with the usual motto, his business was photography at the moment, as the hand went to the brow. The same business, art business, moving around, giving advice, 'I don't care what you say, life is good.' In the places to which he was taken he would say almost anything provided the results satisfied. In London, for instance, he protested that the room was full of Tudor socks and that really reminded him of old times. He was embarrassing when trailing after the Queen like a commercial traveller, he complained loudly in Chicago for three months. He loved things like that. His reputation was for being pretty silly, though he always said he would be called charming, 'After I'm dead.'

THE PHOTOGRAPHER LOVED THE PRINCESS well enough to make a perspicacious move: he tied one hand firmly under her chin, to alleviate feelings of guilt. 'Taking off her clothes is a moral dilemma, isn't it?' Now she is setting off for St Petersburg, and setting up business in such places as Monte Carlo and Nice, where, it turned out, the shops were not quite good enough.

ON THE RIVIERA, the wolfish tone is rewarded with success each year. The rich live in nylon socks and shirts beyond the dim white bay. The police play football close to the big hotels. The world of art suddenly turns over, the tasteful semi-abstract simply exists in the aimless present, enjoyed for a week by those who discovered it earlier. The sun-lovers arrive late, virtue has not anything to do with their lives, these people are subtler and more tempting. The models are looked at and beckoned all night down the obscene pattern of corridors and rooms.

THE PRINCESS DITHERED IN ALL THE EXCITING WAYS: the affluent American bosom in private hands, the new experience, green cuisine in a private garden, the combination of revealing French and Tahiti grey, the pretence of eating a bare man, the clever diet of morsels of meat throughout the year.

TOO INTELLIGENT TO CLAIM SCOTTISH ANCESTRY, she lived with the problem of identity, privately. Coming back on the accelerating train, looking back at the Queen in the north, risking money extremely seriously, she had set foot on the world. The humiliating week did not trouble her much. Whenever she got the chance she superbly lowered her eyes and saw herself rising in the morning for the service of the world.

IN THE ROOM IN THE CENTRE THEY SOLD SALMON, the pink pool exquisite with eggs and cream served with coloured spotlight played on the arms with cucumber and cream on parts of the body, the different twinkle on the wall, blue and red philosophy joined in the brighter whiter production.

THE DESIGNER IS PAINTED BRIGHT RED where possible, he is gently raised above floor level and placed on a lavish sofa, he is completely spoilt in the centre of the room. His furniture of suede is unlike suede, the suede ceiling is his inspiration. He wears his clothes in his room, an elderly girl strokes him admiringly, 'I like to adore him,' he numbers his women, he reels off the list. The ladies enjoy his private life, a cup of tea every three years, perhaps a bit different on Tuesday nights, he uses his mother, he invited his mother quite often, she were a right bore.

THE PRINCESS SWITCHED TO HER OSTEOPATH, the devoted blue eyes were dotty, the giggling waiting in the curious room. 'I get up and stand on the carpet. You need to feel vulnerable.' Eating her fish humbly enough.

IN THE CAFE WITH GREY MIDNIGHT GLASSES, the customers found fault with the length of the tables. The waitress turned round and tugged at the table-cloth, the coffee turned sour. For two hours the crowd shouted, a police officer questioned the people, the important colonel whose hair was short kept his temper because of his beard. The policeman said he believed his colleagues had a sense of humour: 'Every day the bald colonel congratulates me and gives me money.' The colonel said the cracked face of the academic type was his favourite political prisoner, while the man with his hair down the street was put on trial for begging. The gentle waitress stayed in the coffee shop till late at night. The colonel said artists were absurd, committees were suspicion centres, and 'Money is more beautiful than poets.' The minister in charge of the souls of the youth said these sentiments were unacceptable, the colonel had acted without advice, the police should not have acted at all. 'The Christian conscience is the first and greatest aim of all old soldiers. Men give their blood this year to the General in good faith. The rising price of lamb is a measure of the value of the nation.' An American journalist had caused the trouble. To the police he admitted he was wrong. All children agreed that rising prices were lovable, it was precisely the beards that upset the youth movement dedicated to the regime. The need for clothes was created by communism, few people could avoid giving offence. The Government cancelled the red plot, the demand for meat was bloodthirsty and boring, the details of life were not hygienic, the weirdies wrote circulars against the reds, the church was without serious faults, the red representatives were unable to run the country, the army did not deprive the army of its pay, the blows on the side of the head did not look so bad.

eeeeeeeeeeeeee   but surely

eeeeeeeeee surely
eeeeeeeeee we need help
eeeeeeeeeeee the nature of relief work
eeeeeeeeee is non-political
various problems try if you can
of groups who liaise with me
can help first step is write
a letter has been letters again is what we do
sent this is a good time
rapid growth of the move-
ment at Christmas time
in our minds you can't do these things
too much some have done it
if you are set on it teach-ins and debates
he defined the need combine
the point is the cost

THE MIDDLE-CLASS LUNCH is ordered for visitors, the lean man keeps in tune with an infinitely friendly Indian. The players take time to prepare the game. Famine was the subject of meditation by the gay family in the garden. The spiritual leader's laugh was startling, most people appeared at his lotus feet, thousands thought it natural to respond. 'Much as I disapprove of the stock exchange I do admire the market reports.' Booming oil called Yogi, the advertised discussion lasted two years. George Harrison was stained deep maroon, dicing vegetables with surprising vigour. 'Some people don't want to sit pleasantly, and somebody ought to be thinking about that.' Ladies moved in groups, newspapers described a man with beard and jeans, the woman exposed in glory, her sandalled feet manoeuvring, pale skin, crude film, it was all right, the couple were discussed, she attached herself with the originality of an artist, to something foreign, with mood of abandoned humiliation. How many males sat on the brick floor? To teach nothing?

'YOU NEEDED THAT DID YOU?' 'Yes, a sort of pre-death emphasis on sleep.'

told die four weeks unless find thousand pounds depriving someone else seems terrible because the choice of live or die unreal the choice stop the respirator leave to chance oh no oh no cannot switch back natural heart perhaps switch off heart will never take off

THE PHILOSOPHER IN HOSPITAL showed signs of an actor's impatience. He began to shoot questions sternly, making use of rifles and pistols: 'Are you sure you have studied Marx?' His padded luxury women had phenomenal bottoms, his best friends had waited for a decade, crippled by the stiff-necked male, for him to be crucified by bad treatment during the course of an afternoon. Now he found it difficult to question, over and over again, the heavy bed piled with pillows. He paid money to the hospital staff, expecting to be chucked out for singing insulting songs. They sold him seven nurses with one lavatory each. His lungs depended on the murderous reality of the seven horse power petrol engine. The ugly lung was made of iron, it stared heavy with indifference. The shaved head caught in the black scarf smiled daily, the iron tried to imitate the mouth. He kept trying to live in simplicity, to adopt the cult of reason. He wanted to throw the dart board at the flamboyant bishop fool enough to comfort him. Steady of hand and drinking to the end, he left three thousand pounds to an anonymous research foundation.

WATCHING PEOPLE DIE IS A VALUABLE EXPERIENCE, the electric disorder in the chest deflects the pen on the graph.

WE STAYED AT HOME LIKE KIDS, in the stretched arm of exhaustion in August. Father had one day left. He asked about his heart. The doctors told him he didn't have one (slicing salami in various ways).

I GAVE THE NAME WHICH I THOUGHT I WAS. She broke the news. They said there were twins and I was the girl. They advised me to write to the Salvation Army for fifteen years. He put his arm round me and said, 'Hello Glad.'

THE PASTEL-COLOURED ORPHAN looked demure as she reported that there was nothing to it, yet she was muted in the sort of dismal dirty yellow brick hospital that afternoon, coming downstairs, her heart was shut away. 'I'd like you to come and see the piece of cake, it's the kind you see on advertisements, it's on the table in the sitting-room,' she handed him a plate. The calendar stayed on the wall and before lunch they had a glass of water while the young mother with the wedding ring described the details. He was asking what brought her to it, from the physical point of view, when the police reported that the muscles were not tightened yet. The boundaries of irony were reached when the father discovered the child hiding under the table and the naughty girl spent four hours alone in her room before she crept down with hysteria. 'A boyfriend twice your age is understandable, but afterwards, what did you do?' 'I went out and left my baby in the snow,' scribbling in an exercise book the name of her adored one. The matron lifted the baby down, highly-coloured teeth clucking scarlet in her blouse, carrying the carry-cot downstairs with messages to Romeo and the Rolling Stones.

VICTORIA ROAD HAD ALL THE GLAMOUR. Outside No. 66, advertising a drinking licence, the electric light bulbs were running round like a dance floor in Rome. Luck gradually turned and changed the place into a popular basement worth five thousand pounds. The owners were rightly proud, the previous owners had not known their business. The dancers thought they were in the sea among the neon lights and patterned flowers and posters that brought a touch of glamour from under the floorboards.

ANONYMOUS LADIES KNOCKED AT THE BOTTOM OF THE ROAD unexpectedly, they arrived over the wall in the backyard, they marked the road with a sign, and soon the car park began to prosper. Others wondered what was happening: 'Anyway . . . I mean . . . you would . . . if you had hit him sudden . . . when everyone was pissed as me . . .' They jumped on the neon waggon and everyone had a good time when the signs went up all over, young people in all the rooms, the voices of well-shaped women stuffed with blue.

THE SHOWER IN THE ROOF IS SCALDING THE GROWING GIRLS. The flexible bottom is happiest. Anal control is cheaper, and can be used in the seven different positions, though expertise is needed.

who kept him talking downstairs while I was born in Battersea, he just pulled the mattress back across the bed, I did not like to think about the head and shoulders with legs landing in the bedroom, I dealt with the girl cut off by the bottom of the bed, but at that time Barbara said, "Cor dear, I couldn't move, I just lay there,' and we didn't even know there had been one, I wouldn't like to meet that one, I couldn't say I saw him go, somehow nobody thought, they were very much a happy couple, one had read a book, she had imagination, I got to know her later on, I was too busy working to get involved, I should have been working Sunday when she ran into the room, I couldn't afford it at the time and now I'm not living in opulence, it was in August, it was snowing, there was this woman living in sweat in this room, the flats were converted, I got home at one o'clock, the upstairs flat believed in ghosts, the house retained its turrets, and I walked in and there she was, shaking, on the Monday Barbara left and I'm a bit worried that she'll come back along the tree-lined drive like a nervous leaf. I could get her back by telling everyone and this is what I'd say, 'All right Mrs Martwell? Have you seen a ghost?', she said he was living in her room, it was white, no eyes or mouth, I thought it must be Barbara who lived in the three-room flat on the first floor, until she showed me exactly where she saw it the second time, when she got up and put on her imagined things. Nobody was told that, when they rented the two-room flat, while she kept walking round the bed, with glasses on to get a better look, she had a laugh like no one, not even her mother, but the flat on the same floor was where, nothing of course had really

THE EXACT OOF OF THE HIDEOUS THUMP
(exultant thump)
The bride cried in fright
Uncomfortable in her mind
Went very quietly with the officer to the Swedish ship

THE CLOCK STRUCK TWO DEAD. There were trees over-run with dead ground, with the statue of a hotel, a patch of dead shaken with comfort. Two young women rediscovered vegetables, the shape and taste of a pear.

THE WOMAN WHO DIED WITH ALL THOSE EARRINGS ON, her father owned a helmet that would break a wall, he thought he would lean on her neck with the helmet and make her die, he was fearless till he was seventy when he closed that winter, she could not believe it had happened in London as fast as that. Spring came and she touched the wall with her lips, talking continuously in public, this was the thing that caused her spinal injury, the terrific pressure for three years hitting the spine at the top, killed by a fallacy that happened on top of her, the right side over the left side, she knew she would not swing back again, she had to be strong but she was growing old overnight, one leg left out in the rain, agony with boys 'across her path, she showed the strain when her arm was set, something grew out of the wood when she smiled and went away against the wall.

IN THE WOOD, NOTHING BUT HOPE, later on destroyed by polluted water which lay in the quiet hollow. The dark pond suffered most, confident beneath the surface, grim size it was, long, smoking, huge eyes covered with green slime, no doubt sewage weighed yellow, industrial yellow, sold to escape the inevitable. The deep had been left so long undisturbed, it grew worse and we had no heritage. The big brown cold came and the long canal was a sad place. Those streams of green will soon be thousands of pounds when he has died years ago under the weight of trying.

WITH AN URGENCY BEGINNING IN DEPTH, the sun's rays got down to where the underwater grip no longer penetrated. Samples of water showed rich plankton pouring into the sea, the chemical navy floated on the surface, the population of slime had broken down, the food nutrients could not spring up. The artificial nations brought aquanauts to analyse the pools. The continents germinated, the theories multiplied. The shallow seas illuminated new fish, the scientists added to the area revealed. The pinch of horror was felt under observation, starvation showed signs of being choked down, empty stomachs the size of Africa going staring mad in the face. Speaking of financial matters: light up the seas and watch the distinguished explorer suspended for one hundred hours in darkness thick with particles of fish, experimental seaweed in the house for fishermen to catch, goats in a steel ball for seven years gradually stifled, investigating manganese and gold.

HOW ESTIMATE THE COST OF WATER? The sea costs sixty-five million. The sea is softened by marriage with pure water, but nature practises thirst in a way that allows water to become a triumph. Huge tracts of rain are bottled for sale in London, they sell the surface concentration of energy in salt and in this focus of nations in one place, a thousand miles of land in the north are brought to disaster. The savage sea has many tastes, the corrosive attack on the kidneys, strangulation by rock. With little rainfall, or several ounces, roughly fifty million tons is too much as the day drenches the northwest. There is no scientific attempt to emulate distillation, for sea water is the source of fresh water, the process is developing, the nations need salt water, and after all, the water instantly vapourises. He can foresee the time when all those people will live in deserts where the water flashes into steam, and they themselves need him to tap the oceans of water for life. Nature parts water a number of times in succession, by simple methods, from stage to stage, at a rate, and at a price.

THE TRUTH is there is a ritual and skill in earning money, but consciousness begins and ends.

IN THE DAMP CAPITAL OF REJUVENATED MEN who make money work, beauty earns money on the King's Road. Sex is sold from a slot by extremely tough women in out of date clothes. The paper skirt is a napkin splashed with pop colours, foreigners are interested in the powerless city, the dress designers argue for a dollar, the increasingly mobile children make life easier.

THE CABINET IS RULED BY THE BUREAUCRATIC MOUSTACHE. The government manoeuvres without dignity, several ministers have insufficient sleep, three hundred guardsmen keep the roads clean, their silk helmets amuse the inhabitants silently. A dark number of officers drink whisky with agile boys, their job is to peel potatoes. The locomotive is considered a great joke, the driver is expected to kneel on the ground, the passengers are carried round a roundabout and each has kisses prepared for him. A narrow shout is heard from the females stretched on trestle tables whose red fingers are curiously shaped.

WE BUY THEM IN LONDON, DIFFERENT SHAPES OF MOUSTACHE, but we don't want them here, dumped in the parlour, painted in yellow stripes to make the people happy.

THE STREET IS AFLOAT, the mild voice of the moustachioed director-general on the platform, all are committed to a weekend awash with free wigs and wild publicity. The technical excitement of attempting to swindle the people came over strongly, especially the unbuttoned chequebooks with enough power to launch an aircraft against the elements.

THE PUBLICITY ALONE WOULD OUTSHINE LAST WEEK'S EPIC, but no one knew how many would pay for the fun of playing soldiers. The high hopes were anchored when neon signs were banned at night. The skilled man hours jostled to be last to take the risk in the interests of progress. £100 a day, asking and getting the story of the wives, and a few others who'd been missing for three days.

THE STREET PHOTOGRAPHER IN A DOUBLE BED, eating chips magnificently on the second day of the season. He slept like a thousand pounds, he did not seem to be accompanied by relatives, he was eight thousand friends with everyone, he had five teeth to speak of, he slept in a stranger's room for two weekends, and he put the question: 'Which side do you want to know the colour of?'

WHY SHOULD ONE EVER RISE FROM A LONG SEA JOURNEY? No individual decides in fear of his neighbour, to save up for the long journey.

TO THE CATHEDRAL WALLS COME MEN IN RED BECAUSE CHRIST'S BLOOD AND HEART ARE THERE, in the chapel where men and guns enact tragedies, beneath the church. The blood is preserved in the place, in the building he died, the flames died, the word will make them pause. The men for weeks called themselves modern, their error was modern, the old lessons were analysed and elaborated, the crucial experience found between the museum and the tomb. The modern men were fortified by war, the refusal of existence. The famous war was based on the facts of life, the paper conclusion reinforced with concrete. The truth remained in the cellars.

THE ARMOUR-PLATED CATHEDRAL was built in retrospect. Twenty thousand aloetic and catacacious plants were replaced by a cathedral armed with tons of TNT. The church is a strange place, with machine guns in the afternoon. The child is three thousand years old and made of straw, fingers of plaster embroidered with blood. Cathedral arose on the basis of organisation, fifty tons of DDT, the sword of faith, plenty of planning, half a million anti-malaria tablets on an epic scale. The initial scheme was cathedral-warship-orphanage, three in one. Then the military moved in, the war was a hardness in a dry time, the soldiers flocked out there, the tombs were mobbed for a short, uncertain season.

THE CROSS AND NAILS ARE THE FOUNDATIONS OF SOCIETY. Even in London the war helmet is honoured by bishops and magistrates. Jesus was a rich man surrounded by soldiers. The army makes Sunday a holiday. They maintain the normal pattern of slavery in the mines.

THE MOSAIC FLOORS had climbed the shaky dark and the hands in front banged into two eyes in front of him. The reflectors threw light towards the cathedral windows sliding up and down into the darkness, the coloured windows winding over the iron floor. The walls were caught in the copper light and the priest could be felt listening for the signal from the choir. The weights, the drums, the organ sounds unwound like lust dragging a ladder through the air, steel ribbons leaping like a bell-rope in a tower, the heavy bible shivering in his hand. The signal bell fell twice, bellowing down easily. The caged dark settled itself, the bell came down to give warning sound again, as the people travelled into the void. From clouds of unsafe omens, feeling towards the white-lit door beyond the warmth, the priest ran towards the group arriving. 'They don't need me here, not for any sort of job,' the voice behind the darkness talked for a minute. 'No,' he was told. The walls were padlocked to the iron stove, the oven packed with coal on the floor, Christ's blood danced on the ceiling in the heated chapel ringing with men, the noisy virgin with split bosom and buttocks took her fun at the wall and nobody noticed when her cunt exploded with someone else. The wall of stone laughed louder, shaking the bed, swallowing gin in the hope of the new morality, while a wave of thoughts bore into the bone of his shoulder for a moment in the maze of saints in the rows of tombs below the clouds of glass. The signals in his throat slid down and felt cold, the iron hook divided the vertical planking, the foot fixed by a nail, rotten with netting on the further side, there was the Man whose eyes advised him clumsily, holding him, preventing him from falling into his bowels in the pit, stunned, lost, calmed, he dropped without touching the terrified beams.

THE VOLCANIC RESPONSIBILITY FOR THE CUP IN HIS HAND continuously for nine hours. Unparalleled violence ahead. Immediately the memory erupted. He could see no witness. The priest got out fast. He could see the interior of heaven for four and a half hours. Asleep on the outline of water, he had been climbing the night, with mixtures of gas on the way down, his knees returning. The bishop ordered the man back to town. The priest was determined not to. The following day was raining frustration. He refused to continue. The gas was the danger, hacking his way to God and beyond that.

WHOSE BISHOP HAD WRITTEN BOOKS CALLED HOPE, BECAUSE HE WANTED TO RANK FOURTH IN THE CHURCH. He studied science, biology, politics, religion. He said he would be first in the hierarchy through personality. He will be the new kind that has gone to church without religion, without tradition. The bishop believes in London, he might go there for a change, he is so clever. He speaks of his transformation into a saint, his new tie is tied in knots, he is consecrated, concentrated, unlikely to make allowances, he doesn't think it unkind to be accurate. His Anglican relationship grabs the headlines, the popular controversialist has written about his attitude to his listeners, he has digested them. He is an explorer himself (though at times a stiff upholder of the tight circle) a philosopher and a shooter at life. God comes easiest to those in authority. His mathematics sets the river ablaze. He keeps money in the corner of his room.

THE BISHOP IS SWAYED BY THE ADVANTAGE TO RELIGION as he prays for the soul. Known for his love of gifts of gold and silver, he specialised in furs. They are seen together, vestments and furs, smelling of incense and shame: 'We are judged by our jewellery,' he chooses a ring of value, followed by diamond rings, he complains he has no platinum cuff-links, 'I don't get more than one a month.' His corsets are part of his vocation, a piece of silver was a famous symbol, wedding rings come into his mouth, the diamond eye cashing it. Tar more educational than pictures,' they told of 'knowledge and love of the past' and 'all the usual costs have risen.'

THE BISHOP CANNOT LIVE WITHOUT HIS ACCOUNTANTS WITH HIM. He has twelve. There is no problem they cannot solve. He has paintings of religion, he believes that God is sound and light. In the swimming pool he stays with a quiet nun for thirty-six hours. He built a house for God nearby, it has two beds, a medieval piano, and other statuary. 'The Roman Catholic church is my country that made me rich.' He is free, he has a child by either wife, one is the 'son of a friend.' The child is sustained by an electricity socket most of the time, its father is a human female, a photographer of great kindness. Now it is too late for him to travel a lot, the flight to Cambodia is too expensive, though for years his wife made love in the plane. 'The free man must have somewhere to hang himself. I have my church, my religion has many rooms, hundreds of preoccupations, ten thousand songs. God is Napoleon with flats for his staff stuffed with Greeks. He does impersonations, makes jokes against Himself. He speaks to people with kindness when He has time. He belongs to the public. He cannot be a really bad man.'

THE BEGINNING WAS A RIGIDLY RESPECTABLE SORT OF BOW, a wave of things until one of them turned overwhelmingly religious in front of everyone and said, 'I don't want organised church-going, the people tend to hold the hand of the Pope, he gets upset easily, he must go home to bed.' They had chosen for their modern church a striped and lightweight minister. Their rendezvous was known locally as 'on the other side'. He held that the church was at the crossroads, it should have a slightly modern look. The priest held the hand of a fat woman in pale blue, the congregation kept racing off to the notorious 'strip' where women from brothels wept with stones in their hands, covered with trampled dust, the gambling bishop beside her breasts as they grew, arching them up in play, where the easy boozers glittered and shouted at the girl dancing in the street. A few girls got arrested and screamed through the night, walking home in the morning, singing about freedom. They had trickles of blood on their old brick apartment houses and they were lead by Jimmy Anderson, the long and narrow negro, the man aware of his words, his marble head on a pole.

THE RIOT POLICE had a remarkable car. It was a block away when the police department who show restraint when a call goes out rushed the girl to Jimmy Anderson's. A large negro section of men started out for hospital as she lay in bed with a detective from Puerto Rico. One of the poorest got killed by a fire truck, they walked thin in the fourth area, their rooms filled with people as the order went out in the shocked voice of the negro detective who partitioned an area of the big floor space among the apartment blocks close to the water where the few ripples made waves as he tried to hold her hand. The notice over the door said homicide front. They had their place in there, the police controlled it, they had to stand there as the officer fired a little pistol at the girl's sex, with aggravated assault. Naturally they had to take whatever the cops threw at them, they shot her as she fell near Anderson the tall man, older than his considerable amount of action, going under instead of going in and arresting the floor. Instead he made everybody in the store a partner of Groscinski and they understood what he meant. The ring-leaders were eleven policemen who were told to stand still and keep quiet. A tall member of one squad was a lieutenant, five others had the action covered by the district attorney's right to give notice to quit right there because he was dark-skinned, the duty sergeant and fifty detectives owned squad cars and by special order were allowed to use force with a blue shirt and white buttons. They handled on the average one homicide with one car assigned to the particular Mike Canaletto. The Chief grew a new moustache every two days of the year. 'Violence, Marianette?' said the detective, 'Them are called smoking guns, these problems are crimes that come out of the pathos of the human condition because murder is still a trend plotted by detectives in their heads.' Tragedy, the head kind of opened and fell to the floor, then her Daddy came to the scene or was known to be close to headquarters. There they were marking up on maps the numbers of millions of immigrants when the bullet took the cable out of her heart. Others talked of mysteries with coloured pins from all over the world and they stood still, and her mouth clamped shut and the doc couldn't open it and this was comparatively rare. Some police force cars were manned by maniacs, but most of them were struggling detectives from the burglary unit in the gruesome routine of their work, patrolmen in civilian clothes in the least desirable section of town. The girl's father and both men were almost casual, their coats were plain fawn, waiting in the city to get a foothold on life, they seemed composed. 'What kind of messiness is death?' Agitators are instantly recognisable by the police, almost one third of the total have no hair. 'Did you notice his hair?' The cops are not too nice to them in their vehicles, the big chrome spotlight is on the negro, crime is about to be detected. They are soon dragged into the front passenger seat and the police have a duty to attend with suits and briefcases ready for autopsies at the morgue, white eyes and whispery spectacles, ballpoints in gunbelts, a big yellow wallet for the client. Shrinking into side streets in groups of three, one was killed by lack of care. Police organisation is being perpetually straightened by letting them work against the incidence of alien cultures. Would you know the policeman if you saw him in a night club studying the crime sadistics he is thinking of encouraging for statistical convenience? I think I would.

CASSIUS CLAY was summoned by radio police: his house had been ransacked by ministry officials. The boy with bare knees had attacked the man-made menace of the air force officers. Then a rifle had been found on his floor. 'I was going ten miles for a pigeon shoot. It was not to murder or kill.' Cash had been seized in his house. He was accused of acting as courier for the Russians; he had been paid £80,000 for five Turkish divisions; he had broken into the home of Lord Cornwallis and stolen works of art. He said he was travelling to a new job in Adelaide: 'I am pleasing from the start. I can win by-elections. I can win municipal elections. People like me at the start, but see the end results.' He had been talking too long to expect to be taken seriously. He too had been in Hansard several times. Seated in prison, his blue head, a monk without furniture, the unusual words he tried to understand. His last chance to speak had come in this building. The strong interpreter turned to convict, the forced answer contradicted the first occasion, the clear answers tangled desperately, the ruined skull disappeared, the room became upset, the human form destroyed by hatred.

THE PATTERN OF PROPERTY INSULTS WAR VICTIMS. The attitude is clear. While they put stones on graves the army is in Ethiopia, the anarchists are destroyed by antique insects, the price of food is fifty pounds. Lunacy for ten minutes makes its gesture, the poor use public libraries, the pianist dies in the war, the property remains. Teachers are tortured to death, businessmen remember that cookers with frills inside are big earners, seventeen million puppies buy petrol on a winter morning, the gallons are interested in politics. The TV birthrate continues to rise, the elderly faces are frozen, people have refrigerators in a multi-racial community. *The Times* is engrossed in modernisation, the power station shuts at four, the Final Notice has been undeniably effective.

THE SMALL COUNTRY with the impossible standard of living. The dirt grenades are Chinese. Trucks are revolutionaries. Groups of children are shot without resentment. Life was hard. Most of the men stood side by side in small houses.

IMAGINE THE DIVIDED COUNTRY, thousand-mile-an-hour speed limit, disguised motor cars rip around everywhere. The place is white and two-thirds coloured, a strange place two days away, not too sure where the war is, though street signs tell them. They killed natives with a shovel, the Texan general arranged everything. The happy life was plenty to drink, the rain was taken for granted. He is one of these people lazing around, peasants live like waves as well, they draw a veil over labour, they depend on the slow tide.

THE DEEP JUNGLE REJECTED THE AMERICAN GENERAL who went sailing with varying degrees of force into scores of disasters. Victories were disasters, he was a man to shoot communists, the story started in ancient times. At pistol point on foreign soil, the General who was drunk changed his mind. He drank a couple of thousand whiskies guarded by riflemen who shot dice. The winnings paid for military disappointment, the forests lost the last of the war, the roads were as bad as in London, the up-to-date American weapons missed by an inch. The army has its own reward: recently the fighting is over. This part of the jungle was living a million years ago, a horse stumbled over a shell, and rumours of the quiet rebellion were murmured everywhere. Single grenade thrown from a wall. The military base is sited over a land-mine. Two hundred men smudged the shape of the foreign smile with green food, the wooden plate on their dinner table was very fine, the guns were raw, the mortar bombs weighed sixty pounds, a hundred and seventy families felt like people who had lost more than others.

PATROL BEGINS SQUARE IN THE CHEST. Flare makes the sand white. A man can see his feet through the village. Dog crouches in trash, a can in the hand stops his jaw. Twenty booby traps go silent. The physical end of the mother consisted of contact with a modern American rifle.

my fingers found the painful missile
1969   with my blood xxxxxxxxx in place at last
ambulance driver
wax tableau
kill him
everything grows from war nightmare
x   vx   x   v v
second   I extend my hands again
                              mickey mouse
                              minnie mouse
                              two sweeps of steel
see

what I see	time	h
a young	time	o
xxxxxxxxxxx	time	r
mister	time	r
		o
————		r
scrutiny	time	h
		o
————		r
last swoop of love	time	r
no matter how filthy or ugly her	time was	o
I should have a visored cap		r
AB in this space I smelled resin		
ME		
the		
shot		
which		
skinny		
shot		
cold here		

NEWSPAPERS CONTAIN THE SPIRITS OF DEAD PEOPLE. History has all happened and doesn't matter any more. Geography and history have a running track circling round them. The radiogram proves that nothing is an emergency. After the battle of bits and pieces, watch the piles of stones: the Celts killed strangers cruelly in the gloomy morning, the long worms see their dead when killers are about. The spiritualist radio dabbles in life in the scullery where the use of water is forbidden. The tropical torpedo express train goes cold at eighty miles an hour. The garbled message is brought back dead.

GENERAL WESTMORELAND WAS SEEN AT THE SPRING SHOW OF THE ROYAL HORTICULTURAL SOCIETY YESTERDAY. Heavy bombers again pounded the open rock garden, the valley area, especially the primulas. A variety of weapons, for example, showing superbly flowered specimens, while troops were moving towards the Botanical Gardens .

DEATH ON DIFFICULT TERRAIN (during the monsoon rains the authorities do nothing about the mud), heavy American finger, whispy Chinese guided by peasant. The fat General smelled the soldiers' brothel, the poor place was forgotten, the characters followed one life together, the missing child was denied existence. Whisky in one cubicle was a game to play, the married were regarded as renegade. The General fought for the unmarried daughter, with a week's pay from the United States four times a year. 'When you walk with the commander-in-chief you're twenty feet high.' But the girls were changing fast, the ancient film cautiously showed them the sex life of soldiers with no restriction on their movements. The passion of Chinese girls was very welcome, the serious soldier was rare, the beauty from the good family was guided by her ancestors.

I'M TERRIFIED OF FLYING DOLLS. I torture very young people with machine guns, they get knocked down for licking my face, my eyes fall out of the sky, I've been a cradled child for two years, I've had women in the most difficult situations, they lie down with a couple of guys, I lie down, it's very exclusive, I saw a man one morning full of earth, face covered, one made me laugh, the festooned tree of madness, a custom I understand, the broad back gave cover, there was a threat, the dead lie down and think in Asia behind a curtain, candleburning stars left out all night, a dirty off-white body afraid of the sound in the chest.

THE BLOATING AND DEFORMATION ARE INSANE. A striking and disquieting child, she ceases to be charming. Naked female body depends on feeling close, like a pet. Woman's body might envelop a sizeable lifetime. Suckling babes or lovers are curious in extremes. The beauty of hesitation. Quaint doings in wombs. Objectionable mess, paste of white, associated with depressing vegetation. Men prefer women coated with mud, disguised as pies. Add piss to a tin of mud, (the value of piss). Paint with mud made fluid, slightly wet. I prefer a blonde across a table.

WITH MUD ON HER BIKINI SHE DANCED ON AN ARMY BADGE, standing outside the kitchen done up in fluorescent rayon, tempting the boys to follow her into one of the bars, wrapped in a leather jacket, walking round the stage, some of the guys intrude on the girl doing her bit, sitting over her, they take off the tops of their uniforms, the hottest girl sits with them, a nestful of moneyed Americans, in one particular cafe where passers-by join hands and talk at you for a beer, dollar notes are fifty cents each, driving through every doorway, enjoying chili sauce with hot pickled vegetables eating bags of walnuts at a hundred miles an hour, the sincere man says love you, and the boy whose legs are bad wears his open shirt in high places, the best lays are elongated women in the centre of town, a girl sails out with soldiers naturally, she strips from table to table, soon she's wearing white, slowly the girls are brought back and the throaty man says they're back, bikini's on her way and when she strips off her brothers are waiting for the spectacle.

THE GIRL SHOUTED IMMEDIATELY, excessively high. Her ambition was to live modestly, but for the troops she was not pliant enough. Her mind ceased, her conventional thought was a knife in sensitive areas.

THE TALKATIVE GROUP AGREED ON THE NATURE OF WAR.

NO BREAD.

LOAD THE PLANE WITH BOMBS.

SOMEONE STARED AT THE WOMAN like a rabbit looking beneath a skirt. On that incoherent morning, the rain gently destroyed the fire, it was nowhere. But the chin was broken. She was caught and tried to scramble, screamed and floundered, threatened to yell, choked, said nothing. Some stared at the bomb dropped in the street, the swinging shock of explosion for thirty hours, teeth like dominoes laughing, the sun smashed on the road face down as the slam of a shutter. The fall dulled the pain in the arm, kissed the horse's ears feebly, the broken knee talked nonsense about a bomb, the leg against the tongue in the shaking room shaped like a bundle. The light came from tears which supposed companionship and fell into oblivion. When the eyes opened again to crawl between the closed eyes, the light was too hot, the cracks in the head remained and struggled towards each other. The face rusted into private misery, pulled forward, stroking it. Out of the smiling kettle floating before the staring torch, the steam surprised him. The face in the blanket made noises. I thought I saw the left arm out of order, and it seemed to be, I could not be certain, I followed it to one side, with bread in my hand. The body was in good order, it could run a few yards, the pain casually stopped. I offered food on a comfortless handkerchief, lucky egg on dark blue. Brutality touched their eyes, one after the other raised his head to look into the sky.

TO ESTABLISH CONTACT she stood there, now dead, after the skirt had been raised above her head, because the face meant the dribble at the corner of her mouth, I think it meant the mouth of a dummy, the face thus clothed, female muttering, metamorphosed mother, the boy holding her hand, the family would be in the bag she carried, navel cord wrapped round her throat.

HER EYES MADE A WOUND, they were filled with dark, she located him, digested him. For this reason he continued to bleed for a long time, he looked for her and could not find her. He had good reason to suspect her existence, her proximity, he had good evidence.

ON INTIMATE TERMS WITH HER, the memory zigzagging downwards, not yet a person, taking biscuits from the dead, from the corpse of a shot dog, making a mechanical night of it, the boy is made to walk in his Sunday best, noisily in movement, the heavy burial feels friendly, others gather round, they offer him bonbons, herring, stopped her protest with earth.

HUMANITY IS STRONGEST WHEN IT TEARS YOUR SUIT. Would you like me to be a Communist too?

ASK THE FUSILIERS. The flat I had there was beautiful. But these people here they show resentment against the army. I think they are barmy. We work very hard, you might not see us working. But there is a potential for riots. We are forced to respond. We deserve help. Bayonet is a symbol, of family help.

USE THE BONES OF A DOG as a hunting device. The poor dress as a dog to increase strength.

THEY SWEPT DOWN to dynamite the famous tank. For hours a day they hid there, in the long dark galloping with its long guns, as they cut the veins of the young captain.

THEY WERE HALTED ON THEIR WAY. He fired shots. They are my friends,' pointing at them. If we paralyse the city the bread shops will remain closed. He confirmed that his men made decisions concerning weapons. Fired two shots at a helicopter carrying. Asked for and received assurances. He ordered the hand grenades to be thrown. The second lieutenant ran. Fired six or seven shots. Cutting the officer down.

THE MEN WHO DYNAMITE THE TANK MAKE THEIR OWN COFFIN. They plant explosive in a hole in the ground. They gauge exactly the thickness of the crust of the earth. An error of three or four inches will blow you to pieces.

UNABLE TO GIVE THE NAMES OF THOSE INVOLVED.

THE NEED TO KILL WITHOUT EXPRESSION. What have you to say about war? He said today it is a necessity, though here the country unhappily is often sub-human.

IRRESPONSIBLE BUDDHISTS, hooligans and Communists, inscrutable Buddhists, fanatical Buddhists, shaven-headed, hot-eyed, student-cum-hooligan-cum-Communist, suicidal Buddhist frenzy, suicidal Buddhist fanatics, juvenile riffraff, teenage hooligans, Buddhist extremists, fanatical-suicidal-Communist-orientated-Buddhists riding high wide and ugly on a wave of hoodlum teenagers and Communist-paid fanatics.

YOU HEAR POLYPHONY? On either side the sun performs without anaesthetic. Through the jungle blue 3,000 dreams are playing games with a long pole, the bearded child goes into action, wriggling fish are dumped in the mouth, mutilated mushrooms in an iron pot, twenty-four steps towards salvation. Society lives in mud, the water is not boiled, Stalin is the logical conclusion. The round bottom builds her house, the son of God is an army officer, father wrapped in a blanket listens to the talk of frogs.

THE SOLDIERS IN THE NARROW STREETS kept the people away. The chief of police was paid for his part in the physical murder. The widow shouted at the centuries. The major pointed angrily. The symphony orchestra vanished. The major smiled on the phone.

THE TOWNS AND VILLAGES APPEAR TO BE SPLITTING. There are signs of rebellion. Important persons and papers are strewing money in influential places.

AFTER NINE MONTHS' WAR THEY DO NOT BELIEVE IN BATTLE. Several young men have given up the idea of honour.

THE YOUNG SOLDIER was basically ordinary. His life had been hard labour. The girlfriend was difficult to obtain. Others arranged for him to go into a world in which he could 'survive'. The uncommon negro had an American name, his departure was glamourised. In Vietnam he proceeded North, a deliberate act of immorality. He spent six months on humanitarian grounds. He was strangely affected for nearly a year.

HE CONTINUED UNTIL KILLED DOWN IN THE DARK BY MACHINE GUNS.

A YOUNG MAN RESEMBLES AN INSIGNIFICANT STREET ON HIS DEATHBED, the same when he is ill. The exhausted face has no connection with the plump child. His father was a butcher, with the same badge of office, the son had a red carnation at four and a half, and a hand dipping into the chocolates. The boy in sickness is half in and half out of tragedy. The man is looking at the fourteenth century. And so is the river, telling you something two years later. With him, the bleak land died.

OUR CHILDREN KNOW THAT EARTH IS DEATH, it offers the chance to stand at ten to three. This is what narrative events could not do. The round is seen looking at the world. The bullets have glory angles, they understand the kill. The body works like a newspaper illustration, striking the dead lying on their own. The brave learn from the gesture of doing it now, he learns from words who has not words, the light expands or diminishes it. You can do nothing but watch the reconstruction of the past, the face of reality dips his dreaming hand in dye, the future will not come out of the cupboard. But words are heard through the hive of glass and the paper sculptor does the rest: twenty chisels sharpened by fire, red points in the air. 'It is possible to record the family in the garden in the afternoon, or as a vision in the evening. But I expose them to the day. Compare them with other men's faces. Get the terror in the face. Induce sickness by determination. Fix the effect of those who die. When the mind grows tired show the exciting results of drifting faster than words. You can steal the action from the next man's identity, and make a collection of someone else's words.' This trick led him to the light. He fitted beauty into a wooden box by making glass boxes coated with paper in bright sunlight. Hours were needed to force the glass to print and fix the pattern on to paper. Round the walls of the narrow evening the room would not stop talking, the magic possessed the light, and all that nonsense.

THE ROOM WAS FILLED WITH HEAVY AFTERNOONS AND EVENINGS. It helped to be among nice people, nice furniture, a wardrobe belonging to a friend who had gone back to plumbing when he made the grade. A better job was what he wanted. He had a house, he had a car sometimes at night, a small scarred table beside the window. A packet of tea was his habit. He visited a young lady who seemed to realise that unlike everybody else he was not going away. But his form of heating was not good. And when he lost the gas, she moved out. She could not make the grade after a few weeks of that. The bulb was hitched over the bed, his place was in bed with the light on, maybe there would be a crowd in the drunken house, shouting in the centre of the ceiling, walking round the house again at two in the morning. A well-educated man takes time to get a job, he went back again to try the police but they had gone. At that moment he could not see a way, he wrote to his family and said he didn't want them to see how he lived, he did not like the pressure. It was like when he first arrived, now he could not get out of it. He slept late, then he did not lie in bed any more. He was frightened of sitting in a chair, tried avoiding loneliness in bed, listening to trouble on the radio, pulling himself out, because he could not climb out.

A GOOD PLUMBER IS A THEORIST WHO KNOWS PRECISELY WHAT IS HAPPENING.

HIS TWO COATS WERE CLEANED when the weather was good. He took the bus and leaned out and looked, the weather was bad. His cap and trousers smelled in the bus, he came home to his nephews. Half-way back the cracked boots walked home to the old house. Fivepence was found in a locked drawer, the money was washed in a tub and left for six hours, he put the halfpennies in the bank. The small man read the papers and left them outside once a day. The leg lurched to the doctors when he moved, the ordinary man looked after himself. The local children had no money, a face went back behind the door when he died in the crowd. His house by his own standards was already stones, the man lived on his own. The bitter gate had no visitors, his money inside the house was his own. He had no ability or any other gift. His food was regular, he enjoyed the bag of bones at eleven in the morning. He woke early in the living-room, the parcel of coal on the rug. Three panes of glass were a threat to his independence: he blocked them with board. He could do without a jug of milk, the tea he kept to himself. The postman was a human being, an animal intruder: he pretended he was deaf, refused the contact. The social worker would greet him while he was still alive, the hot meal for so long kept him warm, scraping the uneaten newspaper each night, the last chip in the brown bag saved. The hole in the stairs, the hole he had cut in the back, was filled with nails. He held down the cat till it died. The garden grew into the back room, the white loaf went green, the visitor arrived at irregular intervals. He was allowed a reduction in the old age pension on condition he died.

THE TRAMP COLLAPSED on to the shrinking plate, the meal was eaten elsewhere mournfully under the clerical gaze. The bishop's tone of even texture became more true after dinner, the artificial flavour uncompromisingly modern. The cathedral had a budget to work on, the lawns must be kept smooth, there would need to be room for more cars, we must put the poor on a trolley, watch out for the poor, they talk a lot, we must try harder to be friendly. The bishop himself examines how the place is run, he could not be friendlier, he is exacting, he sees the room in the morning, he kneels on the floor to get it into perspective. 'With these people stick to the simple rules: provide them with food and drink. If the tea is moist and the breakfast sticks to the plate they will not ask for more tea. Let your man have an apple in the cold, a place like this cannot always be warm,' as he retired to the lounge where he attended to his devotions.

THE CARPETING IS DARK BLUE, DOING THINGS TO THE SITTING-ROOM. The curtain of apricot is indulgent. He buys a lot of old records. The formal upstairs room has more than a hundred chairs, an irresistible Gauguin for the first time in the lounge. The formal clock is made of paper. The idea is for the clergy to enjoy what they are doing: they spend a lot of time in the bath. The clerical executive has a face, a book, and a job. He was trained for ten days in four stages, he calls himself executive for money. He enjoys his home, he would attract a wife, he will get one, his business gives him satisfaction. He plays golf, amazed by holes, fits in the occasional game with a good secretary.

BLACK DOTS IN SPARE ROOMS. The sound which fits the bathroom is electric tone. The tapestry is interesting. His teeth made a red spot on the piano. The collection of random notes had different names. Growing up is trying. The sound of the past seems dead. The childish lights are flying full of old music. The crosses on the piano crawl across his face. The grown moustache is dining at eight and will not admit he has changed.

IN THE HOUSE WITH THE NEW ROOF, THE BEAUTY DOLLAR FASCINATES. The private room for writing is used in the morning, the bedroom where the long newspapers sleep, the uncomfortable huge room where the guest in bed is moved on to the long table. There is also in the house a hall called Ceremonial, the pink fish along the glass corridor, the guest in the garden, more rooms, more walls. The marble chef has been removed for grilling the bridal cake. Families have parties on the balcony next door.

we should make really	this is bad luck
tremendous effort	within a month or two
who actually	we don't know
does the asking?	it may be a long time
you would not ask for	we are working all the time
money	
from Scandinavian coun-	to release people
tries	
foundations for example	what he says about

the Christian Council is	being attacked in the streets
trying to send a new pair	is true
of socks	when I wrote
we certainly have it in mind	we have been
groups have independence	constantly in touch with
if you can get the money	United Nations
no not now	we would make
when I was in Rhodesia	words
what was happening was	the basis of help

THE SWINGING DIPLOMATISTS in the evening consume their lying officials. The local women find them afterwards, cold on the banks of the Thames. When they have friends it is either where the river begins to narrow, or in the homes of foreigners. The sticky cakes are quite romantic, the quiet old liqueurs cut the throat, their charm is astronomic. Their exotic dinners are served by window-cleaners and black dressed baby-minders in the triangular market-place. Ripe fruit is rare, the sun shines four miles south, the chic little shops washed down by rain make the pram-pushing girls turn grey. The archbishop broods peacefully in the eighteenth-century bookshop wearing his entire traditional costume with attendant women exposing the knee. The display is organised by the clerical service to glamourise the aristocracy. The park is full of police successfully maintaining the law, the flourishing culture of introverted women serves the needs of the rich. The fringe of professional hair becomes an island, the good reputation is impossible to find, the streets are choked with trousers, as they wash their lawns single-mindedly.

ALMOST EVERYTHING WORKS WITH CHRISTIAN MODERN TELEVISION. A friction if you need it, you lover of peace, though of course, 'Go out and buy it.' A viewer pays taxes on human beings, anti-communist he certainly is, and he wants everything that a human-animal-lover, a joinerof-associations could possibly want. There is no quality he does not possess, there is nothing but that which may be possessed. He has the personality of Indian toys and Vodka, he is everything from Finland, he is costume jewellery faceless and flabby, shrunk heads are the formulae which decorate his mantelpiece, an imitation phallus made from pressed-out plastic, sculpture too light for its bulk, brassieres engraved with hearts, imported camel saddles, experimental goods for consumption per square foot, television messages inexhaustibly obscured by the incessantly alternating image, the slogans which existed at the time of my youth, anything to avoid the rush hour, the express change and credo of the road that runs beneath the family man in major cities, the man of property who seeks the substance that remains. On weather-faded crutches (foam rubber will seduce him) the other will carry his crippled master. He will stay in the suburbs, newsagent and confectioner, the utterly forgotten rusty pram, the child will sigh at the sight of the window-pane, discomfort still exists, the worn-out generation is not easy to find.

THE CITY BELONGS TO THE GO AND GET IT. The bread of the rich enters heaven unerringly.

THE PRETTY WAITRESS FROM THE SPIRITUALIST CHURCH began with the vast eyes of a woman in love and the seven nights a week were in her heart handing out endless happiness. Home is relaxed and jiggling with milk bottles. The morning is shared beneath the window, the left arms of stragglers dance on their hips, speaking of helmets and sizzling chestnuts, frost spilling over a field.

SHE HAS ENGLISH EARS. The swinging young understand an advantage of this kind. For her, London was middle-aged; like men and women, love and death were nasty words. Something bad happens when your body is naked, the French have no modesty, the risky Latin brings new rhythm, Lolita in bed has Anglo-Saxon eyes. The surprising experience unwraps the masculine voice, the workman in blue elastic hugs the gutter, his words are a game that goes on all the time. 'Anyway, it's nice to be freckled and gentle, to make a perfect little whole for oneself, best of all at half-past three vigorously with strong wrists till the pain shows wash your hair that must be very hot and very smooth and very clean and absolutely dry.'

THE THOUGHT WAS BORN IN THE SPACE between the bed and the wall, the wall holding the lamp on the other side of those years looking backwards. The years had been hard enough, shaken by crying, lived in rigour.

TIME TO WAKE. The man slept. The girl laughed in the kitchen. The hand sprang from the shoulders. The ritual razor at the mouth, cut the nostril out, he cut his face. The smell of the day at the door again, thick yellow smile, damp bed. He ate love, the egg across the table, pepper lips, people were not in their room, trees on either side of the earth, their heads touching, curved body escaping, hands hot in the house. The homburg hat stepped into the room, thick friendly men, rich fish. The bed in the second room, the place of business, the girl knew nothing. 'When I give her these.' Fifty photographs of girls and money, he was pleased to make money from the house. He made her hold herself, at six o'clock on holiday this summer. The place, the sheets of green in half an hour, her body in his room, the distance to the mouth, the mirror above the bed. He had loved before. The edge of the bed, legs between sheets, paper money in envelope, girl with comb, the comb tangled the red hair, she had her paper toy, red coat. The door answered her question. There were fifteen chairs and tables in the house, a platform supported her bed, the room had two windows. He lifted her body, his nails hurt her, the quick pain touched her, she could not call out. He heard her cool voice, the mood altered, she did not know it. She had ceased to live years before.

HE IS DEFINITELY IN ENGLAND. I sleep with him each night. He was in hospital in Belgium. He may still be alive. As a balance to these hopes. He has been seen, both in this country and in Europe, without official confirmation.

I THINK I LOVE EVERY THREE YEARS SINCE 1938, a couple of weeks before Christmas. Certain natural things are constant. The heat and the sea. Who was it who said? The smell in the nostrils is not unpleasant: heavy containers of hot meals. Beds and sheets, white and clean. And there are bicycles, collars, memories. For me these places are unchanged. Four hundred miles north: sausages, baked beans, Irish stew surrounded by greens. I saw two monkeys for many reasons shouting their messages non-stop and of course I knew they were saying something else. You can smoke, you can take a room, though in that room I never had a good meal, the plates and walls all gold and red. It's only a small town: winding the clocks is work for a month; you see a rat in your bed. The girls are quite unusual along the main street, wonderful green and blue before sunset. When the lights go off she has to like you. The admiral is lost among the famous ladies of the town.

NO ONE KNOWS TIME like a street girl, she goes by nothing much more than a bell. With their flowers these girls have the pride of passengers on the last train of the night. From the outskirts, going to the West End, what they have to offer passes slowly, studied coldly under the clock. Theatregoers at night give the girls a lift because they are there, a woman, then two more passengers squeezing benefits from need. The drops of sweat on the thigh open their short coats with heavy sighs and smells. They need a scarf round head and neck. There are more than thirty tumbling sisters on benches, with rows of others talking late, but there will be nearly seventy men waiting bleakly, not sure why they are there, for people don't offer a bed at the start. The last business of the night lies draughtily between anemones. She shuffles up in preference, for an hour cramped in trust, the dress drawn over her eyes, her lips moving above knee-level. Dozens of fellows walk beneath a poster at dawn, without tolerable purpose.

THE HOT AND HAPPY THREW STONES which hit the patches of grass in the normal pattern of the town. The frightened woman realised how brave she was, proving to herself that she could save money by living near the iron railway, bent in the anonymity of the sea of suburbs at night. She reached her home in the shower of stones slowly out of the dark and turned left into the avenue where the boys threw pebbles in the dust. Her nimbleness was not impressive, but it was light and she could dodge the bullets. She bent her arms double to make them look strong. In her teeth she concealed gold money. Lorries crowded with Irish shotguns loaded with lead carried her along, bulldozing churches on each side of the street in hostile territory. They walked her with them as the crowd refused to move, synagogues tumbling down the broad street, the grey-faced shock threatening like a cloud on the sun, when the shouting started. Machine guns mounted transparent churches with classical obscenities, in a litter of lenses and films of royalty the technique of shots was feared and hated. Bayonets pressed the middle-class town, seized and dragged a girl over the horizon. Under the bridge they beat her on the easy breast worth less than paper, the heavy oval dressed in sweat, her hair wrapped round her heart, high and rounded white outside the shirt, down the street unleashing love, the pretty girls followed with shame in white, dozens of flimsy hearts bent together, almost together, one of them weeping in blue, the sombre elderly huddled ugly while the football racing young men controlled the dangerous place.

A CHINESE STRUCK IN THE FACE BY A CHAIR had a cut on his face. He refused five men, they frightened him when they came, they started smashing and several Chinese lanterns were destroyed. The blade pierced the left arm raised to defend.

THE BLUE POLICE LIGHT FLASHING was danger to the blazing boys. Like bees and minicab drivers they swarmed downstairs. Oil-stove through the window, others milling around with pillows and blankets from the crowded house. The heat built another fire quickly in the building. They found a man dangling, stressing the terrible disaster, in the city designed to have no fire.

PACKAGES OF NOTES were loaded into a lorry. 'I didn't mean to kill the copper.' Police believe the intruder is still wearing roller skates.

THE COPS CAME SKIPPING IN HERE looking for a fight. I was chatting with these butterflies, the room had several, screwed to my shoes. I'm in bed, on layers of old carpets and rugs which my father didn't wear, and by seven the floor was looking pale with sheets of Perspex. The doctor in a dark suit asked if I was ready to go, because my chest had been known to fail. 'Do you ever have trouble with your boots and socks?' They probed the condition of my brain. I found that lengths of plaster made good clothes, my hands joined together to stop them knocking. I examined my jock-strap in the lavatory, I had to study it before I could get started in the business. When I was overweight I cleaned my trousers with toothpaste in the kitchen and left them drying in the boiler-room for two hours. Marlene gave me a hard hug but I did not acknowledge it, from shyness, as I finished dressing. Finding my watch or car-key, at this time, took me thirty hours, while Marlene said my day was empty. So I spooned more sugar into her, with a nose-inhaler. All sorts of possibilities in tubes were opening up with this pretty long-haired blonde. In an afternoon crowded with nervous managers she'd say, 'Everybody's hobby is running for trains.' She relaxed a little when tired through hunger. The junky actress had sausage and mash for dinner. She cost £21 for the night, or the equivalent in steak and mushrooms. She went to bed with a sauce bottle, she had a stock of eight, she was one of those people who dream of them. But probably not tonight, all the time whispering God Is Good, Jimmy, she had vaseline behind the bone, which almost blocked the passage where the sweat flies up. Tired and half asleep, her husband has nothing to lose. The pair of dark spectators had fed-up expressions and gave little whistling grunts inside the room.

THIS FRIDAY MORNING there will be another murder. It will happen in the kitchen. Throughout the afternoon they watch the pretty wife killed, the long moan from the throat, licking her body, there is no reaction, the people have committed suicide. In our homes the crime is talked about, twelve policemen yield $3,000 profit, there is a note of the fact in their Journal.

BILL AND KITTY HAD A GOOD LAUGH ON THE TOP FLOOR. They would not come down. The wife sat quiet at night, and I imagined her half-way down the stairs, or taking off her shoes in the bath with the water running over. When I went up to the top landing there was never anyone there, only the *Woman's Own* on the fire, the smell of burnt paper in the room. Her husband at the back woke up when I was there one night, and that night pieces of ceiling came down and rested at the bottom of the bed, and Kitty got up and did the Lambeth Walk on the side near the window, it was there we had more laughs than anywhere. Her husband was a radio engineer in a food factory till he washed his hands of her. On his head you could see the hair that used to be there. For two years she had been trying to get rid of it. His head had hair till the rain completely devoured it, and what remained fell into the street. For eight years their home was a hard place for her, and when they moved it was down the road with council officials taking the furniture away. They had never seen anything so funny, it was a funny business. 'Derelict?' Bill said, 'So what?' Their child was not even born, they had no surnames, no bell on the front door six years ago. Their baby was born in the back-yard where the little body was found with eight shillings in the cot.

WHEN ALLOCATING DWELLINGS they were always walking past the children playing in passages, the smile is frightened, eligibility in the official view is three in their own flat if you don't touch them. They stick the children with a woman who lived at the back, the neighbours worried so much, the dreadful place was soon evident, the whole family explained the physical disturbances by the woman upstairs, (the clean door does not mean I love it), the little girl is not as bad as that.

MOST PARENTS TALK TO THEIR CHILDREN USING THIRTY DIFFERENT PHRASES SPOKEN MONOTONOUSLY. Educated verbal parents have a grammatical structure. Baby will feed her doll, then boys as well as dolls. Complexities of consciousness, the earlier pivot is underground. Baby boys look for a dolly they can mount. Many adults are able to do this with a doggie because they have practised with children. They use dolls early on. In Russia it is a good sign when a child grasps a doll. Even butterflies educate baby, their wing utterances in higher colour, deliberate labels, spots and stripes. Daddy barely copes with foreign words a twenty-month-old could understand, speed patterns increase the length of the baby's lip, teaching him to use dirty words more accurately.

A FAMILY OF SEVEN CHILDREN lives for years in a council house. The father is selling them for personal reasons. He gambles on a price of £250,000. Other children are being offered by Knight, Frank and Rutley, the agents for the wife. The remaining thirteen are undernourished and dirty. The father beats the boy who was not sold some time ago. The last four boys are living in the fifteenth century. The price of a girl of eleven is £84.

TWENTY TENANTS who had not paid the rent found their melting apartments unrecognisable in the falling building. Their small brick homes with policemen at the door, the blue lawns moved because of their colour. There were several reasons why the demolition date was fixed for so many years, the time was kept secret from the driving crowd of women. The police found the widow in the violent room, and six who refused to move the following morning. They felt sorry for those defeated men, the bad people thrown from the window, the comfortable furniture broken in the home.

THE REGULATIONS DEMAND TWENTY FOOT COUNCIL OFFICERS IN MASTER BEDROOMS OR IN BEDROOMS ON TOP OF EACH OTHER. Narrow corridors strangle idealistic and progressive projects. Front doors are essential. The Norwegians produce pots of paint for £1,000. The country areas are packed with houses, high quality bathtubs installed in one room create pandemonium at weekends. The builders are playing with our living habits. The weekend skiers need not be consulted about ingenious-space-saving-sleeping-on-the-floor.   The   alternative   is   ribbon development. The garden is guaranteed without soil. The solution to the tricky problem of integrating trees is an owlless wall. Karl Kaspar enjoys his open-air kitchen facing a road of communal doors. The English are apt to glance and grimace at each other, yet privacy is not for nostalgic reasons, it is merely that the peasant house is not accepted by the public.

THE SMALL TOWN WAITED OUTSIDE. When I returned I ran high on stilts with loyalty to the particular house. The warm stone house is handsome, but every house is handsome. The central heating takes your breath away.

After being on the road for years with those other travellers, I faced the long wall of rooted people who could not understand why a few weeks' visit was sufficient. I held my glass and watched the grey community blush when I told them about my five years on my own, as the white chunks of ice in their glasses melted quietly. The ice met the ice, penetrated the house. They invited me to complete the pattern of the thing somewhere else. I explained what I had to do. I would not be invited back. I thought I would feel bored sometimes but I had exciting things to do. The attractive English girl, the physical excitement in the intense cold, the glare of the river. Once she approached me after she had been walking in the snow. The wonderful freshness of her education that morning, the air in her throat, I had forgotten, I didn't know what to say. She too had been away for some time, she got up early and told me how dry the air was in England when she graduated. I had forgotten that there was no need to worry or look at the trees, I told her she reflected the bread left out at night on the kitchen table, I thought this was a new way of telling her to come back. But I forgot the water, it was hot and sticky, I felt her thin dry fingers touch mine and I said goodbye to the hotel for a long time. I was caught driving at a hundred and sixty through an open cemetery, with the trees so tall the dead were delighted. And when the squirrels couldn't see the cars I said we'd meet again, stripped to the waist and moving along the road in October. She didn't believe it, she said she'd known painters mostly, in St John's Wood where the leaves were far more colourful, she had to get home before dark. Her lips were like ripe strawberries, her hair had some blue in it, her head shook among the green sentimentality. She was in a position to earn real money.

THE PUBLICITY VALUE OF ORANGE LIPS. The fast actress is quite depressed. Her hair is a piece of coloured machinery, red on the days of racing, following the season for money. She is planning to enter the big money, the international concentration of Hollywood cash, £1,000 a day indulging my love.

TWO THINGS MADE HER FAMOUS: never having been seen dancing, and never having set foot in America. She compressed within her time with easy grace. When news reached her of her past, being one day read in the papers, she never contradicted any story. She appeared to make her life consistent with her past. Being in the company of men from her home town, she lived in a hotel room with a man older than herself. Though she married the Dutchman, her preference was for the beautiful days of her life with her soldier husband.

NAKED, with the additional aptness of a dark, windowless interior, typical luxury, bathing her mood like a slave whose physical allure was capable, relaxed, contemplative, the picture of erotic economy, exciting despite the ruthless contrast of her technique, the honey-coloured hair dominated the white sheets, the restriction of the curtain made her a victim of tent-like embroidery, the single spurt of her lover of the heavy globes of gold water falling like a quick gasp warm around her neck and arms, after a silence of conscious wine the woman was more than naked, the ice vision exploded softly with ermine and ivory hand, the water falling beside her in the room with other people, her limbs were faintly mad, titillating frankly, the ordinary women sprawling on the floor, the erotic properties of a rich garden, the blown fruit of a wilful body burning in an extraordinary way, teasing in answer to the call of a deliberate dream, emphasising the scent of the past, to have some contact with the bed she is indulging her own life, the lines of the city on the curved body, the natural strand of metal placed round the breasts, the lover of globes of gold, the artificial peacock on the carpet, extravagant clothes, her neck and arms, the daylight actuality of the porcelain dream.

HE PACED FOR A FEW MINUTES AROUND THE WHITE PERIPHERY. The tubular detail watched intently. An empty set has walls and floor. This provides possibilities. There were no chairs. There was a box. What there is is noted down. Make sure of the desk painted brown. The money is placed around the woman, an emotional thing which nobody notices. The hunched and sexy sunlight is raised to the critical point of invisibility, the music is absolute. The self-effacing darling settles into melancholy, aware of the leggy girls assembled quietly in the tropical discotheque caustically labelled 'Heaven'. The cream shirt lies over the chair, the passing fancy munches an apple, the pale brown people seem less natural, the cameraman descends from Heaven to the girls on the schizophrenic set. Art is shuttered throughout. The flapping sheeting is stabilised. The place is empty. The girls fold themselves into beautiful young people who are going to be shot tomorrow. Their postures are velvet. Everybody knows what they will need, but they are sitting talking round the room. In the evening the bored groups without talk, fighting to waste the good idea. Fashion goes with moving and now he is talking with energy to stupid people in the cafe where the girl says personal relationships are so important. Emotions will grow more certain, concentrating intensely sooner or later, but this is the party where everybody is deaf and they get more feeble, they say the same thing. 'I want a decent flat, but where?' The girls discuss their hair, sprawling on the aluminium bed, very interesting, the new morality, but not action. The aristocracy looks at the year of the young: 'I do not really like the youth, but then, when death comes . . .' The great museum scares them.

TALL DEAD MEN IN THE WEST END seems inconceivable. The stranger who died has gone away now.

THE DOCTOR DOING HEART RESEARCH is successful because people like being rinsed inky blue after months of boredom.

HE REMOVED THE LUNG IN NEW YORK.

THE DAMAGED HEART WATCHED THE WAY IN. The medicine barrier breaks down. The injection arrived. The shape of the heart, the foreign substance invades the area, Kasparak was suspected of medical susceptibility, the question blocked the way out of the body, the short-lived minutes did well for a time in the body for six hours. The doctors detected enough to survive the ordinary. Unmarked, undisturbed, he was bombarded by diagnosis of intolerable change.

'IT WAS NOT TRUE TO SAY NOTHING HAD BEEN DONE, we sprayed foam over the burning heart, it was a miracle about what happens to the body.'

THE NUMBER OF TOMBSTONES, as far apart as Japan and Turkestan. Enough to hurt the soul.

MANKIND HOPEFULLY LOOKS FOR ALTERNATIVES. 700,000 possible alternatives worth paying for. The concrete train is green. Paris is a disused monastery. Solitude is roses. The wonder of thought diminishes. The light fades in the complex interaction of insurmountable cupboards.

PEOPLE, USUALLY PROFESSORS, big particle accelerators, have grown by more than the factor of one hundred. The decision to build this or that is a strategic decision dependent on the weather. Today is a little steamy, humidly warm.

RESEARCH INTO GLUE teaches that typewriters can be taught to teach. All available buildings, like the British Museum, are to be dissected to fit the new methods.

TRADITIONAL EYES AND EARS have a sense of touch and infinite electronic patience. Materials with names like muscles hesitate to try automatic learning. The appropriate tone of the fully-computerised voice gets sterner, the book has taste and smell, the do-it-now information moves fast. The most expensive go wrong often. Gradually the impact of the picture is sputnik-shocked, each typewriter is like a long boring bicycle. The old wear earphones to test the new American picture, any number of minor brains are packaged for the market. The latest computer points to the dog and forms a giant. When asked to do something about it, the child does with a pen, the patient voice expresses concern. The striped people are simple gadgets built for experiments, they push the button marked America and their developing doubts are suffocated logically. Miniature power is expensive, but scrambled peanuts in cheaper classrooms will soon be available. The size of the dollar equips five continents, putting together diverse classes, with people and masters arranged in pairs or in groups.

THE SUPERSONIC PARADOX creates chaotic survivors. Poverty is being built. The anti-American car is unthinkable. There are facilities for the child to learn love for money. Frozen food is the start of the bigger car. With high-pressure advertising he sips wine early in the street of addicted children. The very young will grow up to drink from a flask at atomic research centres. The impressive number and poor quality of cars is one thing, second class domestic appliances are another imposed upon the European nation. The English do not need more space in the crowded university, education is free to harness the power of the sea three years after the boy fills in a form. The Americans spend half as much again: the big manager remarks that the government dotes on him. State-owned statistics come fresh or tinned, the cancer advertisement follows the law, a few people drop off the line, prolonged suicide is expected naturally to expend itself one day in seven. The suicide pill is sent through the Post Office. Vietnam is always being worked out. The chaotic intelligent read the leftish weekly for the elite who are non-political. The obscene Americans have money, the straight and personal nut is on TV, Parliament is fitted into slots, freedom is too flowery, only the girls are real when so many things are wrong. The well-paid writer agrees the final figures, the free wife comes in monthly dollops, sex fantastic is accepted as an instrument of state. The girls rely on trade guarantees and in controversial moments produce a polite suppository. Because she is not a virgin the younger girl will be obliged to use the telephone, while the physically violent woman advertises on cheap notepaper: Six guinea syphilis, the western disease.

GIRLS AS RICH AS COWS, SELECTED NAKED, we have photographed them before, like the cereals shown on page twenty. She is established in your house. She is best, lean, thousands recognise her uniqueness. She is fed on fish and left alone. Her breasts may be pointed or rounded, they may be naked, they are there for you to use, six times a day for a few days. It depends on your conscience. Remember the sloppy breast of milk in a dozen colours, I wish she were more serious. As one little girl said: At what age do you acquire your bosom? Any time after ten, there are a few signs, girls are different, they vary. A lot are growing after ten years and three months, which is nice. Another group may develop with maturity, this raises important questions because after about three months they know they will be plagued by bouncing for years: they must be ample. They feed themselves double for growing breasts, the body weight of mother warmth is irreplaceable. Thousands of town girls have been taught by mum. The clean, slightly older girl will slide into a woolly coat. Hours of love-play help development, I have seen them protect their limbs, their underparts. When they grow less shy, they command high prices.

THE MASSAGE PARLOUR IN THE NEWSPAPER OFFICE HAS ITS SHARE OF

LEFT-WING ANIMALS, untidy men with no weapons, apart from eight-inch implements. Highly-political men are breaking the peace. The whitewashed telephone is broken. There are crowds of spies in department stores. Sandbags at night and doors of sliding steel when tension produces a bomb on the tracks. The Eastern Police make an arrest. You will be protected in the building.

THE PRESIDENTIAL PHOTOGRAPH fell with the noise of glass spinning rain on the panes. The prisoner's head thumped in the bath, the electric lamp appeared in the middle of the ceiling, the electrode buried in the skin. The hot weight fell, dull iron, faint sound, the jaw of a cat, cold in his ear, the valve between the inner and outer ear insulated from shock, we hold history, the limp cat tied with rope, the hissing ceased, the size of the earth observed no change. He had not bothered with his sandwiches. The cat's body exposed the jaw, the wound below the head, blue flower, face in air, regular sound of sun, fibres of metal paralysed, down the broad way, metal dust, rubber honey, tubes, seeds, paper, dust.

ANIMAL opened its eyes. The heat was asleep at one o'clock in a stone bath. The slow cold moisture from the floor of the gaol.

THE METAL constantly forced into a torture frame as he dreamed, arrivals forced the doors, everyone said no. Stretching to touch the opposite side, pressing the wounded leg to the door, he heard the voice of a man he knew. The prisoner's indistinct underclothes were moist against each other in the cellar and no one minded how long he had been unconscious. The voice in the doorway felt in his pockets for half an hour, his fingers asleep. The voice stooped in his ear with white-faced questions that followed all night, his feet over a bridge did not reply and he felt the pain in his arm tell the truth. A flared match showed a small cut in the neck, the dim feeling as the hand brought the point of a knife against the flesh.

THE RETIRED POLICEMAN PERCHED ON HIS STOOL. His manner was blank indifference. The gush of blood from the neck was very funny really. He would not worship anything. He had too much chin. He would not burn to death. But he had the dead look in the eye, stereotyped and shocking.

THE PRISONER raised his hand, the insects were taking over, colonising the Virgin Mary, ambushing the white telephone, doing tremendous damage to her ear, the big teeth smiled at the wires hung on the wall, the man with white clothes put his hand to his chin.

AAAAAAAAAAAAAAA
Hanoi
extreme left wing
non-violent?
no name
never stop
we
been arrested in a round up
excuse to repress and silence
pressure from abroad
weeks afterwards
the shooting
hero
in touch with us
released
we have not been able to
say

your earlier mouths
you have to spend money
reduce the number of
prisoners
within the group
torn to pieces
to mention
what has been
going on in Greece
hit us hard
emotionally
I think we have
done a great deal
the figures are
terrifying
do
anything

THE RADIO KEEPS FALLING APART, the life insurance man snaps in two, we don't want war in June, the bored and confused shadows of an army dying of poison of the foot, the stretch of land moved slowly, the land began ten foot thick, the sun travelled at night, the physical problem of history traversed the broken storm across the seas, the personal red line of blood was featureless for three years. The war tax is witness to the casualty figures, the heart ends in the neck.

THE COMMUNIST NECK crumbled coldly, hoping. The chemical cloud was devised to hide what had happened. The confused day was final. Seven million comrades returned to join those who lived in danger, the thickening cloud in North Vietnam followed, searched out the moist feet far down the road. Kicking the noise of the guns, the rain was lame, soaking the three or four others, one carried by men, the lost communist supported by a rope. Breaking his arm in two, the other tied by them, holding his heels uselessly, the arm received a cut, continuous struggling anger below. Few were what they seemed to be. The invaders took a road, and another and another, and reached another bridge and another road and it was not the finish.

TRAPPED IN VIETNAM, the wife's head crinkled green. The name of the murderer stayed on the cross, imprinted in black, coming straight at you, warning you never to attempt to describe the hideous dead which had been there for a very long time.

CROP DESTRUCTION. C.B.W. Law of war. Kinds and degrees of violence. You can defeat your enemy. Lethal. Allow you. Decide ahead of time. You have other types. Attack the mind. Paralysis, type of thing. Discuss in detail. In Geneva, 1925. Britain's own, in Wiltshire. Smokes are thus preferred. Burning eyes. Within seconds. Soldiers driven mad. Both were hurt. They have found eighty pounds of C.S. Riot control. We took away a grey powder. Mask of plastic. That is, C.S. He observed lethal effects. Report of secret industry. Many died. Skin blisters. Asphyxiation.

WILD FLOWERS BEGAN IN THE WAR.

THE LONG GRASS in the evening spoke of smoke, the under-growing thinner sack illuminated the distant potato, the prickly feet appeared in leaves, the floating ice threw expanding blancmange that you could touch.

THE YELLOW-BROWN SKIN OF THE RAILWAY TRACK, river of peaches, I went down the river of boredom to see the upsidedown trees and after passing through towns with smoke, going across country, now I am getting nearer, another patch I've seen before, I can see the advantages of colour, the trees thick with people. It was important that in the summer of 1949 when I graduated, I left that country where the sun caught them colours like the local coloured paper and a few days later I knew I hadn't a chance, when the coloured scenery got its picture in the paper. I sailed around but it did not excite me to pass my driving test, I couldn't understand why I was made to feel exceptional, I wondered why a racing car should make me want to go to Europe with twenty-five other young men! I saw that the trees looked fine in the distance, carbon copies of years earlier when they had looked better than any other. As I drove along things became harder, I began to come close, I could see the leaves fade behind the house with servants, I decided to go back. All this splash of the town left behind and faded out with relatives who were later to die as I was having another look. It was the colour that belonged to death, it was pleasant for a while to be back with the mortician's art, far more interesting than this good country where novelty began to wear thin. I was more touched by something splendid in April, my mother recalled the old feelings of dullness when people drove down-river seeing local people in the sitting-rooms of their houses, and isolation returned. All I wanted was to see the end of winter merging with the breakup of the family. She said get out, and I did. A few more years to see things elsewhere. I got the sense of being back in second-hand England. Again the nostalgia for the lived-in, drab, wooden community.

THE ENGLISH EASTWARD CALM WAS BLUE, the boys at school seemed in summer where cricket was playing Chopin's E flat polonaise, and the lake curved on a different scale too. There the upper half of the sun broke over and over, loudly on the horizon westwards to the forests' tall and bristly haircuts each evening to play illicitly with the magnolia air. Protected against winter they walked in blue, like smaller stones closed in soil. The sheep is deaf, with impaired speech, goats in the care of nuns can feed themselves. The stone neighbours envy the full stomach, the school is overawed by stone, the big man is a great delight. The country house will move slowly, the headmaster has children, the white fur coat will walk around the garden. Acres of stretched orchards and jackets of apple trees stood to applaud the smoke in autumn, the energies of these months in sunshine, their clear hot shoes filled with apple wine. The shrewd captain from the Crimean war met the heavy thick-soled farmer marching round the seasonal fields. Living in winter had taught him why the yeast was stolen from the kitchen.

IN THE LONG DISTANCE THE BOY OF FOURTEEN SHOT A BIRD, the kind he had seen drawn at the top of a pole. He brushed aside the sound of school, shooting at the English air. Now in the sky the target moved, his ability changes with the wind, the strength of the sun did not matter. The boy barely murmurs, the paralysed wings are shot, their broken feathers are refinements that distract. The boy knows the regulations, shooting with care and discipline.

WHEN THE CHILD VISITED LONDON SHE SPENT THE DAY INSIDE A DEAD TREE, she lit a lamp inside the box at the age of twelve. When she left the house she cried when she remembered the chair she had burnt with a match. At lunch her father had a hole in his side, the factory worker was covered with sores, the family helped the husband when he put down his tools to keep his hands warm in winter. Sometimes he stayed away from work to make decorations on the sides of a box, thinking a man was a piece of wood in particular shape.

THE MANUAL LABOURER SANG IN THE CHOIR for the last ten years of his life, he gained a reputation, he was thanked by the church. 'We can't forget that song,' then he turned against his own and was put in a mental hospital where he decided to become a monk.

I NEVER KNEW THE MAN. I understand he actually lived, he worked in his own way, allowed no curve, it had to be clean at the edge. In a sense he knew what was there, he was there, he was illustrating an emotion. The problem was physical, fetishes, images, objects. 'Personality is (a question of) form. I want to do it with nothing (that old stand-by) to have sailed (stretched) so far and not fallen.' His courage was automatic, he didn't escape, he acted through his fears. Offered a head still breathing: 'Were this your head I would draw it.' The bone dictated the line.

HE WAS BORN IN OVERCROWDED SUFFERING SOCIETY FILLED WITH NAMES. With himself central to his thinking, art was good, men evil. This recurring theme, art against evil, he saw figures conscious of themselves in time of crisis, he drew them with the energy of a prophet.

HISTORY WAS TOO TRAGIC. Dostoevsky was an absurd experience in a disused basement organised by students publicly thrown out of college in 1962.

THE GENIUS THREW SCRIBBLES ACROSS A PAGE. Increasingly fragmentary construction is a solitary occupation. The accidental imagination passionately battles, the blind man guides the black ink on silk, the desperate man is a work of art.

JAMES JOYCE IS A FAMILY BUSINESS. The people have heard of him. Ulysses takes a taxi back from where he was going.

THE TRANQUILLISING DRUGS CARRIED A RED-PAINTED NOTICE: We cause the dawn in the deep water. Killed instantly by fatal damage to stop the man moving, the unexpected collapse is caused by flooding, the anger blew up, psychiatric patients ran down the main street and ripped through the fuel store with absolute madness, the houses and bungalows were shattered, the patients hit by flying glass, the continuous treatment involved thousands of tons of gravel across the roads with blast and fire, the damage occurred progressively, cars were up to the axles in boulders, this secondary effect intensified rapidly, something should have been done three weeks before the doors came flying across the street and other disorders.

THE ASYLUM WORD IS SWEPT AWAY. The psychiatric shudder is different today. Anxiety behind doors for years involves a magistrate, the human patient takes a turn for the worse. Repetitive jobs make wild men sane, the Hollerith machine leads to executive suicide. The glamorous parachutist tries to kill the service chief, the suspicious and insecure have no particular love for the Queen.

I CAME OUT FOR THE WAR, but stayed for the funeral of a friend, carrying a basin for a man in a cemetery, he had harmony, a boy was struck by a stone, it lay thinking, it had become real, real beginning, it gave the name of people, it made a dent in the grass.

THE MORTICIAN AT HOME SURROUNDS HIMSELF WITH SKULLS, because he longs for slain enemies. He leaves the wall of granite to rot, the fragments of bone are decorated. The sun tips behind a black rabbit, the grass is seized by an owl, the skinned yellow-eyed dead inhabit the grave of grass ten feet away. Hawks stand on the works of man. They hover, simple, resilient under the ice, useless wings with long effort. The dusty road wooden beyond the rock, the fence posts are ramshackle, trees on horseback. The clouds' soft camel feet obliterate the man and touch him with earth.

EVERYONE HAS A CLUMSINESS IN THEIR ANSWERS contained in a story somewhere in their family. Their sinister immunity comes from that which has been added to the night, cloudy and still as an exhibition in a church. Among the graves of the first dark shapes drifting in, she was the first woman to be brought there, lying among clothes, when the wreckage flames carried back the bullet to earth, behind the black village church with bearers handing the box to the man who worked in the office. The sky was green above the crowds, but the mother in an instant signalled the end, the memory of the triumphant cheer caught in the light as they swirled over the defiant voice. 'We had a lovely view.' They remembered the astonished cloud. The shape caught by the slow spring, bent in two and sank out of sight.

AT NIGHT PAST THE WINDSCREEN, the only cat was the size of a house. A piece of paper as sharp as an instrument, everything was a name lost for three hours in the racing cold.

A JOURNEY AS TOUGH AS ART. They travel the road heavy with

burgomasters, the painted box ablaze for miles, the buildings images of dominant trees, each trunk white as a cloak, the arrival (of the insect) is enjoyable, the face of the town hidden by rocks.

DRIVING FAST was the big danger and now it is past. Speed has a meaning of its own, speed lets off gases which are determined genetically, distinguished from the static. Like a fire, there are moral implications, as well as circular and triangular patterns.

THE MOTORBIKE pressures the skyline, the black horse turns green, the girls disintegrate fast, the mobile restless people wear flowered clothes, the young grow slow, women release on their knees, the sociological dog says Jesus while scarlet shapes explode.

THE DEATH in the car on the hill at a spot. There was blood on the road. These two came and were tricked that evening. Both were victims, the two were known, and their knowledge brought them close. The disclosures were true and the answer was yes, and that was all. The car had knowledge of the victims and there was no case. The car was told and owned and they drove to the spot on the plain, the crash they planned in the field, it was day. The tap on the window wound down and words were used to persuade the car to go away. The need to leave the field was recognised, the keys loaned to the victims were handed to them. They rattled. The watch said time and did not say what he saw. The days were soaked with rain, but he was a man who did not look at the time. He had the keys and his wristwatch stopped, with only a few minutes in it.

THE PRISONER DIED AS RESULT OF THE SKILL OF THE CONSTABLE. The Lord Chief Justice 'could see nothing incongruous'. The widow was no worse off, she would travel first class at no extra charge. Her husband had been killed by the police driving straight at him. Her new car would contain picture windows individually controlled, she would reap tremendous benefits, she would recover damages from the insurers. Yet she rejected proposals yesterday that would cost 15,000. Despite the apparent absence of the recommendations to be published shortly, this would result in a nil award because she had failed to complete formalities. Her skill must have been impaired by the amount of alcohol consumed. The error of law was not the result of the law. A second and third car would be examined, and crashed about an area occupied by spectators and other observers.

THE DANGER OF PAVEMENTS. A hundred and eight are known to have died.

NOW GO SILENT, fast, flexible, by train slung from pillars above streets. The rocketing acceleration is limited only by what (passengers) can accept.

THE SULLEN TRAIN CRUMPLES SUICIDALLY. The carriages abound with names, blankets, trousers, falling soot and dusty remnants, hell of old life, tiny smoke-black blankets disinfected by mountains, the necessary stony shore, vertebrae and rusted bottles, their faces have sheep's heads, the wild weather as the rails lengthen, there are no chairs and faded curtains, several million people travel with exposed wires and random glasses levelling off in the whipped wind roaring in the middle of the nowhere wire, poles of tin whirl over the beginning to darken invisible grey geese, the headstones hurl in the drunken sky with no warning, the wife is thrashed in the air for a minute, the graceful foot is pressed to the earth of smoke, the hard ribs crack, you can hear the fires warn each other and the firewood and skins for thirty seconds died among orange flares. The bride is incapable of swimming, she has changed her eggs in the supermarket for mutton chops and she travels to her house for basketball. She leaves the rows of scrubbed crosses in the shrinking land, the antirrhinum rustle of sheep who say to each other there is no grass there is plate glass for two weeks without stopping. Their eyes refuse to lamb in modern purple, the price is 3/6 a pound. Proudly the bride's fingers are ice green, her prize-winning children will be born there, the other wooden wife buys work in winter, the ancient lady is deep and crinkled, four dogs stand in the lake at night, the horse is thick with blue ice, the house is covered with metal, you see men on the roof blown down from the clouds and grumbling at the hail half a mile wide.

SURVIVORS OF THE VOLCANIC AGE before industrial eruption thrust them, forced them to fall, into the notorious soil. They had the convulsed glass feeling of the coming of steam that destroyed the green mountain. Not only this, but the one who fell thought he was five miles from the floor. His lump of a wife had disappeared, he was left, a man of fifty-seven, with two sisters, two goats who came to him when they were cold. He faced the difficulty of desolation, the solitary tiny. He saw something new against the hill, its face was glass.

THE GLASS CONSISTS IN GLASS, spaces, six abstract people, several psalms in one character, a screen against which the modern angel grew. Through the window and miles away for a long time God ran from the frightened face towards his own, at least once and probably more times. (Remember, he came down.) Cathedral colour-skills are different from a house, the cathedral contributes fire to keep God alive. In the green field, the common ground, he is alive and well. The glass is divided, stretched across the floor in the form of water, the effect and texture of a town. I come back deeply drawn, the wool in the window holds out the light, a surface can never be flat, strong reflections confuse the problem of light. I must avoid prayer, the mad experience.

'OUR HOUSE IS NICER THAN CHRIST'S.' The Cardinal is right. The Pope has to put up with 180 rooms and a series of witty tapestries. The rowdy cheerful Pope is untouched by his exotic environment, he pours tea, his lady is willowy, the Christian executive has bony knees. His Christmas is as big as Selfridges (he is a Roman Catholic) where he cooked a turkey recently. He spent the war with the Duce hugging the bust of a beautiful young woman. He never fully recovered from his wartime experiences. What remains is plenty of Holy Roman Empire, and statues which Mussolini used for target practice. His grandfather was hung by the state, now he lives in a hall of mirrors. He is asked to give weddings to the Texas Division of the US Fifth Army and when he returns from these outings, with the people lined up all day for the ceremony, he puts on his hat covered with the signatures of the Commonwealth Cricket Club. When they see him coming the Guards vanish down the corridor with loud shrieks, and he says, 'You can't blame me for that. They accepted my invitation to attend,' and it is true they survive unharmed.

THE SOBER SWISS ARMY LIVES ON FISH, not that it matters.

CARESSING THE IVORY CARVING, THE STONE POPE HAS NOTHING TO DO, only private pleasure. He puts the glass down gently, turns away the image, finds the one he has just left, examines the next with the same technique. Mouthing rubbish, the Pope circles the delicious object, enjoying the amorous proceedings in public.

BEAUTY UPSTAIRS, part of the glamour of private amusement, the sexual enjoyment of angels. The infant Christ is well-advertised, the postcard business keeps your eyes open to the theme of legs and reverence, a nun walks through to find the apartments closed at noon.

THE CATHOLIC FAMILY IS PAID BY RESULTS, judged every month by performance: we believe in sixteen million kids getting really fat and big.

EVERY TIME GOD GRINNED THE WOMAN SAID SEX. After one suicide His family made a million. Human is what he was. Jesus is ninety-five per cent the sexual thing. Heaven is an adult relationship, hell a dead loss. Confession is wish fulfilment. Naked women murder children, a Rolls Royce is an abomination. His face is covered in jewels. 'I can sit for hours with a young man of forty-five.'

EVERYONE LAUGHS TWENTY-ONE TIMES when the Pope gives something away. 'Like hell', when his secretary told him he earned 50,000 a year. Convinced that he should be in an infirmary, his solemn bank manager says the kids adore him. He is ill, he is crazy, he is unique. Whenever he is not feeling well, they talk about success to cheer him up. It's a deal he has with God, a giggle in hospital. When his eleven-year-old boy fell from a tree, nobody said he was not dressed decently, a sweet was placed alongside his head. His hair was dyed or dying, but you could never detect it from watching.

IN THE DANCE HALL HE WAS INVITED TO LAY HIS HANDS ON, full of the sounds of sex and the dangers of money, hungry for youth, for the sixth-former in extraordinary clothes. The concrete cock grew naturally, the priest was mucking about with her tits. 'So I asked her to come and see me, to have a talk with me.' And a lad passing says, 'Why don't you wear a mini?'

WHEN THE BLOND PRIEST bought a flat for his 'Mother', the effect was fantastic. The Duchess distinguished herself, she appeared in church in her uniform, carrying a teddy bear and wearing white trousers, shaking her head as he walked by.

IT IS NECESSARY TO DIVERSIFY PEOPLE. Every dolly has a tremendous personality. In their young days they wore trousers. The girl was teating a small boy of ten, he remembers being taken from his mother. It was the horror of war, his home was under guard, he was taken before he could escape quietly. The qualified doctor set fire to the empty building. The patient having a baby wore a large flowered hat. The policeman was called Lilian: 'I enjoy a long skirt,' he says, 'being pregnant is very primitive.'

I WANT TO TALK TO YOU (ABOUT MATHEMATICS). I want to if you like express the impossible. I believe in luck. If luck goes against you, you've made a mistake.

I'M A FAILURE. I have the least reason for surviving. Poverty is part of the punishment. There is little doubt that the Board ensures that my family does not starve. My wife anyway. My wife and I were children in whose mind the need did not occur. No money, she not being here. Everything seems to come to me for bills. You can assume that the suburban machinery has broken down, the broken plaster lying for months, my poem on the poverty of the land stretching down the length of the room. I don't know, I think I would have gone mad. I have grown used to it now, but when you go out you see faces skipping at you, you know, you know what's in their minds. Besides, I don't know many people in London at this point.

HE THINKS WITH A POINTED BEARD. He is conscious of skill and tone. His friend and rival lives in Wolfe Street, Dundee. His poetry experiment is a verse a day. 'I never use I, it is never the right word.' When friends arrive he goes out for a walk around the block.

HE STUDIED THE WORLD WAR IN A LIBRARY. He formed a friendship with war for ten years, he was considered austere and regular, he showed himself geometric, oblique. He was born in Europe, especially Paris, his home was broken and dispersed. In a New York hospital he was invited to kill a man, he said OK, his postcard asked for expenses, and a first-class hotel. A gun became part of his life, he lived on the edge of a knock on the door, that would come in and start chucking everything around.

MEN IN STOLEN FLYING SUITS: 'WE ARE HERE TO KILL AND WE ARE GOING TO.'

SHOOTING IS STILL A DANGER, although the risk is scientifically acceptable. A policeman in London is inclined to disbelieve statistics. In one sense he carried a gun to murder, but he was stopped from making too much of the experience. He was armed, he killed a man accidentally on principle, his first step in the war against crime. 'I believe in arming Britain's police,' he said. 'We cannot simply refuse guns.' He saw hundreds of policemen killing a man, the cornered body was armed, some 5,000 pistols were issued, either nervously or fatally (anyone could take a gun into one of the finest schools in the world). The criminal was ill-informed about his death. His ignorance had two aspects: in Brazil they had shot off his legs, they were careless in the use of the pistol.

THE POLICE had come down to the bar to seize the staff of the hotel. Television on a shelf of bottles was a landscape which had not been seen before. The police were accused of kidnapping. No one would talk in the night club. The gang two years ago was a menace to society, each man took his gun to a separate town and stayed there for a period of up to five years. The local police had seen the commercial possibilities. They had taken a party of villains for traditional roast pork and a diet of bombs al fresco. The situation of the mountain people was dangerous, they had done something wrong, the donkeys had drunk too much of the fascist landscape. Their deformed lawyers were mentally deficient, their savagery was concentrated in the poorest region. The Marxist politician began to tell his two kidnappers that he had seen his cousin shot for carrying a photograph of Gagarin. The murder of a man a hundred miles away on the steep hillside made the lawyers' fortunes in the summer heat. They made sixty million a year from the heat and dust. When it came to money-making the island was like nowhere else, for the mountain children there was no change. The top-secret and successful church appeared in essence the same as the old-style bandit. The police seemed indifferent so long as tourists were shot for austere reasons. On August 12th a priest shot his wife then killed himself, but that confirmed what the Communists had been calling him for a decade: a highwayman, an extortionist. And no gun was found.

SHOT DOWN IN GUN PLAY before he could be brought home to his suburb in June, reconciled to justice, coaxed out of crime before he veered south, he followed the brilliant windfall. He knew the signs of property deals, the profits in killing. Now forty-three, his impatience was apparent, Ky created the brutal occasion with anyone. His capacity for elastic violence outwitted his bodyguards. His property company unearthed large numbers of murdered men and in the poor light attempted to sell two hundred. Last Wednesday, when the rotting bodies were delivered, the actual state of the poor quality meat was defined by the English. The language used had been obscure, the legal owner had an imperfect right. The alternative argument noted the antecedent death, and this was taken as a sign of progress. Since they had fallen behind with their payments that morning, the bodies of two men had been disintegrating rapidly. I don't suppose that they were killed by killers.

HUMAN BEHAVIOUR IS ABSOLUTELY JUSTIFIED. You cannot argue with war. The edge of the rope will not keep quiet, the intimidated child will say things to you until silenced by slaps and threats. There is no point in arguing with people, they are too frightened.

HONG KONG IS A CLUTTER OF WAR TOYS. The body-building industrialist wishes to live for a hundred years, as long as his business instincts flourish. He packs his pills in bags, the new-style heated ceiling mats have conquered death. Last year was the year of the low table, fish were guillotined on the low table. He is able to buy beauty, colour magazines are his hobby, daintiness can be recognised in his home by the smell alone. One of the bonuses of the Vietnam war is that he can rent a home for life for 1,000 dollars, and death, for some, means happiness. Six hundred years won't stop that war: business needs fragile peace for a year, then violence every year for ten years. The industrialist says that people who do not rush about are lazy, they can do nothing, they are defeated by a single blow. Though this man avoids the trials of war he puts four lumps of sugar into his opinions. His enemy resists by doing nothing. 'There is a war on.' And that is what he needs, everyone defends the war, the landlord must have it, the government is elected for war, the soldiers give stability. For taking an egg you go to jail, the practice is not modern. The people are too ignorant to own a coal mine but gangsters do good business, they run the roads and ports, the puppet makes money from the ideal way of life. Do not talk peace with the cruel people, the lips of the big stomach will learn nothing. The word in the room is calm and remote, the war talk screams overhead, the police drink pale tea, justice is expensive everywhere, it filters through the barrier of names. The soldier is called patriot until the sudden sea of fire stops the semi-red street. Petrol pours down the paper-thin man. The bar-girls add to the flames.

'CHEMICAL GESTICULATIONS OF CHAOTIC HUMANITY IN THE VAST AND

SHATTERED EAST.' The official explanation is back to normal. The flooded river is remembered for seven hours. The sun forgets about human beings, in the cool green coma in the middle of May.

SUNSHINE PAINTS THE SIDE OF THE MOON. The new name dazzles from the bottom of the street. Indisputably British faces blossom in the trading centre, the bourgeoisie is growing at the root. Non-military rifles are sold on the open market, the pale-skinned recipients show a profit, the damp white ladies are diminishing, the attractive Indian is a strategic asset. Things were going on with loose grey discipline everywhere except on the other side of the street where the communists carried guns in their trousers. The Chinese years ago knew the smell of rebellion under the floorboards, now the plastic bomb had liberated it. They sniped with guns in the streets, from the gloom of the girlie bars the net scalps shone scented white, nipples ringed by orange lights, two breast areas each clean stone. Police were riding cars down the corridors between houses, despair in forms was being announced, the smell of the European produced order, the people sprang back out of existence, nihilism made a series of steps past boats of earth, the government was going to dump the rebels into the sea.

OFFICIAL FRANTIC DISCIPLINE IN A BLUE SHIRT GREETED EVERYONE, the Governor at the bar accompanied the martial music, as he gripped the bottle the tropical shrubbery fell into the ammunition box. After the Governor was killed by broken glass the government fixed the price for rooms without windows. When the widow went north to visit the man who owned the best hotel, she was made to swim for it. Beggars from the street dragged through her hair, she saw the dead man loud and grinning, and several hundred miles of grease above the royal photograph. When each bottle of water costs six shillings it is not hard to kill a man with a budget spent on keeping lice abounding in his hair.

THE FELLOW WHO IS LOW KEEPS HIS HEAD TO THE GROUND, but the speculator practises self-reliance. He is someone who makes a study of money throughout his life. He trebled his million in ten years. His hands are brighter than we have, the rare millionaire of the dream, the fizz of the boom, disease of the brain. Regardless of the tricky figures he is totally involved in money more than ever, the solid gold plates are for his pleasure (his customers don't want to lose him). His crocodile boots get bigger, give him a fiver for his gold-plate watch, he has four cars, a song and dance in the office, aeroplanes outside his house. This individual exists as a prototype, he can weigh as much as four. His business is creative work, making something out of nothing. He cannot think or feel without absolute dedication, since the day is his own to feel whatever he likes in the place he has devised as an extension of himself. On his way down the street, on the subject of misleading those who thanked him, the advertising man kept four bottles of good blended sales drive. He took care of his mail and won the friendship of at least one big dealer, a sleight-of-hand middle-rank salesman whose company ultimately suggested the broadest big stock profits. His personal secretary had been wrapped up in a happy device for altering the rental property which seemed the coming thing. Blanche went heavy when she had worked out the corporate salary rises formally before she left the office. The conference was over before anyone could gather from his call to his lawyer that his account of his daily expenditure had been underwritten by an insolvent operator. It would be legal, for a few minutes each day, if his plans were successful.

ANYWAY, HE HAD KNOWN TWO QUEENS, both typical of their day, and each in her way was best. He has sympathy for the kids who go out to work, in good weather and in bad. In his small office in Lower Regent Street he is pretty pleased with the way the girls wear their hair long, he likes the way they're shaping.

LIQUID GREEN HAIR IS ABSURD. No, don't.

THE CROTCH EXPERIENCE was different, soft fastenings at the thighs, hold the shoulders, ankles emphasise the impact of school-girls in school-buses, seeing them makes him quickly fatigued, the single-decker is best, their windows wide, he identified them standing in the aisles, but still, this was manufactured reality, totally new, still in the experimental stage.

LAST YEAR HE WATCHED THE GIRLS ON THOSE MODELLING JOBS, more than a dozen of them in his sights. He laughs at the behaviour of the female. He is somebody who contains few problems, musical talent instils values. His successful childhood is framed above his desk slowly and clearly, he had that much realism, he isn't enjoying his daydreams any more. For ten years the driven male slowly and clearly through each day. The wealthy fanatic exerts pressure, what counts is pressure, but where does the mind wander to?

THE GAME OF OBJECTS, newspaper illogicality, the female attitude towards fun, the accurate instrument indicates blemishes, pursuing the man in his own house.

HE SPENT UP TO FIFTY DOLLARS in a French restaurant with the girl who came for two hours' study, his sports jacket shouldered with vice and corruption, as the furred girl explained the geography of Europe. In the capital of the gold city they had fallen in love as they stared out of the windows at the river police.

HE EXPLAINS WHAT SHE SEES, familiar with the words she does not know. His voice prevents her from joining the group. He tries to remember the talking of his children, as they draw the young shape, the brilliant green minute. 'I have watched Maureen many times,' the painted grin, the serious steps in the room, the voice says, 'Dear, it is doubtful whether she will understand.'

REGENT STREET HAS A WHALE'S JAW. A small sunset attracts trade, horizontal layers of Dunlopillo keep the place prosperous. When the street is decorated for Christ, fruit is stuck to the windows in the morning.

HE REMEMBERED THAT THE ROMANTIC YOUNG LOVED MONEY, the snowing and the snow go hand in hand, the Victorian bandstand was red and yellow, the long people walked back slowly, the windows would like to see them, they walked through orange snow, the street lights shone on white cardboard, she said she wanted sleighs to appear in the shop window, with floodlights at night. Her kisses were from Europe, and other things were changing, perhaps it was to do with his money.

PRAWN COCKTAIL BLOWN AWAY.

SHE WAS NOT LONG AT THE OFFICE OF POLITE THANKS AND REFUSAL. He drove to her place when something was wrong. They had one beer in his lovely automobile, and soon they were moving around the blocks they had seen before, as he told her carefully of his love and rage. She enjoyed meeting the troubled folding days, she thought progress was like putting on a suit. 'I missed you,' and she said other things behind the chauffeur's back. 'I will take you, since you remind me. I want to talk to you after dinner.' He swallowed before he drove to where she wanted, with difficulty. She felt at home in the Mercedes. He thought she said she had fixed a time, and decided on coming to his flat. Since dinner this had happened several times. Perhaps she was going to murder him in his office: he was going downhill emotionally. He received a message after watching the Mercedes take her back to the cafe where she had gone for more time. The quick horn handle at the side, the Mercedes was pregnant, the pedals covered with flesh, the bucket seat looked chic, the coloured beautiful automobile drove narrow like a dirty knife. The motor sound was faint, it would go better, thank you. It was necessary to be some distance away, her expression was too much, the worry would prevent him from thinking, he talked of whatever it was he feared from the conversation. He was silent until after he was sure of the road, bringing the flowers and lighting her cigarette, saying nothing to the car door. The effort of keeping his voice low helped contain the tones of the well-shaped head of the girl sitting beside him. The pressure from the corner of her mouth made her nag the bucket seat. Women were graceful branches spreading over us to protect the sun from the wash from our mad shock.

IT'S HARD TO FORNICATE IN YOUR OWN HOME, IT'S BETTER IN THE PARK. One of the reasons is the horror of women indoors. The girl friend of the reserved Englishman has waited until today, when men and women are kissing in her back-garden. The roadside picnic is the strangest revival since Chinese became fashionable. The dull and careful park-keeper has a job on the public payroll, and his determined alcoholism is unquestionably moral. The majority of park-keepers have a certain lightness of spirit: he will assume the old-fashioned homosexual to be buying flowers. But sex and drink in a public place is a vice.

A SMALL, QUIET SQUARE, YOU UNDERSTAND, a shop on the edge of a joke. Step out of the sun into a drink. Inside the flat there was half a melon, a jumble of fascinating coffee-spoons, four doors painted scarlet, a refrigerator cut in half, yesterday's pile of pussy's pieces, a cat in the middle of the refrigerator without moving its feet. He turned the dove-like fish whose voice was higher on both sides, the blood flowed over, he kept the blood inside the bowl, then took off his coat.

THE COATS ON THE BED ARE BUSY TALKING. Girls of eighteen must be married in a dream in a mangled room. She was warm with doubt and shy in areas of life. The gloomy morning blossomed, he knew everything every her and what they were, her lovely skin gave him enormous energy. They had a discussion for hours that winter, the most beautiful naked body sensation, able to bath together and get married. It was one of those middle-class things.

THE TWO TOOK THEIR WORDS TOGETHER BY THE USE OF LIPS, he cut the words out of her nose, he would prefer her teeth. Her heart was a sound in his opinion, with infinite possibilities, her moving parts worked well. The police were involved in the business, they arrived at his office to discuss the extortion case, she knew nothing, her eye was ruled inadmissible. The trial for rape was the same. The allegation was withdrawn before the offence was committed.

BAD WEATHER is the opportunity to opt out of Saturday nights, and for newly-weds this encourages saving. The heating bill is high, the snowball escapes from the rosy houses, the instructions to the thermostat are hazily defined. The girl in the green bath looks ridiculous, glaring up and turning round, asking who made her wear her clothes in the bath, thinking there was no reason, at least so it seemed to me.

WHAT HAPPENS USUALLY WHEN YOU MEET? Special display in the gardens, the glamour of contemporary art. Meeting is a reproductive process, behind a row of misty bicycles, where the observation of death grows older, and women are easily available.

RUMOUR ran and never stopped along the corridors of the tennis clubs, youth hatching plans under lamp-posts to catch the eye of female cars with noisy open doors. The art schools made plots to run away and hide with flimsy girls swooning on number plates. They were friends of such wild occasions, discussing the history of civilisation and ideas. He decided neither to leave her now nor to support her nightly at 9.25 p.m. in his soldierly arms in an orange daze of whisky drunk warm in the brewery.

THE GIRL IS A PURPLE DRUG substantiated by fact, the same social escape as drink. Parents on the other hand make no difference, especially when they are married. The fascinating child will wish to marry her father, she will avoid an abortion. Many girls wish to marry their own child, interestingly many girls pass through this stage. The tendency is towards the ideal. Progressive girls take care of the figure and tend to live as if they were pregnant. Some of them wish to marry their father, some of them never tell the truth, freedom prevails, the pattern is provoking.

A SINGLE MAGAZINE IN AMERICA SOLD 30,000 COPIES LAST YEAR: write and tell them why their pretty pictures and all those dreary things reflect the times. The first pornographic thing all over made £300, the imported American production is enjoyed in cinemas in Ireland, the coffee bar delights in it. Already Warsaw is famous for racy drawings and subtle catching literature. The connoisseurs of the developed bust between boots helped to shape the appetite for everything, for heavy leather anything, delighted with globes, the actual balls are mostly vulgar, the bit of sex is unintentional. I've had a very visual wife for years, my wife Margaret had the formula right, always picking the size that sells, encouraged by her coloured personality.

THE ULTIMATE CAN BE VERY DREARY, the law recognises the likely lass, most get prosecuted after all. Eighteen female persons are in the area of police operations, they don't have to walk through the common gateway any more, they don't have to fight each other with fists. The lawyer in the courtyard is well heated, he visited the women in their living quarters, the restaurant is as hygienic as possible. The good health girls also exist, though on a cold day they are not permitted beyond the glass barrier. The young blonde girls are very desirable, they sell milk, the men are not allowed to drink while they lie in the girls' wombs, though they're very keen on coffee. The middle-aged wall-paper, fawn furniture, the walls are sadder than before, the cuddly blouses are divided between nine. 500,000 women are too cold, for five days they happen naturally, that's nice, but they expect a profit as well.

SEX-AND-VICE IS THE COUNTRY'S BIGGEST INDUSTRY. Most towns have some local area where they keep their little girls. Luckily for their fathers most things happen where lots of allegedly sexy sights are concentrated: they know where they stand. The famous street, the mystery of oho, no one knows much or cares less, the streets are full of theatres. The street is a street that smells of sex. The dead food is all hamburgers. Natural people's minds are caught by wicked sausages. The automatic crook is a food machine. Dodgy doormen look like single women, the square pavements say what they would say. A very clean dwarf took my shoulder and gave me welcome in the afternoon. It's bound to happen decently. The girls have huge neon signs till they are pulled down. Sex maniacs are fascinating to experts, their scattered illusions are differences that separate the breasts. The gentlemen arrive from the Oxford college, but the nights are designed by gangs, successful lads reach everything new, the stained hand breaks bricks, their fists go round the block, they invest their money in women.

THE CENSORSHIP BOARD HAS FIVE HEAVY BREASTS but bouncy noise is not its way to happiness. Sex is pain in a brown paper bag, a product of very thin people. The Scottish cuntry expects nothing better than sex by manipulation, and this is permissible, particularly in public life. The over-eager student is banned officially or unofficially, the passionate dissimilarity of boys and girls is attacked by the right-wing MP. The unfree member at nine o'clock on Saturday makes money enthusiastically, he gets up and leaves the room, he desires life in ignorance, he wants something which sells in a shop. The business of sex is understandable; it is unpleasant; the joyless depend on the local brothel and not much else. The talentless politician is not going home, his personal history is disheartening, his hero is a fish, he has regrets, he misses the pop influences, he needs his dream of glory. He thinks the boys will get tired if a book is banned for nine years. The influential persuader says no, and authority in a black cap says don't marry a nun who has been pepped up. Thirty-seven per cent of the people are curious about sex in a churchyard and smile at the thought. The mind is clean till it gets its hooks on a book.

THE LOCAL MAGISTRATES were misfits, eccentrics, boozers, who would say anything for money, with a function not unlike the man who does not get worried when he takes over a haunted house.

CYRIL CANNOT BE ALONE. Best with someone, old or young. It doesn't matter which. No opinion is comforting: too sophisticated or too simple. Even for Admirals the sky grows darker, and he had discovered that for vicars, headmasters and others the sea rises higher. The prudent institutions remain alone like saddened women. During the years he had felt dispossessed, without allies, not in the right place. He had written articles seeking to help materially, or dealing with matters spiritual, but everything had been said in the universities, and the various churches were unhelpful. They all believed in the erosion of property, while he was growing richer. The infernal unions produced astonishing struggles every year. These people were neither patriotic nor honourable, and they became more dangerous in the summer.

THEY ACTUALLY PASSED A LAW SAYING THAT UNION JACKS MUST BE WORN IN THE HAIR, and all girls must be inspected or thrown in the lake. The pretty girl drinking with the millionaire refused and was most emphatic, her red hair done up in magnificent black. For three days repeated excuses had been provided, as they danced to the river-pattern riffle in the garden. The politician's wife had her hair multicoloured in the morning, the magistrates were dancing easily, the stuffed skirt waiting for them under the oily talk about culture, the moist pressure of flesh behind the bar, the official sound waves mixing with the gurgling music, the drunk flow of music with young ladies swung upon the water throng. The lovely girl turned red and white with fury, the beautiful main street swept towards the lake, down the avenue of hills on either side of the flags of the progressive nations. While the Indians submit to the whip, the Queen in diamonds looks like a god, the fizzy orange has a fine head. The mother country shall be in the headlines drinking beer, the banana war (Britain's unique contribution to the history of stink) the banana war is what you've got to do.

THE CUSTOM OF AFRICA has since been written: Can we eat boiled sticks? He walked a few feet then whispered: 'Four tins full of flour, please.' The motorised flour weighed less than forty-five pounds.

READY TO HURL YOURSELF INTO AFRICA you may end in your neighbour's lap with four large dollops of droppings of elephant. The black cook misread the sinister clause, and burnt down the house without noise, there was no sound from the branches being moved across the room, only the groaning from the child in the high cot. Night is impossible, you gaze at it, weaponless. From the window of your vehicle, wait the night (no movement going round in circles), a rare, black, swift African dawn came down, boring in Kodachrome. In ran fifty elephants, a battered tree stuck in the mud, pedestrians with inflamed faces stared rudely at the ladies' legs. The black-headed chauffeur made fruity sounds, spicing the sandwiches the most expensive way. The choice is yours. Bodily intimacy in the morning, the first exposure of the child's cock, the animal noise was terrible, thousands of addresses mumbling in the atmosphere. They fell together in the six foot hole, a hundred yards of whispering windows open to the rain, exhaustion loaded on to black handlebars.

THE STREETS NAME THEMSELVES AFTER LAVATORIES, the discipline of classes is always in use, to maintain the power of the bottle-drinking Queen.

NOW WAS THE OPPORTUNITY FOR INTELLECTUALS TO SALVAGE THE IDEA OF THE HONEYMOON AT WINDSOR TO INCREASE THE PRESTIGE OF THE QUEEN. Limelight gets results, American confidence assures support, the frigid Queen is managed with dynamism and skill but it is doubtful if her compatible partner will keep his mouth open without talking too much. The enigmatic grin is more aggressive than arrogance and the immediate issue has become the equality of manual workers with peeresses in their own right. Now waiters will expect similar treatment, the government is so feeble. Morality is about money anyway, the church collects its income tax, and the transition from the absurd low-grade civil servant to those who rule the land, is unpredictable. The mechanical eye of the chairman of the board sorts figures and writing, official contraception is bought cheaply, the country seems sinful, the police are sold at 100 per cent profit, men found impersonating royalty are sent to

Scotland, raspberries wear an expression of natural nobility, the unmarried girl waits outside the liquor store penetrating the marked man with gleams of sunshine.

IN THIS CHAOS THE SCOTTISH PRINCESS WAS COVERED CARELESSLY WITH YELLOWING MEDALS. Twenty minutes later she murmured from the window-sill because she was so pretty, 'I should have shaved there,' (pointing), 'like the French girls do, then you would have loved me in the garden.' She said she was never fresh enough, though she ground her teeth herself, it was so easy. 'Like other girls I wear short skirts, I am light and fluffy like the English.' She was not against old photos, souvenirs and maps, but she liked to meet new people.

OF COURSE WE ALL KNOW HER INTIMATE OPERATIONS.

SHE BORROWED PERFUME FROM THE BISHOP'S YOUNGER DAUGHTER, she had wanted to enter the church countless times. In Liverpool she had switched to theology, it was frightfully interesting to hit the headlines, the huge amethyst on her hips, her gloves were of particular interest, living in a council house, dressed in a purple cassock, reporters all over the place.

WITH CONTEMPT FOR DARING NAKEDNESS (modern children were undressing too quickly) she said amusing things. She did it perfectly. Playing the adult beautiful, she behaved like a pound of bacon.

HER NEWEST MINI-SKIRT HAD A MOUSTACHE FOR THREE WEEKS. Then her stomach began to woman, rejoicing in the sense of permanence. On weekends she worked for charity, and every Saturday night she stayed in bed and opened the big ones. She made a lot of money because she looked honest. 'I may sell my mother, we shall see.'

WITH THE ACCENT ON DIFFERENCE, the long, low, solidly-built sturdy original fabric was the choice of a lady. Timber structure, brilliant white, front door facing pretty against the trees. Like Mrs Murphy she is not interested in the fifteenth century. She said it in the village near the church, a neat clean woman reading potatoes. What is death? Two signs pointing down a hill that isn't there. She stared at water the colour of opal. Beyond the gate was a wonderful wood. Her private glimpse of modern furniture and film in colour hour by hour, the same was true of all the other houses, the curtains fell in peace in nearly every case, with only a pattern in sand remaining. Towering weeds strayed across picturesque beds of air, at breakfast time a man knocked, all he wanted was sixteen pence a day. The decision was wearing her nightdress, the mistress was glad to offer four thousand pounds. A man offered sacrifices living in the open, the lodger living in the third bedroom stepped over the frontier and everyone smiled, the white bird moved off with part of the fireplace, there were no sounds in the hall. And only one addition had been made to the magnificent sands.

JELLIED EGGS AND CREEPER-COVERED BEANS, the garden was her bed, the lawns a bath of fire. The flute was one of her hobbies, the wooden stave closed over the glass door leading to the sea. The August dress looked marvellous, it was time to change behind the lawn, seven people had a bath, the lady's tie was gay, a lot of people had lived in that street but now it was nasty down there. Her grandmother died, smothered in ivy. The great romance of her life was an artist who worked a petrol pump. The lonely man had never married.

THE COUNTESS DID NOT MEET HER FAMILY. How would you like to have her superiority?

THE FIRST PAPER MEMORY IS SOMETHING LIKE A HOUSE. My father's father wore a paper hat but was more interested in plates and cutlery. He went off to live in America because the ideas of the eighteenth century irritated him.

BALLOONS ARE BLOWN UP ROMANCES, the frantic dance-floor of a war-time film, the northern girl in a trouser suit, the customers in little paper hats.

NOBODY KNOWS HIS OWN FATHER, HE FINDS HIM LOST IN A BAG: he looks sad, he wanted respect for values, he begins his work for civilisation on Friday night, depressed by the ignorance of the *News of the World*.

HIS HABIT was to go to a place for years to have his own reactions. He did not want to be told, he wanted to know. The primitive eccentric has lost his memory, his strength to find huge ships on a piece of paper, he looks for his feelings and finds a horse, the river may take years to isolate the ocean.

THE RIVER FLEW PAST THE FUNNEL FROM TIME TO TIME.

RIVERS OF BRICK, curved red patterns dive and fall north and west, lining the roofs with weeds. The walls climb into petals of change and stress, the sign of the road crosses the various bloods and different risings of ancient people. The path is paved with years. Bright hunters shelter in the green valley and the home is painted with purpose. Unnatural wealth is a green fog, the heart seems interior, cathedrals on cliffs like brave omelettes blast the town to bits. The road falls on the town, the church of glass collapses, the unity of time and lime destroys the lives of kings. The driving lights are lit by Ulysses, the gardens shine for miles splashing white peach.

IT IS THE LARGE CITY. It lies in the middle, at an average height above the sea, between the coast and hills, bounded by plateaux, between the two lies a valley. The river has its source, it flows through lakes. It is so large. The highest point is an artificial hill. Subject to changes in temperature and differences in rainfall from year to year, forests occupy the area, it has trees. The surface was shaped by ice, retreating water carved valleys, valleys connected by gullies, split by the blanket of lakes. It occupies the land. The marsh is now a garden. There are few hills. From the rubble of hills, remnants of woods, the nucleus, the absorbing and transforming expansion, the rulers advanced the boundaries to the sea. Lines of streets connect the gates. The wide circle is now complete. The metropolis is built. The factories form towns. Sewage spoils the lakes. The exit road is the favourite part of the city. The office of Mayor forms the centre of the zoo. The famous court and prison afford lovely views over the airfield, intercourse is not allowed, though permits are issued for limited periods.

MILLIONS LICK THEIR WIVES. The death houses are bricked up. Police protect their lives. Energetic foreigners increase trade, the quick-witted work in the central market. The city is force, the Minister of Order determines policy with the concurrence of representatives. The constitution is operative. All meet the government for consultation. The city cannot feed itself. Cows are edible. An abattoir was set up. Water is purchased by the municipality, from wells within the area. Electricity is supplied, the modern power is fired with dust. Horses are abolished. There are private cars. Trains go in and out. The underground is low owing to the low ground.

THE LEAF AT HIGH ALTITUDE withers before the cold, the less delicate stay soft and pliable. The grey spout rises, the forkful of snow is thickened with beer, the systematic cruelty of cold increases. As the ice-like mountain forces the shiver of weakness, the sunsilk hair uncurls its beautiful colours, the menthol-fresh actress in her spring flush spurns the unlit set, the hair on the young buds brings unhappy memories of milk, for six minutes she seems less strong, she looks for milk in her memories, her delicate years are used, the years ago are prized, the lemony feeling is warm and long.

MONLANGUOROUS, VERY. The hair falls apart and the amused actress exploits herself eating fishes. Now I do not know what else to photograph. She hopes her knees go click each time. Her fierce look shows her juicy inside. (She keeps her honey in a sponge bag for a time.) Massage of the bottom might be necessary, if you can reach, probably in the morning, certainly at night.

THE DIRECTOR sat down on a chair on a mountain, the numerous megaphones shouted: 'He is not here.' The palaces were tipped upside down when civilisation appeared, some of the buildings were in pandemonium, the white stone stairways would not reach up, hundreds of new brick homes appeared, ten fortresses were locked and guarded by well-paid men, the experts said the city built by men was now in ruins, the extras who lived on the other side had to knock to gain admission.

TWO SWISS CAMERAMEN, WITH PANGS THAT ENDURED, PREOCCUPIED WITH THE FICTITIOUS IMPOSSIBILITY OF PURCHASING REALITY, TOOK PICTURES OF THE MORNING SWIFTLY. The character of God they were substituting for money, the money involved in God, the idea was for Him to be driven by car, and someone had to change the wheels, provide the tyres. God was in his late forties, short, dapper, and very likeable. Sure they paid, more than for anyone except the Queen. 'Just look what's at stake. We can't afford any cuts, or the sound will not be heard.' They shared His belief in His mass-pulling power, His insistence on starring in the power-movie. But there would be mistakes in rainy weather, they must wait for sunshine, spending dollars entertaining the actors overnight. Or He might get killed in one hundred and ten explosions each equivalent to disaster. The money must still be found, both for union recognition and for insuring His face against damage to His business. 'If you're interested in nuts, we're trying to avoid the possibility of disaster. We're in a competitive situation and people have an idea one way, sexing up the scenes, mixing up the races, going too fast and claiming to play the game with the story of what is happening. Every year somebody does, somebody risks, he will be "more authentic". But we're not worried when somebody else gets vicious currently at fake speed.' They were shooting the world in the insanity of it, contracting to re-equip the superstructure whatever they felt. They were careful to remain boring, nothing compared with the tedium of the plain. Their confidence was gone. 'But we can make everything: Names, owners, machines. Everything we've got is good as gold.'

THE TRUE GOLD IS GOLD EACH YEAR, it is a simulated black gold market supplied by the scales of London. Zurich weighs three-quarters of a handful of coins, non-communist Vienna has a couple of bars tucked away. What will happen when the demand for coins is confined to the chap who mends the road? The market is secret, the gold itself is kept in kilo bars. I know lots of people over the Pyrenees worth £800,000 an ounce. The banker suggested £3 an ounce. Most afternoons tons of gold vanish into the cellar, the son of a wealthy soap alone spent £167 million in Spain, with plenty of money left in fibre boxes. The Greek remembers the armoured train: 'My daddy said to buy it.' How great the desire for the globe. Bargaining the family, changing their money, others in Europe also see gold inside the vaults. We have less money, and less death. We have seen the electrically-operated door, sovereigns hidden in Eastern Europe, it is possible to buy gold, with gold. People are forced into gold. If a man dies with gold in his pockets, his son quickly removes the coins.

THE MONEY HIDDEN IN SWITZERLAND was left there by Germans who had turned the landscape into lead.

THE GREY ROCK FLUTTERED ACROSS COUNTRY, the pine trees suited the occasion, thousands of extras evoked joy, the skylines of cliches were ugly with church spires, the calm identity of love secreted in glaciers.

GREY SUITS, ALL CONFIDENT COPIES OF PARIS THE CITY OF PLEASURE, unfolded in the morning as policemen shut the gates on teen-age wings. While Byzantine spectators cheered, the statue from the shaded park was taken to its place on the shores of the lake.

THE FILM SYNDICATE is synchronised and linked, their costs are up one per cent, disaster is happening all the time, £10,000 is regularly lost. Elderly men in hot night clothes paint Bardot in neon, her breasts are remodelled in concrete. 'We never stop trying to have the stars knocked about. I expect we will end by having them torn to pieces.'

SWING IN. With a zoom lens blot out everything above, the level of energy and time from all angles focuses in your hand one evening. You can point personally. The specialised space gives you a child's room. Work on a big scale. A lot of activities become possible. You can show detail in a way that precipitates a revolution. Then every year for five years, tackle big schemes, use progressive methods. Three cameras encourage imagination, detail sustains interest, choose your subject, the death of Kennedy, the cheap hero. Fill the space on the white wall, discover you can do what television cannot do. Like Cassius Clay, the drawn, torn philosopher, you are too big for the windowless screen. After all, all you need is a girl in a van on the verge of stripping her cotton dress, and the mastery of new techniques and technical mysteries.

MARLON BRANDO WATCHED HAMLET, laughed at a phrase in it, held the world in a drink, ran from the office in tears.

EVERY MOOD RECEIVES A FEE. He is an experienced actor whose identity is submerged. Burdened with his bags, his secretary's function is to carry his equipment. There were perhaps a dozen bags, and these enormous weights had to be out by eight o'clock, borne by the slightly built girl in dark blue, who was thus burdened with full responsibility. The film star walked straight out of the hotel and on to the set. She slammed the bags down. All that day he looked like a wrestler, he held out his hand to the taxi-driver, grabbed him by the ear and thrust his head down a hole.

THE OBSOLETE ACTOR WAS IN FACT A DUKE BORN IN GREECE.

THE WOMAN SECRETARY SAID THE DUKE WOULD GO TO BED ANYWHERE, TOGETHER WITH FORMAL PRAYERS. He would do it in the car, anywhere, in the face if she didn't, for an hour and a half on television, with a bottle of sherry and three empties. She married after three years. Then this was something her husband and the Duke took turns at. He spent a week with his wife this summer.

HE WAS ALWAYS IN THE NEWS. And you've got to know that it is not unusual for a familiar face to look this year like an arthritic ready with the right answer. The Duke's your man. When you talk to him he disappears for a month or two, thrusting his hand back into your pocket. His advice inspires you to shut up. He returns smiling with the news that has already been announced. Well above the usual tone, he has been around the world in general. The usual offence for men of this class is failing the tradition of a good family (a load of rubbish in the circumstances). Why should he waste his time and money on those who serve?

HE CARRIES AN ASSORTMENT OF COMPLEX EQUIPMENT AS A FORM OF SECURITY. His tape-recorder felt slightly depressed, the wire crawled over the wall. A piece of masonry formed a secret sign. The occurrence in the taxi held religious meaning.

CONVINCED THAT THE WORLD SHOULD LOVE HIS HUGE FAMILY, he needs the help of women to be poetic. He has eight children by friendly women. The star was free on the Riviera, away from amorous adventure for eight years, reading Time magazine till dawn, hearing the other sounds of the twentieth century thing. It is hard to believe the town suit can still create such sounds. The fix resolves the contradictions. To meet his yellow public he comes to London, his stomach is lifted out and broken, his body distresses him. His tall hands thank the man, talking of brothers and thanks.

NOW HE CAN EAT HIS THREE BANANAS. He helped himself at one o'clock in the morning, his mouth of fruit foaming over himself. He forgets his name, he fools the new life in him, his chin holds up the world, the fatigue in his eye crosses the other eye. The world follows the primaeval order. He preserves fear of himself at four, but there he is between the living thing and the sea. Until he is dead his family lives too. An aeroplane waits in front of his hotel. The guest-book makes an O till his silver money is found. The American crackles in chapel, destiny can read and write. He will kill the famous chef, his arms gone, he has kennels full of bananas, he encourages photographers, it was he who felt overwhelming in New York.

HE HAS ALWAYS ENJOYED THE TEXTURE OF A HAPPY MARRIAGE complete with grotesque cripples (the reason why he is labelled master) avoiding the large inhuman ground with tilted shadows.

THERE WERE ELECTRONIC CLICKS OF LANGUAGE as he talked to his wife. The operator had charm. The conversation had a Spanish hand over his face. 'Okay,' but he was suddenly different. She knew who he was. 'Yeah, it's me.' It was clear he had been betrayed. It was all right. It was unimportant. He had received and not answered a letter. The lousy dinner encouraged him to stay in New York. The continual rain worried him. He knew he was not there with her good wishes. He got through Paris successfully, the passenger gangway smelled of kerosene. 'I told you about my trouble. The painful thing was cured. When I passed through I felt free.' He remembered years ago when he slept with his Washington wife in different positions. She liked to cook, but now his wife was five and a half feet tall with sandy brown husband and respectability. She had been wearing a white linen suit, it had been announced that she would be wearing white. Her relatives had trouble in selecting the guests and telling them to shake hands. In the double room he had a couple of drinks with Anne Marie and said in passing, 'I appreciate those rags.' The glass contained comfort enough but not enough. It was a hell of a life with no roots. They told me to keep going on as before. Yeah, I said. In 1957 I found something: the advantage of staying in hell. But a permanent girl asks lots of questions. We were running around most of the time, then we moved back to Paris. I found it best to get her out of the way first. I remember her cheerful questions. The answers wouldn't come. Then she stopped writing, and the lawyers were saying . . . For Christ's sake! She stayed some time before she went away.

IT WAS THEN HE PRODUCED HIS PLAN TO SPEED UP LIFE: there were only three terms of life and 'It seems to me that we are a hybrid race able to increase speed for ever.' He laughed out loud at the remarkable thought.

HIS SISTER THEODORA WAS MARRIED THE NIGHT BEFORE in his castle lined with armour. The groom carried a bouquet of bread in his buttonhole. They had four daughters and a son the next day.

A COUPLE OF LEGS WERE STUCK IN THE WAISTBAND OF HIS TROUSERS. In the village below, he swallowed a bowl of soup and chocolate mascara. His voice was ricochetting thirty miles from Salisbury when his wife flopped in the snow. His capable hands one at a time were eating bread and cheese, carrying on the noisy war in Welsh, with shaved head and fur boots.

NOW HE EXPECTED TO SEE THE KILTED PIPE BAND OF THE SCOTS GUARDS marching and cheering over the mountains and being shot through their old battlegrounds. He cabled the casting director with controversies all the time, he learned that the Guards were not tall enough to shift the tons of sand against the wall, he was asked to help but he was tired. He placed his boots on the table, switched the direction of his bulk on the bed, stripped off his military shirt.

HE STAYED IN HIS YACHT FOR 250 DAYS, fastening his teeth on to a paper cup ravenously. He landed south of Nice, then tripped over a giant tree.

THE SHALLOW SEA OF GREY SMILING MATERIAL prolonged the day, he carried the night in his overnight bag. The young woman on the telephone promised the fully-equipped recreation he demanded. Next day the well-built delegate from Britain, wearing pearls in his hair, a devotee of silver, made plain his deep respect for private aircraft. Peter Sellers certainly seemed funny trying on his trousers. The lounge filled up with Germans aware of her Swedish shape at the dead end of the long hotel, pursuing her legs between the sheets from spiritual motive. Her bosom grew bigger and bigger until she stopped breathing altogether. 'In South America the young women last two months. Here it is possible to strike lucky with loads of francs and make the girl last longer.' David Frost laughed joyfully in the great hotel, his little joke a forlorn attempt to create nothing whatever. He had totally subdued his daisy. Frank Sinatra stated his preferences too. The courageous younger sister distrusted him. For three days she lived on cups of tea alone. Christ, he was a Greek sculpture, and like Jesus he smoked hash on and off. Apart from getting high on sacramental wine he had no personality problems, he had a dynamic wish to play a leading role in public affairs. David Frost was bloody rude to a blonde actress a few minutes before, he finished with a terrified smile, he'd been playing poker with Yvette Mimieux and Gypsy Rose Lee by mistake. He said goodbye to Ted Hill who loved good conversation.

THE TOUCH OF INSANITY MULTIPLIED HIS FANMAIL FIFTY TIMES, his incoherence puts him among the biggest. For a year he did his weekly show of gibberish which it is, it is all beyond reason, putting on the mindspin, the open secret signs of the bigswing each Saturday. Younger Europe is big enough to force him towards the idol industry, getting ready for last year's anarchy. A million dollars develops messiah though his supporters claim none of this is relevant, frequent hysterics build his talent with speed, throwing out business like maniacs, the wilder blurs are loved, the blowing howling conflict business with the psychedelic motorbike and that's where the audience met him on Saturday night, sexily monstrous, obviously there. 'I choose pop, I wind to fit the mood.' He began to sort through thirteen girls, plastered with lunch and placards. He was a landslide for hours on end, stretched out all over with the longwave slogan, promising to bring back commercial things like reversible eek radio and immediately win eek or the new girl's climax. 'Then I'll be all right and conscientious in all this and wrap things up the way I want with hardly anything for hours on end. When I have Europe I'll spread for hours. I came out alive and worldwide in the end. I'm going again like I did this afternoon. What's the point, money's the blahblah maximum point.' He has direction, his assistant Sam has a million dollars in the bank and his personal photographer has quit, and the rest of his engineers and secretaries plus assorted life-educating flesh shrieked amazingly. The rich and successful man in his chair sweated like he had a sergeant-major on top of him. 'All this is mine,' neurotically on the floor. His cars were a good show, his career had flair, he made himself. When he came on the air he sends out the sense of man was mad, the producer got out of the way, he started right on his night, the mad show eleven till two, the same wave as the afternoon, all hardwork length, he had a fast dinner but tonight puts on an average fifteen hours, sorting the swingkids, preparing his pile in fleets of cars, the full fanclaim producing jungles that careered his special trade right across town to eat 500 separate cassettes, the restaurant in his mouth with marvellous food and this when he began to suck it, all of this became really expensive, he went berserk with his head for the first time, swinging the waitress on her back, flirting with spirit, insulting himself, she brought him bowls of plums, there was a fight as hard as ever, he was burning time with endless morning music, fifty girls in twenty hours, maniacal by now, a dozen wires and tubes in corners, three more hours hanging on, he pissed on his photographer giggling in a corner, he stripped most of his girls to the waist, his knees screamed, he howls his eyes open for the eye-opening ultimate climax putting in

THIS MAN WITH CRIMINAL TENDENCIES became mentally ill. He was aware of the colours of his friends. He swiftly attained his object. His stability increased. His own feet were a pleasurable lump of mankind.

HE TELEPHONED HIS LONG-DISTANCE WIFE. 'Independent means we're able to lead independent lives. In a bright green bed we go our own ways. Without a sound it's good for us to play quietly.'

AFTER THEIR EVENING TALK his superior mind slides towards the wordless night. He listens occasionally, her admiration looks at him, he breathes faster, she has moved the dead, her mouth has said nothing.

OUR LINE IS DEAD. A night telephone can cost twelve pounds. Exactly. Yes. Can't do a thing about it. Check each girl in town. Literally impossible. You try to check all those in one night. Can't be done. Inadequate machinery. Going now.

HE RODE TO HOUNDS IN THE MORNING. His three gardeners were loaded with arms and ammunition.

THE DAYDREAM DISCOTHEQUE remained in need of the professional lavender shirt, picture the noise, adolescent Annabel with shock smile exercises on the staircase between songs of intimate toiletry on recording tape. Half-way men with two women coiled around the jockey seat permitted the mother of twins to stumble through the door every four weeks. He replaced his head on the rack, a bit shaky, silky personality sprouting hellos on the home service. He had forgotten the whisky, the melancholy smooth, as silence sinks in the toothless mouth.

LOOKING AT A TELEPHONE means that a woman is an individualist as long as her face works. Her history is another matter that should be opened and written down. The paradox of her reason leads to division of labour, the law and nature of language is involved, the collaboration of telephone and man.

HIS LIBIDINOUS EXPLANATIONS KISSED HER NECK and said: 'I'm having a haircut now in Las Vegas tonight.' She was often unconscious until quite late at night, she continued to evolve rather than revolt, she possessed mixtures of pain in her bedroom, the badge of the wife of a torturer. Aware of his envy of her hair, she learned the correct way to decorate her transvestite uniform, to cultivate the state of not give a damn.

I'LL LEAVE HIM AT THE RIGHT TIME.

SHE PRACTISES HER LITTLE BIT OF ANGER. But her family responsibilities are indestructible.

THE NEXT DAY HE WAS INJURED IN A PLANE CRASH. His intellect and sensitivity explored those regions after midnight, the practical man his tie was off, he was killed in action with the physical courage of one strong hand and other disasters. The dirty work is done with sophistication, the silent cufflinks charged with electricity, there's no mistaking the coloured shirt in the flames. The copy of Look was a poem. The U-shaped body was getting very mean.

THE WATERS SWIRLED BEFORE HE DIED WITH A KNIFE, the police recorded he was not dead. For twenty-five years his wife had time to gasp, the breakfast on the table turned tragic.

HER FLAT IS A USELESS TEXT-BOOK TWENTY YEARS OLD.

THE FACES AND ATMOSPHERES OF WOMEN LIKE ACTRESSES.

THE FUNERAL CHAPEL FROWNS ON THE DOG LEFT AT HOME. To protect old ladies from the past, the future is picked out on a die.

DEMOLITION BEGAN AT THE CENTRE OF AN ILLUSION: women in a vision of cloaks and coaches, hotels release their men with the last lights of the night, mincing photographer, noisy princess, two canes walking. Thirty street corners were pulled down, the anxious earl overlooking the clattering park as the town houses toppled too. The duchess wanted to speak, the unfashionable people had assassinated the eighteenth century, those who survived danced in offices. The world war was a party in fancy dress. The accidental and esoteric fell like unrecognised bombs at the death of the famous cafe. The magnetic prostitutes clustered for protection, the gold dresses up and down. They were six in a circular garden, behind the disorderly street of ritzy flats, their house remained a private dwelling.

SKI TROUSERS BREATHED PALE VIOLET. The incredible Jewish room became so hot. The child was swung in the air soon after dinner began. The cook is dressed in black silk, she loves jewels, she doesn't care for the food, her gown would not match the goulash.

THE BROKEN HOME TURNS BROWN. The bottle of love is lost. Lust is brought indoors, to the horror of women whose desires are released in private. They continue to dress in downcast dress, in strained and sober costume. Women in velvet uniform (grey actors) avoid striped poets and fluorescent shock. They miss the adventurous festoons of last summer.

HER BODY BURST AT LONDON UNIVERSITY, an instrument changed her. Without hair or clothes, she moved house, she threw stones at her sister Kath. There was no reason for the groups she had begun attending, the drinking session is reserved for barbarous women, her husband forgot the astral plane. She picked up a living in Ealing, and afterwards in Brighton. The glorious welfare worker could not be drunk, technically.

THE PROBLEM IS THERE ARE NOT ENOUGH FLATS ALLOWED TO EXIST. It is homes. And we all know there have been explosions in families condemned by the government. There are tremendous bangs on council estates when a flat gets given to a family. The trouble starts when race relations reveal themselves. After all, the pink will continue to exist in family swellings. The families wait for a flat contrary to humanitarianism. The lower classes are rivals at the moment in England and only eight out of twelve cities are occupied. The smashed windows are coloured. The family is too dark to afford the rent. 'I said good morning to the ladies many years ago, she looked at me, she can't explain the feeling of removal. The children may be wrong, it may be against the law, but words frighten them.' 'Why the hell should they dare to have plaits in the hair?' The decent council flat is out of sight, the wife is too small, flattering one bedroom, the nasty neighbours could leave, the plaits are better in Paddington, the gentle negro has one son crushed by smashed children. 'But not at home, they're shy after all, they've got to, I'm not going to, you say you wouldn't, we didn't realise Mrs Longville wouldn't mind next door but then we wouldn't know perhaps.' She sat on the sofa and the gentleman had his arm round her for ten years, she shouted she was born there, the camera smashed the photographer's mind, the scared children won the war with gentle manners, why should I speak when it's bad for them? The practice was to make the flat like everyone else. When they were given a nice flat with no distinction of tears everyone could see how this all started.

A NEARBY SLUM IS NOT PITIED, clothes over the floor, six prams allowed: loving in the neighbour's garden is better than playing in bed. The lawns for a time needed talking to: the children do this in quiet voice: 'I am now hanging in space. Automatic me sallies downstairs and swerves around the nasty quiet. I am convinced of many monsters. In my face comes the funny face. I make big friends when I know my parents.'

THE REST OF THE MORNING IS VERY HARD. Arching the back with particular skill, the boxing instructor tends to hit very hard as often as possible. 'Then he started beating me on Saturdays. When I was six or seven he beat me, he would get so angry. I would stand against the garden fence and he would beat me, slashing as hard as he could. Oh yes, he got it off his chest that way, aware of the rest of my life.'

THE GARDEN WENT ROUND FOR TEN DAYS. Tiny babies refuse to eat when beaten, ignoring the breast for the same reason. Only the mother dares not sleep for fear of the salacious cry in the night. The floor rears itself up in strain and dies with the brown paper parcel tied to the boards. Even those impersonal children crawl downstairs to wonder how long the rabbit will be there in the blue box, with its own nose twitching.

THE SECURITY OF A DIRTY ZOO. Find your stinking child sitting on food, building a nest of experience, committing suicide at the end of a chain.

THE CHILDREN HAVE BEEN EXHAUSTIVELY INVESTIGATED. A committee plans unpleasant experiments. They push them to the limit, each individual limit, using himself again and again. The ethics remain tricky. Their motivation is explained, some are over-keen to take part. After ten weeks of isolation, put the question: What makes them do it? This may mean they enjoy some technique of hidden disease. They are connected to a machine which works in a fairly unspectacular way. The actual sensation is of woolly slippers over the face. The clip on the nose sounds alarming, the effectiveness of instruments is fifty-fifty. Human subjects pay a shilling a ride. Ministry officials are not appointed, the medical idiot is enough.

THE EXCITEMENT OF LIFE. The longed-for box of chocolates. Very slowly eight boys and girls go to sleep together.

'WE HAVE A ROOF THAT BOTHERS. We have few things. We hope to live cheaper. How?'

NEW PAINT FOR SIX YEARS HAS NOT BEEN SEEN. 'Without compensation we would not be here.' The wall-paper is forbidden to telephone apologetically. The room is prepared to receive the mother, to prevent deterioration as far as possible. The control of the child is not worth the dirty stuff the mother left there. The first morning is unthinkable. The lively evening is shut on return, the nightmare was absolutely necessary, the electric plug is cut from below, the plastic hand has disappeared. Again the shaky morning comes unsuspecting, the rapidly opening window looks like the dawn, the exterior-looking wintry dawn that waits downstairs.

THE THREE PERIODS OF GLOOM, the time of the birds flying in V, the fleet swimming in the field of air in the column of rising air. It never stops officially. Drinking is the last resort, though the rainwater is occasionally dangerous. The people wept soup, drinking the world's heart. They love children, is it not strange they ran out of money?

THE BLOCK OF HOUSES WAS AN OVEN. Like a hospital, separated by fences, there was no sign of a room wrapped in thick sleep. The heat of flesh heard four strokes through the floor, the room was filled by a wall, the nine years felt heavy on the shoulder, the red basin of glass was covered by coal. Her hands noticed the tight gown tattooed by white soap, grey gums weeping with soap in them, the body moved the foot which slipped in childhood, the eyes watched the basin through the air. The window could see the man opposite, he was shouting information with his bones, the room breathed with slowness buttoning his jacket through the door, the feet in the room began yelling, the flat face was frightened by his arms in the middle of his clothes, the ceiling went on talking slowly fit to choke. He brought her down to the floor, yesterday the head moved in the cupboard. The coffee was boiled cabbage gradually, the words drowned in the bed whenever she liked, louder than anyone else in the warm bed. The expressionless moment, the soup colour downstairs under the wooden feet fallen in the room asleep in the iron oven to cover the fire at night. It was green with cleanliness, the sand and chairs on the wall were soldiers in the light room, the pink box filled the ceiling, the door was another leading to onions and hot coal pondering in the cupboard. The door appeared in the squat house banging into the night asleep in the pit, the door opened on to yesterday's ground swallowed in the corner, blown out and locked up, shutting the door behind, a last door banged in bed, the shadows folded their arms along the road.

and hundreds of numbers of trams on the road, and you have these poor guys swinging and beautiful, and he eats nuts like a dream, and straw is turned over the whole country, there isn't one house unexploited, everything loose would fall on the doorstep, he says I've told you the dream, fall down, mock it, he hates what it was, the arrogance of war in which he was obliged to show pity, when he lived in a loft for three blank years. Now he faces the freedom of the mother who would be an artist one day, each beginning with days locked up in freedom. When he came in he said that is why I will go and eat bean soup, back from the war passionately painting his mother on the bed asking where he had been.

THE DAY IS MARVELLOUS IN INDUSTRIAL LONDON. Every city is there in the land of Paddington, grey as plastic tomato. The acres of pleasure cost fifty shillings a week, excluding food, electricity, and nervous breakdown.

OTHER PEOPLE LIE DOWN, BUT THIS WIFE HAD HER SHOCK STANDING. She is too young for Britain. The bodies of newcomers are bought and sold, bit by bit, for green cheese and powdered milk. The wife wanted the whole house sprayed white, she was spending her time sleeping with a dog and three bloody cats, she was looking for a bit of land to raise vegetables. She said she had seen an advertisement for soil: 'Now they've sent me the wrong sort of soil!' She offered her belly to the city three times a night, at four o'clock, six, and eight.

THE MAN IN THE CAR HAD A QUICK SMILE WITHOUT A SMILE. She found the squeezed and concentrated movement exciting.

WHY NOT DRIVE OFF STRAIGHT AWAY? One and a quarter hours. How long between him picking you up? And you? He talked about people he knew. Are you married? Yes. Something. I've got something that would. Quieten you. Struggle. I shout for help. He terrify me. Face frightened me. I moved across. We talked for a bit. His manner changed. Physically I could have stopped him. Talking for a bit. After. Kept saying I wanted coffee. Didn't want coffee particularly. He let the driver's seat go. I fell back on to the passenger's seat. He just sat there for a while. The second time was he gentle? I didn't really. Notice? I was trying to push him off. Offered me a cigarette. I kept telling him he ought to go.

SHE DIDN'T. Discourage me. Went further. To see how she reacted. It wasn't a definite no-go-away. Would have taken her. Minutes if willing. Yes. You know what I want. Wait to see. Kiss and cuddle.

IT WAS A COMPLICATED PLACE FROM ALL OVER THE WORLD, five colours on holiday, humming from a lorry. Now look back: the cars moved easily, as a man with big animals, restless, mobile. The careful glare is shaped aerodynamically, reducing the cost of exploitation. The apostles of speed despoil the atmosphere, the city is floating in foul gas, but 'the entire town is suffused with natural charm.' Two hundred grey people live on radiant platforms, the overwhelming success of pre-cast concrete cells recalls the splendour of a century ago.

THE MOTORCYCLE ATE A SEVEN-YEAR-OLD GIRL; a few people used a telephone.

A CERTAIN CAVITY LIKE A TOMB, the skin is left like a girl asleep. His hands climb up her, play a game with the shape of an idea faltering in the curve as he talks.

THEY HAD THE TEACHER DISMISSED. They frightened him by the lasting method, drawing the blood of the child.

THE BEAUTIFUL YOUNG LIVED IN EALING, the dog had a glamourous waistcoat, the princess cried in the fog, the child was asleep in her bed, she looked from the window but it was not wide enough, the unthinkable window swam with nails, shouting children hung out flags which said things silently, the child changed little, she seemed very beautiful in the place everywhere with portraits and flowers and gowns that gasped in velvet frames carefully tended in the old-fashioned way. So much greenery was deplorable. The shopping was no longer amusing. The Lord remained the same, a friendly chimpanzee. People came to dinner with a thousand advantages, when the bus passed the door before the war.

NOW THE SAD CITY CANNOT BEAR THE YOUNG GROUP THERE. It makes me think I'm forty but I'm not sure. I know I'm going to end, I know I was born, I remember my youth in flat language. This is the first time I have studied architecture to still the tension. A vague gesture of empire crushes my stomach. I go to these parties for the genitals, the heart

SHE HAD HER OWN WAYS, SHE TOLD ME. 'My chief job was to look pleased.' I have found five dazzling model-girls by the amateur method. I collect names to put in your eyes. The girls' idea of looks is to succeed in New York, they are new, very new. Sally in pictures likes to work well, people like English skin, fashion is still a trick, you have to highlight London, the idea is to wear paint at a party. You can't catch Marianne Faithfull, her mood is important. The end result is complete personality with the virtue of mouth. The melon-shaped personality of a first-class technician warms the director's heart: professional women look more female, the angelic mouth is an invisible export.

BOTTLES BULGED UNDER TARTAN SCARVES and gin was consumed in the white-tiled lavatory. Certainly the Scottish scholars acted the part of conquerors, but the orgy of overcoats in the female premises looked like planned festivities. Their accomplishment was to colonise by force. With buttresses of alcohol after cheerless weeks of sober work they tended to wish their revered parents in Northern Alberta.

A WARNING VOICE WAS RAISED ON BOTH SIDES OF THE ATLANTIC, the hazards of war lasted 35 years, the young people were not worried.

THEY LEFT THE TOWN AND TOOK A BUS TO EDINBURGH, they queued for dates on New Year's Eve, with the blackflies grinning.

LIKE THE MAN IN TOLSTOY'S STORY, they were satisfied with a monthly ration of pretty girls each as large as the Ukraine. What the young man wants is most of the world, he finds it easy to be strong, provided he can seduce his great-grandmother.

THE MONOTONY OF RIVERS, immense things in Edinburgh, champagne in the back garden, 20,000 spermatozoa and this is all right. At half past eleven the adored one in bed, all sleeping in one bed, they did not care for their companions, the foot odour became apparent.

THE PECULIAR PROVINCIAL CITY was shocked by spinach in a hotel room, the undergraduates were masters of the old world, T. S. Eliot was assumed to be a Martian, their future was to prevent the blowing up of the galaxy, through the summer night they stuffed newspapers into bottles and knelt in private prayer.

MARIANNE FAITHFULL STARING AT 7.15 A.M., DOTTED WITH DEAD LEAVES, GREETING EVERYONE AT THE DOOR, brushing and burning the town, 'We're so happy as it happens,' enjoying all morning with the boys.

The phantom officer last year did not come. One knows what is going on: in the late afternoon teenagers drinking at parties again, maybe your best friend shuffles out of the kitchen, and here we go against the wall, praying to Oedipus with his two daughters. There is so much hash at the welfare agencies, the stuff is handed round, people arrive with wheelbarrows, cultured families prefer meditation as a substitute, the vast area of science maintains the leisure problem, people dump their garbage in the language laboratory. The seventeen-year-old is shallow, filled up every three months, keeping alive with sweet delight, freedom shows on her records, at the first passionate parties down there a crowd of young people hung on a tree one night with bored bottles of beer.

MEN WITH WOODEN CLUBS CONTRADICT ONE ANOTHER. Within a few days they return to London to learn how to kill properly.

THE TRAIN HOME TO CHARING CROSS SMELLED OF URINAL, this national problem instantly became a way of life: 'Well—wasn't it nice?' No. They approached the corridors of houses. The waiting for cream and sponge cake was over.

THE CAPITAL INCREASES. From the train comes the sound of the hills, it is a red rhythm living there. The wealth of London does not wait. The hotel was not the same sixteen years ago.

TOP-LEVEL WINDOWS LIT WIDE GALLERIES, THE CHAOS WAS WIDENING, the palace was designed to close, everyone could see the end, everyone kept moving, we knew our chaos. About the city, over and against the city, the father seen as cloud shadow, the urban myth centred on the figure, the European recognised and overwhelmed, the great northern city communicates shock. You realise the wave moves on, atoms disappearing, the child killed, hung in the centre of the city square. Anyway the children knew, there were so many of them, they could play their games without time limit or restriction.

EIGHT MONTHS AGO THE NEW DEEP CARPET WAS SCRAPED AND PAINTED. The dead city miracle was better than ever. They had already forgotten what had happened. The city dignitaries had promised the central heating once again, the government had given 300 for a library. Tanks had delivered guests to houses all over the town, with gifts for each shop-keeper and businessman. The fried housewife hunts the market regardless of season, asparagus breaks down kitchen walls, cooking rare fruits in fluorescent light. The scars on the slums were deep and formless. The big premises were fully functioning. The banks were still earning and sometimes money at thirty-three per cent was rushing away with itself. For ten years people in truck-loads had been taken off to sawdust-covered destruction, now they were split down the middle and loved by officers in smart uniforms. Dogs were dried and varnished, cats were saved, the centuries' muck this summer was cleared away. Books were collected in basements black with oil, the pages buckling slowly. A thousand dangerous pages were thrown on the fire. Grandiose schemes laid floors into the future, the sun burnt blue, for those who worked in small rooms the money was slow to come. Antique tables had more glamour than contemporary art, the museums alone had hope. The tragedy stretched over the family, all jewellery in the city belonged to the church. For the first time the crucifix in the hospital was daubed with oil, the people had slept in mud for six hundred years. Thousands of walls were bulldozed for the people. There were only two cups in the new laboratory. The hotel was beautiful and welcoming for £50. Soldiers patrolled the ruins, they pinned medals on firecrackers. A thousand men gathered plastic strips to exchange for girls for sale in shops, tied together and placed upright, each face covered over. For the special display of money in the Gardens, fourteen million pounds arrived, there was so much goodwill, the names published and inscribed on a stamp. You can talk to the people, no one can accuse you of superficiality, the ministers sit in the ministries, the yellow restaurant squats on holiday waters, the culturally-minded buy books, she wakes screaming in the morning, they may break down the door of her house, the city is glutted with money, the sky looks normal, it explains the growing feeling of fear.

THE PROMINENT BUILDING WAS CLAD IN ALUMINIUM SUN-VANES which were polished at least once a day. The curious structure had wide shady roofs, each one collapsed while it was being built. Other perspectives were rising inside the fabric itself which stood on slightly rising ground, and towering behind the main construction most of the block looked like something grandiloquent made of money. The slab-sided bone block contained no apartment smaller than a prestige project, the brilliant achievement contained the sky.

THE SIZE AND STYLE OF A DWARF WHO SPRANG AND PINCHED THE STRANGER, the millionaire impressed the spacious suite. On the edge of fresh roses every builder was going bankrupt. The dream of size was predictably inadequate for the nonsense dream-palace designed to show where the roses came from. The luxuriant imagination dazzled Paris, only the raised and covered roads convinced the excited buildings that they were wrong.

FOUR OR FIVE TIMES A DAY THE RECORDED VOICE IS VISIBLE FROM THE TALLER BUILDINGS. 'Oh, don't go there,' twice a day across the road, from police officers investigating infiltrators. The local automatic experimental officers check their instruments sooner or later, each with a telephone and delicate equipment around the neck. They sit close to the measured mast, their life in the limelight, examining a small mechanism. One man inscribes numbers on a ticket of orange steel. On a fine day the men sit on the roof, full of blue, until the spots of rain fall on the toy windmill. The highest roof has three tin cans tied to it, the copper rain inside the cans relays messages by radio. John bursts his parachute and brings it down patiently to his office on the forty-fourth floor. Fourteen times a day he looks at the clouds and can tell you the time by counting the specs of rain in his eyes. Suspended from a tall government tower a balloon soars to the other side of the world. (It travels to China and meets problems when it gets there.)

IN WASHINGTON THE NUMBERS OF PIGEONS SAILING ON THE WIND ARE USED FOR INFORMATION, as they whizz round the top of the Capitol. In a way it's scientific. The investigators can calculate the number of lawyers framing alibis and decide whether to prepare a new dossier before lunch (their salad and sausage stands ready behind glass). A computer takes over from the men, personal news is the rare exception of the occasional day, there are devices by which they control it. The computer decides the pressure of the world, it produced future changes, man had ten ways to feed him, the radiosonde was faster than any existing, the mysterious balloon imitated reality for forty-eight hours. They study the charts in detail, next door rare instruments are used. None of them knows the sound of the language used by the rest of the world.

TREMENDOUS MONEY IS TRUE LIKE PRESIDENT KENNEDY, magnificent individual, altar joy working at winning belonging. Magically intimate feelings leap forward into happy mouths. Five hundred sporting skills communicate directly. High quality psychology operates on sub-conscious blocks. Natural people are developed by Arthur Sloan. The hidden eye in the office raises its hand when it wants a drink. The taste of western business says yes to the innocent. A million Americans in America alone, enthusiasm for America is planned, American joy, vitamin-enriched, protein-based, true.

THE CHAIRMAN OF THE AIR FORCE ABOUNDS WITH BOYISH ENTHUSIASM: he makes a special appeal for the young to be transported into the sky. 'We need people able to spell, reliable witnesses of the sound of the ripped-off wings.' Thirteen in one night volunteer for the adventure. Roger who is eighteen looks into the sky for six hours a day, he reaches for a drink at noon. The Chairman apologises for being late, he thinks his pilots are missionaries, he quotes the names of the Gospels with particular emotion, with no interest in lesser people.

A BOTTLE OF WHISKY IS LOGICAL. The terrified senator tries to alleviate the disillusioned poor. His wife carried a bomb, her hair tied to the handle. Books and papers stop suffering. I think it's shameful to castrate the state attorney.

YOU EAT THE FORMULA. It makes you slim more-or-less normally. It has an excellent effect on what you don't eat. The idea is to consume your calorie-intake. Food which swells is known to be good for you: biscuits for instance, and steak. The taste of bread will give a lot of people a comfortable stomach. In 1965 he had two children cooked and tasted, as an experiment, they tasted something like egg. Poached baby is a nice little meal—he is very secretive about the curious cooking process.

FOUR HUNDRED MILES BY MISSILE: FRANCE MUST HAVE HER OWN.

THE PARIS POP SINGER WAS HELD IN PRISON FOR TWO MONTHS, he broke with the cominform, his anti-totalitarian father changed his name and found work with the tourist trade. I wish Cardinal Stalin would die. God resigned from the party, he must have been an atheist at heart. The arithmetic director for three years was a communist, for five years the wrong kind of communist who could not control himself, then for four more he was what the party wants, and then for thirteen he contradicted.

The party wants how many more years?

DR ZHIVAGO WAS MURDERED ON THE WAY, the corpse was a foreigner, the governor replied: 'I don't know.' The Doctor's family was abolished, the author lost, meanwhile his father was walking home from prison.

PRISON IDEOLOGY WAS CLOSE TO HERESY, so he went to extremes of discipline, he was correct, he became an alternative candidate, his boots and papers belonged to the socialist alliance, the party remained in control of the right, the bureaucratic policeman arrested the whizz kid politician, Noel Coward said 'I'm not sure', with a portrait of Marx in his pocket (he had had a better life before the revolution), he had known Germans who were really good, now they could not be found, there were worse things planned for the future, he would become depressed in prison with other anarcho-liberal elements.

THE FRENCH AUTHOR LAID HIS GREY FACE ON THE MARBLE STAIRCASE OF THE PRIME MINISTER'S SALON, the successful poet had atomic power, smile of esteem, he had been a communist in Spain, he was asked to explain, politics on vague faces, tributes paid to his face, several thousand dollars, he is being paid by *Life*.

GOERING LAUGHED. He overkilled a second time and became angry. The arithmetic country has no leader. The best-selling radiation meter confuses inner thinking on important issues.

THE OPERATIONS-ANALYST TRIPLE-CHECKED THE ACCURACY OF THE AIR FORCE ACCOUNTANT, the New York government got on the hot line to Iceland, Russian space material was responsible for the attack on Rhode

Island, the President wiped out North Carolina, the area office rejected the suggestion, action delayed from 9 a.m. till 11.30 p.m. then prolonged indefinitely, ten colleagues lost face, lectured on the destruction of peace, they would provide a clean war in place of dirty peace. The lesson of the bomb was to kill the President, press all his buttons even if this meant his hands were raised and his reputation lowered. The importance of planning five years ago against Chinese policy: publicity changed the approach to hydrogen bombs, a softer sell to improve the image. Alarmed by graphs he refuted thinking, he believed discussion created personality differences which would not arise on an uninhabited planet.

IN HIS CELLAR THE RICH ALCOHOLIC ATTEMPTED TO REBUILD SOCIETY. His consultants corresponded with government officials in each case and concluded that the H-bomb would not be a catastrophe for the chiefs of staff. A system of H-bombs attached to boot straps would restore a nation's dynamism, a rigidly programmed computer might emerge as a great power, Russia would lose her credibility, German humans would be used as slaves, Kennedy would withdraw from the United States, the world would decline into crazy history.

A DOT ON A GRAPH IS HAPPENING.

POLICE SHOUT OUT A STRING OF WORDS as they march down corridors. No one spoke as they dragged the body from the rim of the great stadium. The chief of police was prepared for next winter, his men lined up for duty. All this was being rehearsed, he had disciplined some of them, their equipment was ready to go, his assistant gave out tickets for the show, everyone bought one, the veterans demanded two.

ENDLESS EXCLAMATION MARKS FORM A TOWER FOUR YEARS HIGH,

REACHING TOWARDS THE GREY.

THE POLICE HIT THE STUDENTS FIRMLY AND BROKE THEM UP, the swear words made these guys mad, they curse together, policemen yelling, short-skirted girls get hit where it really hurt, you can bang them against the wall when we beat them later, cracking bones every few seconds, a ton of muscle driving into peach and honey, he shoved his hand in, hammering athletic, they cry as they hit their necks.

THE OCEAN GASHED THE LONG WHITE GLASS, the sailors rolled right over, the pane of glass was blind, three nurses on bicycles ate pie and ice cream with a twist of the hips down the lavatory, long pink baby under the arm, the physical husband asleep on a heap of parcels. The vegetarian girl with yellow hair winked at the Baptist minister in the bright shirt, she didn't understand the conventions, she had seen his cock from 300 miles away, playing with figs, eating ribs of beef with her nail clippers, plaiting her hair in the lavatory, she fed her baby the end of his wet cigar, the cow rolled over, with twelve big pieces of coconut bar, sick on the grass, she posed on a heap of parcels, photograph her pussy for ten dollars, her lips moving with the landscape, leaving off her winter silver buttons, she met two fellas suffering from haemorrhages and suchlike crippled hippies.

SCORCHED EYES FULL OF WHIRLWINDS, the old dark difference teases you, lorries talk of work, caged assassin in an uneasy place, drunks for sale, a starched-blue gun in a pitch-black window, grabbing documents and pecan delights. The assassin could buy a Mustang and skid along the western rim, a man's got his hands on the back wheels, the uniform escape route, you need to know the highway's questionnaires, pattering on about curing racial unrest. Who was the driver behind the soft American car? She seemed to be giving him some relief, the piece of pie alive with pickle, guns everywhere, kneeling with relief, Mustangs everywhere, cops pining to grow up, evidence of yearning, the driver driving westwards into the land itself, seven, eight, yellow and blue highway, I'd shoot locomotives, a black new Mustang, rocks in mad shapes, this guy gave me trouble, it keeps the costs up, he stops to eat a wax cigar, he paid extra for the waitress, the explosive mark on her thigh: 'I know I'll end up dead.'

LEAN DEATH IS A CONFLICT BETWEEN MONKEYS, the word has seventeen letters. Monkeyshock of deliberate approach, a wife fifty years in the house, grass inside the kitchen, trees at the birth of the baby. The parents' coats are taken away because things have gone wrong in the connecting corridor, birth is expected at any time now, birth is a triumph of climbing and roaming, spontaneous escape. I have entered birth and survival, equipped with ropes, at the social level climbing is the principle of difficult living.

INTERVIEWED IN CAGES, madmen tell the world: fists flail to hammer the wall, the head is built in hate. BLAST those men who have the name of parents, DISGUST tears them apart, SPECTACULAR MONSTERS, TWENTY-THREE THOUSAND DISCIPLINED ROWS of animals fifty miles north. FLUMP FLUMP FLUMP FLUMPFFF.   KON. KNOCK THEM DOWN.

ON THE HOT BRIGHT DAY OF ATOMIC CONSTERNATION, they furled the night. The meteor snapped the end of the centuries, the clouds shouted and pulled their shaped nets in haste, tearing the sky before dawn. The puppets in the city of low wood and paper grabbed paper madly and covered their eyes, Christianity went on as always towards their shore. The old men, birds' heads wild with fear of political menace, were wary of the sudden intruders, but on the beach the women appreciated the dramatic foreigners, they went with buckets of water to the American arrival on the self-conscious doorstep to buy the country. In the shops the bright day came quietly, the comfortable officials were well beyond reach, the crucifixions were done indoors, the slaughter stared at the black and gold for forty days, while ornamented women attempted to live by trade. Their silk night series of silks shivered with fires lit on the head, everyone returned from abroad towards the ocean of impotent seclusion, old women along the coasts blew the intruders away, and these strange sights said no.

ONLY THE AMERICAN ANTHROPOLOGIST SURVIVED. He was busy on a good thing.

LITTLE IS KNOWN. Man hides. Ape qualities grow. Avoid the female. Change. Low, thin, with a jaw, and teeth. Dog head. He eats eggs. Hunt animal. Pain. Shriek.

HAMSTERS ARE MIGHTY PUPILS. Instead of memory they spend years of life in a box.

GRASS SKY. Green sun. White distant sound.

CRYSTALLISED BLACK DELIRIUM, metal-white terror, singular stone mania, mineral illness, inexplicable earth, hills of stone, changed leper, green sun, dense bright green swollen bodies, pulverised heart, heart thump, illness, science at each step, give oxygen, horizon on the margin of a strange thing, the use of the knife.

ATOMIC RETURN TO THE ENORMOUS THICKNESS OF ICE A MILLION YEARS BEFORE THE SOLID ICE DRIFTED APART. The theory of distances and patterns of drift. Quartz ice, sack cloud, storm force. The answer is impossible.

THE BRIDGE OF EARTH, the movement of the roughly triangular land, link between lands. The high face will turn, the road will have been a slim column of extreme lightness into the hillside, it will turn quickly over the sloping land, concave lower down in spite of the concentration of concrete. The pattern of tight curves can be anticipated, the grey green lane will resemble the natural flow.

THE WOODEN CITY NO LONGER EXISTS as the green children approach. The child has changed. Weakness ensures continuing shock, patches of bright money float in mattresses, the children sell guides to the old city. 'We could earn more at games.' Life becomes meaningless deliberately, get a job repeating rhythmically, paint the mind clean.

POVERTY ENDS IN VIOLENCE. They make a revolution for entertainment. The big money kids catch the goddam' boy, now they go murderous, meet death the day before.

WATCH THE BREATH OF PATIENTS. The hospital has a temperature of 120 degrees, the blood flow slackens. The hospital was struck by lightening. The five ton lorry stuffed bread into her dress. The large families made their big move.

VISIBLE EMOTION GOES SLOWLY BROWN, bundles slide continuously in efforts to avoid the years. The situation is expensive: urgent applications for washing machines are accumulating. Reporters split families with well-constructed questions, the doctors would like to see more response, the threads again are running in the air, the baby yells up the steep ramp hour after hour. The two sides cross, a counter-movement cautions, the trickle disturbs the even flow, tens of soldiers guard the area.

MRS CARTWRIGHT WAS TRAMPING THE PAVEMENT WITH OVER £2,000 after an order by the Leek County Court that cash and cheques could not be used without permission. Her Post Office money was lost by Mr Harry Clarke, the husband of a wholesale greengrocery concern. 'The public are obviously in favour,' said His Honour, before he climbed into his telephone and drove off.

BUT SUCH IMPRESSIONS CAN BE MISLEADING. In America today there are more than a hundred churches open for the thirty-three million rich today. Religious books attract the well-educated, the best three million are published by the church and Christians are able to get higher certificate on Sunday. The certificates are obtained by force or fraud, the price of orthodoxy is high. The sharp and clever are sold in hell and heaven looks shifty to some, but the church is used to people who believe that thought has ceased.

THE PAINTER HAS EATEN THE JUNGLE, the dream of the rocking chair dream has evolved, the theme of traffic into street, the tight pattern of poles around the people, imagine people rewoven a thousand times, he is now deep in his Victorian bed to sleep in the street instead of working, his dream bed seems ugly in the road, he does not count his love, the remote new is shown in summer, the rare is rarely found in town, you should be in Europe by the roadside, there is an edifice, go there! In spite of himself in autumn, his bicycle glorifies the dream in mocking it, the ten dazzling towns he knows, the ten names too are stolen from the railway, he has been smeared with the extended parts of his dream. Of course he doesn't like the political idea, the electric one at the top. Pop soothes women with light, he excludes them from his dream, nobody need be sold in his world. The dollars museum is all around there is, there let the poor thunder, the dream paints new signs for two years, he smiles when questioned, there is enough space for two to lie together, inseparable from his dream the wealth flows in friends together, the same numbers of gold and minerals, friends in barns together crammed with wheat to burn, the significance of human abundance photographed by Vogue with the name of the motor oil quoted in conjunction with every place. Look at the next scene:

THE MAN ON THE ROAD WAS ACROSS THE PLAIN, he could make the ground black, and the sea-ice was a flat tree on the straight land. His coat was held at home and he was cold with intense day for an hour. The red air was pain. The cut fence shut the track, the grass had a roof on, the light was a smoke eye caught by a block of light, the hanging sound penetrated the pit, the fire a shadow emptying. The man was a horse waiting, sleep worked the lever, the eye said who he was, the dark shook, nothing interrupted the pit choked by coughing. The ground was over there. The big horse with six legs was blown up by fire, the squat head sticking up ready to devour the world. He saw there was nothing on the road in the morning, no door. The horse shouted misery in America, the howling darkness named the people, the western burning threatened, the horse was harnessed to empty tubs, the young space blew death by the hundred and the oven burned blue in the sky of iron. Time had brought three sheets of metal and the glad accident had a strangler's face. The name grinned three times when the skin of the frog was roasted. The fit of white light with blue neck and hands like a horse, stone ears scraped the pit, then a man's legs perished and a doctor fell out of a bucket. The foot could not move without shouting and the hammer went on banging the carcase slowly. He had known the strong flattened by rocks, three sons had got out of his skin and the kids found something to eat. The windows felt cold as they were lowered into the pit. There's money! The horse had started again downward, the journey wiping the foam off the wind. The man moved in a ball in space roasted by fire, a dog in darkness, dead ovens red with history, its meal of flesh.

HARD TIMES FOR A CUP OF TEA! The wild Irish sing down the Edgware Road while others are waiting by the mountains to be caught by soft voices in tired mist. The bays are filled with fishermen, the old life is brightly painted, a mile trip is a big event planned for father: 'Will ye no be comin' by train?'

CHRIST STAYED GOSSIPING FOR A FEW DAYS in the cluster of villages, the place had a cultural outline, the homes of zodiac signs. He journeyed six or seven miles: the rich travel only when things go well. He wrote his book about the world, the idea of the parallel world, the world of order in the future, preserved in a book. He was attached to the old world of interest in minds and lives, sometimes more, sometimes nations, classes and so on. The prejudice swerved towards its target, the blast turned on him with force. But he kept separate from the world of fixed interests. His old world replaced it.

BEST RELIGIOUS SYSTEM IN THE WORLD. AVRO State Service. Big staff, catholic enterprise, against the excesses of socialists. All schools and doctors in one system. Christians have manifest faults, but their aggressive approach, their ruthlessness, transmits profits from far afield.

A PERSON IS HIS NAME. When he needed a new name he turned however indirectly towards bread and wine. When he had been reinforced by his family name, the remote midway name, when asked his name, he had heard the slight danger sound of the high accordion. Now Jesus was taking chances. He needed the radio link with revelation. He remained for a period of eighteen months, a distance of several thousand miles. Finally he needed neither name nor food. He had a glimpse of the only compost a man's house needs, and he in his turn was allowed a glance under the warm surface. The spirit came to call. He responded as to a woman, with the type of behaviour in which it is a dance, holding together with no rivalry. It was also secret. The maternal caress of watchful warmth. It ended in violence softly. The original family of man did not forgive the other. The blood improved in wood like wine, it cost nine shillings a bottle, was sent twenty miles away, given the identity of God.

there being of glass on walls, clouds over, glass cube but this is rare, composed of cubes, they fit flat, in the frame of brass, glass, coloured glass, in order that the light should shine through, yes this is so, each one of thousands, the effect of spacing, irregular, the effect is almost dull, the size changes, flesh in glass, in the form of wrinkles, parchment, with green or red written across, grouped, important, church propaganda, confined to windows, use glass of particular richness, you can see below, allow this dome, the shape of church, allow curved space, the lines of an octagon, use fewer, the best, apple blue you see, please the people, attempt illusion, crucifixion of the frontal figure, the theme is refined, very graceful, please as well as strike, you have to look up, hinting below, began with the eye, globe of eye, separate the two, wider, humanity of head droops a little, so gracefully, remembered, theme repeated, bring the mind, within, procession of people, tribute to the king, propaganda, presenting gifts, bring god, for a moment, less in size, minute, moved about, the only way, in larger form you find fascinating, particularly in decline, it costs less, personal piety, new style, stone source, astonishing quarries, the experiment succeeded, obviously, suited by complexity, a colourful thing, it is sensational, the pattern within, the individual, worth examining, it has character, if you look, you will find Him, it is no accident, this is where you belong

now you ask
the thing would collapse
the archbishop is certain
a person killed in Turkey
he tells the tradition received
this takes you back
the meaning does not turn
dead memory
now how they came to the
nothing depends on what
after all
he never assumes
in some sense
the shattering thing
and then the thing stopped
standing and talking
this is continuous
say on the sea-shore
there seems to be
he was buried
he has got up
took his clothes with him

no reason
the essence of the matter
you must believe there was
how reliable is the evidence
when you come to think of it
the strength of the evidence
on physical remains
a new situation
conviction is a question
happened
yet he never mentions
we will disintegrate
what we should call
vaporised
finished
allowing them to touch
don't you think
this to a lot of people
elaborate stuff
he was dead
revived
they would have stripped
  him

suggests to me strongly
at best one might say
but for me
the fact that matter and energy
it opens one's mind
becoming

reconstituted
some kind of possibility
great shock
are equivalent
there are possibilities
not solid not permanent

all sorts of contradictions
in a strange way
has been found
generalisations
it goes beyond the particular
you would say he is alive
we have to
everybody knows about electrons
because the effects were
yet
when he was asked
to be subjective
and this is what I believe
in mental images
and I think that hmm
and yet
but to him
one knows
existed
his moral position
like his or like I thought
extraordinary experiences
although I knew
like my husband next to me
and the joy
and this was an experience
a symbolic statement
obviously
yes but there have been
but presumably it seems to
    me
unlikely
it depends on what you

this thing
experimental
laws of science
man made
nonsense
because you see
the classical example
without seeing one
a long time ago
what does this mean
I think
as a person
firmly
in pictures
an agony
fundamentally
I feel it so because the fact
in a sense it never
what it comes down to is
I find myself
his was
so near me
like another person
I had such a wonderful
and all I could say was
it was so real
in the sense that

instances

I should have thought it was
what one person said
do not think

so far as we know
people say that
people make statements
I might interpret
or another
all one can say is
how do they explain
I would think that
of presences
it doesn't seem to me
as a body
no

when we die
very happy and content
that indicate
inside us in some sense
I don't mean literally
here is an instance
they certainly
people have seen all kinds
all this kind of thing
I can't see the end
as a human being

WHEN THE TIME CAME FOR HIM TO GO to a place where he was needed he explained that this requirement limited the possibilities in that the circumstances would create their own environment ultimately qualifying the manner in which he would or would not execute the exceptional tasks burdens and functions appropriate to his intangible and contradictory situation. The ignominious conclusions resultant and consequent on instantaneous conversion created an equation of spontaneity which obscured the necessary impossibility of significant action.

THE STRANGEST THING IN THE SKY JUST NOW IS THE STARS. Possibly visible as faint blue stars they are precise in the sky.

AROUND THE EARTH THE PLANETS, each marked the state of the modern scratch-signs in the sand. After twenty-two days the Pope will descend from the why. He said that getting and fitting the crown would be a major task, his voice faltered, one of his girls appeared, he was very sorry, but he had had a good year, he did not want to be singled out, it was a team job, he was superbly backed by society (although he wore a Party badge, he was not and never had been a member).

THE CONE   Bobby Baker
electricity   Baby Boko
simultaneity
inter-galactic intelligibility (so many eyes)
research which leaves intact
the attack on lives

GOOD BOYS DISCOVER NEW CONTINENTS. The blue steel nut shell starts calmly. Ten machines tell a good story. The dangerous trap is a slight misfortune. The craft runs away from earth. The volunteer for a few minutes pretends the pressure is greater. Astronomy makes him stagger slightly, he needs oxygen between the stars. The sun mystery has two eyes, green and blue, this bright thing because he is happy has the silent beautiful body of a woman in a newspaper, he looks at her, defenceless. Beyond the air is something else too far away from earth where it becomes impossible to hide, his feet in ice for four years. The distant human watches his health intently, to detect the moon anxiously asking questions. Gods and heroes die in space, the explorer does not think of it. In 1988 in the sky in the morning, his eyes on a stick in space. He says yes for fear of failing. The attraction of the moon is 150 miles long, streams of moon provide the opportunity for seismic activity, the moon's heat is enormous, the moon's face is perfect boiling water, no, the moon is replica of rock.

THEY WANTED TO STRAP HIS LEGS AS AT BIRTH, minute jolts and gleams delivered into blue space like surprised eyes heavy with gold and dollars knocking around for years.

THE BRILLIANT SCIENTIST FROM THE SPACE AGENCY scrapes eggs from the skin.

MINUTE BY MINUTE, THE TECHNICAL FACES LOOK AT HIM.

LOOKED FOR HIS LEADERS. NO REPLY, NO REASON. Stars became mysterious chandeliers above dark members of an unfriendly family. After the burnt frenzy in the area that separated the narrow dark room from the back of the craft he had no doubt. The transformer was burnt out, and that statement was made from comprehension that his craft was a room without its own plant. That did matter. That was where the deficiency lay, the only part of the story that was not news. The young scientist excused the reporters who did no work, all had made the prophecy of failure, to ignore them was to fall from a tower into a trap. The absurd words meant simple death. A piece of steel was folded into the curved roof. In that, a minor error was made: it did not fit. The violent pattern of green disappointed and fatigued, and in the end the yellow and green edge caused disaster. The news was not a hoax, the flies buzzed in and out with sadness. The trip was definitely on and would go on. The barbaric and religious photograph of the President became the true goal. The group died at the stroke of prestige absurd against a wall. The yellow colour of successful dust meant nothing.

HIS MOTHER SPOKE ITALIAN. She had five pieces of bread. The time was the end of the month. Pieces of evil outdoors, inhuman beings in stainless steel polished by the twelve foot sun, the colour of the sun was dull green, the colour of common nature under the influence of science, and don't forget that nobody understands.

FIX THE POSITION OF THE RADIO ASTRONOMERS MORE PRECISELY.

MEN ARE OPENING THE MOON. Streams of wheels have springs of space. The rim of the system was the wide discovery of unintelligent activity. Lovely men remained untouched by many winds from space. His vehicles have enormous wheels. Individual effort evaporates in space. A million years of rain reflect the skill of space. His perfect skin will be watercooled, his undergarments bear the marks of convulsive birth, advantage can be taken of his need to stay cool. Inside, the lesson is learnt without expression. There is no gloom. The white kitchen defines the cotton contemplating man as cool as cotton. Like a plump young girl it is possible to make everything up. The cream silk conversation lies on the surface, the mind totally engages the calm tragedy, the mind turns pages, there are flowers at the limits of comprehension, gauge the outlines once again, again the complications have always been calm, it was even the family drabness in the plain landscape, the face of decay, fragmented intellect, the American failure is no surprise, in his mind the personal death is fifty years ago, his brother dead, he has no urgency, his habit is gone, five years past he had nowhere to go, now he is left, man as man.

THE PERFECT WREATHS GIVE INTENSE SATISFACTION. Stomachs take risks with highly intelligent champagne. Inspired by space, he received a medal for working for the sons of the rich. Like the gladiators he risked his blood, and throbbing spectators expect their sons to follow him.

AS LONG AS HE STAYS IN HIS CHAIR, happy in the clutches of the air, to risk his life twice. (You rarely find people on the moon.)

CHARACTERS:

Waitress	Models
Drunks	Prostitutes
Chef	God
Priest	Negro
Italian waiter	Jimmy Anderson
American woman	Detectives
Eamonn Andrews	Riot police
Police	Groscinski
Ladies in gaiters	Marianette
Children	Daddy
Babies	Immigrants
Duke of Windsor	Mike Canaletto
Vice-Admiral	Agitators
Bolsheviks	Cassius Clay
Miss Hueth	Russians
Scottish sexologist	Painters
Housewives	Dylan Thomas
Intellectuals	Photographer
Criminals	Princess
Bishops	Designer
Archdeacon	Osteopath
Duke	Colonel
Chief Constable	Weirdies
Widow	Indian
Queen	George Harrison
Household Cavalry	Philosopher
Barbra Streisand	Nurses
Mrs Kennedy	Salvation Army
Jesus	Orphans
Billy Graham	Rolling Stones
Mary	Matron
Betty Lou	Barbara
	Mrs Martwell (who saw the ghost)

Mrs Davey
Persian girl
Rumanian Dean
British Council
Africans
Prime Minister
Terrorists
Reporters
Theodora
Frederick Forsyth
Diplomats
Baby-minders
Window-cleaners
Archbishop
Spiritualist
Lolita
Bicyclist
Theatre-goers
Marlene
Bill
Kitty
Knight, Frank & Rutley
Council officials
Norwegians
Lord Cornwallis
Anarchists
Chinese
Texan general
Communists
Mother
Mickey Mouse
Minnie Mouse
Celts

Boys
Tough women
Guardsmen
Millionaires
Director-General
Soldiers
Magistrates
Accountants
Burglars
Gangsters
Governor
Salesman
Voyeur
Maureen
Chauffeur
Park-keeper
Homosexuals
Tennis players
Girl in the bath
Connoisseurs
Dwarf
Censors
Sex maniacs
Right-wing M.P.
Karl Kaspar
English girl
Actress
Film Director
Heart specialist
Kasparak
Professors
Prisoners
Headmaster

General Westmoreland
Royal Horticultural Society
Chinese girls
Fusiliers
Captain
Buddhists
Fanatics
Stalin
Chief of police
Butcher
Sculptor
Plumber
Tramp
Bandits
Marxists
Property developer
Industrialist
Landlords
Yvette Mimieux
Sam
Sergeant-major
Gardeners
Annabel
Mother of twins
Torturer
Transvestite
Pilots
Earl
Kath
Welfare worker
Mrs Longville
Boxing instructor
Ministry officials

Farmer
Dostoievsky
James Joyce
Patients
Mortician
Lord Chief Justice
Bride
Pope
Mussolini
Commonwealth Cricket Club
Swiss Army
Policeman called Lilian
Gunman
Telephone operator
Scots Guards
Peter Sellers
David Frost
Gypsy Rose Lee
Bankers
Byzantine spectators
Brigitte Bardot
Jack Kennedy
Marlon Brando
Cripples
Astronauts
Painter's mother
Marianne Faithfull
Students
T. S. Eliot
Oedipus
Arthur Sloan
Air Marshall
Dr Zhivago

Boozers	Noel Coward
Vicars	Goering
Bishop's daughter	Malraux
Naked women	President
Mrs Murphy	Vegetarian
Petrol pump attendant	Sailors
Countess	Madmen
Ulysses	Mrs Cartwright
Mayor	Others
Cameramen	

'Essay' from *Beyond the Words*[*]

I cannot write a manifesto in the abstract, I can only define my ideas concretely in relation to my work.

I began writing short prose pieces in a rather pressured, affected style, trying to say something significant in each sentence. One piece was about digging a hole in the ground; one described a man rowing a boat. I started with something seen, then isolated and intensified it. The pieces were nearer to poetry than prose. Looking back I find them literary and a bit absurd. I remember writing in a lined exercise book in light blue Quink, a poem about a horse galloping across a stony beach. I'd seen the horse and the beach separately and put them together. I kept the poem for a long time. One verse described the horse like the sea 'breaking across the beach'.

I realized I could hang around forever waiting for things to happen that would trigger off precious paragraphs. Then I saw a photograph in a shop window, of a man and woman kissing. It recalled the relationship between my mother and father and between them and me, which I had tried to define but had been defeated by its complexity. I solved the problem simply, by describing the photograph, the image. This was the key to my being able to write my first book, *Buster*. Using my memory intensely, I found I could review my life in pictures and describe them in sequence. At the same time I discovered I could lie. I had been held up by

---

[*] *Beyond the Words: Eleven Writers in Search of a New Fiction*, ed. Giles Gordon, Hutchinson, 1974. Contributors were invited to write a brief description of their literary aesthetics before their short fiction pieces.

the need to tell the whole truth. Now I described the couple in the photo as if they were my parents although they weren't really. I could invent fiction.

The snapshot method worked best with the earliest memories when all I could see was a series of 'stills'. As I brought the story forward, nearer to the age I was, I remembered more and could tell a connected story. It was interesting the way the form changed, the narrative became more connected, as the boy in the book grew older.

The bit of *Buster* that led to my later work was a passage where the boy gets hold of an old typewriter and writes one word: Onion. He looks for the word most remote from 'onion' and hits on the word 'man'. Hoping to find total disconnection, he writes 'onion man'. The two words connect to make a phrase with meaning: a man who grows onions, or maybe sells or eats them. Thus at that early stage I was considering the question of connection and flirting with the notion of disconnection. In the next books I continued to see how far apart I could make succeeding images and yet connect them by ingenious or devious or extravagant or so-called surrealist means.

Disconnection fascinated me partly from an immature wish to shock, go to an extreme, make a break, an iconoclastic need to disrupt or cock a snook at the body of traditional literature. There was also the element of game, to set myself a puzzle, to stretch the two arms of a metaphor and still find a link between. The further I pushed the thing the more striking it became. I was also showing contempt for what I was doing, almost trying to write badly, from disgust with myself and with Literature which is not life but only marks on paper. Plus a political rejection of bourgeois art as a self-indulgence irrelevant to the struggle for social justice, which, by playing the bourgeois art game perpetuates a system based on exploitation and greed. Disconnection also expressed my own social estrangement, my distance from others, with the dual sense of superiority and yearning for closeness. Paradoxically, the act of wrenching images apart expressed a need to hold them close, like people. The couple kissing also made a connection in the sexual sense: I delighted in their closeness, envied it, wished to get away and leave them to it, desired to join in and be close to them.

My parents were separated by my mother's death. My elder brother and I were separated by his early death. The consuming nature of this experience showed itself not only in the disconnected form but also in the content of my work. *Europe After the Rain* is concerned with brutality and physical extremity but not with pain. Much physical damage is done but there is little emotional or psychological response to it. The characters seem numb. The climate of detachment reflected my own numbness in the face of two deaths. I had a particular delight and relief in writing that book, which derived from seeing that my most destructive fantasies could be transcended and used to make a book.

The story of *Europe After the Rain* was close to mine: a young man killed and a family broken, in a landscape of war and purposeless suffering. Yet I did not use introspective methods to gather the material. I came across it by chance. Three accidents happened: I saw the Max Ernst painting of the title, at the Tate. In a second-hand bookshop in Lyme Regis I found the verbatim record of the Nuremberg trials, and in another shop in Axminster I bought a journalist's report on life in Poland after the war. This last provided most of my background material. I had this badly written guidebook on my desk and I typed from it in a semi-trance. My eyes glazed and in the blur only the sharpest and strongest words, mainly nouns, emerged. I picked them out and wrote them down and made my own sense of them later. I dug up characters from that book though as a mere travelogue it hardly contained any. Perhaps some of *Europe After the Rain*'s 'numbness' derives from this distanced technique of writing from the unconscious. Painters often screw up their eyes when looking at a landscape so that in the blur they catch the essence.

In *Celebrations* I used other random methods, variations of the cut-up technique. Given this, I showed a strange consistency in my choice of characters. With no preconception or conscious decision I repeated my family pattern. Powerful father, absent mother, slaughtered son, surviving son, one woman: 'the woman about the house' as my mother was in our family of five. Whatever random techniques I used this pattern remained inescapable.

Celebrations grew from a mosaic of fragments written with no concern for ultimate plot connections. Delaying until the last minute any notion of what the book was about, I gradually assembled a series of heavy public rituals: marriages, funerals, wakes, steadily growing grander until they tipped over into absurdity. I got away from the bare, staccato style of war and found a full, baroque form to suit the content. I was disappointed that the book's reception was not what I had hoped, but pleased that my work was getting across to a slowly growing circle, notable among them John Calder, Bryan Johnson, Robert Nye and Angus Wilson.

After *Celebrations* I began again with fragments, so far apart as to make nonsense. In a succession of re-writes I pulled the pieces together. I could have re-written *Celebrations* to make it more coherent and acceptable but I stopped where I stopped. With *Babel* perhaps I stopped too soon. What defeated many readers of *Babel* yet gave it the quality I wanted, was that not only the narrative but also the sentences were fragmented. I used the cut-up method to join the subject from one sentence to the object from another, with the verb hovering uncertainly between:

> General Westmoreland was seen at the Spring Show of the Royal Horticultural Society yesterday. Heavy bombers again pounded the open rock garden, the valley area, especially the primulas. A variety of weapons were on show, superbly flowering specimens, while troops were moving towards the Botanical Gardens . . .

If the form of *Babel* was obscure, the content was clear: it was about the power of the State. How in every street, every room, every shop, every workplace, every school, every institution, and particularly in every family, the essential pattern of power relations is dictated by the underlying rules, assumptions and moral principles of the State. *Babel* described not the obvious apparatus of dictatorship but the hints nudges nods assents implications agreements and conspiracies, the network of manipulations that envelops the citizens and makes them unaware accomplices in the theft of their liberty. In *Babel* the crude despots of the earlier books, camp commander, factory manager, death, are reconstituted in the subtle dominance of the amorphous State.

My play *Palach* combined a number of themes explored in earlier work: the boy victim; the poignancy, bravery and senselessness of his sacrifice; state power. The 'numbness' of *Europe After the Rain* recurs as the trivial, indifferent chat of passers-by. From *Celebrations* came the use of rituals, like the boy's birthday and the drawing of lots, as substitutes for personal relating.

Babel had used press cuttings as raw material. Clearing my desk of these cuttings before starting a new book, I saw the possibility of reproducing the headlines themselves in a visual collage. Off-set litho printing enabled me to do this in *Dreamerika*. Babel had gone to unrepeatable extremes in the fragmentation of narrative, now I latched on to the story of the Kennedys whose characters and activities gave the reader easy reference points to help him through a sea of disparate images. I played hell with the documented facts, made crazy distortions of the alleged truth, in order to get some humour out of it, and also to raise questions about the nature of documentary realism. Screwing up the story made some very undocumentary truths emerge. Like when old Joe Kennedy buys the United States for 17 billion dollars . . . It was not until I had finished the novel that I realized the parallels between the Kennedy family pattern and my own: the same dominant father, the same martyred son.

After *Dreamerika* I gave up writing from the subconscious, making a mosaic of found pieces. I had written four books that way and the fun had gone out of it. But I was unable to sit at a typewriter and make up a story without raw material to work on. I was grounded in a method by which I found patterns and connections in a mass of indiscriminate stuff. I could no longer use journalistic material so I had to find something else. I hit on the idea of using a cassette recorder to record many hours of natural speech. I transcribed the cassettes and used the resulting material as previously I had used press-cuttings. I made a collage of voices. I carried over from *Dreamerika* the use of a well-known story and set of characters to create a framework and points of reference. The result was *The Angry Brigade*. Again I set out to free myself from my obsessions and again I was trapped. Same pattern: powerful State, youthful sacrifice. Like *Palach* the book was about physical action as opposed to mere discussion. From *Babel* came the anarchist ideology and its concept of the State.

In 'Wonderland', my contribution to this book, I have fused factory, hospital and work-camp into an all-purpose institution to represent the power of the State.

'Wonderland' from *Beyond the Words*

Ancient Roman mythology tells us that Venus, the original Goddess of Love, floated in from the ocean on a huge sea shell, fully grown and in possession of all that beauty of face and form which was to make her the darling of the gods and of all earthly males.

When I say working class, it's a good phrase, though it's a phrase I never use, to sum up people who live in three rooms because economically they have to live in three rooms. We use the social security and the health department to our advantage. The middle class do just as much damage to their children but they will not accept help or advice. When you say to them if you go to the children's department you can get a grant and you may get rehoused it doesn't mean a thing, they don't think it applies to them. They can spend £200 trying to undo their marriage or take another flat, they have quite a different set of problems.

My kid was snatched into care. After I got him back he never went for walks, for instance, in case he might get snatched from the crocodile.

I worked as a builder in those high rise flats where you can earn a tremendous amount of money. I brought home fifty, sixty, seventy pounds a week in notes. I gave my wife thirty straight off and the rest I drank, when I was drinking (I'm not at the moment). So there was no shortage of money, but we lived in three rooms of a rather run down house down the bottom end of Holland Road.

Hollywood mythology tells us that a modern Goddess of Love rode into Beverly Hills pedalling a lavender bicycle, dressed in tight-fitting lavender pedal pushers and a tight-fitting lavender sweater.

We were attached to Dr Garvin. He had a large practice mainly Irish, down the road there, and the trouble with the Irish and the main reason it was difficult to unwind his practice (because he was dealing in drugs) was they don't carry cards. When they return to Ireland the doctor might have five thousand patients on his books but there's no check. This all came out afterwards. He was pushing amphetamines on his patients to keep them quiet. My wife was on these things for three years through no fault of her own. She became hooked doing what the doctor said. He got sent up the hill for two years. While he was in there he ran the practice through a system of locums! Then somebody local, one of those do-gooders, tried to get him out! He was transferred to the main block where he would be safe, but he continued to run the practice from there, taking the money through these locums. It took three years to get the practice taken over. A very good doctor, Dr Bell, runs it now. He said it was the tip of the iceberg, he'd no idea how many people were using the things. After he'd got my wife off the pills she turned to drink because drink is very catching. If one member of the family does it the other usually joins in.

I'd got the older boy with me and was waiting to get the girl when she was old enough. They were well brought up children but very nervy, and yes, they'd been bruised. I daresay children don't mind physical violence, they prefer it to being ignored. That's why drugs are worse because parents cut off from their children completely, which tends to frighten the kids more.

The agent who discovered this Hollywood goddess, the myth continues' could see as well as any normally sexually oriented male that this luscious blonde was also fully grown and in possession of that provocative

face and figure which would enable her in a few short
years to become the darling of the cinematic gods and
the earthly, but frequently wealthy mortal males.

I had this feeling that everything was going wrong. I was drunk, my wife was drunk, and when I went looking for her on Friday night I knew I should have got in touch with someone. This is one of the mistakes I made that sits on my mind. Over the weekend I knew there was going to be a bust up and I tried to contact someone but the switchboard closes at six o'clock and they don't publicize the night number which is only for emergencies. I rang again but they refused to give the emergency number. They said they would send a car round to my address but I said don't do that, it will precipitate a row that isn't necessarily going to blow up. My wife had left the kid with a neighbour when she knew I was coming looking for her. So the neighbour rang up too. Apparently — this came out at the meeting we had afterwards — the neighbour had been involved with Dr Garvin at one time and now she claimed she'd slept with me! She threw it in my wife's face, saying anyway your man's no good, I mean, I've had him, everyone's had him. And she had a boyfriend in the office, though they tried to hush this up afterwards. They're very crooked up there, not all of them, but that lot, they're renowned. So I couldn't do anything, though I have the night number now. It's the main block, you ring the main block and they get hold of someone in your area. It's a long way round but they can't man every switchboard in the areas. They back you up legally too. When I said the child shouldn't be left at home with a drunk mother they said just sit there and lock the door on her and we'll be round. They can be very good. But the neighbour called them and said the child's grossly neglected, the mother hasn't been home all night and the father's gone after the mother blah blah blah. I said 'I'll be round in fifteen minutes, I only need to find a taxi.' They said, 'No, we're taking him into care.' Well they can't do that without a Mental Health Order. I don't know a lot about it but I know that. They shouldn't have done it without deciding whether the home was bad or not (the neighbour knew in fact it wasn't). But they took the boy away and put him in a Home so the two kids were in two different Homes in North London. Normally when this happens the kids stay with me, though it only happens about once a year. If it had been a weekday the boy would have been with me and I would have said no, you can't have him. I wouldn't allow any number of cars to take him away because I just don't let my children go into care.

> The year was 1953, the place a Wonderland called Hollywood. A crisis had struck Columbia Studios. Rita Hayworth, the reigning love goddess, after an epic argument with studio president Harry Cohn over money, had flounced out on her contract, leaving the studio not only with a stack of expensive film properties which had been purchased for her, but no one to compete with Marilyn Monroe who was under contract to a rival studio.

Of course my wife came back. They found her. She was dead drunk. I went in and beat her up and broke her nose and blacked both her eyes and injured her spine and kicked her in the stomach. They'd phoned me that morning and said they didn't release children at the weekend. Once they're in the Home they're in the Home. God I was furious. Sunday morning I went round there and we had a general meeting about what we could do about it. When my wife walked in you've never seen anything like her face. It shook me rigid. I thought, that's the result of not making a phone call. It was chance. I didn't have the number I should have had. They didn't give it me when they should have done. They took the boy and I came back and found him gone and I took it out on the wife. I think it frightened me so much that they could take my kids away and they might not give them back. If one can point the finger at the villain it was that particular man on duty that night, the boyfriend of the neighbour. They said it was something that will not happen again. They said they had reason to believe she had friends in high places, someone who said, 'I'll deal with this, I know this family.' He triggered off the situation, a man who didn't know enough to know he should not have done that. I don't think he was in the car that picked the boy up, I think that in the office he said, 'I know that lot, you go and pick up the kid,' under the Old Pals Act.

> There were a number of things Cohn could do to get even with the uppity Miss Hayworth. He could black-list her. He could suspend her. He could tan her goddess-like fanny with the riding crop he always carried.

In fact my wife looks forty-five, she's thirty-two, very hardworking. When we married she looked like a well-behaved little girl, always clean, turned out in a cotton frock with puffy sleeves, like a nanny child. That fits really. When we lost the kids she went to live with her sister. They both soon got what I call hatchet-faced, with dyed hair. Other than that they didn't look the part. They never made much. They lived in a flat and two constitutes a brothel. The villain was the bloke in the office, he was running them, which was fair enough. They don't get the women usually, they're not out to harass the women, they want the man who makes the money out of them. If a man's running four or five girls he's going into the protection racket and he can build up quite a trade. You get him putting pressure on the shop round the corner. Those are the villains in those cases. The money gets siphoned off into big crime, that's where a lot of big crime comes from.

They didn't go after the real villain because he was one of them. They went after me. They were on the house for three weeks. I was livid. I don't like cars sitting outside, coming in late and finding cars outside. It was usually a disguised car but you know what they look like in their regulation flannels reading their regulation newspapers, you can tell them a mile off. You get the feeling, I've had it once or twice. I walked up to one and said, 'What you want today, mate ?' 'Waiting.' 'You can't do that. I've got some stuff being delivered and you're bang in the middle of where I want the truck to come.' At first he was a bit shirty, then he said, 'It's not much of a job. I don't like sitting here any more than you like me sitting here.' He was all right, straightforward, short back and sides, only they all look neat and tidy whereas most people don't. After that they said they'd come and see me to sort it out. It was a time when I had a lot of trouble so I said call at teatime when I thought I wouldn't be too busy. It nearly emptied the place! One guy who ran a strip joint couldn't get out the door fast enough, several went out the back, the most surprising people disappeared.

It was harassment to make me co-operate. They had to pick up someone, if not me. One of them asked me to help at least put the two women out of circulation. I said no. He said if we take her to court will you say she's not a suitable mother. I said indeed I will not. I never go into court. I do sometimes but not for you, that's the distinction. He wanted to know who my friends were, he asked to see my address book, but I wasn't having them go through the book saying 'Fancy him being here' with any name they knew. I think that's wrong. It's my right not to have them going through my friends. When I said so he was quite reasonable. I said, 'You don't do me any good coming round here.' He said, 'Why?' in injured tones, with his flannels and his white shirt sleeves rolled up to here precisely. I said, 'You don't look like friends, let's face it.' He laughed and said, 'I suppose you're right, we can't get away from it.' He gave me the name of the man they wanted. I said, 'He calls here sometimes, I'll let you know. But I don't like it. It stinks.' He said, 'He's done seven years for grievous bodily harm, if it interests you.' I said, 'Yes, it does.'

> An ominous silence descended upon the Big Man's inner sanctum, a silence broken only by the angry whoosh of the riding crop as bald, beefy, powerful Harry Cohn, teeth clamped savagely on a cigar, strode across the heavily carpeted office between rows of golden Oscars standing at attention on his king-sized

desk and the rows of nervously expectant underlings
standing before the desk.

When the man did turn up, the funny thing was he looked about
nineteen. He still had acne. I couldn't believe he'd done seven years. I
thought, what do you see in those two old bags, they can't bring in much.
I rang through and said I'll keep him talking but you'll have to be here
inside three minutes. We more or less did a deal. I said if they left me
alone I'd help them pick up their man. Then they got into a traffic jam
and didn't arrive on time. I was pleased and I showed it because the whole
scene stinks. I'd tried to safeguard the children by offering them what
they wanted. Otherwise they'd have broken up the flat in the middle of
the night and then I'd never get the kids back. A cut and dried decision
over these things is very hard, you do what you feel will cause least harm.

One thing was clear: something had to be done. When their car arrived
late nothing happened, they weren't put out. They said next time you see
him give us a ring, we must pick one of you up, so make it soon.

When I phoned them I took care to phone from a call-box. I wanted to
ring up and say I would lead them to the guy if my kids were left alone,
but they traced the call and a car arrived. I said you shit, you've radioed
the cars, because he had promised over the phone not to. He said, 'What?'
I said these cars have arrived at the phone box. He said, well there's
plenty of cars. If I'd put the receiver down I could have walked off, but the
man was listening on his little . . . Then they arrived and held me there. It
was about eleven thirty, I'd just been to the cinema. They held me until
their boss arrived. They were quite rough. I don't blame them, they have
their job to do, but they weren't gentle. I had to stand on the pavement
with them punching me, until a big car came up and I was shoved in and
driven off.

Suddenly Cohn stopped. He turned, his eyes gleaming
with self-righteous anger. A triumphant smile twisted
the corners of his mouth. He brought the riding crop

down in his desk with a resounding whack of decision.

We drove out of London on the M1 and I saw the work camp on the left, a factory with a tower like a giant Heinz baked beans can with horns sticking out.

> 'So we don't have another dame with big boobs on the lot,' he said. 'So what. We ain't got a star? We'll make one!'

Reception was a front hall, a waiting room with magazines. That's where visitors waited, well away from any peculiar sights or sounds. Then you walked down a long stone passage to the main building. The passage was beautifully done, with carpets and wallpaper and fireplaces in the alcoves. Apart from the telecommunications tower we'd seen from the road, the main building was divided into two: the main block which had got people forever in it, and an oblong building with those who hadn't gone really wrong yet. The oblong building was about five thousand yards long and two thousand wide, covered by a series of pointed roofs, A-shapes placed side by side. In that were all the shop floors: machinery, toolsmiths, tinsmiths. Two levels, high level and low level (because the place was built on a slight hill), and a subterranean level where they did the plating.

> Thus the decision was handed down from Mount Olympus by Jupiter, king of the gods. It had only to be carried out.

The oblong building was a bit like a school, you got the sort of freedom you get in school, yet you were not free. You had to do a certain amount of work but you didn't do a lot of work. There was no piecework at this stage. It was guiding you and training and canalizing your mind in all senses: how to use a file, how to use a turret lathe and a centre lathe and a milling machine and all the other machines — bending machine — that one would use.

You had to do ludicrous things, like file down a block of metal into a two-inch cube. It was a very rough cast lump of metal, you had to cut it and file it and emery cloth it and then it was put — the best ones were put — in a glass case! Look what he's made! He's made this incredible two-inch block of metal! The best workers wore neat overalls, their hands were clean, always covered in that Swarfega stuff you put on your hands before you start work, it was very tacky and they'd be shaking their hands up and down to dry it out.

They gave me a job taking burrs off heavy frameworks, two-foot, three-foot frameworks. A burr is a piece of metal left behind when a high speed drill goes through it, it's the rough bit and it cuts really bad. There were many different kinds of scraping tools to get these burrs off and I learned to handle them. They were very heavy. I remember the incredible heaviness in my hands after doing that job all day.

We worked at benches, the tops of the benches were armour-plated eighth-inch thick. We worked angle-iron, H-iron, L-shaped iron. I went on to mark out control panels. A mark-out means getting a piece of iron and the drawing that goes with it. The drawing shows what size holes must be put in that bit of metal. You get whitewash and a whitewash brush and you whitewash the metal. You wait for it to dry. If it's not too rusty you mark it out. Then you centre-pop it with a centre-pop and a hammer, ready for the man with the drill.

The windows didn't open, or they opened a bit, so a man could not get through. All the windows were blacked out, the lighting was fluorescent strips and the strips flickered. After three days I got splitting headaches from the noise, the smells and the lighting.

Four times, three times I was shunted about. My job in the plating department was soul-destroying. The platers wore rubber aprons like mortuary attendants. There were three hundred men there that the manager, who was a sort of friend of mine, wanted to get back outside, but they couldn't. They had no families or their families had gone or they couldn't get proper work. They could have made it reasonably well if they'd had some support from a family.

As my father had a greengrocer's shop they said I'd do better in the time-office. I collected the clocking-in cards and entered them in a log. Managers' cards were orange, the rest were white. The work was peaceful but boring. I picked up the cards from the clocks in various places, took them back to the office and then redistributed them. So I made contact with all sorts of people, the people one was working with, which was useful. The time-office helped me back to life, I could begin to come out into life.

> Max Arnow, Columbia's chief talent scout, spotted a young blonde at agent Louis Shurr's office. He arranged a screen test that had the blonde encased in one of Rita Hayworth's old gowns, standing in front of a prop fireplace, thrusting her ample bosom at the world, murmuring, 'I want love . . .'

The man who ran the time-office had been in the Air Force, in the battle, I don't know, he'd been brave, he'd known fear and failure. I'm a socialist and he was a fascist, but I don't believe in these labels: each of them I find I am. He was fed up with the work, he'd too much work on, he couldn't get it done. I only saw him about once a week. Well once a week isn't bad is it? Enough to keep in touch. I was absolutely rock bottom the last time I saw him, and he boosted me up, telling me what a great person I was, and I ought to do this and I ought to do that. Boosted up? Boosted up really on lies.

I went on to work on all the machines. By then I was on piecework. You had to do Christ I don't know how many an hour. There was a flat rate. A rate-fixer fixed the rate. You had to do two hundred an hour to get 5 per cent bonus. You would get a batch of material, maybe a thousand items, and you would have to do a job on those items. The pressures of piece-work were enormous, it was impossible to make any of the jobs pay, that means make any bonus on them. That was the great crime because the whole point of using cheap labour, which is what we were, was to get as much out of us as humanly possible.

There was a very good fitter who used to take a pride in his work. When he did a job the Inspector needn't go near it because it was always right. Unlike nearly everyone else who would bash a bolt through with a hammer, he would file the hole to make it fit tight. He was a proper fitter. This man was asked to work overtime. He never worked overtime, he had no need to. The pressure was on this particular job but he said no he wouldn't. The manager came down and had a word with him, and he still said no. That was all right. It happened a few more times and each time he said no. That man was taken off that job, he was forced out deliberately. They didn't want workmen, they wanted exploitation fodder, you had to do it their way or get forced out. Unfortunately that poor geezer was sent to the main block. All the ritual began. Someone appointed himself chief collector and all his possessions were collected up. The saddest thing of all was the raffling of his tools. It was like the end of the man, all these worn hammers, these dividers and rules and spanners, in a box, and raffled. He had a fairly expensive watch and that was raffled as well. The money went to his wife.

> Meanwhile, the casting department placed the blonde
> in a quickie 'B' picture. A good amount of fan mail
> resulted. Gambling on the audience interest shown,
> they put her in another picture. The mail came in like
> a postal Niagara.

The job was not beyond me, it was that I had no interest in it. Had I knuckled down I could have done that side of it, the physical side, but the other side . . . Oh Christ I don't know how long I did that for, I think it went on for six months before I was shot across the road to the main block.

We went through the shot-blaster's hut, it was a large but and inside was another but with a big iron door. The bloke wore a mediaeval sort of helmet, with a little slit, huge gloves and a great iron pipe. It was the start of the horrors. It shook me in there. You go through two sets of doors, unlocked and locked behind you. You can't have any belongings because people just take them. I wanted to get out. I didn't belong in there. But you can't get out. They said to me, the new manager's on his way, when he comes don't annoy him, get undressed and have a bath, you're filthy, you've had a long day, you can talk to him, he'll ring up someone and get this sorted out. It all seemed very easy. I went and had my bath and I came back and everything had been taken, my clothes, everything, and there I was.

> Harry Cohn thought again. He signed the new blonde
> to a $100 a week contract. But he continued to look
> around for a new love goddess to put on the vacant
> pedestal.

They kept my clothes as a punishment, like in school, I suppose any institution gets like a school. You're deprived of your rights like a child. Without clothes, coffined in a dressing gown, it was humiliating.

Even the telephone didn't work, it was on a padlock and you had to ask for a key. When the manager came he just gave me a shirt and dungarees and put me on the line. There was nothing I could do. Everyone lined up and I had to line up with them. We'd had no breakfast, we all stood in a queue. Some of the young workers looked pretty frightened, they'd been told that when they got back they'd be all dopey and wouldn't remember anything. They hung on to each other and said they wouldn't go but when the charge-hand said 'Ready' they all climbed into the lorry. The ones who'd been before tried to cheer us up: 'Not to worry, it'll all be over tonight, you'll be back here having a pint, you'll be OK, you'll feel fine.' They don't reply, they repeat themselves, won't go, won't go, but there was a sense of powerlessness because you've got to go. The charge-hands can force you physically, they're chosen for their size. If people get bolshie they are held down and injected. Horrible thing. People screaming and shouting. Five minutes later you see them calm enough.

The skills required were not great. You only had the physical thing, the tactile thing, how to turn the lever. The human element was taken out. At five thousand an hour something would go wrong if the human element was allowed in.

If you've got a terrific noise and pain everywhere, all day long, in your hands and in your head, you're so furious with yourself you try to externalize it. That's very different from trying to kill yourself, odd cuts and stuff, which people seemed to spend their time doing.

The line makes you lose touch with any kind of reality, you're in this quagmire, you can't remember your past, your memory's gone. You can't remember your best friend's name, you can remember him but not his name. You don't know if he's married or whether he's got any children. He's just a space, though you know he is your friend.

> Cohn paused to take another look at this blonde he had
> dismissed so lightly. He took a long, appraising look at
> her. She had a good, firm figure, and a pretty face —
> but there was more than that. In a town saturated with
> pretty girls there *had* to be more than that.

It's not self-hate it's self-love. If you don't reach their standards you break down. It turns to hate because you can't bear doing what you are doing.

I made slow progress. I used to copy the charge-hand in front of me. He was a huge, fair-haired, white-faced man, a clever man, I suppose he was, he must have been. I did whatever he did because I didn't understand the work at all, or rather I understood more when I started than when I'd been doing it for a week. In the break, seeing him sitting eating Spangles while I worked to catch up, it was so futile, I used to shit myself.

Like everyone else I waited for what would happen that night, I lived in anticipation of getting out through those doors. Several times I went out,

I crept out, and got razor blades or something. I never thought of it as anything odd. It never disgusted me, when I tried to cut myself. When other people did it it was appalling.

One guy, Charlie, was only seventeen, he'd lived in orphanages and special schools all his life. Every time he'd got to like anyone in one place he was passed on somewhere else. He was very violent. They said he'd already put two men in hospital, and he had, with a broken jaw, and one had a broken arm I think. Suddenly, he used to work very tensely, staring at his machine, suddenly he got out of line, he went over and put his hands through the windows, then he broke a bottle and grabbed the glass. We were hours trying to get him to have his arms bandaged. Then he threw a cup and hit someone in the face. Three others put their hands through windows and broke bottles. There was all this glass. I can't explain it. It was mass hysteria. I wanted to do the same myself but I realized it would be crazy.

They put Charlie back on the line. After six weeks no one knows where the brain goes, or the mind. He did not speak for a month. If you lifted his arm or his leg, he sat or lay there, the leg would set in an impossible position, like a yogist. When he started speaking again he just quoted things. He said he was a friend of Henry Ford. His face, suddenly you would see him, he would be working and the whole thing would stop, his face would be rigid, and his hands, as if he had dropped out. Two minutes later he'd be back. I don't think he'll ever . . . He was seventeen. I don't think he'll ever . . . He was very intelligent. He had those eyes which are half shut but still crazily bright. He'd had a breakdown over his A-levels. I got to know him, began talking with him. He said, 'You don't think I'm mad do you? Don't think I'm mad just because Henry's my friend.' After four more months on the line he didn't know if he was French or English. If you asked him a question in English he would reply in French, and vice-versa. He had TB but he took up smoking French cigarettes. If you gave him a fag he'd take it and if you offered him another he would take that too, he'd have cigarettes between all ten fingers. I'd say, 'Want a fag ?' I'd wait, and then I'd say, 'Voulez vous une Gauloise?' Then he burnt himself all over his hands and arms with cigarettes and he finally got out.

> There was an indefinable sexiness about this one, coupled with a childlike innocence that intrigued as well as titillated the male gland. The hazel-green eyes were seductive, the full pouting lips were like welcoming beacons that murmured sensually, 'I want love . . .'

The works manager was female, she trained dogs and she treated us the same. If you weren't trained well she was bloody. Though she was a woman she was never shocked. If you told her you'd killed your mother and raped her when she was dead, she'd say yes, I must make a note of that. It was her job. When Charlie came back with his hands bandaged she just said, 'You stupid bastard, what the hell have you been doing to yourself? If you give me a tenner I'll cut your fucking arms off.'

She had a terrible job with the work-freaks. She said she had the opposite job to usual: people overworked because it seemed the only thing to latch on to. She had the job of shaking them out of their work mania. They could be very funny, suddenly going from being depressed to being as high as kites. They acted like they were roaring drunk the whole time, working like maniacs, laughing, they'd do anything. One guy worked himself to exhaustion, he swore he'd never work again. Next free day he was digging in the garden, digging was the great thing, digging holes and filling them in. In the middle of the night-shift that guy had an epileptic fit and after it was over, horrible sight, what was so tragic, everyone laughed, you had to laugh, people did such crazy things.

For me the work pressures built up and up. I saw no point and no end to it. It builds up over a period and you shake it off. I fought it off by going wild. It was my last chance. When I felt the drop coming and I knew I was going to roll down the hill . . . I went high. I knew it was going to happen so nothing mattered.

> In his forty years as a movie maker Harry Cohn had
> learned that what the public wanted was sex. If they
> thought this blonde had it, he wasn't going to argue
> with them. The girl's experience was slight but she had
> the diamond-in-the-rough qualities of a potential
> movie sex goddess, and Cohn was prepared to polish
> and shine her into a star until she radiated from movie
> screens the world over.

The point is I didn't want to run away, I didn't want to go anywhere. At that time I didn't want to do anything, but I didn't want to go back on the line, that was it, that was what I ran away from. I walked near the wall when I was leaving work and slipped through and got on a bus. They ran after me but I'm a good runner. No, it sounds cunning, but I'd got a torch and in place of the batteries I'd slipped in a knife, a pen-knife, and they'd discovered it. So when they said they would put me back I ran down the corridor, out and over the wall, through the bushes, and got a lift from some old guy buying petrol.

After a day I wanted to go back. People don't want to leave, in the end. They come in fighting, drugged, deluded, against their will or because they can't get anything else, and in the end . . . it's such awful protection in there. If you want to go berserk you can. Anything goes. They need you so they watch you. You can have hysterics on the line but you're still valuable, you can be sent away and repaired, they can still use you, you are their property, so you'll always be taken care of.

> He called her back into his office. 'Don't get involved
> with any of the guys at the studio,' he cautioned her.
> 'They can't help you like I can help you.'

I went back but I would not work. If you don't work you don't eat so I didn't eat, I only drank water. At first nobody tried to make me eat. Then they made me go in to meals. They dragged me in. I had five men carrying me, I was fighting and biting, very undignified, childish. So I got some broken glass. I broke a bottle and tried to cut myself and when someone came I threatened them with it. I would never have hurt them. But I sat there with this bottle.

They put me in a room on my own, bare room, completely bare, nothing to harm yourself on, nothing to climb on, nothing to break. No furniture except an iron bed. It's amazingly difficult to do anything with an iron bed bolted to the floor. The windows had nothing to hang anything on, no curtain rails, just unbreakable glass with bars outside. They didn't need bars with that glass. The room had unbreakable glass, everything unbreakable. The panic it instils in you, the fury. I banged on the door so hard, in the end I said I was sorry for disturbing everybody. They said it was natural to want to get out of a place you didn't want to be in.

The door had no handle, it was smooth and bare, it opened the wrong way, not inwards so you could bar it with a piano dragged across, but outwards into the corridor. They gave me plastic plates and cups and no knives. I slept because they gave me pills, pills all the time. You feel so hopeless in there, the idea is you'll be begging to get back on the line.

Someone stayed with me all the time, think how much it cost, and it didn't do any good, it wasn't getting to the root of the problem. It was protecting me from myself they said, but it was protecting their property for them. Whatever they did made it more of a challenge, because I was determined to do it. When you have someone following you they follow you everywhere, when you pee and when you shit, you leave the door open, they're with you every minute.

At last they gave in, made concessions, we struck a bargain. They would let me alone if I would go back on the line. As I seemed to get back to normal they put me in with the slow workers and the violent ones and the difficult ones like the guy who sat and masturbated all day and that was all he did. I was so frightened of doing something wrong that I did something wrong. One night they were playing the gramophone too loud and I wanted to sleep. They had a fixation about a certain record: WHAT

HAVE THEY DONE TO MY HEAD MA? WHAT HAVE THEY DONE TO MY BRAIN? They played it again and again. I said if you don't turn it off I'll throw the gramophone through the window and I got up and I did throw it through the window. Next day they didn't remember anything, they didn't hold it against me, they just laughed.

So I tried to kill myself. Once I'd preconceived it and arranged it and I knew the time and how it would be I was tremendously peaceful because it didn't matter.

Then I was in bed, I don't know how long for because I was drugged. I'd cut myself. I'd lost pints of blood. I had to have transfusions, it went on and on, each bottle takes an hour. I had eight pints, you're only meant to have seven, but for some reason I had eight.

My kids were so shocked when they came to see me. They said I was never to talk about it, never say I'd been in such a place. When they came to collect me they brought their dog. They had to lock it up because it kept barking at people. Everyone seemed to have something wrong with them, I don't know, their bodies were a bit deformed, or they walked funny, and they laughed when the dog wouldn't stop barking at them.

Saying goodbye was agony. I didn't say goodbye. I said I'll come back and see you next week. I gave them presents. I was too sad to say goodbye. I'd got to know them. There'd been no conversation in the way people sit and talk about the weather, we'd none of that.

> With his fatherly advice, Harry Cohn lifted the blonde to the pedestal left vacant by Rita Hayworth, and the publicity department began informing the unsuspecting world that Kim Novak, Goddess of Love, had arrived in Wonderland.

People keep in touch tremendously with each other and with the camp. If you go down there they'll always tell you, someone's got a card from someone.

(Acknowledgements to *Kim Novak, Goddess of Love* by Charles E. Fritch, Monarch Books.)